HOT RUN

DECEPTION IN THE DEEP

BY: T. STEVEN SULLIVAN

Mark,
As I look back
you were usually involved
in some way when I was
gettin' in trouble!
The good ol' days!

T.

Acknowledgements

First and foremost, I have to thank my wife Amy who has always supported me on many crazy adventures and endeavors. Thanks for being my best friend and the love of my life. To the guys I served with in the Navy, I wouldn't trade that time for the world. To my fellow bubbleheads JJ Henson and Eric Swalla: JJ you are a wealth of knowledge, thank you for being my human Google search during this project. Eric, thank you for your opinions, they helped me to craft a better story. To my brother-in-law Lt. Brian Lapp, my father-in-law Tom DeWolff, and my friend Suzanne Kosik, thank you all for your feedback. To my friend and amazing artist Jon Pinto, it is always a pleasure to watch you create exactly what I ask you to. Thank you Tony Elam for being the engine driving me over the finish line, your motivation and advice has been invaluable. To my fellow dreamers in the Dream Builders Network, let there be…

…and finally, thank you Mom and Dad for always believing in me.

This book is dedicated to:

My brothers of the Silent Service whose unseen and unheard missions keep us safe.

PROLOGUE

Three months ago…

"If I die tonight, you and I are going to wrestle!" Staff Sergeant BJ Maddox screamed the challenge to God as he crouched, taking cover behind a man-sized boulder as a layer of earth rained down upon him. The dirt, which pelted him, had been thrown up by both rocket propelled and hand thrown grenades. Every time the dust cloud would be kicked up by an explosion, he would use the momentary cover to change positions. Surrounded by his fellow fallen Rangers; he checked the number of rounds left in his M-4 carbine. He had started the battle with the larger M240 machine gun. His powerful frame never had a problem wielding the M240 as agilely as other soldiers managed their lighter M-4s, but he had run out of ammunition, even though he had employed conservative short round bursts since the onset of the battle.

Matthews had been the first to go down, the victim of a lucky shot from an undisciplined fighter's AK-47 spray. Next, Gutierrez, and then Faulkner, both unable to get sufficient cover from RPGs. BJ, after burning through his entire cache of M240 rounds, had moved from body to body, picking up each dead friend's M-4, and using it until it was emptied. He had just scooped up Gutierrez's bloodied weapon when he dove behind the large boulder for cover.

Pulling the clip out, he grimaced, finding only two rounds remained. Counting the round in the chamber, he was left with only three shots. He tried his radio again, "Ticonderoga, this is Knox, over!" He checked the power on the unit for the eighth time. "Ticonderoga, this is Knox, our situation is desperate," he shouted into the transmitter, still referring to his unit in the plural.

BJ was part of a six man Ranger Unit assigned to the western region of Afghanistan. Intelligence reports had led them on, what many in the unit considered, a wild goose chase. Their reconnaissance mission in the desolate western regions had come after months of intense skirmishes large and small with Taliban and Al Qaeda fighters along the Afghanistan-Pakistan border. Now, they had spent the last few weeks crammed into dusty rock crevasses silently observing goat herders prod their mangy animals down desolate dirt highways.

On this particular evening, two soldiers in BJ's six man unit stayed behind at their base camp, both complaining of digestive track issues. BJ and the other three did not give them any grief about hanging back. They knew they were tough soldiers who did little, if any, whining. It was just as well, they all agreed. Nobody wanted to deal with a guy who was stopping every five minutes to pollute the mountain side.

When the trucks had come rolling down the road, Gutierrez grunted, "Jax and McAllister will be pissed; first signs of life outside the dark ages and those two are back at base camp scrounging for soft leaves." The mood quickly sobered when the four Rangers realized it was a heavily armed convoy.

As the trucks barreled toward their position, Gutierrez got on the horn to alert Central Command. After hearing Gutierrez attempting to raise somebody for the third time, the others began to take note of the distress in his voice. "I think we're being jammed," he reported. BJ snapped his attention away from Gutierrez's puzzlement as he heard the rumble of the trucks come to a halt.

Matthews, who was peering over a rock at the convoy, began reporting, "It looks like two dozen SUV's and some..." BJ tried to pull him down but it was too late. The mountainside was lit up by an AK-47. When Matthews slumped to the ground, it was apparent he was gone.

"They must have night vision," Faulkner screamed.

"And jammers!" Gutierrez added.

"Twenty six minutes," BJ exhaled as he checked his watch. It had only been twenty six minutes since that first burst of shots had taken Matthews and now BJ was cut off and alone. "Three shots, make 'em count," he said as he slapped the magazine back into his weapon. "No preliminary bouts, it's you and me," he reiterated his challenge to God. He took three quick breaths, kissed the scope, and then jumped up from his hidden position. He quickly sighted in on a man with an RPG. "Pop." He squeezed off a round which struck the man in the throat. "Pop." His next shot went wide of its intended target, striking only the dirt. He slowed himself. Let half a breath out, then held it while he zeroed in on a man who was crouched on one knee. "Pop." The shot hit dead center, barely noticeable to BJ, who earlier had seen men cut to pieces from his M240. However, as he was ducking back behind his protective boulder, he did notice the man slump over.

He tossed the smoking M-4 to the side, then, gritting his teeth, he pressed his back against the boulder testing to see if he could get it to budge. He let out a hearty laugh which stayed off tears. The task of rolling a boulder down the side of the mountain at his attackers could be deemed a desperate one, by a desperate man. He eyed the radio again, but decided just to throw it in the air as if he hoped it would be picked off like a clay pigeon.

He looked over at Gutierrez, whose body lay about six feet from his position. Gutierrez's eyes seemed to be fixed on BJ's. His jaw, which must have been broken either from the explosion or the impact with the ground afterward, was pushed out and upward in a grotesque under bite. Oddly enough, BJ had seen him make this face upwards of a hundred times. In their down time, Gutierrez would entertain the guys by jutting out his lower mandible in an exaggerated underbite impersonating a slightly disfigured cousin of his who claimed he could continue drinking due to the fact that he had both a right and a left liver. The sight of his friend, eternally wearing the face he would put on to make everyone laugh, knocked the air out of him as he tried to restrain tears.

BJ reached down and removed his knife from its sheath strapped to his thigh. He cut the straps of his vest and it fell to the ground. From one of its pockets he retrieved a small transmitter. "I'll buy the next round," he said to Gutierrez. Then looking up toward heaven, he gave one last warning to God, "It's me and you big man, bring your A game!" He started to get up, then paused and looked up again, this time almost whispering "I love you, Dad." He stepped out from behind the rock.

He wasn't cut down instantly, as he might have expected, but a cloud of dust, still lingering from the last barrage of bullets to sweep the landscape, extended his cover. He started down the embankment at a slow trot. As each footstep fell, his momentum multiplied and the determination in his countenance became more hardened.

In the ravine, the men's eyes widened in horror when they saw the ghost like warrior emerge from the dusty vapors as he careened down the crag. He flew at them as if he were the very shadow of death itself coming for them in the night. They were frozen, until BJ screamed. He probably intended the sound to be like the roar of a lion, instead, whether it was the exhaustion and stress of what he had already been through, or the knowledge that these would be his last moments, his vocal cords tightened. The shrill cry came out like an '80s glam rocker. After the initial shock wore off, the waiting men raised their weapons. However, at that moment the first light of the sun leapt over the mountain. Its fingers of light shimmered off the whites of BJ's eyes. This, contrasted by his darkly painted face, gave tremors to every hand on a weapon.

One by one they began firing. If a bullet had struck BJ at this moment his momentum alone would have carried him to their feet. As fate would have it, not a single bullet hit him during the charge. He heard bullets tear the wind as they passed within millimeters of his ears. He even felt the friction of two bullets pass between his arm and his body as he ran. The men firing at him saw the ground behind him puff with the impact of the bullets and it appeared as though the bullets had passed right through him. A few of the men melted off the front of the line as they dropped their weapons and ran.

When events started, there were nearly one hundred and fifty fighters engaged against the quartet of Rangers. Now, the enemy number was below ninety. Even with the superb kill ratio on his side, and the frontline dissolving, BJ's last mission was hopeless. He did not get close enough to touch one of his assailants with his knife; instead he made a beeline for the lead transport vehicle.

As he passed through the middle of their line, three men were mortally wounded by their own crossfire. Two bullets ripped into BJ's right leg tearing apart the meaty portion of his thigh. Then the firing suddenly stopped. Even though the men showed no discretion in firing their weapons when their fellow Jihadists were in the crossfire, they did not fire at or near the transport truck.

BJ hopped on his left leg the last few meters to the truck. He dove at the left front tire sinking his knife deep into the sidewall as he collapsed into the wheel well. The only sound to be heard was the hissing of the tire, as its air escaped into the night. After a moment the men all began to laugh at the American Soldier's fruitless attack. What went unnoticed by all who were in observance was the slight ker-thunk as he magnetically affixed the small transmitter, which had been in his left hand, to the underside of the truck's frame.

One week ago...

The muscles in Miguel Sanchez's back strained as he lugged a box of flour containers up the brow of the merchant vessel, the Santa de Juarez. He shuffled up the steep plank in a procession of his fellow cooks. Normally, the cooks would have their pallet of food loaded in a matter of minutes with the help of the ships crane. However, on this morning the crane was being reserved for reasons not disclosed to the kitchen staff. The cooks' grumbling became louder with each trip up and down the brow carrying the food stores into the deep bowels of the ship as they watched the crane sit by, idling. "We could have been done an hour ago and their crane would still be sitting there wasting fuel," the cook behind Sanchez mumbled in Spanish.

Sanchez did not respond. He was not being rude; he was accustomed to saying little. He could barely concentrate on the menial task of carrying box after box of food stores. He had come a long way since his days as a beat cop in Miami. Currently, he looked more like the felons he had been locking up back in the day, with his pony tail and his coca field tattoos. However, he told his wife that he felt this was the case that would bring him back stateside. It could possibly bring a resurgence to a career which seemed to stall some time ago.

He had already sacrificed so much, his strained marriage, his relationship with his daughters, but the thought of getting a promotion so he would finally be running operations from the DEA command center had him working harder than ever to make a historic bust. He may have been taking more chances than he had in the past, but in all the time he had spent as an undercover agent he never had more than a mediocre bust. Now, long after the passion for the job had worn off, passion which had been fueled by the helpless feeling of watching his brother consumed by the underworld of drug pushers, he found himself working with renewed zeal to get out of the surreal world he had been moving in for the last six years.

During the early hours of the morning, while sifting through records in the ships business office, he had come across a bill of sale for the Santa de Juarez. It seems the merchant vessel was purchased by none other than Hugo Chavez's top military commander. Assuming the news would be considered a major development in his case, he made contact with his operations director requesting a higher level of surveillance to be placed on the ship which was preparing to embark that afternoon. His director received the request with luke warm enthusiasm and told him to make contact in four hours and he would have an answer for him.

Sanchez was enraged. His director acted as though making contact was as simple as picking up a cell phone and ordering a pizza. Cell phones were forbidden aboard the Santa de Juarez, which happened to be the first sign to Sanchez that he should try to infiltrate the vessel.

Each time he made contact with his operations director, he was putting his life in the gravest of danger. Under normal circumstances, he might make contact a single time in a one or two week period. Now his director was asking him to take the risk for the second time in the same morning, simply because he didn't have the backbone to wake his superiors.

It was now two hours past the time he had been told to check in. His back was killing him, yet his nerves were his true detriment. After his discovery of the bill of sale, his heart rate was racing as if he was a rookie agent again; having to force himself to mentally filter every reaction and response he was having so as not to come across as a bundle of nerves to the men he was working around. He was itching to get back to the utility closet where he had his encrypted communications device stashed, but found himself held captive by manual labor.

As he reached the top of the brow, Sanchez couldn't help but glare at the crane operator. The operator sat in his air conditioned booth with the window slightly cracked, while he lounged back in his seat smoking a cigarette. Suddenly, the operator, as well as the rest of the crew was brought to attention by a sharp whistle.

An armed guard had blown the high pitched attention grabber through pinched fingers. Sanchez had been standing just a few feet away from the man and his ear drum throbbed after he was finished. He shifted his dagger eyes from the crane operator to the impolite guard. The guard pointed to Sanchez, "You cooks, get below!" Sanchez studied the man's filthy chapped fingers. He couldn't help but stare at the guard in disgust as he watched him put the fingers back in his mouth to repeat the whistle.

"But we're not finished," Sanchez protested.

The roar of an eighteen wheeler coming down the pier signaled the crane operator to fire up his mechanical arm. Sanchez tried to take in every detail of the truck as it barreled towards the ship. To his detective's eye, the one detail which immediately screamed at him was how low the trailer was riding on its axles, as if the cargo were of an extremely dense nature. Before he could make any further assessment of the approaching vehicle, a hand grabbed his shoulder and shoved him towards the hatch leading to the interior of the ship. For a man with as much self defense training as Sanchez, it was an exercise in monumental restraint not to drop the inept excuse for a security guard to the ground with his wrist pinned between his shoulder blades.

After the guard pushed him through and shut the hatch behind him, Sanchez dropped the case of flour he was carrying, spilling the individual canisters all over the deck. "That comes out of your pay," said one of the other cooks, who had no authority over him or his pay. Sanchez said nothing in response; he simply stooped and began to slowly clean up the mess. Once the other cooks had made their way down the passage and turned the corner, he kicked the canisters aside and ran down the stairwell taking the steps three at a time.

He made his way to a utility closet deep within the ship's inner corridors. Shutting the door behind him, Sanchez jammed a broom stick against it, making a post between the door and the outer wall of the closet. He squatted on the floor and pulled a half dozen boxes of latex gloves off one of the lower shelves. Hidden in the bottom box was a blackberry sized satellite encrypted communicator. He pulled a mop bucket out of the corner to reveal a piece of conduit with a two inch section removed exposing the wires it was intended to protect. From the communicator, he pulled out two wires with alligator clips at the ends and clamped them onto two of the wires exposed by the missing strip of conduit. Dialing in his frequency, he made the call to his operations director.

The lack of enthusiasm expressed earlier in the day seemed to be just as prevalent in the afternoon. "It's a no go on the increased surveillance," his director informed him, "give us a call back if you find out anything else that might be of use."

"But I already have," Sanchez tried to express his emotion without bringing his voice to a level which could be heard by anyone passing the closet. "As we speak, they are loading something onto this ship that seemed to be of great importance."

"What was it?" the director asked dryly.

"I'm not sure; they kicked all nonessential personnel off the deck when it arrived."

"Well, why don't you see if you can turn yourself into an essential person?"

"I'm not out here picking daisies. I'm trying to give you something."

"You're not giving me much."

Sanchez tried to impress upon his director that the feeling he had on this case was different than any other cut and dry narcotics operation he had ever been on. "At least pass along the information I've given you to the DOD; they might find it interesting."

"Will do," the director said with no reassurance in his voice, "you're doing good work, just continue doing your job."

"I am doing my job," Sanchez snapped. Acting as though the promotion he had been seeking had become secondary to this case, he repeated himself, but didn't stop short this time, "I am doing my job, why don't you do yours?"

Sanchez abruptly ended the communication session and returned the utility closet to its unmolested condition. He was about to shut the door behind him as he left, when he paused to grab a broom and a dust pan.

CHAPTER 1

Petty Officer Thomas Quinn sat rolling his bishop back and forth between his thumb and index finger. The slow rocking did not seem to sooth Petty Officer Jason Scarpa who opposed Quinn across the crews mess table. The cramped compartment was buzzing with sailors taking advantage of some precious down time. The crews mess was the only recreational area on a submarine, and its five small tables were filled with sailors reading, studying, or playing hand held video games. In the center of it all, Quinn and Scarpa sat transfixed on their chess match.

"Do you think you are going to make a move before I have to reenlist?" Scarpa grumbled.

"Reenlist? I never took you for a lifer," Quinn piped back with a smile. The smile was Petty Officer Quinn's trademark. Over the last five years in the Navy, he had used his smile to win over his superiors, as well as his subordinates. It was a smile that Scarpa despised. Quinn seemed to ooze military bearing, always having a fresh haircut, wearing military creases even in his working uniforms. While the only thing which appeared to ooze from Scarpa was bearing grease. Being an Auxiliary Division mechanic, Scarpa spent most of his time down in the bilges of the submarine tearing apart sanitary pumps or changing o-rings in the boat's auxiliary diesel engine. He did not own a uniform without one kind of stain or another on it.

Quinn slowly moved his bishop to a conservative position on the board. Scarpa immediately moved his rook, as if the game were on a timer. Quinn rubbed the back of his four fingers across his cleanly shaven chin as he took in Scarpa's last move. "This is the last time I play against you!" Scarpa snapped.

"That could very well be true; I leave for OCS after these next training ops," Quinn softly reminded him. Scarpa's jaw clenched as he stared straight at Quinn. Quinn could see Scarpa filling with rage. Scarpa had been a Second Class Petty Officer when Quinn had arrived on board as a Seaman Apprentice. Now, after nearly four years, not only were they equal in rank, but Quinn had earned his bachelor's degree and was accepted into Officer Candidate School. Scarpa seemed to be contemplating jumping across the table to knock a couple of Quinn's teeth out, just for the satisfaction of not having to look at that infuriating smile anymore.

At times, those feelings of rage had gone unrepressed in Scarpa, which was part of the reason why they were, at present, the same rank. After nearly four years, Scarpa was still a Second Class, mostly due to the fact that he had been busted back a rank in a Captain's Mast hearing for locking a junior officer in a torpedo tube. The officer had since left the submarine force due to a previously undiagnosed case of severe claustrophobia.

However, it wasn't the fear of being demoted again which kept Scarpa from lunging across the table at Quinn; it was the fact that Quinn was an All-American wrestler and more recently had some success on the mixed martial arts circuit. Scarpa, who had grown up fighting on some of Detroit's meanest streets, seemed to know that underneath Quinn's pretty boy exterior he shared the same thirst for alpha dog violence that he did.

Also, Quinn was part of the boat's dive team. Being part of the boat's dive team himself, Scarpa knew firsthand the type of determination and willingness it took to completely exhaust one's body both mentally and physically in order to get through Navy Dive School. It was obvious, with Quinn, if it ever came to blows, it would not be a battle, it would be a war, and for Scarpa that war would certainly be over something a little more worthy than his annoyance at Quinn getting to go to Officer Candidate School. After all, he acted as though Quinn was his only equal among the crew in both mental and physical aspects, and treated Quinn strangely enough, like a friend.

"I'm not an officer yet, quit staring at me like that," Quinn chimed, "your Jedi mind tricks won't work on me."

"They will once your spine is removed in Officer School," Scarpa replied. Before Quinn could once again defend his decision to abandon the enlisted ranks, the entire crew was brought to their feet by the high pitch scream of the flooding alarm.

The alarm was followed by the crackle of the 1MC, the interior shipboard communications system, and a voice screaming, "Flooding in Main Seawater

9

Bay! Flooding in Main Seawater Bay! Damage Control Team respond!" Immediately after the announcement, the banshee like screech of the flooding alarm reverberated in the small compartment once more.

Instantaneously, the sailors were on their feet lifting the lids of the bench seats they had seconds before been relaxing on. From the benches they pulled army green canvas bags adorned with stenciled markings of "Damage Control Kit" and "Flood Patch Kit".

Scarpa tried to lift the lid to the bench he had been sitting on, when it slammed shut. He looked up to see Seaman Apprentice Kyle Schmidt trying to scoot his way off of the bench. Scarpa grabbed a handful of Seaman Schmidt's uniform and threw him to the ground. "Move NUB!"

Schmidt cowered on the deck like an abused animal waiting for the next blow, but it never came. Scarpa had grabbed a tool bag and bolted out the aft door of the crews mess. Schmidt scampered to his feet and followed.

The wheel on the water tight door of the Main Seawater Bay spun counterclockwise with inhuman speed. As the hatch door flung open, sailors poured in like fire ants coming out of a disturbed mound. They quickly descended upon the steel jungle that seemed to be spewing water from half a dozen pipes and valves. The first sailor to come through the hatch was Petty Officer Bradley Stopper. Stopper was known to all on board as Rubber. It was a nickname given to him in the first few minutes of his arrival on board the submarine. As a new Seaman just out of submarine school in Groton Connecticut, he was introduced to the off-going Commanding Officer. "Seaman Stopper," the C.O. exclaimed, "I suppose we should just cut to the chase and start calling you Rubber right off the bat." So it was, even though Bradley Stopper had made his way up the ranks and had shed the moniker of Seaman, the name Rubber never left him.

Immediately, Rubber located a small metal box affixed to the bulkhead and began to don the sound powered phones it contained. He plugged the phones, which had not had a design change since World War II, into the receptacle adjacent to the box. Depressing the metal button on the mouthpiece, he made his report, "Control-Main Seawater Bay, the Damage Control Team is on scene."

As Scarpa and Quinn came through the hatch, Rubber listened intently to the response from the control room. "Control wants to know who the senior man in charge is," Rubber reported. He knew very well who the senior man was, but he did not dare pipe back to Control that it was Scarpa before Scarpa had given consent.

Scarpa glanced down at Quinn's left arm. It bore the insignia of second class petty officer, as did his; however Quinn's wasn't nearly as faded as Scarpa's. "You made rank well before me," Quinn said to Scarpa.

"Would you rather have me turning a wrench or barking orders?" Scarpa replied, making no attempt to hide his disdain at the reminder. There was no question in Quinn's mind what Scarpa should be doing. Scarpa was a mechanical genius.

Quinn handed off his tool bag to Scarpa as if he were a Quarterback handing the ball off to his star fullback, "nobody turns a wrench better than you."

Acknowledging the back-handed compliment, Scarpa snapped his heels together and threw up a sharp salute, "Aye, aye sir!" As Scarpa leaped over the deck railing into the rapidly rising water in the bilge, Quinn knew Scarpa was obviously mocking him but he had no time to dwell on it. He swung around on his heel, pulled one of the earphones away from Rubber's head and yelled his orders right into the junior petty officer's ear.

Trying to compete with the deafening sound of the ocean rushing into the boat, he yelled, "Phone talker, to Control, Petty Officer Quinn is the senior man in charge!"

"Petty Officer Quinn is the senior man, aye sir!" Rubber repeated. Quinn's eyes snapped back from assessing the situation and caught Rubber's with an icy glare. The officer harassment from Scarpa was no surprise, but to have Rubber tack on the title *sir* to the end of his repeat back, implying Quinn was already an officer, was an unexpected slap. Rubber, obviously realizing what the glare was for, quickly duplicated the repeat back, absent any titles. After getting a quick nod of approval from Quinn, he cupped his mouth with the receptacle in a vain attempt to filter out any of the background noise and gave Control the update.

As Quinn returned to the assessment of the situation, he couldn't help but wonder why he would take so much offense to Rubber's use of the word "sir." In a few weeks he would enter Officer Candidate School and from that point on, the protocol would be enlisted men referring to him as "sir." Besides, he had once shared a barracks room with Rubber and knew his friend never said anything to try to upset anyone, even in jest. Quinn's thoughts ate at him. He tried to wrap his mind around why he glared at Rubber the way he did. Rubber obviously added the "sir" on at the end of his repeat back because he already thought of Quinn as an Officer. There were no ill intentions weaved into the comment, only admiration.

There had been many great officers throughout naval history who had risen from the enlisted ranks; Quinn had been reminded of this by every officer trying to seduce him into applying for OCS. It seemed as though he would have to get used to the no man's land that he had entered, never again being accepted by the enlisted ranks as one of them, while at the same time he was not sure if he would ever be fully embraced by the commissioned officers because of his status as a Mustang, an officer who was formerly enlisted. Quinn did not want to admit to himself, his problem wasn't with Rubber; it was with his own doubts about his forthcoming commission.

Suddenly, Quinn had the Dr. Phil slapped out of him when he realized he was doing as little as Seaman Schmidt to improve the current situation. "Schmidt, what are you doing?" Quinn yelled, trying to cover the fact that he was momentarily absent himself.

"I, uh," Schmidt couldn't even stumble through an excuse before Quinn assigned him a task.

"Get down there and help Scarpa with that monster leak," Quinn pointed to the bilge were Scarpa was attempting to clamp down on a pipe patch by himself. "That's a twelve inch pipe with a hole in it the size of Texas," Quinn had found his rhythm. "That leak alone is beyond the capacity of half a dozen bilge pumps."

Schmidt cautiously climbed over the deck railing and down to the pipe where Scarpa was set to work. As other sailors seemed to read each other's thoughts while they worked together trying to sustain the catastrophe, Schmidt looked as though he were thinking he had made the biggest mistake of his life when he volunteered for submarine duty. At seventeen, he had never been more than ten miles from Decatur, the mining town in West Virginia he had grown up in. As timid as he was, he probably never should have said yes to submarine duty at the recruitment center; however, his ASVAB scores were high enough, and at the time, it sounded like the furthest place in the world from his dirt-bag stepfather. So he raised his right hand, made an oath and now found himself in a place he referred to in letters to home as the "metal hell."

By the time Schmidt made his way down to Scarpa, the water level in the bilge had risen so rapidly it was already up to his chest. Scarpa was riffling through the tool bag he had hung on a flange bolt the size of a bagel. Schmidt timidly asked, "Anything I can do to help?" After asking, he flinched as though Scarpa had become the new embodiment of his stepdad. To his surprise, Scarpa slapped a chain wrench in his hand.

Having just come from Submarine School, he should have been very familiar with the modified vice grips. Looking as though he expected a rebuke from Scarpa rather than any sense of trust, he hesitated. Scarpa pounced upon the delayed response, "It's a chain wrench! You use it to clamp down on this pipe patch!" Embarrassment and anger seemed to flash across Schmidt's face. He looked like a high school kid, letting the teacher's pet answer all the questions, receiving the kudos, while he sits, too afraid to assert himself even though he knew the correct response.

Instead of trying to reassure Scarpa that he knew what it was, Schmidt simply responded, "Okay!"

At that moment, a fire seemed to ignite inside of Schmidt. He had been handed confidence by Scarpa but he let it wash away. He puffed out his chest and whispered the words, "It's do or die." He watched as Scarpa slammed a massive steel patch against the enormous pipe which was chiefly responsible for filling the bilge.

"Schmidt!" Scarpa screamed, his voice barely audible against the roar of the rushing water, "Clamp that chain wrench over this patch!" In a burst of adrenaline, Schmidt cast out the chain like a pro fisherman. As the chain wrapped around the pipe, he blindly extended his left hand, catching the chain perfectly in his palm. In the fashion of an old sea dog, he threaded the chain into the open teeth of the wrench and clamped it down like it was in the jaws of a pit bull.

Scarpa looked momentarily impressed. He had seen sailors with years of experience struggle to do the same maneuver in two minutes, and he had just witnessed a kid, still wet behind the ears; pull it off in just under two seconds. Without stopping to show any amazement, Scarpa kept the momentum moving, "Good, now I'm going to move the patch up so the chain splits the stream, then we'll rotate the patch over the hole."

The simple use of the word "good" from a hardened sailor like Scarpa visibly grew Schmidt's confidence, probably more so than the nine weeks of boot camp. Quinn noticed the progress Scarpa and Schmidt were making on what appeared to be the worst of their problems. At first, he had been apprehensive about sending such a fresh sailor down to work with Scarpa, however, now it seemed to be an inspired decision. He thought it was the type of split-second processing he would have to do every day, if he was ever to become a Commanding Officer.

He watched as Scarpa and Schmidt rotated the patch over the hole in the pipe. Even though the patch was fastened securely with the chain wrench, a good deal of water still sprayed out from all four of its sides. "Hold it there," Scarpa yelled, "I'll get the bands to seal the patch!" As Scarpa stretched out his arm, reaching for the tool bag which was hung closer to Schmidt, Quinn read the unfortunate situation perfectly before it unfolded.

Quinn could see such an eagerness to please in Schmidt's eyes; he could tell he was going to grab the bag for Scarpa. "Don't let go of that wrench!" Quinn's plea was too late to be heeded. Schmidt let go of the chain wrench and tried to reach the tool bag for Scarpa. Like a gun with a hair trigger, the moment Schmidt let go of the chain wrench, the sea pressure overcame the patch. Without a firm grip on the wrench, its chain sprang free. Having no time to react, the pipe patch rocketed off, grazing Scarpa's forehead.

Scarpa grabbed his head as he stumbled back and slid underwater. Quinn hopped over the parapet and down into the bilge to pull him out of the water. As Scarpa went under, Quinn could see his eyes, which had been rolling back in his head, flash back to alertness. The frigid water seemed to push away the black shadow of unconsciousness which would have been enveloping his vision. The bone chilling cold seemed to reawaken Scarpa's senses. He emerged from the depths like an African Croc. As Quinn reached Scarpa, he found his rescue mission was no longer to save the injured sailor but rather to restrain him so Schmidt would not be torn to pieces.

Schmidt saw Scarpa's murderous eyes fixate on him as his blood soaked head came out of the water. Schmidt raced out of the bilge as if he had seen the fabled bilge monster lurking in the greasy water. Scarpa screamed at Schmidt while Quinn used every ounce of his body weight to hold him back, "I'll kill you NUB!"

Suddenly, the eerie glow of the emergency lighting was replaced by bright florescence, and the relentless roar of the rushing seawater slowed to little more than a trickle. Scarpa and Quinn stood in the blood slicked bilge and peered upward to an observation window. The large placard underneath the window read: Naval Base Norfolk Submarine Damage Control Training Center. In the window looking down upon them stood Master Chief Paul Hackett. Master Chief Hackett was the Chief of the Boat, or COB as the position was traditionally referred to, for the USS Key West SSN-722, the Los Angeles class fast attack submarine the sailors were assigned to.

In the submarine force, the COB, typically being the most senior enlisted man in the crew, was the liaison between the Officers and the enlisted men. There was a rumor among the sailors aboard the Key West that their COB was the oldest enlisted man serving in any branch of the U.S. military. The rumor, however, was solely based on the fact that the COB looked like he could have served under John Paul Jones. In actuality, his leathery face and a stringy white comb over made him seem much older than forty six. However, the combination of three decades of submarine service, two divorces and only six years of sobriety along the way, made him *seem* twenty years older than any other man in uniform.

At that moment, the COB's face, a deep shade of crimson, was a stark contrast from his white knuckles which strangled the microphone. "I've had turds stop up water better than you lady boys!" He looked down upon the shivering mass of sailors in their wet uniforms as they stared up at him fearfully. He constantly griped that these guys were children, not grown men. Yet, he had been repeatedly reminded with all the new restrictions in the Navy, he couldn't even discipline them as harshly as he would a child. "If it were up to me," he continued to lecture, "I would come down into that simulator and hold a couple heads underwater. No one would ever let go of a wrench under pressure again."

"However," the COB paused just long enough for a bit of pressure to be relieved off the pulsating vein in his forehead, "we have regulations in place to make sure no mothers receive any tear-soaked letters from you wussies. Who cares if you kill yourselves when we're at sea, just as long as no one's feelings get hurt!"

For now the only resource he had to try and teach them to avoid fatal errors was to yell, and he had just attended a two day seminar addressing the inappropriateness of using "offensive" language. "You'd better write your Mamas and tell them you love 'em, 'cause with incompetence like that you'll never make it back alive!"

"I always tell your mama I love her," Quinn quipped under his breath. The comment seemed to warm the shivering mob and they separated from each other with subtle laughter.

The COB noticed the change in the men's posture. He had been at the game long enough to know when a smartass was in the crowd, even when he couldn't hear the comment. He also knew this group well enough to know exactly where the salvo had been launched from. He cranked the microphone's output level, "Quinn! Don't make me put my foot in your mouth!" A couple of the sailors stifled a chuckle.

A few years back the comment would not have sounded so ridiculous. Back then, the COB would have illustrated his intentions with a more uncomfortable orifice. He may have even chosen an expression that would have implied a change in Quinn's gender, but then that would have gone against the lessons he learned from the sexual harassment training video he was forced to make his crew watch semi-annually. It was beyond him as to why he had to show a video of the world's worst re-enactors portraying a Tom Selleck wannabe Navy Captain harassing his civilian secretary who looked like she belonged on the hood of a car in a White Snake video.

He was sure the moron in the Pentagon who came up with that one would not have appreciated the scene on the crew's mess as the entire duty section got up after their forced viewing of the video and goosed the COB as they went about their day to do something that actually mattered. The COB just rolled his eyes for about the first ten guys saying, "Yeah, yeah, I got a room full of Benny Hills." After a while the joke wore off, at least for him, and the last few guys out of the space had to duck to avoid the punches he was throwing, but every last one of them managed to goose, or at least smack him on his backside.

In reality, he of course knew the training was Navy-wide and the surface fleet did have to deal with those types of issues. The Pentagon couldn't just institute separate policies for submariners, no matter how off keel they were.

"At least we don't have to deal with women on submarines yet," the COB muttered to himself, but as he looked down on the generation of sailors brought up in a world dominated by Oprah Winfrey, he relented, "well, maybe we do."

"You lady boys get cleaned up and back to the boat," he snarled, "we've got a weapons load to finish up before we head out to sea in the morning." The COB turned to head out of the training center's control room. As he started to go through the door he paused. "Hit 'em again with the water." A weaselly looking petty officer sitting at the control board was all too happy to comply.

"Hit 'em again with the water, aye Master Chief," the petty officer whistled through his overbite as he began flipping switches.

The COB waited with one foot out the door. He heard the roar of the flood simulation pumps as their RPM's cranked up like his 1978 Corvette Stingray coming off the line. Instantly, the groans of the unsuspecting sailors in the mock Sea Water Bay matched the volume of the pump motors and rushing water. He closed his eyes and listened to their grief as if he were sipping a brandy while enjoying a symphony.

CHAPTER 2

Captain Michael Maddox leaned on a crate of dehydrated food stores, which was waiting on the pier to be loaded into the Key West in preparation for its underway the next morning. He sipped coffee out of a nondescript ceramic mug, taken from the boats galley, as he watched his Weapons Officer coordinate the loading of torpedoes aboard his submarine. Captain Maddox let his mind drift absently as he stared at the sub. The Key West wasn't the most impressive submarine in the force; far from being a Seawolf or Virginia class submarine, it wasn't even a 688-I, one of the newer Los Angeles Class submarines. However, that was of no consequence to Captain Maddox. He knew how to drive a boat better than any other skipper in the water. He was able to train up a crew which could take on the newest class submarines and make it an even playing field. Even though the Key West was handicapped by older technology and the cumbersome fairwater planes, the disciplined crew Captain Maddox was able to mold kept the aging boat a formidable weapon in the U.S. Navy's arsenal.

Most young Commanding Officers would run around their boats like mad men micromanaging their Weapons Officer as his division loaded weapons on board their submarines, but Captain Maddox wasn't a young C.O. He was the oldest captain in the submarine force. In his lengthy career, he had dealt with just about every problem a C.O. could face and handled it with a coolness that made him the best Captain in the undersea realm. It also helped that his Weapons Division Officer, Lieutenant Commander Dominick Copaletti, was emerging as the new stud in the submarine force.

The Weapons Officer, or Weps as the crew called him, was not an Annapolis man. He, in fact, had graduated at the top of his class from Boston's prestigious MIT. Unlike most of his fellow graduates though, he had no lust for scoring a position with the highest paying engineering firm. For him the desire was to lead men in battle. It was as if in long generations past, the Centurion soul had been so tightly woven into his DNA, another millennia could pass and his descendants would still have a heart for war. Yet, even with his warlike tendencies, he still had the mind of an engineer, and fast attack submarines seemed as though they were designed for him. That is, they met every desire of his heart, except for comfort. At six foot five, the Weps wasn't exactly cut out for submarine duty. His broad shoulders, chiseled chin and thick black hair made it seem as though he would be more at home in the pages of a comic book, rather than continually hunched over in a nuclear powered sardine can. Though his stature made men want to be led by him, it was the fact that he treated men of all ranks with even handed respect which kept the sailor's devotion to him undying.

It was for different reasons that Captain Maddox could not have asked for a better subordinate. The Weps was a great naval strategist. His split second decisions during multinational naval exercises over the past two years helped in furthering Captain Maddox's reputation as the most dangerous and feared opponent in the sea; a fact that Captain Maddox felt should have come up in Washington during the recent senior officer promotion boards. Boards which he hoped would finally promote him to Rear Admiral.

Captain Maddox watched the Weps direct his men as they loaded a Mark 48 ADCAP torpedo down the weapons shipping hatch of the Key West. Behind him, came the growing whir of a golf cart motor as it approached. He paid it no attention until he heard the squeak of its brakes and then the clunk of its parking brake being set. He turned to find Rear Admiral Victor Perry stepping out of the golf cart which was chauffeured by a young sailor. Captain Maddox took no notice of the woman in the cart talking on her cell phone, all he really focused on was the warm hand extended by his oldest friend. Before shaking hands though, he gave Adm. Perry a quick but lazy salute. Keeping with protocol, Adm. Perry returned his salute but with a little more snap.

"It's good to see you, Mike," Adm. Perry said as they met in a familiar handshake.

"Good to see you too, Vic," Captain Maddox responded softly. As they exchanged pleasantries, the sun's light reflected off of Adm. Perry's medals which adorned his dress white uniform. The reflection forced a squint to sour Captain Maddox's face. While Adm. Perry talked, Captain Maddox couldn't help being distracted by the medals. Most of the medals represented the worst six weeks of his life, the first Gulf War.

In those days, Captain Maddox had been a young Lieutenant Commander serving as the Executive Officer aboard the USS Chicago, the fleet's Hot Boat, that is to say its most decorated submarine. Its crew was headed by Captain Jay Dalton. Captain Dalton lived and breathed submarine warfare, and LCDR Maddox had been his right hand man. Together they led the Chicago to every top award in the fleet. As the world was leaving the Cold War to the history books, Captain Dalton, with the help of then LCDR Maddox, was preparing to show what fast attack submarines meant to 21st century warfare. Unfortunately for LCDR Maddox, the twisted hand of fate sidelined him just before operation Desert Shield transformed into operation Desert Storm.

The night before the Chicago was to leave its port in Crete and track south through the Suez Canal to join in Desert Shield, LCDR Maddox was racked with kidney stones. The pain was unlike anything he had ever felt, and according to Navy regulations, even if he had dragged himself down the hatch, he would not be permitted to go to sea while afflicted with kidney stones. When Captain Dalton consulted him about whether he should have one of the department heads take over his duties, or if he should request a replacement be flown in, LCDR Maddox recommended his best friend and biggest rival from the Naval Academy, LCDR Victor Perry, take his place as the X.O. of the Chicago.

It was not just a favor to his good friend; it made both strategic and logistical sense. LCDR Perry had recently begun a stint on shore duty in La Maddalena, Italy and LCDR Maddox knew being stuck on a base with a war on the horizon was killing his friend. Besides the fact, there was no better qualified officer for the job; he was only three hours away by puddle jumper. He could hop on a plane and be in Crete that evening, ensuring the boat would be able to get underway in the morning as scheduled.

The next morning, as LCDR Maddox lay doubled over in pain on the floor of his temporary barracks room, the Chicago went to sea. Captain Dalton could not have been more pleased by LCDR Maddox's handpicked replacement. After a flawless trek through the Suez Canal and the Red Sea, the Chicago prepared to pass through the Straits of Hormuz. That night, as the submarine crept past the coast of Iran; Captain Dalton retired to his state room early complaining of a migraine. At zero four hundred, the messenger of the watch entered Captain Dalton's stateroom and instead of delivering a report from the Officer of the Deck, he found the man lying face down on the deck.

So it was LCDR Perry took his place as XO and two weeks later found himself to be the Commanding Officer of the USS Chicago due to the untimely stroke of Captain Dalton. The very evening of Captain Dalton's death, as his

T. Steven Sullivan

body lay atop of the crew's frozen goods, the Chicago emptied its arsenal of tomahawk missiles. LCDR Victor Perry not only became the youngest Commanding Officer in the fleet to take part in Desert Storm, he also sank three explosive laden merchant ships Saddam had intended to sail into U.S. naval supply depots in Bahrain.

Those few short weeks not only accelerated the career of young LCDR Victor Perry, but they did the same for any officer who had been aboard a submarine which launched missiles into Iraq. Whether it was a C.O. or a junior officer, it did not matter; if they were on a boat that launched birds, they had a chest full of medals. By April of 1991 there wasn't much room on the fast track for an officer who spent the Gulf War launching calcium rocks from his urethra.

Captain Maddox forced his gaze to scan the harbor, trying not to expose the petty jealousy he had of Adm. Perry's uniform. The somberness of Adm. Perry's tone brought his attention back to the conversation.

"The Presidents words about BJ in the State of the Union Address," Adm. Perry began as he too gazed out over the harbor, "made the whole country proud."

Captain Maddox still hadn't found the words to respond to the masses of well wishers trying to console him for the loss of his son. He found no response at all would keep the prying questions which followed at bay.

"Did you see Kathleen while you were in Washington?" Captain Maddox asked.

"I did, she seemed to be doing well," Adm. Perry replied, seeming to notice his friend's aversion to talking about his son.

"I knew she would be," Captain Maddox said as he turned his attention back toward the submarine, "She's the real trooper of the family." Captain Maddox knew his wife would be able to handle events stoically; she handled everything in stride, even the state of their marriage.

While they were not divorced, nor would they ever be, the years of him being at sea and with the success she had in Washington, first as a congress woman and most recently her election to the Senate, their lives were separate, but they remained friends.

"There's a rumor on Capitol Hill that she is a shoe-in to chair the Senate Intelligence Committee," Adm. Perry informed him.

Captain Maddox was not trying to be rude to his old friend. His lack of response was simply due to the fact his mind had been racing at flank speed lately. Adm. Perry seemed to take no offense at his friend's standoffishness. The events of the last few months would have worn on any man, no matter how strong their character and the news he was bringing him was not going to improve the situation.

"Mike, I need to talk to you about something," Adm. Perry's voice trailed off, as if he didn't really want to start the conversation he was about to. "I know it's not the best time."

As Captain Maddox turned to face Adm. Perry, the sharply dressed blond woman, who had been waiting in the golf cart, moved with executive grace toward the two men.

"Excuse me Admiral," the woman said as she brushed him aside, "Captain Maddox, it is an honor to meet the father of Sergeant BJ Maddox. On behalf of everyone at my network, I would like to say how much we appreciate the incredible service your son did for our country and what an honor it is for me to ride along on your ship." Ms. Stephanie Collins delivered her prepared statement as she stood with her perfectly manicured hand outstretched as though she were waiting for Captain Maddox to kiss it, rather than shake it.

Adm. Perry finally had Captain Maddox's full attention; although it had been won in a way he most likely did not appreciate. "Ms. Collins, please wait in the golf cart until we are finished," Adm. Perry firmly requested.

She let her hand linger in the air a moment, and then as if she had an epiphany, she cheerfully stated, "I'll wait in the cart until you boys are finished." Acting as though she were completely unaware of her imposition on the conversation, she spun around on her stiletto and shook her way back to the golf cart. As more sailors on the pier began to ogle her, the swing in her hips became more exaggerated.

"You were right Vic, it's not the best time," Captain Maddox coldly stated.

The pain on Adm. Perry's face, should have queued in Captain Maddox that the trivial news that Ms. Stephanie Collins, America's favorite morning news anchor, had been given clearance to tag along during the multinational war games the Key West was preparing to partake in, was just the tip of the iceberg. Unfortunately for Adm. Perry, since he had insisted on delivering the news from the promotion boards to Captain Maddox personally, the task of dumping Stephanie Collins on him was passed off as if it were some sort of reconciliation prize. There could be no doubt however; it would be like kicking dirt on a man's grave.

"Mike, I've got the results from the promotions boards," he started. As Captain Maddox whipped around, there was a glimmer of hope in his eyes. It was a look that hadn't made an appearance since the cat and mouse days of submarine tango with the Soviet Block. As quickly as hope made an appearance, so did it dissipate, once it met the anguish in Adm. Perry's eyes.

"Oh, come on, Vic! How much longer am I going to have to keep pushing these pigs around the ocean," Maddox said in anger, "they're not going to give me many more chances."

Standing there, the two officers, who had at one time stood shoulder to shoulder, dressed to kill as they made the ladies swoon on the D.C. social circuit, looked as though they weren't even in the same military now. Adm. Perry had managed to maintain his lean muscular frame over the years but Captain Maddox had lost his athleticism along the way. In fact, in his working khakis, absent any medals or ribbons, slouching posture, with his gut pushed out over his belt, he could have been mistaken for an old elementary school janitor.

"There aren't any more chances Mike," Adm. Perry said softly, concern filling his face. Maddox did not seem to be processing what he was telling him.

"Of course there is," Maddox motioned wildly with an open hand as he spoke, "I just have to drive this God-forsaken hunk of metal around for another..."

Adm. Perry interrupted, "They're giving you a pretty generous buy-out package."

Suddenly, Captain Maddox's fiery gaze seemed to lose focus. The sun's reflection, rippling across his eyes, betrayed subtle tears beginning to form. He did not try to hide his face in shame, but turned on his old friend.

"You mean *you're* giving me a generous package."

"Now that's not fair, Mike."

Captain Maddox poked Adm. Perry in the Chest. "You could have gone to bat for me!"

"I did go to bat for you," Adm. Perry retorted as he backpedaled. He did go to bat for him during the boards, but the fact was, Captain Maddox hadn't made things easy for himself over the last fifteen years. While he was undoubtedly loved by the men that served under him, he had a way of getting under the skin of his superiors.

The terms of the retirement package were generous. For the Navy, the last thing the Brass wanted was for Captain Maddox to be hard up for money and take a job as a cable news military expert. One of the main arguments for not promoting him over the years was the higher his rank, the more credibility it would lend him if he were to become an outspoken critic of the Navy. But now with his wife's high profile position in Washington and his son's even higher profile death, he could be a Seaman Recruit and his criticisms would be taken as scripture.

Captain Maddox had known for quite some time this day was coming, in fact he was dead certain two years ago that he would be forced to retire, but to his surprise they kept him hanging on. Now, the news was no shock to him, he was simply going through a dance which he had choreographed long ago. It was just as he imagined, being told by his best friend, on the pier, in front of the crew, the only thing he hadn't foreseen was the Chihuahua in the golf cart fixing her hair.

He didn't see that one coming; after all he was a strategist, not a prophet. But still it distracted him. He had a whole speech about how it should have been him driving that boat, how he should be the one with all the medals. However, the moment seemed to slip away. He wasn't sure if it was the death of his son which made it all seem a bit theatrical, or if it was his own plans for a retirement, plans that would make the Navy's retirement package seem like a meager uniform allowance. Whatever the reason, he didn't feel like staging a grand production the way he had done so many times before in his mind.

He pulled his hand back, snapped his heels together and tossed up a salute, "Good day, sir."

Adm. Perry attempted to bring it back to a personal level, "come on Mike."

Captain Maddox simply held his salute firm, stared straight ahead and repeated himself, "Good day sir." With a sigh of both defeat and relief, Adm. Perry returned the salute. When it dropped Maddox turned 180 degrees and walked away.

When Ms. Collins saw Captain Maddox walking across the brow to the submarine, she hopped to her feet, "Wait! You need to take me on your ship!"

Captain Maddox ignored her. When he had disappeared down the escape hatch, she turned to Adm. Perry, "Geez, he seems pretty grouchy for a guy whose son saved millions of lives."

Adm. Perry spoke almost to himself rather than acknowledging her, "There was only one life Captain Maddox wanted to see saved." He turned to her, "Come on, I'll introduce you to the COB. He'll take care of the arrangements for you and your camera man."

CHAPTER 3

Captain Maddox sat in his stateroom with the door open. At eight feet by eight feet, the Captain's stateroom was the largest personal space aboard the submarine. It was adorned with the standard wood paneling which made living areas aboard the submarine seem like a small fishing cabin. As if designed by a pop-up trailer engineer, there was a bunk, or rack as submariners call them, which would fold up into the outer bulkhead to reveal a small table and two bench seats underneath. More often than not, Captain Maddox would leave the rack down, preferring to work at a laptop size desk which folded out of the stateroom's aft bulkhead.

In the forward bulkhead there was a door which led into the head. In keeping with the camper motif, the head had a broom closet size shower, a sink no bigger than a soup bowl, and a standard submarine toilet. The entire head, including the bulkheads, was constructed out of stainless steel giving it a frigid appearance. Even though the space in the head was limited, it seemed a bit of a luxury for a submarine, since it was only shared with one other person, the X.O. There were two doors for the head, one forward and one aft. The forward door led to the XO's stateroom.

On the bulkhead just above Captain Maddox's desk, there hung two frames. The first frame displayed his diploma from the Naval Academy. The second was an eight by ten photo of Captain Maddox, in his dress whites, with his arm around a thick necked kid in an Army Sergeants dress uniform. The young soldier was BJ Maddox. The photo was taken the day BJ graduated from Ranger school at Ft. Benning, and the only thing in the picture broader than the handsome young man's shoulders was the smile on his father's face.

Captain Maddox found it very hard to accept that BJ did not intend to follow in his footsteps and take a path that would lead to the Officer Corps of the Navy. When his son informed him that he did not even intend to go to college, he nearly threw him out of the house. The final straw was when BJ told him he had enlisted in the Army. Captain Maddox could not get past his own ego and believe that his son was joining out of a sincere desire rather than spite. However, as time went by, he began to realize that the Army had been able to do what he never could, harness BJ's seemingly infinite supply of energy. When he saw his son serving with a passion greater than that of his younger days as a junior officer, he became BJ's greatest pillar of support.

There came a knock on the frame of his open door. Without looking up from the reports he was reading, Captain Maddox commanded, "Enter Nav."

The boats Navigator LCDR Arthur Hage entered and shut the door behind him, "Excuse me, Captain."

"What is it, Nav?" Maddox barked.

The Navigator jumped. He was a fidgety man, although he had not always been so unsure of himself. The stress of being a Navigator was surprisingly more than he had expected. Before being assigned to the Key West, he had done a brief stint as the Engineering Department head on a trident submarine until it collided with an undersea mountain. Although he had nothing to do with the ship's control party during the incident, the entire board room was removed from the boat. Most of the senior officers were discharged. He, however, was lucky enough to be reassigned.

Unfortunately, the only department head billet which was open to him was the position of Navigator aboard the USS Key West. After seeing how the Navigator of his former submarine had been strung up both in the world of Naval Politics, and in the media, he did not relish the thought of taking the position. However, at the time he thought taking another department head position aboard a submarine was the only way to salvage any sliver of hope for his career.

He never realized how good he had it as the engineer. If he didn't want the Captain to find him he had a whole engine room to hide in. As the Navigator though, he was constantly under the Captains thumb, and usually the first to feel the brunt of the Captain's temper.

Yet, it became apparent to him, as the Key West had many successful missions, his fellow department heads received many accolades from the squadron while he did not even receive one citation of merit to be placed in his service record. He knew, as did the Captain he stood before, both of their careers were dead in the water.

"Captain, is the mission unchanged?" the Nav asked in a hushed voice.

"It's imperative we complete it now more than ever," Captain Maddox stated as he looked over his reading glasses at the Nav.

The Nav stepped closer and spoke in a whisper, "But Captain, I have a few concerns."

Captain Maddox tossed down his clipboard showing his displeasure, "Now why am I not surprised?"

The Nav, who had become accustomed to that type of tone from his Captain, continued to press, "Is it true Stephanie Collins is coming underway with us?"

"Yes," Captain Maddox tried to formulate an answer that would appease the Nav, "but she will be staying in the XO's stateroom which, when the time is right, will become her cell." He could tell that the Nav was not set at ease.

Captain Maddox would have preferred to bring an officer like the Weps into the loop, but as neurotic as the Nav was, he was easily manipulated. "I still don't understand how we are going to keep the XO and the other Department heads in the dark," the Nav persisted.

"I told you I've got the XO taken care of," Maddox said in a calm voice trying to reassure the Nav. "If there's one thing I know about that squirrelly little man, it's that after two days at sea the only thing he can think about is popping his head out of the hatch and taking a breath of fresh air." Captain Maddox knew the Nav could go on all night with his interrogation, but he had neither the time nor the patience to listen to him. "If you'll excuse me," he got up and left the Nav in his stateroom to question the bulkheads.

Emerging from his stateroom, it took just a few steps aft for Captain Maddox to enter the submarine's control room. To his dismay, the COB was giving a tour to Ms. Collins. He wasn't sure which ate at him more, the fact he would have to deal with her incessant questions over the next two weeks or that her short skirt seemed to distract every red blooded sailor she came in sight of. Even those sailors who didn't see her were equally distracted, as her perfume melted through the dingy stench of the synthetic air which always lingered throughout the submarine.

The control room was buzzing with activity; Stephanie Collins had a worried look, as if she were questioning whether it would be safe to go out to sea the next morning, not to mention submerge. She looked around at a number of sailors with electronic gear pulled apart. Some had themselves buried half way into pieces of equipment which, to a novice eye, would seem as though it might be vital to the submarine's operation.

In the center of the control room, Scarpa stood on a stepstool between the two periscopes using a pneumatic grease gun to cram the bluish green lubricant into the scopes' grease fittings. Every five or six seconds the relief valve on the pneumatic gun would pop, immediately followed by a startled flinch from the petite reporter.

"Master Chief, is the ship really going to be ready?" she asked nervously.

"Don't you worry your pretty little head missy," he said in a tone which seemed to be an octave higher than his usual growl. Sailors throughout control room exchanged uncomfortable glances. They had never heard the COB talk in such a soft voice; it was as if he had been a victim of some parasitic alien using him as a host body.

Quinn entered the control room just in time to hear the COB's most earnest attempt at being cordial. He could tell Ms. Collins didn't realize she was actually being treated with the fairest amount of respect the COB could muster. So Quinn took it upon himself to save her, not that it was any sort of sacrifice when she was so beautiful.

Using his best John Wayne impersonation, Quinn injected himself into the conversation, "That's right little lady, don't you worry your pretty little britches, this ain't a ship, ships sink. This here puppy's a boat, and boats submerge." Quinn could see Ms. Collins trying to hide her laughter. It was hard to tell if the COB truly wasn't amused or if he just didn't make the connection as to why the John Wayne impression.

Her curiosity in Quinn seemed to be piqued. All afternoon she had witnessed, not just enlisted men, but also senior officers treat the COB with kid gloves. Yet, before her stood this handsome Second Class Petty Officer, treating the COB as if he were his stuffy older brother. Because of her success in television and popularity with the tabloids, she usually intimidated men of her own age and tax bracket, but here was a young man who seemed quite confident around her.

Quinn knew exactly who Stephanie Collins was, even the Amish probably knew of Stephanie Collins. He was surprised how attractive she was in person. He thought the TV types were all about hair and make-up, and while she was made up quite nice, she had a natural beauty to her that made him forget the rest of the work he had for that afternoon.

Maddox noticed Ms. Collins falling for Quinn's charms just as easily as everyone else who met the kid. He took the chance to sneak past her. Unfortunately, the COB had a way of disrupting the spell Quinn was laying on.

"Quinn! I've had it up to here with you today," the COB said holding a hand, trembling with frustration, level with his forehead.

"I wish I were that tall," Quinn casually remarked as he fired off a wink at Ms. Collins. She probably would have fallen under Quinn's spell completely, had it not been for Maddox trying to duck past.

"Oh, Captain Maddox, a moment of your time please," she snagged his arm as he tried to dart away. He stopped, signaled his surrender with a sigh, and finally addressed her.

"Yes, Ms. Collins," he said, regretting every word as it slipped past his lips.

"I was wondering if we might get together for dinner tonight," she blinked her beautiful brown eyes at him. "I could do a preliminary interview with you." Her charms, however, were better suited to be used on the rest of the crew. He perceived her presence as a cruel twist of the knife by the Navy bureaucrats; making him suffer through his last underway, being nagged to death by the little Chihuahua.

"I think Petty Officer Quinn is better suited to entertain you tonight, Ms. Collins," Captain Maddox said to Quinn's delight. "I'm afraid I have too many loose ends to tie up before we get underway in the morning." Captain Maddox hoped that Ms. Collins would fall under Quinn's spell and be distracted by him for the next two weeks. *Hell,* he thought, *she might even do an expose' on him and boost his promising career.* "How about it, Petty Officer Quinn?" he deflected, knowing any story she'd put together on his own tenure would end up sounding like a eulogy.

"You heard the man, Ms. Collins." Quinn put out his arm for her to interlock with, "Do you prefer line dancing or Salsa?"

Captain Maddox could see her eager eyes accept even before she put her arm through Quinn's. *The Kid is smooth,* he thought to himself, satisfied that his impromptu plan might work. His small victory was soon diminished when he met the sourness of the COB's gnarly face.

"Well thanks a lot skipper," the COB griped as Quinn and Ms. Collins headed out of the control room, "you could have sent her to dinner with me." He pouted in a way none of the crew had seen before. "She's closer to my age than Quinn's." Captain Maddox jokingly ducked as if the COBs words rang out like a gunshot.

"Don't let her hear you say that COB, you wouldn't want to insult our guest," Captain Maddox said with the first visible smile of the day. The Captain's smile quickly reverted back to a scowl when LCDR James Stanton, the boat's Engineering Department Head, posted himself in front of him. The Eng did not wear his confidence as humbly as the Weps. Fittingly, it seemed to rub everyone in the crew the wrong way, everyone except for the Weps. The two men, whose positions should have set them up as subtle competitors, were as thick as thieves. Off the boat they competed in everything. Whether it was in a pick-up game of basketball or shooting pool at a bar, their ferocity with which they tried to top one another had landed them in hot water numerous times.

However, while at work, the two understood the necessity of accommodating one another in any way they could to reach a common goal. Each of them realized that the better their submarine performed, the further their own careers would be excelled. In happier days, Captain Maddox relished being in their company, the same way an old war veteran enjoys the nostalgia of buying a drink for a young serviceman. The two department heads reminded him of Adm. Perry and himself in their wonder years. The Nav, who was still grieving the loss of a promising career, could barely stand to be in the same compartment with, as he put it on more than one occasion, the two prima donnas.

"What's the status of the Engineering Department, Mr. Stanton?" Captain Maddox snapped, as his mood slipped back into the quiet rage which had been eating at him for the last few months. He knew he would have to prod the Engineer for the status report. The man was like an impetuous child who had just done something polite for the first time in his life, and would wait all day to be acknowledged for his good work.

The Eng proudly flipped through his report, "The Engineering Department is ready to go to sea, Captain."

"Very well, Mr. Stanton," Maddox's response completely lacked the enthusiasm with which the report was given. "What time is my reactor going to be started?"

"The startup watch will be stationed at zero one hundred hours sir." As the Eng made his report, a short stout chief lumbered his way into the control room.

The chief, apologetically interrupted, "Excuse me, Eng." The confident Engineer did not appear at all happy to see the dumpy man.

"Yes Chief Monroe?" he begrudgingly asked. At this point in the day, the only reason for one of his department's Chief Petty Officers to interrupt him, would be to report bad news.

Hesitantly, the chief delivered, "I'm sorry Eng, but the evaporator just quit." The Eng, obviously upset with the news, clenched his jaw in an attempt to conceal his emotions.

"What do you mean it just quit?"

"Are we going to be able to get underway tomorrow Mr. Stanton?" Captain Maddox prodded. The Eng, remembering he was in the presence of the Captain, tried to make it seem as though the report did not worry him.

"My team will have it fixed in no time, even if I have to stay here all night."

"Good man," Maddox said, letting the Eng's rouse remain intact. He of course knew, without the evaporator online there would be no fresh water for the reactor, meaning the boat would not be able to go to sea. He could see the Engineer wanted desperately to go assess the situation in person but did not want to let on how urgent he felt the matter was by bolting out of the control room. Captain Maddox decided to have mercy on the Eng and offered a way out.

29

"Well Eng, don't just stand here, go fix *your* evaporator!" The Eng didn't make the Captain tell him twice before he shot out of the control room.

As the Eng headed aft, Captain Maddox exchanged a quick glance with Scarpa, who was still on the stool greasing the periscopes. It was quick, but a lack of reaction from either man would have made any observer think it was intentional. The Nav was observing, and the apparent collusion kept the Nav frozen in place as Maddox headed out the aft door into the navigation equipment space. As Scarpa's gaze shifted to lock with the Nav's, it seemed to thaw the man and he hurried after his Captain.

The Nav caught up to Captain Maddox just as he was removing the safety chain in order to head down the ladder to middle level.

"Captain," the Nav hoarsely implored as he grabbed his Commanding Officer by the arm.

Captain Maddox just stared at the grip until the Nav regretfully released it.

"This is not really the place, Mr. Hage."

"I apologize Captain, but I need to know."

"Need to know what."

"I need to know if Petty Officer Scarpa is in the fold," the Nav pressed Captain Maddox for details on his plan more than he had up to this point.

"Yes," Captain Maddox curtly replied.

"I don't think that is such a good idea."

"I don't think it's any of your concern."

"Yes but Captain…"

"Down ladder!" Captain Maddox tried to end the conversation by simply continuing on his course, but the Nav persisted.

"I don't trust him."

Captain Maddox held up with one foot on the top rung of the ladder. "This operation isn't based on manning it with the most trustworthy personnel."

"I know that sir, but Scarpa seems…" the Nav hesitated.

"Seems what?"

"The kid seems evil, sir."

"He's down right sadistic Nav, but he's the only one I can rely on to cause enough havoc in the engine room to keep Stanton out of our hair for the next ten days, without causing a reactor melt down." Captain Maddox stared into the Nav's eyes until he saw the Nav capitulate. "Down Ladder!" he repeated the warning then continued on his way.

CHAPTER 4

The early morning mist rose off the water in Norfolk harbor, giving the sleek black submarines a ghostly appearance as they steadily swayed in formation moored against the pier. As the first light of the morning sun illuminated the harbor with red iridescence, a lone topside watch could be seen patrolling the deck of each submarine, except for the Key West.

Sailors clad in both khaki and working uniforms swarmed about the Key West and the pier where she was moored, making last minute preparations to get underway. Some were loading last minute stores; others were disconnecting the heavy shore power cables. The reactor was hot now and the Key West no longer needed support from the pier.

As Quinn and a few other sailors came across the brow, Scarpa climbed out of the forward escape trunk dressed in his diver uniform, using just one hand to maneuver the ladder, carrying a tool bag in his mouth and swim fins in his other hand.

"Scarpa, we've got a half hour before we station the maneuvering watch," Quinn beamed. "You turning over a new leaf?"

"I'm trying to get the next Blue Jacket of the Quarter award." Bob Newhart was the only other man on earth who could have delivered a line laced with that much sarcasm yet still keep a straight face.

Quinn noticed Scarpa's scraped and swollen knuckles as well as a fresh black eye. "My guess is you had a little trouble last night and now you're trying to avoid the COB, eh." Quinn noticed the anger flash across Scarpa's face. At this point he was able to read the many degrees of Scarpa's anger, and he knew he had touched a nerve simply because he was right.

"Just don't tell him where I'm at."

"Where who is at?"

"Me," Scarpa said indignantly. "Don't tell the COB where *I* am at. Do I have to spell it out for you?" Quinn couldn't understand why Scarpa took simple matters so seriously. He had not had things as easy in life as Scarpa would have liked to believe. Scarpa, as well as most of the crew, looked at Quinn as if he were a spoiled rich kid who probably was forced to join the military when a frat prank had gone too far. This was not the case at all for Quinn.

Quinn's parents had died when he was five, and he was shipped off to live with his Uncle Cal and Aunt Vicki on their run down farm in northern Indiana. His Uncle Cal was a Korean War veteran who suffered from severe Post Traumatic Stress Disorder, or at least that was the excuse he used when he would beat Quinn with his belt or any other farm tool that was close at hand. Quinn suspected the fits of rage were brought on more by vodka than war flashbacks. It didn't help that his Aunt Vicki showed her affection for him too readily, which only acted as a catalyst for his uncle's rage.

Aunt Vicki was a sweet woman, but even the love she had for Quinn wasn't enough to keep her around. When Quinn was eleven, she left. As her car disappeared from view, Quinn said nothing, he just waited. What he was waiting for didn't take long. Before the dust settled in the driveway he had been knocked down. His head crushed into the dirt, as his uncle's full weight pressed down upon him like a mill stone. As he tried to gasp for air, the dirt, mixed with his tears, snot and saliva formed a mud that caked around his nose and mouth.

Quinn was not sure if he had been choked until he passed out or if the blows to his head had caused him to be knocked unconscious. He finally came to when a sharp pain in his left hand kicked his neuroreceptors into overdrive. He tried to pull his hand to his face to inspect the pain but he found he could not free his fingers from whatever had clamped down on them. He pulled harder, but then his fingers were pulled equally hard in the opposite direction. Forgetting the pain in the rest of his body he whipped his head around to find his uncle's prized pig trying to gnaw the fingers right off his hand.

It took six or seven hard blows to get the seven hundred pound hog to relinquish his hand, but when it finally did, Quinn managed to back into a corner of the sty and inspect his fingers. The gruesome sight of his mangled fingers brought on a bit of wooziness, but he managed to keep it together by focusing on the positive aspect; they were still there.

He heard the hacking laugh of his uncle. "You want a drink, boy?" Uncle Cal cackled as he stood in the doorway urinating into the thick mud which covered the floor. "You and Neddy awt get real close, bein' roomies and all." Then he began throwing rotten apples and other spoiled food at Quinn. Defiantly, Quinn picked up an orange rind and sucked the last remnants of citrus still clinging to it.

The old man dumped the rest of the bucket of spoiled food into the pig's trough. Then he closed and locked the door with a heavy chain. Immediately, Quinn set out to find an escape. The search, however, proved to be futile; he found that the sty had obviously been fortified. He couldn't help but wonder how long his uncle had been planning to make it his cage.

The throbbing in his fingers reminded him he had to get the wounds clean or the infection, which could set in, would become the worst of his problems. It was clear he wasn't going to be receiving a first aid kit, so he used the closest thing he had to a sterile wash to clean his wounds.

Luckily Neddy's bladder seemed to be ten times larger than his own, so even if he was half way across the sty, he could still make it in time to give his fingers a good dowsing. While washing his wounds with urine wasn't pleasant, he was already an experienced hunter and was used to the foul smells that came from within animals. The most difficult task during the healing process was keeping his fingers out of the mud.

After about a week it was clear that his fingers would heal fine, with the exception of a few mangled scars. However, like his other scars, they would diminish, somewhat, over time.

He wasn't sure how long he would be kept in the sty, and he hadn't thought to start keeping track of the days until he had been there two weeks, or was it three? To his best guess he had been there about four and a half weeks, when Neddy seemed to grow territorial as it came to sharing his food.

Each morning, when the old man would come and let Neddy out, Quinn would take advantage of the solitary time to eat. At first, he had been able to bully the giant hog, but as Quinn became weaker and weaker his blows began to have little effect on its thick hide. One evening, when Neddy was let back in, the hog, after examining the empty trough, charged Quinn and pinned him to the ground with his massive slobbery snout. The pig seemed to be taking on the sadistic persona of its owner.

Quinn knew he needed to escape, but found he was too weak to make any real attempts at a break out. Then, one morning, as hope seemed to be failing, he noticed Neddy chewing on the support beam in the middle of the sty. The previous evening, Quinn had used the same six inch by six inch piece of timber as a shield from the rotten fruit his uncle hurled at him. The hog's insatiable appetite left no scrap behind, even if it was imbedded in the grooves of a wooden plank.

The first four feet of the exterior walls of the sty were cinder block, so the plan Quinn came up with would have to focus on the one interior wall of the sty which was made of wood and led to the rest of the barn. The next desperate afternoon, as Neddy was out wallowing in the sun, Quinn began to smear scraps of food on the wooden slats which made up the base of the interior wall. It took the pig no time to set to work on the slat once he had cleaned up all the scraps Quinn was attempting to eat. Before long, Neddy had chewed a small hole through the plank. As the pig's powerful jaws made the pine planks seem as if they were balsa, Quinn couldn't help but think his bones would soon be snapping just as easily if the pig's appetite kept increasing like it had been.

Once the pig was finished and had moved on, Quinn was able to kick out the board. Though he was small, the opening still wasn't large enough to enable him to escape. He knew his uncle would surely notice it in the morning, so he tried reaching through to see if he could grab a hold of anything that could help him.

The next morning when the old man came to get Neddy, he let out his call as he entered the barn. "Soooui! Soui! Soooui!"

When the familiar grunts of the pig did not return his call, he rushed to open the door of the sty. Quinn had always thought it appropriate the old man and the pig spoke the same language. When the old man opened the door, he dropped to his knees. There, lying in the mud was his prized pig, its underside completely sliced open with its entrails scattered about. The only thing that kept the old man from lunging at Quinn was the bloody sickle Quinn held firmly in his hand. Knowing full well he was going to take a beating for his deed, Quinn stared straight at the old man, as his eyes danced with a savage fire.

Quinn did receive a beating, but not until his uncle's shock wore off later that afternoon. That was the last night Quinn ever spent in the sty. It seemed his uncle had gotten the majority of his sadism out of his system, or at least reason had won out in his uncle's mind. Cal was too old and had lived too hard to run the farm by himself. The farm barely scraped by and he couldn't afford to hire any hands to help, so Quinn became the foundation of labor he depended upon. Though he never treated Quinn with anything resembling kindness, he did move him into the loft of the barn and life in the loft opened up a whole new world to Quinn.

In the latter part of the nineteenth century, the barn had been used as a school house. Though it had long since been converted into a shelter for animals, the loft contained chest upon chest of books. Quinn had never been to a formal school. When he was very little he had gone to a preschool or a daycare, he couldn't quite remember, but his mother had given him a good basis for learning with a lot of one on one time before she passed. Then, when he came to the farm, his Aunt Vicki had taught him the way she had been taught as a little girl, at the kitchen table when her farm chores were done.

Under her guidance Quinn quickly learned to read. Before long he was reading anything he could get his hands on, it didn't matter if it was the manual for the John Deere or one of Aunt Vicki's recipe books, if it was on paper, he would read it. The treasure of the library in the loft was all the escape Quinn needed for the time being.

As the years passed, Quinn's shoulders became broad and his muscles hardened from strenuous work and the massive amounts of protein and vegetables which were the staple in the diet of farm life. Because of his growth, the physical nature of he and his uncle's relationship became less one sided. The abuse, however, did continue, though now it was more verbal than anything else. As Quinn devoured the books that filled the loft, he began to realize what a shell of a man his uncle was.

Though he did not attend school, the library in the loft not only filled the educational void, but it far surpassed the fast food style curriculums he would have received going to a traditional school. He was able to learn about American and World history through biographies and published letters. He read classic literature, as well as the writings of Aristotle and Virgil. *Plutarch's Lives* kept him fascinated for months as he read it over and over. He read of Roman history, the Napoleonic wars, and what fascinated him above all else was naval history.

He read and cherished the signed copy of Theodore Roosevelt's *The Naval War of 1812* and was enthralled with Britain's earlier rise to naval power. One day he sat on a log at the edge of a cornfield and read Robert Southey's *The Life of Nelson*. While most kids his age only knew the work of Southey through an uncredited-modernized version of *The Story of the Three Bears*, Quinn was more engaged by the creator of Goldilocks' account of the amazing life and death of Britain's most celebrated naval hero, Vice Admiral Horatio Nelson. To Quinn, who was quite used to, but not fond of, the fragrance of a freshly fertilized field, reading of the Battle of Trafalgar and Nelson's breaking of the combined French and Spanish fleets seemed to put a thirst in his soul for the smell of salt water. However, being on his own and not answering to anybody, Quinn didn't consciously realize that he was identifying, not with great leaders like Nelson, but more with the rogue Captains like Britain's Lord Cochrane, whose pirate-like seamanship earned him the nickname Sea Wolf by a frustrated Napoleon Bonaparte.

His uncle probably wondered why Quinn never ran away. The fact of the matter was, Quinn was quite content to handle the duties of the farm, so long as he was left alone. For the most part he was, but every so often, when his uncle would tie one on, he would come looking for Quinn.

One evening, when Quinn was fifteen, he was returning from an afternoon of fishing when he caught sight of his uncle. He could tell the old man had it in for him. Quinn saw the familiar look of payment due in his uncle's eyes. Even though Quinn had been doing more than could be expected or wished for from any hired help, his uncle started ranting about some trivial task that had not been completed. By now, Quinn could predict the old man's every move. As expected, he started the same way he had for years, with a right hook. Quinn was quite near the old man's size now. Though not tall, his muscles were solid and quick to react. He bent at the knees and waist, lowering his level while at the same time stepping past the punch. He dodged it with very little effort. Then, like the strike of a rattlesnake, he lifted his knee then shot out a hard kick. As the heel of his work boot struck his uncle's knee from the side, he could hear what sounded like a thousand pops as every bit of connective tissue in the old man's knee tore to shreds.

The old man fell in a crumpled heap on the lawn. Quinn could not hold back his rage; it had been pent up too long. His uncle was doubled over holding his useless knee. Quinn straightened him out with a kick to his face. He knew he was crossing the line of what was considered honorable in a fight, but then the old man had never shown any honor. Quinn pinned him down with a knee on his chest, held him by his throat and rained down punches on the old bastard's face. He only stopped when his hand began to throb.

As he lay in his bed that night, he could hear his Uncle Cal whimpering in the yard. The next morning, Quinn wasn't sure what exactly happened to his uncle; best he figured the old man was finally able to drag himself inside the house at some point during the night. It wasn't until later that evening when he saw the flicker of the television coming from inside the farmhouse that he knew for sure.

He didn't see his uncle for another month. When he did emerge, he was walking with a crutch. His mouth drooped when he talked. Quinn wasn't sure if it was because he had had a stroke or if he had broken his jaw during the fight and it had never healed right. Though he never did talk to Quinn again, Quinn would hear him mumbling to his pig, Neddy II, on occasion.

One morning, when Quinn was seventeen, he found his uncle dead in the pig sty. His fingers, nose, lips and ears had been devoured by Neddy II. Quinn figured he had had a heart attack in there, but after the coroner examined him, he said due to the amount of blood loss, it was more likely his knee gave out and he had a heart attack quite some time after the pig had begun to eat him. Quinn would spend the rest of his life trying to figure out if the guilt he felt was for having been a contributor to his uncle's death, or for the absence of tears to shed for the man. Whichever the case, he never told anyone he was the reason his uncle had a bad knee.

Quinn was taken in by a local family and attended high school for his senior year. The classes bored him, but the assimilation into the normal teen culture didn't take him nearly as long as he thought it would. The traditional model of schooling didn't interest Quinn in the least. He much preferred to read a book, and then move on to another once he had digested its content. Listening to a teacher regurgitate what he had already read in the text book seemed like a colossal waste of time. So when all the other students would talk excitedly about going off to college, he just couldn't picture paying money to sit through the same type of lecture.

His life's heading was set the day he saw the gleaming white uniforms of the Navy recruiters come into the school. He was eager to discuss naval firepower and strategies with the men of the Navy. Disheartening as it was to realize the men knew nothing of any great naval legends like that of Lord Cochrane, they did however present themselves as a key to the world that Quinn was eager to see.

Quinn understood why many of his fellow shipmates thought he came from a privileged background; he was always engaging the Junior Officers, who had recently been through the Navy's War College, in conversations about strategies of past naval battles. Strategy was not something most enlisted men thought about. The men of the enlisted ranks had jobs to perform, tasks that would keep the submarine operating smoothly. Their job was to provide senior officers with a machine that would operate precisely as needed when called upon to bring glory to those in command. The enlisted men in return would be able to tell their grandkids how they were a part of something that mattered in the world.

Quinn didn't find himself dwelling on the obvious differences he had with his counterparts, yet as the time came closer for him to rise above the enlisted ranks, he couldn't help but long for the feeling of unity he once shared with his shipmates when he first arrived on the Key West.

CHAPTER 5

The COB lumbered down the command passageway toward the control room. A quick glance into the Captain's empty stateroom as he passed, told him the Captain would most likely be in the radio room since he could also see the Captain was not in the control room from the same vantage point.

The COB entered the control room and spoke into the overhead as if he were talking to God. "Captain, are you in Radio sir?" He was actually speaking into the open microphone that allowed the radio room to hear everything that was being said in the control room. This system allowed for immediate communications with the radio room during critical moments.

The communications box above the Conning Station in the center of the control room crackled. "I'll be right there, COB. Is the Eng with you?" The COB saw the Eng hoisting himself off the deck, having just come up the ladder from middle level. The Eng looked like he hadn't slept much since the day before.

"He's right here, sir." They could hear the slam of the heavy door to radio as Captain Maddox came out. Had they been underway the Captain would have taken great care to ensure the door did not make a sound as he shut it behind him.

"Captain, are we ready?" The COB held the 1MC microphone inches away from his lips. Captain Maddox looked at the Eng.

"The engine room is ready for sea, sir," the Eng said, lacking any of the previous day's bravado.

"Station the Maneuvering Watch, COB."

"Station the maneuvering watch aye, sir." The COB keyed the mic and spoke with the grandeur of a ring announcer, "Station the maneuvering watch!"

The boat came to life. Every sailor aboard had a station to be at for the maneuvering watch. Men in their dungaree uniforms scrambled to get to their stations in order to safely maneuver the submarine away from the pier and make the trek from Norfolk harbor, through the historic Chesapeake Bay and out to sea.

Quinn jumped into the line of sailors filing aft through the crew's mess making their way topside via the forward escape trunk ladder. He carried his swim fins and safety line in one hand as he climbed; as with all submariners, climbing ladders with one hand had become second nature. As Quinn emerged topside he noticed Stephanie Collins stifle a laugh as she and her camera man came across the brow. Quinn knew exactly what was making her so giddy, it was his dive shorts. As one of the boat's divers, his job during the maneuvering watch was to be the safety swimmer, in case any of the line handlers fell overboard. This meant he was outfitted in his dive uniform, which consisted of a blue and yellow reversible t-shirt, neoprene dive boots, a dive knife Rambo would be proud of, and the ever impressive dive shorts. The navy's standard issue dive shorts had been designed for unrestricted movement of the legs. In short, they would make Daisy Duke blush if she put them on.

"I wouldn't have let you drop me off so early last night if you had been wearing those."

"Don't laugh," Quinn said with mock embarrassment as he held out his hand to assist her descent, "besides, I wasn't the one who said they had to cut the night short to lay down some voice tracks."

"I'm sorry," she said, biting her lip as if she were a teenage girl, "I'll make it up to you as soon as we get back." Their conversation was drowned out by the roar of the crane's diesel engine as it started up in preparation to remove the brow. "Just don't forget the shorts," she yelled as she tugged at the snug waistline.

In the control room, all of the equipment, which had been previously covered for security precautions, was now at full operational status. Everyone seemed to be waiting patiently at their stations ready to take control of the boat as soon as it was away from the pier. The COB entered the control room strapping on his life vest. "Chief of the Watch, report."

From the ship's control panel, Chief Meyers pulled the phone down from his mouth. "Everyone is on station with the exception of line four, they're missing a line handler." The COB went to the periscope and swung it aft. "I'm trying to find out who is supposed to be on that line now, COB," Chief Meyers continued. The COB looked at the stern line. He could see three sailors standing about, waiting to heave off their line.

"Stoney," the COB softly growled as he began scanning the end of the pier where sailors were smoking.

"Say again, COB."

"It's Petty Officer Stonefeld; he's supposed to be on line four." The COB continued to scan the pier, "Find his LPO, see if he was at muster this morning." There was no sign of him loafing at the snack bar, and then as he began to make a visual sweep of the parking lot, something caught his eye in the distance. He rotated the handle on the scope for greater magnification. "Son of a blue-eyed fart!" The COB zoomed in on the roof of the submarine barracks, where he could make out Stoney, sitting in a lawn chair, drinking a beer and watching the activity aboard the Key West through binoculars.

Chief Meyers, still on the sound powered phone, asked, "What is it, COB?"

"Chief of the Watch, do we still have a land line?"

"Sorry COB, we pulled it at oh seven thirty."

"Radio, get ahold of Shore Patrol. Tell them we need some trash collected off the roof of Carter Hall."

Quinn and Scarpa were near the water line at the stern of the boat. They had just taken off the ballast tank vent covers when Quinn noticed the COB come storming out of the hatch. "COB looks pissed," Quinn observed. Scarpa looked up as his hair blew into his eyes. He reached down, cupped some water in his hands and used it to slick his hair back. When they were in their dive gear, Quinn and Scarpa were not required to wear their ship's ball caps. Normally, this was seen as another special privilege of the divers, but in Scarpa's case, it exposed the fact that he had not had a haircut in a few months.

When Scarpa slicked back his hair, Quinn noticed a deep cut on his forehead held together by butterfly bandages. "You look like you were trying to find a date at the SPCA again," Quinn sniped, trying to get a rise out of Scarpa.

"No thanks to your Nub," Scarpa reminded him. Quinn grabbed hold of Scarpa's chin and turned his head so he could take a better look at the cut. "Don't touch me," Scarpa said as he knocked his hand away, "at least not 'til we've been underway at least a week."

"It does have a sense of humor," Quinn said not as a jibe, but as a true statement of amazement. Scarpa never joked around with anyone. The resulting effect was a cone of isolation from the rest of the crew, which seemed to be Scarpa's intended purpose. Being on a submarine, it was nearly impossible to stick so many men in such a stressful-cramped environment, and not find them reverting back to a preteen form of crudeness, where the world seemed to be one big locker room and the fart joke was the ace of spades.

Yet, everyone in the crew knew not to joke around with Scarpa. Ribbing Scarpa was like checking for a gas leak with a match. As much as the officers complained about the immaturity among the crew, which seemed to spread like wild fire during long deployments, they knew the alternative would be a *Lord of the Flies* scenario and Scarpa was subconsciously voted most likely to smash someone's head in with a rock.

Quinn knew he was poking a bear with a stick every time he goaded Scarpa, yet there was a part of Quinn that thought poking a bear with a stick sounded like fun. The fact that Scarpa would not only tolerate, but sometimes even play along with Quinn, put him on a level no one else in the crew seemed to attain with Scarpa. Quinn was under no illusions that Scarpa considered him a friend, nor did Quinn consider him one, but he did seem to treat him with less disdain than the rest of the crew, which always remained a mystery to Quinn.

The COB did not zero in on Scarpa as Quinn had predicted; he posted himself at the edge of the brow with his gaze fixed to the end of the pier. Soon, all of the sailors topside found themselves staring in the same direction without even knowing why. The answer soon presented itself as everyone saw the pier sentry lift the gate to allow a Shore Patrol vehicle to slowly make its way down the pier. It came to a halt right in front of the Key West's brow. The COB's stern posture did not change as the shore patrolman opened the back door and hoisted a handcuffed Petty Officer Stonefeld to his feet. Stoney was in no way prepared to go to sea. He needed the help of both shore patrolmen to cross the brow. When the trio made it across, they uncuffed Stoney and relinquished him into the custody of the COB.

As Stoney stepped down onto the deck with bare feet, he did not help his circumstances. "Request permission to stay ashore, COB." All the sailors topside had let curiosity draw them in from bow and stern and they could see the COB was as close as he had ever been to throwing someone overboard.

Instead of the COB losing it, they witnessed the rage withdraw from his face. "Permission denied, Seaman Stoney," he said in a cool voice. The surprise on everyone's face was readily apparent. It seemed they had all expected the COB to go off on a diatribe that would surely leave Stoney with a saliva soaked face. "In fact, *Seaman* Stoney," by giving special emphasis on the word "seaman," the COB had forgone the formalities of the forthcoming Captain's Mast and already demoted Stoney, if only in conversation, "it will be a long, long time before you set foot ashore."

Technically, if it did come to a Captain's Mast, Stoney could argue that he had not missed ship's movement; in fact, he was only about an hour and a half late for muster. In most cases, if a sailor showed up late for duty, even a bit intoxicated, the COB would have sent them to their rack to sleep it off for the morning, then made them work it off in with some EMI, Extra Military Instruction. EMI usually consisted of working like a dog for the COB, doing some menial, but humiliating task with the expected outcome being the sailor would take on a more militaristic attitude. Stoney was very familiar with the EMI form of punishment, probably more so than any other sailor aboard, yet he was arguably the most un-militaristic sailor in the squadron at the very least.

"Get below," the COB said softly. Quinn knew, as many other sailors did, that the COB's sudden softness was like a great white shark disappearing after it had circled its potential prey a few times. It wasn't good. They knew they had better get Stoney below decks before the COB ate him alive.

As Stoney was helped down the ladder his voice resonated up from the hatch. "Dead men tell no tales!" Quinn could see the COB had not been especially satisfied with the lack of fear from Stoney to the first threat of punishment, but he knew, in the weeks to come, the COB's new hobby would be torturing Stoney. Especially if he was made a captive, restricted to the boat, and unable to escape the wrath of the old man.

"Get back on station!" the COB roared. The line handlers quickly made their way back to their posts. The COB gave a loud whistle, and then waved his hand in a circular motion over his head to signal the crane operator to take the brow away. As he started to make his way to the bow he stopped in mid-stride and pressed the earpiece of his walkie-talkie into his ear.

"Take on the tug, aye, sir. Line one, take on the tug!"

The line handlers caught the line from the tug and fastened it to one of the boat's foremost cleats. Once the tug had been secured to the boat, the COB called out, "Throw off all lines." The COB's booming voice ensured the order was carried out by all the line handlers simultaneously. As the thick mooring lines slapped the water with a sharp smack, a deep bellow came from the Key West's glorious foghorn. The submarine lurched away from the pier, slowly righted itself, and with that the Key West was underway for Captain Maddox's final voyage to sea.

As the foghorn's deep echo faded, it was replaced with the whining high pitch of sirens. The transition of the two sounds melded so smoothly, the Conning Officer in the bridge looked down at the horn he had just operated thinking it had some maintenance issues.

Two additional Shore Patrol cars raced down the pier with their sirens blaring. They came to a screeching halt at the head of the pier. Four shore patrolmen emerged helping three marines out of the cars. The marines looked as if they had come from the base hospital. One had his arm in a sling, another hobbled on crutches and they all looked as if they had taken a vicious beating. The COB immediately looked at Scarpa, who gave no tell, one way or the other, whether he was the guilty party or if he had even noticed the commotion on the pier.

The marines, however, noticed Scarpa. They seemed to momentarily forget their pain as they clamored over each other pointing him out to the shore patrolmen. A naive shore patrolman used the P.A. system in his car and called for the "ship" to come back in so they could speak to the ship's diver with the long hair. The shore patrolman obviously didn't understand the costs involved in running a billion dollar submarine with a nuclear reactor in operation, not to mention the fee for the use of a unionized tug boat.

The COB cusped his large hands astride his mouth. The amplifying effect he achieved nearly matched the decibel output of the Shore Patrol's electronic system. The COB's first priority, in true bubblehead fashion, was to correct them on what to call his submarine. "It's not a ship, it's a boat! Ships are targets!" The COB may have not been thrilled with Scarpa's idea of a good time the night before an underway, but first and foremost his loyalties lay with the submarine community. "Screw the surface pukes," was the sentiment he most often espoused. "We'll be back in two weeks. Until then, he's mine."

The shore patrolmen looked dejected, as if they couldn't believe that the world of Naval Operations didn't turn upside down for them because they had a P.A. system and eight cans of pepper spray between them.

As the warehouses and the piers of the base seemed to drift by, the line handlers cast off the tug then set about overturning the cleats to leave a smooth surface topside that would yield no cavitation once submerged.

As Scarpa looked on while the last of the deck clearing operations were performed, what seemed to be a bear paw wrapped around his arm, just above the elbow. The COB's finger's dug into Scarpa's arm just below his bicep. He pulled Scarpa in close to his body. "You got lucky this time," the COB snarled. "If they had been here five minutes earlier, you'd be headed for the brig."

Scarpa said nothing, even though he probably knew he would not have spent a minute in the brig. Those Jarheads had attacked him; of course he had provoked it by egging them on all night long while they played pool, but they were dumb enough to jump him in the parking lot. The bar where Scarpa had been hustling pool bets was in a shopping center which had a sufficient amount of security cameras covering the parking lot. The cameras would have provided a fully detailed view of his ambush and the subsequent beating he gave the Marines. Had they jumped him inside, where there were no cameras, they would have had an easy time finding fellow Jarhead witnesses who were just as sick of Scarpa's drunken belligerence to back up whatever cockeyed story they fabricated.

Scarpa stood sheepishly, and let the COB finish. The COB's frustration again grew as Scarpa showed no emotion. He finally let one last threat fly, "If you don't cut that hair you'll find yourself hot racking with Prescott and Nixon." At that, Scarpa's posture changed. The COB could see he finally struck a nerve. Hot racking was a system created out of necessity on submarines. More often than not, when a submarine set sail, it went to sea with more sailors than racks. This problem was addressed in two ways. The first and most preferred way was to outfit racks in the torpedo room. This would be the case if the submarines payload was light and left space on the torpedo stowage trays to do so. More often than not, the torpedo room would be full and the option to turn it into a berthing area would not be on the table. When that was the case, sailors would have to double up in their racks. Meaning, two sailors who had opposite watches would take turns using the rack, or three sailors would share two racks in a round robin fashion. The practice, not relished by anyone for obvious reasons, was something only the most junior sailors were subjected to.

Quinn knew the thought of sharing a rack with another sailor was bad enough, something which Scarpa had not had to do since his first year on the boat, but having to share a rack with Prescott and Nixon, considered to be the two vilest creatures aboard the boat, was unbearable.

The COB saw that his threat had worked. He released Scarpa's elbow and undoubtedly expected to see Scarpa with a freshly cropped head the next time he saw him.

CHAPTER 6

Stepping out of the forward crew's berthing compartment into the middle level passage way, Quinn unconsciously adjusted his balance to account for the slight list to starboard the boat ran with while submerged. The submarine did not rock from side to side as surface ships did, at least not while it was deep. However, the torque from the powerful main engines was enough to give the boat a constant pitch to starboard as it sliced its way through the deep waters.

Quinn approached Petty Officer Johnny Sparks whose massive body was sprawled across the deck as he tried to work on some impossibly placed electronics gear. Sparks' whole face and body contorted as he tried to reach under, up, and around, to work on the back of a piece of equipment that looked liked it had been placed in the bulkhead during the world's most expensive game of Tetris.

Quinn was just about to step over Sparks, when he noticed his friend's face turn red, then nearly purple as he held his breath, gritted his teeth and hopelessly tried to perform a task that only his fingers could feel. He let out a groan as if he was in the throes of death, then dejectedly he exhaled. As the blood drained from his head, he wriggled his arm back out of the bulk head.

"Who designs these things?"

The question was rhetorical, but Quinn shot back with, "Oompa Loompas." Sparks let out one forceful laugh. The joke was especially funny to

Sparks who was the tallest sailor aboard the submarine. At six foot six, Sparks should not have been on a boat. There were only about three places on board where he could stand straight up and give his back any comfort. There wasn't even a rack on board that was long enough to give him a moment's rest without bending his knees, forcing him to sleep in a semi-fetal position. He could have taken one of the racks in the torpedo room where his feet could freely hang off the end, but sleeping under a torpedo tray would only give him about two inches of clearance above his nose and turning over was impossible.

Quinn tucked the chess board he was carrying under his arm and extended his hand to help Sparks to his feet. As he pulled his big friend up, Sparks forgot to stop in his hunched position and cracked his head on the light.

"Ow, damn it!" As Sparks pulled his head away from the light cover, Quinn noticed a few strands of his hair left behind in the cover's screw.

"Your recruiter must have hated you," Quinn laughed.

"If I ever see him again, I'll strangle him."

Suddenly Quinn's senses were heightened. Sniffing the air like a wolf, he asked Sparks, "You weren't doing any soldering were you?"

"No, do you smell something?"

Quinn's eyes squinted as if to say "yes," but he wasn't sure exactly what. Sparks began to sniff the air as well. He pressed his nose up against the bulk head. "It smells like cigarette smoke." Quinn stepped closer to the bulk head.

"It does," Quinn agreed, "but who'd be smoking up here?"

Quinn followed the bulkhead aft, then turned the corner and peeked in the door to aft crew's berthing. Inside the berthing compartment, he witnessed the boats two mess cooks, Petty Officers Joe Carter and Herby Grant, with EAB masks (emergency air breathing masks) loosely sitting on top of their heads. The EAB masks were lifelines on the submarine. Being such a confined space; if a fire ever broke out while underway, the boat would fill with smoke quite quickly, choking out any breathable air. In the most severe cases, the entire forward compartment of the submarine could be filled in less than a minute. The emergency air pipes ran throughout the overhead in every occupied space of the boat and were outfitted with a series of manifolds every few feet.

The manifolds had four receptacles on them, enabling four masks to be plugged into them at one time. Each mask was designed with a regulator which works similar to the way a scuba regulator does. It takes the high pressure air fed from the emergency air pipes and reduces it to a breathable pressure.

Quinn silently watched the two mess cooks pass a cigarette back and forth, taking drags off of it and blowing the smoke through the curtain of one of the junior sailor's racks. Quinn recognized the rack as belonging to Seaman Schmidt, although he could not be sure the prank was being carried out upon Schmidt, since Schmidt was hot racking with two other Nubs.

Quinn did not interfere with the prank. He knew, just as hot racking was something that young submariners had to endure, so was hazing. The Navy had cracked down on hazing as had the other branches of the military, but as long as the military was filled with young men it would never be totally eradicated. Besides, Quinn thought it a necessary part of submarine life. Of course, he understood, as well as most sailors, the Navy could not let malicious sadists be allowed to run rampant through the boat doing whatever their sick minds could come up with and try to sluff it off as hazing. However, there was a certain level of mental stress Quinn thought viable to put a new sailor through, especially if he or his fellow shipmates may have to depend on one of the Nubs to save their life at some point. Yet, in the relatively short time Quinn had been in the submarine service, he had seen a major crack down on hazing; and from the stories he heard from older sailors, there had been an even greater decline before he was even a part of the submarine service. He also noticed a decrease in the feeling of community and bonding among the newer sailors. They no doubt were part of something larger than they had ever been in their lives, so a concrete bond with their shipmates was most certainly formed. Yet, it seemed to take longer for the younger sailors to become a cohesive part of the unit, of the family, as dysfunctional as it was.

Quinn watched as smoke filled the rack. He could hear slight coughs coming from inside, where Schmidt's pleasant dreams, which were probably rare as a Nub, were most likely turning subconsciously to panicked dreams of asphyxiation.

"That's enough," Grant whispered to Carter as he reached up and placed a hand on the EAB mask. Carter nodded a three count then they pulled the masks down over their faces, which immediately produced a mechanical breathing sound reminiscent of Darth Vader. They ripped back the curtain of Schmidt's rack and blasted his eyes with an extremely bright damage control flash light.

Carter yelled, "This one's still alive!" Schmidt sat straight up, cracking his head on the underside of the top rack. In the midst of his panicked confusion, he screamed. Regrettably, his scream came out sounding like a teenage girl in a haunted house. He toppled out of his rack and crashed to the deck at his pranksters' feet. Not realizing the air was quite breathable, he clawed at Grant's legs grabbing hold of his belt trying to pull himself up to the unmerciful figure.

Quinn watched the events unfold with amusement. Then he slowly reached up to the overhead and shut the valve which fed the air manifold Carter and Grant's EAB hoses were feeding off of. Immediately their masks were sucked tightly against their faces, not having a fresh supply of air after they exhaled. They ripped the masks from their heads, wincing, as the rubber straps tore at their hair.

They heard Quinn's laugh and saw his silhouette turning away as the door closed behind him.

Quinn found Scarpa sitting in the crew's mess, reading a book. Scarpa had taken the COB's order to heart and shaved his head. There was about a quarter inch of dark stubble left that seemed to accentuate the patches of smooth scarred skin in a dozen places.

"So, who was your barber as a kid, Freddie Kruger?" Quinn jibbed.

"I'm just trying to look like a four dot oh sailor, like you," Scarpa said as he rubbed his hand slowly from the front of his head to the back. "You never know, I might actually win the next Blue Jacket of the Quarter."

"I'll tell Satan to pull out his snow boots."

Quinn noticed Scarpa crack a smile as they set up the chess board for their ongoing game. Quinn knew it wasn't just his joke, although it truly would be a cold day in Hell if the Chiefs on board gave Scarpa an award for being a model sailor, an award Quinn had won six times since he had been on board. No, Quinn knew he was smiling because he was comfortable. Some sailors found it relaxing to be underway, and Scarpa was no exception. For other sailors though, a few days underwater in a tin can would have them clawing at the pressure hull, but for Scarpa, it seemed to be settling. The soft whirr of a thousand different machines, all working together to push them through the ocean, had a slight taming effect on Scarpa.

"Is it your turn, or mine?" Quinn asked as he set up his last pawn.

"You only ask when it's my turn," Scarpa replied robotically as if he had answered the question a thousand times.

As each man scanned the board one last time to make sure their pieces were in the same positions as they had been two days previous, Carter and Grant came trouncing through the crews mess stuffing their EAB masks back into their storage bags.

"Man, Quinn, why'd ya have to mess up our little prank?" Grant asked in his southern drawl so thick it screamed, *I'm from the hills.*

"You forget Grant, that was my Nub you were messing with," Quinn said as he noticed Scarpa making his move obviously thinking Quinn was distracted.

"We know that," Carter jumped in, "we just thought he might need a proper breaking in, seeing how it's his first underway."

"Consider him broken in then," Quinn said as he turned his attention back toward his match.

Carter and Grant headed into the galley, unwilling to let Quinn's less than jovial attitude dampen their spirits. "Did you see the look on his face?" Grant asked as they relived the moment with each other.

As Carter opened the door to the galley he belted out the Navy SEAL battle cry, "Hooyah!" It was a battle cry which was quickly seconded by Grant.

Still hearing their play-by-play, though it was now muffled by the galley door, Scarpa rolled his eyes, "Idiots."

"Come on, Scarpa," Quinn pleaded, "they're harmless."

"They're a couple of SEAL wannabes."

"Everyone has to have goals," Quinn said, again trying to get the issue to blow over. "Besides, I know if I was in a tight situation, those two would probably be the first to come to my aid. It's truly not worth getting worked up over," though he could see Scarpa was doing exactly that.

"The last time I checked, the SEALs weren't forming an Abbott and Costello team."

Quinn let out a slight laugh, which he felt a little guilty about, but what Scarpa said was true, the pair did resemble the late comedy duo. They both intensely desired to become SEALs, but Carter was just too fat and Grant just too skinny. As boys, they had both watched entirely too many Steven Seagal movies. Their lives had been on parallel courses until their paths merged in the Navy. Since the day they met, they had been inseparable. The only apparent difference between the two was that the longer Carter worked with food, the more of it he consumed, and the longer Grant worked with food, the more it repulsed him.

Before Quinn could make another move, the game was interrupted by the General Alarm, followed immediately by an announcement.

"HOT RUN IN THE TORPEDO ROOM! HOT RUN IN THE TORPEDO ROOM!" Then there was another blast of the general alarm. Quinn, Scarpa and the other sailors wasted no time pulling out the EAB masks and heading out of the crews mess.

The sailors made their way down the ladder to lower level and amassed at the door leading to the torpedo room. Behind them came Schmidt, stumbling down the ladder. Quinn could see the panic in Schmidt's eyes when he realized there were no available plugs on the air manifold. Before the young sailor could turn in a vain attempt to retreat up the ladder to the manifold he had just left, Scarpa grabbed the end of Schmidt's air hose. "On the belt, Nub!" He inserted the hose fitting into his mask's spare plug on the belt clip. Like a desert Nomad at an oasis, Schmidt drank the air. After a few breaths had calmed his nerves, Quinn could read the disappointment on Schmidt's face for forgetting about the spare plug on the belt regulator.

As before, Quinn found himself to be the man in charge and he slipped into the natural role of giving orders, "Phone talker to Control, Damage Control Team is on station in the lower level passage way, we are moving in to secure tube three." As the phone talker gave his repeat back, Quinn assessed the team. "Scarpa and I will secure the tube. Rubber, you start securing the

Weapons Control Panel." Looking at Schmidt, he tried to think of a task that seemed trivial, "Schmidt, you make sure the flood control valve is shut."

"Okay," Schmidt said as his eyes darted across the faces of the confident sailors crammed into the space with him. Before Quinn could correct his vague response, Scarpa grabbed ahold of the hose on Schmidt's mask and pulled it in so close their face shields touched.

"Okay!" Scarpa yelled. "Okay, what? Okay, you're going to go get us some coffee! Okay, you're going to go change your diaper!" Quinn lightly put his hand on Scarpa's shoulder. Gently, he pulled him back trying equally to calm him and keep him from turning and pouncing. Quinn felt as if he were trying to stop a tiger from chewing on a piece of steak.

One of the reasons Quinn had emerged as a great leader was his uncanny ability to empathize. It was as if he could get into the minds of other men and create such an exacting picture of what life was like in their shoes, he was able to treat everyone truly as they would have wished to be treated. To Quinn, he was unrecognizing to the fact that his mind worked differently than others. In some instances, he wanted to coach guys on how to talk with each other in order to filter out what to him seemed like incredibly simple stumbling blocks in communication. In his mind, he could place himself in senior officers' positions and sympathize with the pressures they were under. This made him a go-to guy for a lot of these officers. On the flip side, it also made junior sailors flock to him for his patience and understanding. Empathizing with a Nub came easy, because he had lived through that hell not too long ago.

Scarpa stopped screaming but did not yet yield his grip on Schmidt's mask. Seeing Schmidt cower from Scarpa's spit-covered face shield, Quinn remembered being in that position. He remembered thinking, *don't these guys get it, haven't they ever been scared? Were they born knowing exactly what to do in an emergency on a submarine?* He knew at that point, Schmidt wanted to curl up and hide, but this was a submarine. There was nowhere he could go without being more than three feet from another person.

The kinder, yet still stern, voice of Quinn brought Schmidt back to the point of functioning. "Proper repeat back Schmidt," Quinn said, "you should know that by now." He knew adding that dig in at the end would enrage Schmidt. Even though he could empathize, he couldn't hold the kid's hand. He had to start a fire under his butt; otherwise if he didn't get up to speed he would find guys like Scarpa hammering him every day. Even if he had been upset at the moment with Quinn, the fact was, in the short time Schmidt had been aboard, it was Quinn who had taken him aside most often and taught him things which would surely help him earn his Silver Dolphins sooner than any of his Submarine School classmates.

When a sailor came aboard, fresh out of Submarine School, they had approximately one year to complete the qualifications to earn their Silver

Dolphins, the coveted submarine warfare insignia pin. The Silver Dolphins are one of the oldest special warfare insignia pins in the Navy and undoubtedly the ugliest to all but those who wear them. With its two carp-like dolphin fish which have their tails curled up as they look inward while sitting atop a wake made by the center piece of the ornament, a submarine sail jutting out of the water with its periscopes raised high, the insignia isn't nearly as dashing as the winged insignia of the aviators and does nothing for the production of testosterone as does the SEAL Trident pin. Yet, the months of studying, pouring over schematics, learning how to produce, from memory, one-line drawings of every system on the boat, from its sanitation systems to the workings of the nuclear reactor which provides the life blood of the boat, all of that first year's collective efforts, tears, and frustrations produce an insignia pin that is worn with no less mental and physical toll than any other in the world.

Back at the barracks in the evenings, Schmidt would hang out with some of his former classmates from Sub School and they would compare notes about life aboard their respective boats. To Schmidt, it must have sounded as if he were the only one who had a person on board their boat who could be considered a mentor. Quinn would teach things to Schmidt which no one was taking the time to teach his classmates on their boats. So in those evening meetings, usually held over a game of pool, Schmidt would transform into teacher to his friends. The blind leading the blind, Schmidt had begun to call the sessions when he would explain a key portion of a vital system in a one line schematic drawing. In actuality, teaching his friends made the lessons more concrete in his own mind and he seemed to be retaining information at a faster rate than his friends. He would probably sit for his submarine qualification boards months ahead of his counterparts and, more importantly, earn the right to wear the Silver Dolphins, shedding the pejorative of "nub."

Still, he must have been irritated at Quinn for reminding him about using a proper repeat back, he might as well have been yelling, "Two plus two is four!" The proper repeat back was one of the first things drilled into every sailor's brain at boot camp; it was the most basic of skills. Even so, Schmidt let fear take over and it slipped his mind. In all likelihood, Quinn could have asked him what the sum of two plus two was and the very same feeling that he was about to crap his pants would have prevented him from blurting out, "four!" The only solace Schmidt could possibly take in the moment was that if he did indeed lose control of his bowels, everyone was wearing a sealed mask so it would not have been known immediately.

Quinn looked Schmidt straight in the eye, and very deliberately said, "Seaman Schmidt, when we go through the door you stay in the aft portion of the torpedo room and verify the flood control valve has been shut."

Schmidt listened intently to the order then repeated, "stay in the aft portion of the torpedo room and verify the flood control valve is shut, aye." As

51

he exhaled the word "aye," there was no air to replenish his empty lungs. Panic returned to his face, as he looked down and saw the end of his air hose lying vacant on the deck. Scarpa had released his hose with no warning; not exactly the way it was covered in training, but now was no time to wonder why nubs were expected to follow all the rules, while those who were reiterating them the loudest were not holding themselves to the same standard.

As he scooped up his air hose, he could see the others had already penetrated the door to the torpedo room. He followed, but the others had already made their way forward to secure the tube. Suddenly, the panic in his face deepened. It was not uncommon for a young sailor to completely blank out on the very order they had just repeated back. Fear had a way of turning the mind to mush. It had been a mere three seconds and already he seemed to be searching his mind for the words which moments before had passed his lips. Like a heavenly ray of light bursting forth through rain clouds, the words "flood control valve" seemed to involuntarily escape his mouth. He smiled, but then quickly rolled his eyes at himself, "Great, I'm as sharp as a goldfish."

As he said the words there was no air to replace the breath with which he used to say them. His lungs apparently jumped on the mental treadmill. He looked to the overhead. It was a mess of hydraulic pipes and electric cables. It wasn't natural. In buildings, architects took great care to keep these materials hidden, but here all the inner workings were nakedly exposed. It would have been suicide to make it any other way. Aesthetics were not a consideration in most areas of the submarine, especially not in a critical area like the torpedo room. It was the same on surface ships too, but Schmidt had never been on a surface ship. In fact, until he set foot on the Key West, the only other water vessel he had ever been on was powered by oars. Presentation was of no concern, being able to work on a disabled system that has the dual power of being able to kill or save a crew was all that mattered. Having the ability to see the problem and begin to work on it in a fraction of a second was paramount. For this reason, Schmidt could see a part of every system in the overhead except for the one he needed most, air.

As his eyes scanned the overhead, he seemed to be fighting the urge to look down. It took some getting used to for nubs, not to look up when that was where the air manifold would be. However, once they overcame the need to try and decipher the different piping systems in the overhead and looked down, the emergency air would be easy to find. As Schmidt finally overcame his novice instincts, the red four inch by eight inch non-skid sticker on the deck signifying that there was an emergency air manifold overhead seemed to stand out like a blinking beacon. And there it was, the manifold he needed to plug into. His eyes must have scanned over it a thousand times in the previous four seconds, yet he did not see it, even though it was brightly painted red so at a mere glance a sailor would find it.

As Quinn brought his team forward, he saw Stoney laying face down on the deck without an EAB mask on. "Quinn!" Rubber yelled, "It's Stoney."

"Nothing we can do for him now," Quinn said coldly as he stood over Stoney's body and set to work on securing the torpedo tube. "We need to get that torpedo shut down or we'll all be dead!" As Quinn said these words he saw the COB out of the corner of his eye.

The COB reached up, grabbed the 27MC and keyed the mic, "Control-Torpedo Room secure from the drill."

Quinn heard the control room acknowledge the COB and then over the 1MC the announcement went out to the entire boat, "Secure from the drill." Like dominos falling, the normal lighting was restored, the damage control lights went off, the ventilation system kicked back on and Quinn ripped off his EAB in disgust.

"Ten more seconds and I would have had it powered down, COB!"

"Doesn't matter," the COB shot back, "you never shut the flood control valve."

Immediately everyone's eyes shot to the back of the room. "Schmidt!" Quinn yelled, "Get up here!" The confused sailor, still wearing his EAB, peered around the corner. He began to walk hesitantly toward the forward part of the torpedo room until the air hose from the belt clip went taught. *At least he was wearing the mask right,* thought Quinn, *otherwise the poor fool would have had his face catch the slack.* Instead, Schmidt had the mask's regulator clipped on his belt as it should have been, so the tug which prevented him from advancing any further was felt by his hip. Realizing he was still plugged in, he went back and unhooked himself. This time as he headed forward it was with more urgency, since he was now apparently concentrating on finding a new manifold.

As he rushed forward, Quinn was feeling some pity for him and he planned on letting him plug in then gently telling him to take off his mask. Scarpa took no such pity. Even before Schmidt could start to look for a manifold, Scarpa ripped the mask from his head. "Drill's over nub!"

"That's right Scarpa, so there's nothing we can do about it now except learn from it," Quinn said stepping to the defense of Schmidt. Quinn had positioned himself so Scarpa could not reach Schmidt. Even though he was protecting him, Quinn flashed the young sailor a look to show him he was not pleased. Scarpa stood breathing heavily like a lion deciding if the kill was worth the fight.

Suddenly, their faces were illuminated by 1500 watts of camera lighting. "Emotions run high as sailors train just like it was the real thing," Ms. Collins said as the camera panned from the trio at each other's throats to the softer features of her face. Scarpa turned and headed out of the room. Ms. Collins cameraman, Dave, turned off his light and lowered the camera.

"Beautiful," he said as if he was reading right out of a cameraman's guide to looking cool.

"What was that guy's problem?" Ms. Collins asked.

"He's got some anger management issues," Quinn said as his mood was easily lightened by the presence of the lady. It would take some getting used to for most of the sailors, the idea of there being a woman aboard. It meant they had to be on their best behavior. Quinn had it quite easy though, most of her attention had been focused toward him thus far, so he didn't have to battle the subconscious urge to get noticed by her. Their cruise ship moment was abruptly brought back to the reality that they were on a sub when the COB laid in on Quinn.

"So why did you kill us, Quinn?" the COB asked in a blatant manner which was obviously intended to degrade Quinn in front of Ms. Collins. Quinn realized that he was the one who ordered Schmidt to pull the flood control lever without first verifying if he knew where it was. To the COB's surprise, Quinn didn't try to brush it off.

"I'm sorry, COB, I should have personally made sure flood control was taken care of," Quinn relented. The COB seemed to be taken aback by Quinn's humbleness, and eased his rhetoric as well.

In a moderate tone, the COB corrected him, "It didn't necessarily have to be you personally." Quinn knew this of course, but he didn't want to appear to the COB as if he thought he had all the answers. He knew he needed to let the COB be the COB. "What you need to do," the COB continued, "is have complete confidence in the person you designate the task to."

Before the little scene could be played out any further, the Captain came over the 1MC. "Listen up, crew. This is the Captain. That drill was the initiation of Operation Eel Hunt. This is a training exercise where our mission will be to destroy the Teddy Roosevelt battle group. Over the next three days we will be hunted, ambushed and snared in sonar traps. Our job is to evade and destroy. We will be joined in this exercise by some of our international partners, notably the French Navy's newest experimental attack submarine, the Poignard. She will be a deadly enemy; it's the first of its kind. Equipped with the latest in hydrogen fuel cell technology, the only things in the ocean that will be more silent than her will be dead. We will still be faster than her and I know her crew will not be half as capable as mine."

Quinn could swear he felt the pressure in the boat change at that moment as 120 sailors took in deep breaths to puff out their chests. Captain Maddox was a great leader and knew just how to get the most out of his men. Quinn only hoped that one day he would have men that would follow him with such deep loyalty.

The Captain continued, "There will be two parts to this exercise. First, we are the hunters, targeting the battle group. Afterwards, we will take a three day break to take care of housekeeping issues. The second phase will begin when we come back to the operational area. We then become the hunted." The mic clicked off. Before anyone could return to their business, the 1MC keyed back on. Everyone paused, but they heard nothing, then a sigh. The Captain began to speak in a much more subdued tone, "Men, you have been a good crew." Quinn had to admire such a simple statement. He did not know what Captain Maddox was about to say, but whatever it was he had the crew's attention. One of the most important lessons Quinn had learned about leadership from Captain Maddox was that praise did not have to be poured on lavishly to gain the respect of the men serving under you. Compliments were only as good as the source. Being told you were doing a great job by somebody too incompetent to know what a great job was meant nothing. On the other hand, having a man like Captain Maddox, who time after time earned the respect and trust of his crew, giving them even the simplest of kudos was a currency valued in the undersea realm more richly than Spanish Gold.

The men were ready to do anything Captain Maddox asked of them, including Quinn. "You are also my last crew," he confessed. "It seems there are too many men behind me and not enough room in front of me. This is my last underway. When we pull back into port, this old sea dog will have to hang it up." Quinn looked around at his fellow sailors and could easily read despair and frustration on their faces. Everyone aboard the Key West knew their skipper was the best in the fleet. None of them could grasp the reasons why their Captain was never advanced. For the most naive of sailors, this was their first bitter taste of naval politics.

Quinn thought Captain Maddox must have seen the same forlorn looks upon the faces in the control room, for his speech changed gears. All traces of self pity vanished from his voice. He began to speak with renewed vigor. One would have thought they were about to fight for the very blessed freedom the country's founders fought for, rather than a simple training exercise to test a few new systems and tactics. "But now, men, I would ask you one thing," he continued. "Let's stick it to 'em! Let's show them how clueless they really are. Let's destroy them." That was it. He had them. He could have added "with real torpedoes!" and the crew probably would have complied. As it was, they were just as happy to take out the surface fleet with exercise torpedoes to show the Navy they were about to lose a damn good man.

"Come on, Ms. Collins," the COB beamed, "I'll get you an exclusive with the skipper."

Quinn couldn't contain a laugh, "You'd better hurry COB, I just got word Chief Moore is racing up from the engine room with Anderson Cooper."

"Well, Mr. Slick Pants," the COB growled," unlike you, I'm sure Ms. Collins is interested in doing her job, or do you think she would rather delegate her interview to an unqualified nub?" Quinn's face reddened. It wasn't often that Quinn made such a blatant error in judgment such as he had, but since he spent so much of his day being smug with the COB, the COB did not let the opportunity slip by without rubbing Quinn's nose in it.

"Actually, I am here to get an interview with the Captain," Ms. Collins said, feeling a little awkward, "so, I'll catch up with you later." She turned and headed up the ladder to middle level trailed by her cameraman and the COB.

"Can I get up now?" Stoney said, surprising Quinn, who was practically standing on top of him.

Quinn stepped to the side, "I thought you were sleeping it off."

"At least you didn't stand *on* me," Stoney said as Quinn helped him to his feet. "It's nice to know you're not even gonna check my pulse in the event you find me out cold in an emergency."

"Stoney," Quinn started, "seeing you out cold is nothing new to me."

Stoney got to his feet, opened one of the bench seats in front of the Weapons Control Panel and pulled out a tool bag which had been filled with TDU weights. Not having a gym aboard the submarine, the torpedo room became the unofficial workout room. The sailors had filled tool bags with weighted plates from the Trash Disposal Unit space and used them as makeshift barbells. As Stoney began his workout, which consisted of four pathetic arm curls, Quinn noticed Schmidt trying to slink out the back of the torpedo room.

"Seaman Schmidt!" Quinn called out putting an extra emphasis on the long e sound in the word seaman. It didn't take young sailors long to figure out when somebody calls out to them and puts any sort of special emphasis on their title it was not good. The only thing worse was if somebody in Khakis, that you didn't know, addressed you as "shipmate." The word shipmate was never followed by terms of endearment. Schmidt's eyes were fixed on the deck plates as he slunk back toward Quinn.

Up until this point, Quinn had been very patient with Schmidt, but this time, Schmidt must have thought he had pushed him over his limit. Quinn assessed Schmidt as he stood in front of him. He was sure that at this moment there could not possibly be a more pathetic looking sailor throughout the Navy.

"Look at me, Schmidt," Quinn said in a steady voice. Schmidt looked up and found Quinn's expression to be stern, but void of any anger. In the same steady tone Quinn said, "Schmidt, verify the flood control valve is shut."

Schmidt just blinked in surprise at first, but he responded to the order, "Verify the flood control valve is shut, aye." Quinn looked at Stoney as Stoney shook his head in mock disappointment.

"Wrong!" Quinn said abruptly.

Schmidt thought for a moment, then started to attempt it again, "Verify the-"

"Wrong!" Quinn cut him off this time. Schmidt looked wholly confused. Quinn could tell Schmidt was replaying the words in his mind, trying to figure out what was wrong with his repeat back.

Seeing Schmidt was not going to find the right answer on his own, Stoney spoke up, "Why are you saying you'll follow an order you don't understand?" Schmidt's face went flush. It was obvious he was upset by the fact that he hadn't understood what Quinn was asking when a terrible specimen of a sailor like Stoney had seen it so easily.

Schmidt swallowed his pride and asked in a defeated tone, "Petty Officer Quinn, I don't know where the flood control valve is. Could you show me?" With that, all the sternness that had been in Quinn's voice melted away.

"I thought you'd never ask. Come on, I'll show you," Quinn said cheerfully as he headed to the aft part of the torpedo room. Schmidt followed Quinn to the flood control lever. His face went pale when he saw Quinn's hand resting on the Hydraulic lever labeled "Flood Control" just inches from the EAB manifold he had been plugged into. He could not hide his shame when Quinn shifted his hand over and patted the air manifold and said, "You were probably plugged in right here while you were looking for it."

"Don't worry, Schmidt, I probably looked as pathetic as you do right now, when Petty Officer Sullivan pointed out the same thing to me years ago," Quinn said, trying to keep the kid from beating himself up too much. "And Sullivan probably looked the same when Kloetzke was making him feel like an idiot." Schmidt looked as if the self deprecation was easing a bit. "That's the circle of life on a submarine; one day you're a Nub, the next day you're teaching one."

Quinn turned and headed back to the forward part of the torpedo room where Stoney was still hanging out. As Schmidt was following, Quinn talked over his shoulder, "The easiest way to piss people off around here is to not ask questions."

Stoney added his two cents, but this time Schmidt had been too humbled to be bothered by his comments. "If you don't understand something," Stoney began, trying hard to take on the role of a mentor, "just ask."

They stood silent for a moment when Quinn gave Schmidt a slight push, "So?" Schmidt still said nothing. "Come on Schmidt, I know flood control isn't the only thing about that drill you didn't understand."

Schmidt thought for a moment, then he seemed to dismiss whatever it was he was going to ask. "The only stupid question is the one not asked," Stoney said, seemingly prophetic. As much as Schmidt must not have been in the mood to hear clichés, it was the encouragement needed to make him speak.

"Okay," Schmidt said reluctantly, "what *is* a Hot Run?" He searched Quinn and Stoney's faces. There were no exchanges of glances. No suppressed smirks, no sign the previous statement about there being no stupid questions might be reneged.

"A hot run," Quinn started, "is a very serious situation for the boat." Schmidt listened intently. "A hot run is when a torpedo starts up but does not leave the tube."

Schmidt no longer held back, "Can it explode?"

"No," Quinn answered, "there are safeguards in place to prevent that." Schmidt must have shown some relief in his expression, for when Quinn continued he added a grievous tone to his voice that was absent in the initial description. "However, the type of fuel it consumes burns so hot the exhaust gases can weaken the torpedo tube's breech door. If it is weakened to the point its watertight integrity is lost, the sea pressure could overcome the door. Then you've got a hole in the boat nearly two feet wide. A hole that size will fill the boat in a heartbeat." Schmidt shuddered.

"That's not what the judge told me a hot run was," Stoney added, quickly lightening the mood.

"I'm afraid to ask," said Schmidt.

"Don't have to," Stoney offered, "I'll tell ya." Quinn settled in, sitting on the cushioned lid of the trash can which was designed to serve as a stool as well. Comfort took on a new meaning after being on the submarine for years, he barely noticed anymore when he would lean against the bulkhead and one type of valve or pipe mount would dig into his back. There was the comfort of the world, and then there was the comfort of life on a submarine. The sailors made do with what they had.

"I found myself standin' in front of that Texas judge," Stoney reminisced. "He said, 'boy you shoulda known better than to try and pull a hot run like that in my county.'" A smile appeared on Stoney's face as if he longed to be back in a world where justice seemed fair now that he was quite familiar with the military's version of justice. "You see, I had been busted trying to ride my bike across the border."

"Since when is it illegal to ride your bike across the border?" Quinn asked right on cue, having heard the story upwards of fifty times.

"Since earlier that day, when I stuffed the frame with the cheapest pot I could buy."

"So, how did you get busted?" Schmidt asked, seemingly happy the attention had been taken off his ineptitude.

"You see, Quinn, now the boy has no problem askin' questions," Stoney observed. Quinn smiled at Schmidt's obvious annoyance with being called "the boy". "I got busted because I was trying to play it cool," Stoney said as he fished a Marlboro out of his pocket. "I was going to try and look like I had nothing to worry about by smoking a cigarette." Stoney slid his cigarette under his nose taking in the fragrance as if it were a Cuban cigar. "Thinking about it now, I guess it's a big tip off when a seventeen year old, who looks like he's fourteen, is smoking a cigarette, especially when it turns out to be a joint."

"Wait a minute," Quinn interrupted, "I've heard this story a thousand times, you never mentioned that it was a joint!"

"I usually leave that part out 'cause it makes me look stupid."

"You are stupid," Quinn reminded him with no malice.

"I recognize that," Stoney relented. "In fact it was so stupid, my dad found out about it when he heard Mike Huckabee mention me by name on the radio."

"Did your dad kill you?" Schmidt asked.

"He was so pissed; he was on lunch with all the guys at work when he heard it, so all my sneakin' around trying to keep it from my parents was out the window. He made me fire the cheap suit lawyer I hired and when the judge told me I had a choice between jail or four years in the military, my dad was almost held in contempt for giving the judge a standing ovation."

"And here you are," Quinn said, beaming.

"Had I met the COB that day I would have taken the jail sentence," Stoney confessed. "At least there I would have had a chance at parole." Quinn was always amazed at the different reasons and circumstances which brought guys to the boat, but at the heart of them all, they all were seeking adventure. Instead, they found drill after drill.

As if taking a mental cue from Quinn's mind, the general alarm sounded followed by the announcement, "Man Battle Stations!"

CHAPTER 7

The Santa de Juarez

Sanchez stooped behind a stairwell, taking advantage of the dark cover it provided. Even at 4 am there were still a few men on the deck that Sanchez was trying desperately to avoid. Standard black fatigues would have been more appropriate for a stealthy operation; however, he settled for the black t-shirt he wore under his apron, and the black and grey checkered pants which were the standard dress for the cooks. This way, if he was seen, he wouldn't raise too much suspicion. He stuck to the shadows as best he could, trying not to put himself in a position to have to explain what he was doing skulking around on the deck at such a late hour. He moved swiftly from shadow to shadow. On a previous excursion two nights ago, he found the containers in the same condition they had been since they left port, but earlier in the evening he had been on the helipad smoking a cigarette when he noticed two forklifts had not stopped rumbling on the main deck the entire time he was topside.

Now, as he approached the area of the deck on the starboard side where the containers had been, he noticed they were missing. In their place was a tarp covering something massive on the deck. He sat in the shadows observing patrol patterns of the deck guards trying to find their rhythm. They were not disciplined though, stopping to chat with each other for thirty seconds here, or two minutes there. It was almost a curse they were so undisciplined. He would not be able to formulate a plan with specificity as to how long he would have to inspect the contents concealed beneath the tarp. When the guard he labeled "Mr. Chatty" on his note pad had just walked past his position, he must have assumed his chances would be best to make his inspection, because the man had a habit of stopping every other guard as they strolled by him to tell a lewd joke.

Sanchez made his move. He darted out, taking a gamble no one would notice him as he sprinted across ten yards of illuminated deck. When he reached the massive block, he squeezed as best he could into the thin shadow it cast upon the deck. He found that the tarp was not tied down securely; rather it was held to the deck by iron plates, taken from the ship's workout room, and laid across the loose ends. He slid a few of the plates to the side and poked his head beneath the tarp.

"What the hell?" the rhetorical question escaped his lips in a whisper. Two pallet-like structures held stacks of large steel cylinders. The cylinders looked to be about two feet in diameter and approximately twenty feet long. They were stacked three across and three high to each pallet, giving a total of eighteen units.

They were the strangest type of container Sanchez had come across in his years of investigating narcotics smuggling. He did not have any more time to ponder the uniqueness of the cargo however, hearing the boisterous laugh of Mr. Chatty, signaled him that it was time to go. The laugh meant the joke was over. Mr. Chatty would be thoroughly entertained, and the victim of his incoherent humor would be laughing politely and turning away, rolling their eyes.

Sanchez returned the weights to their original position and stole back to the shadows. His excursion had not gone completely unnoticed though. As inept as Mr. Chatty was, he managed to catch a glimpse of Sanchez's retreat. Seemingly unsure of what he had just seen, Mr. Chatty began to investigate for himself. No guard, especially one as insecure as Mr. Chatty, would invite ridicule from his fellow guards for sounding the alarm due to a stowaway cat.

Sanchez noticed the guard tailing him. Ducking behind a capstan, he watched to see if any other guards had joined in the pursuit. No other guards seemed to be joining Mr. Chatty, so when his foot practically set down on Sanchez's hand, Sanchez popped up and shot out a jab that crushed the guard's Adams apple. Mr. Chatty instantly released his grip on his weapon and pawed at his throat, as if his hands could do anything to alleviate the internal swelling of his larynx. As the man staggered forward, Sanchez came at him from behind, wrapping his left arm around Mr. Chatty's neck and locking up the grip with the crux of his right elbow. He flexed his left bicep and forearm as he squeezed. Within seconds, the anaconda like choke had cut off his carotid arteries causing him to instantly black out.

Sanchez felt the man's body go limp in his arms. He lowered him to the deck softly as to not make a sound. His eyes desperately scanned the decks to the left, right, and above him for any sign the struggle had raised an alarm. Satisfied Mr. Chatty had been the only one alerted to his presence, he returned his attention to the matter at hand. Mr. Chatty lay on the deck, his breathing became heavy and slobbery as oxygen returned to his brain and he started to come to. Sanchez, needing to get off the deck as quickly as possible, could not afford to linger topside strangling the buffoon until he was certifiably dead. He hoisted Mr. Chatty on his shoulders in a fireman's carry and heaved him over the side before he was lucid. As he tossed the man, Sanchez unintentionally made a loud grunt. Between the grunt and the splash, he was sure someone's attention would be drawn, but both noises must have been merely amplified in Sanchez's own mind due to his heightened senses.

After loitering a moment longer, Sanchez was satisfied his cover had not been blown. The excursion would only be evidenced by the missing Mr. Chatty, but Sanchez could take comfort in the thought his missing presence would be relished by most, and the list of suspects would be too broad to cast any focused attention on him.

Mr. Chatty, or Miguel Torres as he was truly known, chopped at the water with heavy arms and legs, a look of horror splayed across his face like a child woken from a horrible dream. As he gained more control over his breathing, his flailing limbs calmed to the more rhythmic circular motions of treading water. His wits seemed to be regained, but then the look of horror returned as he began to spin around looking in all directions. When he spotted the ship he tried to cry out for help, but all he could manage was a horse cry which was easily kidnapped by the westward wind. Each time he called out, he would wince in pain as his throat seemed to close up around the words.

"Turn around!" he grunted. "Turn, turn, turn!"

As the lights from the ship shrank in size as they raced toward the horizon, Miguel began to cry. "I'm sorry mama, I'm sorry," he begged for forgiveness out loud. "You told me not to go to sea, but you were so sick and they paid so much. I'm sorry mama, I'm sorry."

Miguel was quiet when the single point of light, which was the Santa de Juarez, blinked off as it disappeared over the horizon. He resigned himself to his fate and made peace with God.

USS Winston S. Churchill

In the sonar room of the USS Winston S. Churchill DDG-81, an Arleigh Burke class destroyer, a sonar man sat doodling on a note pad. Intermittently, he would glance up to check his screen, but most of his attention was focused on the sketch in his lap. Only one of the headphones he was wearing barely covered his left ear, and it was pushed back so far it would have been debatable whether he could hear any sounds emanating from it. After making another cursory glance at the screen his gaze dropped again. As he returned his attention to the tattoo he was designing, a light started flashing on his screen.

A young sailor walked past carrying an empty coffee mug. The sonar man, without taking his eyes off his paper, reached over and pulled his mug out of its holder. He held it up above his head, "As long as you're going that way."

"Sure," the newly designated coffee boy replied as he studied the hideous design," how do you want it?"

"Blond and sweet," the doodler answered. The blip on the screen finally caught the coffee boy's eye.

"What's that?" he asked as he pointed to the screen. The doodler looked up and jumped with surprise. He slid the headphones to their proper position.

"Oh man, Oh man, Oh man," he repeated while he began to perform his duties a little too late. Snatching up his comm. mic, he attempted to alert the bridge, "Torpedo in the-" Grunting in frustration, he tried again, this time keying the mic. "Torpedo in the water bearing two-six-zero!" he screamed.

A school of grouper fluttering in the black water scattered as their biological sonar systems gave warning. The moment they split ranks, an orange torpedo zipped through like a fullback blasting through a hole in the line of scrimmage. The torpedo cut through the water as it closed the distance to its intended target, the hull of the Churchill.

In the panic-consumed bridge of the Destroyer, the Captain ordered, "Activate the NIXIE!"

"The NIXIE's not deployed, sir!" the Conning Officer admitted. The Captain was about to retort, but then his lips tightened into a scowl as he accepted the inevitable. Earlier, permission had been requested by the Conning Officer to pay out the AN/SLQ-25, a fiber optic towed cable, known as the NIXIE which emits diversionary electro-acoustic ship noises in an effort to confuse incoming torpedoes to explode over a thousand feet behind the ship, but the Captain had denied the request on the grounds they couldn't afford the time to slow the ship to make a safe deployment of the cable.

Now, there was not enough time to begin to give the orders to deploy the Nixie; the torpedo was within the threshold of striking. Running its predetermined course, the exercise torpedo went directly underneath the hull of the Churchill. As it did, it emitted a shockwave. Even though the shockwave was simply an electronic sonar pulse meant to signal defeat, it hit the hull as if it were the massive clapper of Notre Dame's south tower's famed "Emmanuel" bell.

T. Steven Sullivan

Sailors in the compartments below the water line of the Churchill dropped anything they were carrying and covered their ears as the energy of the pulse transferred through the thick steel of the hull and into the air.

USS Kalamazoo

Captain Joseph Scott, the C.O. of the USS Kalamazoo, stood on the bridge of his ship studying the battle board. Flanked by the silent Adm. Victor Perry, Scott tried to convince the old submariner his battle group was closing in on the Key West. "He'll slip up. It's just a matter of time." Adm. Perry simply shrugged as he watched sailors move the scale model ships on the battle board, updating their most current positions.

The Kalamazoo, a previously decommissioned replenishment oiler, had just been pulled off the moth balls and gone through a dry dock refurbishment where it was updated to be a command center. It was outfitted with some of the military's newest hardware; however, anyone who had served time in the Navy could tell the real attention had been put into the amenities. It was quite obvious the real mission of the Kalamazoo was to impress dignitaries and congressmen. Its staterooms seemed more likely to be found on the Titanic rather than a supply ship. The entire ship took on the feel of a luxury yacht.

The crown jewel of the Kalamazoo was its battle board. The Battle Board was a hybrid of cutting edge electronics, and scale modeled warships. The surface of the table was a ten foot square deep blue ceramic tile covered with a high-gloss sheen. Inlayed in the table were fiber optic lights. The tips of the light threads were so minute, when not illuminated they were virtually invisible. Once illuminated they created a grid which could be set to divide the board in as little as four quadrants to as many as one hundred quadrants. There were also five separate sets of scale model ships. The different size models could be used based on the size the grid was set to represent. If each square was set to be indicative of one nautical mile or if it was set to one hundred nautical miles, there was a correctly scaled model for it.

The norm was to see the midrange settings used, due to the gaudiness of the larger model ships, and the wimpy feeling everyone had when using the micro-models.

"I wouldn't underestimate Captain Maddox," Adm. Perry said as he admired the pile of model ships which had already been removed from the board.

At that moment, a frantic report came in from Radio. "Bridge-Radio the Churchill has just been sunk!" Captain Scott pounded his fist down on the cedar rim of his precious battle board. Like a craps dealer retrieving a lost stack of chips, a sailor with a 48" rattan stick pulled the Model representing the Churchill to the sideline.

"The Churchill was only twelve nautical miles northwest of our position, sir," one of the Quartermasters informed him.

"He's close," Perry warned, "you might consider bringing the Poignard down this way." Scott's eyes flamed as he studied the positions of his diminishing Battle Group.

"Radio, send word for the Poignard to be especially vigilant," Scott called out, "the Key West is coming after the Roosevelt."

"I'm just an observer here," Adm. Perry stated smugly, "but the Roosevelt is all the way up in the northern most quadrant."

"Yeah," Scott began suspiciously, "and I just bet you'd like me to think he's not going after her." He turned away from Adm. Perry. "Helm, bring us to course three-five-five."

"If he *is* coming after us," Adm. Perry again gave his best common sense observation, "you're making his work easier by closing the distance for him."

Scott's face flushed with anger. "He wants the aircraft carrier. By going after the Arleigh Burke first, he was attempting to use reverse psychology and you're trying to help him by using a reversal of reverse psychology."

"Correct me if I'm wrong, but wouldn't that bring us back around to strait forward psychology?" Perry pointed out.

CHAPTER 8

USS Key West

As the Kalamazoo made its way slowly through the choppy night sea, Captain Maddox could make out men moving about the surface ship's deck through the periscope's highest power setting. He could see the lookouts, who seemed to be more engrossed in their conversation than alerting their bridge of any potential threats lurking in the waters. He could also make out shadows on the bridge of the Kalamazoo. They weren't giving off much light, yet the Key West was much closer than most CO's dared to get their boats to surface ships. The safety of his crew was all Captain Maddox was concerned with. Most CO's put a higher value on their careers, which kept them much further from any potential collisions than true safety required.

"Weps," Captain Maddox said without taking his eye off the scope, "Do you have someone standing by in the three inch launcher space?"

The Weps turned from the fire control center and addressed the Captain, "Petty Officer Quinn is on station, sir."

Captain Maddox strained to turn the scope, "Very well, Weps. Chief of the Watch, inform the Eng he needs to get someone from A-div to take a look at this scope next time we're on the surface."

"Inform the Eng to have an A-Ganger look at the scope the next time we're on the surface, aye, sir," Chief Meyers said as he was picking up the phone to contact the engine room. Before Chief Meyers could finish his call, Captain Maddox was piling on the next order.

"Chief of the Watch," Captain Maddox said, completely aware that Chief Meyers was still on the phone, "have Petty Officer Quinn verify his pressure on the launcher."

Chief Meyers hung up the phone as he acknowledged the order, "Have Quinn verify his launcher pressure, aye, sir."

Chief Meyers turned to his messenger of the watch who was sitting cross legged on the deck behind the Chief of the Watch's station at the ship's control panel. Captain Maddox pulled his eye off the scope briefly and glanced over at Chief Meyers quietly reiterating the Captain's order to the junior sailor. Not having men like Chief Meyers around was one of the greatest misgivings of his forced early retirement. Captain Maddox always measured a CO's ability to command by the level of competence of his crew that served under him.

Over the years, his fellow CO's learned anyone who had served on one of Captain Maddox's boats was worth five sailors. Captain Maddox had a habit of driving his crew to the brink of collapse, only to carry them on to greatness. He had always driven Chief Meyers hard, never letting Meyers finish passing on an order before piggybacking another on top of it. Meyers had an uncanny ability to speak and listen at the same time. It was an ability that Meyers had developed so well, Captain Maddox found himself stalling his orders until he had another to give right on top of it, just for sport. Many chiefs who stood the same watch station tried to emulate Meyers' abilities but failed to come close. Chief Meyers was always flattered that Captain Maddox seemed to take so much pleasure in trying to trip him up, but he had developed the skill at the age of sixteen working the drive-thru window at McDonalds. So by this point in his life, it was second nature, and try as he might, Captain Maddox was never able to put more pressure on him than a bus load of high school jocks with chipmunk metabolisms.

The three inch launcher space could not have been more appropriately named. It was exactly as its name implied, just a space. No bigger than a public toilet room stall, the space also served as Doc's office, and a storage facility for small explosives that were kept in a temperature controlled safe. Quinn and Schmidt were on station in the space. Schmidt pressed the phone earpiece tight against his head then keyed the microphone in response, "Verify pressure, aye." Quinn was already tapping the pressure gauge of the launcher when Schmidt began to respond to the Chief of the Watch. Schmidt looked at the gauge then keyed his mic. Before he could get a word out, Quinn put his hand over the mouthpiece. Schmidt looked up in surprise.

"To Control," Quinn told him with his hand still over the mic, "the three inch launcher is pressurized to fifty psi above outside sea pressure."

Schmidt looked in protest at the gauge that clearly read 500 psi above outboard sea pressure. Quinn slowly repeated himself, "To Control, the three inch launcher is pressurized to 50 psi above outboard sea pressure." Schmidt stared at him for a moment, pleading with his eyes for Quinn to change his mind. When he saw the resolve in Quinn's expression, he relayed Quinn's response to control.

Chief Meyers was bent down listening to the soft remarks of the phone talker, then he announced the report to the control room. "Officer of the Deck," he belted out, "the three inch launcher space has verified the pressure of the launcher set to 50 psi above outboard sea pressure."

The Officer of the Deck responded, "Very well." Then he looked to Captain Maddox for the order.

The Captain, who was looking out the periscope facing directly at the port bulkhead, gave the order without looking up at the Officer of the Deck. "Fire!" Like a domino effect the order fell though the control room.

The Officer of the Deck gave the order to the Chief of the Watch, "Fire!" Chief Meyers dropped the order to the phone talker, and he gave it over the phone. Instantly came the concussion of the three inch launcher as it blasted it's flair out like a rocket.

Everyone in the control room jumped. The deafening blast of the three inch launcher was clearly louder than any had anticipated. Captain Maddox watched through the periscope as the red flare, which was supposed to lob high over the bow of the Kalamazoo, shot like a missile right into the bridge of the surface ship, lighting it up with a blinding red phosphorescent torch.

Schmidt's face was as white as a ghost. Even Quinn's was one of surprise. At times, he couldn't resist pushing the envelope. The urge was usually primed by the knowledge he would be able to charm his way out of any consequences a less politically adept sailor would face. This time, however, he had pushed his mischief further than he had in the past. The concussion the launcher cycled with seemed loud enough to shake loose Quinn's armor of charm.

Through the ringing in his ears he heard his name being screamed. Captain Maddox was still in control, but like the three inch launcher, his volume had surprised Quinn.

Quinn scurried up the ladder to the control room and posted himself in front of Captain Maddox, who was still on the scope. The Captain peeled himself off the scope as he was yelling for Quinn again. Finding Quinn standing in front of him, he cut himself short. Quinn wasn't sure if this was going to be the straw to break the camel's back. Angrily the Captain said, "Okay, Jackass, why don't you take a look at what you've done?"

As Quinn stepped up to the scope, he felt Officer Candidate School slipping away. Captain Maddox, who had been his most ardent supporter in getting him accepted to the program, was now steamed. While the use of the word "jackass" was pretty harmless in the world of expletives, for a man who did not use, nor tolerate the use of foul language, it may as well have been an F-bomb.

Quinn looked through the scope. He could see panic ensuing on the bridge of the surface ship. While he could not make out any facial features, he could see sailors silhouetted by the brilliance of the red flare. One sailor was beating the flames with a coat only to catch it on fire, while other sailors tried to dowse it with fire extinguishers. This only added to the chaos. The whole thing had an air of the Three Stooges about it.

As Quinn stepped back off the scope, expecting the worst, he was met by a smiling Captain Maddox. Quinn hadn't seen that smile since before Captain Maddox's son had been killed. Captain Maddox slapped him on the shoulder.

"Great shot, Quinn!"

Quinn felt relieved. OCS wasn't slipping away after all. He caught Chief Meyer's eye. The chief was shaking his head in disbelief.

"I guess you'll have to calibrate that gauge, Quinn," Chief Meyers said, reminding Quinn how lucky he was that Captain Maddox wasn't holding mast right on the spot.

USS Kalamazoo

The flare had come to a stop when it became wedged between the base of the battle board and the deck. As the flare continued to spew its self-fueled flame, it began to char the beautifully hand crafted drawers which held the model ships. Captain Scott began to twitch with anger as he watched the marvel of his bridge being scorched.

Le Poignard

Aboard the Poignard, the French submarine, Captain Philip Reno stood over the LCD screen which made up the submarines plot board. In stark contrast to the outdated pre-digital paper charts the Quartermasters used aboard the Key West, the Poignard's system looked as if it were an oversized iPad. Merging real-time satellite video feeds with transparent navigational aid overlays, Captain Reno was able to utilize the touch screen to easily zoom out and, in turn, remagnify different quadrants of the operational box the exercise was taking place in. He looked over to the tri-screen monitor system which displayed the feed from the fiber optic periscope. The Teddy Roosevelt cut slowly through the water as its main task was to act as a target for the first part of the exercise rather than the powerful floating air station that it was.

Captain Reno stifled a yawn as he watched the big aircraft carrier cut crop circles in the ocean. Even though he, as well as the rest of his crew, had not had much rest over the past three days, his appearance was still sharp. He was part of a new generation of French Naval Officers. In its bid to become known as the military might of the EU, France had all but done away with career advancement based upon a collection of political connections, and implemented a merit-based system.

Reno looked more like a young CEO than a Naval Captain. At twenty-eight, he was the youngest Commanding Officer in the French fleet. His role in ending a rash of hijackings and sabotage of French owned oil tankers by Somali pirates partly won him the coveted position of being the first C.O. of France's prototype hydrogen fuel cell submarine. The fuel cell France had been able to produce far eclipsed the output any of the world's top shipbuilders had been able to produce in an electric submarine. It was the first of its kind to use fuel cell technology for propulsion rather than just for auxiliary power. Besides the power plant, the submarine was equipped with the latest technology the world had to offer, and Reno was hungry to use it all. In simulator test missions, many of the officers vying to become the sub's new C.O. complained that it seemed too much like a video game. Reno, on the other hand, celebrated the fact it was videogame-like, and expressed his disappointment when the simulator programmers informed him there were no "difficult" levels.

"I have bad news, sir," Reno's executive officer Michael De Panafiue said softly as he stepped out of the radio room. "You were right." Reno looked disappointed, but not surprised. "I sent it to you, sir." Reno touched an envelope at the bottom of the screen and an authentication window appeared on screen. He touched his index finger to the fingerprint graphic in the window and then typed in a code on the virtual keyboard which accompanied the box. Once the code was accepted a message popped up on the screen, the contents of which seemed to further displease Reno. He closed the message with a swift tap of his finger, as if the computer would register his disgust with the increased pressure. As De Panafiue watched, Reno flipped back to the satellite feeds and zeroed in on a quadrant in the southeast corner of the op zone. De Panafiue looked on in apparent amazement. Reno worked with the deftness of a user who had been integrated with the system for years, rather than just a few weeks.

Reno brought up an image of a surface ship. He flipped through images as the time stamp on them worked its way backwards. A few of the images showed a red flash on the ship. He set the images to play forward. He and De Panafiue watched as the choppy pictures showed a red flare shoot out of the water less than a quarter of a kilometer from the Kalamazoo and make a direct shot into its bridge.

"He was close," De Panafiue observed.

Reno's snarl transformed into a subtle grin, "I like this American. We may have to use everything we've got, especially our brains."

CHAPTER 9

USS Key West

As Quinn walked down the command passage way toward the control room, he heard the Chief of the Watch announce, "Surface! Surface! Surface!" The announcement was followed by the crowing of the klaxon alarm. The Key West was unique in the modern nuclear navy, in that it used a traditional klaxon horn as its diving alarm rather than the digital squelch the other boats of the fleet used. Chief Meyers, being a traditionalist, had scoured eBay in search of one of the old klaxons off of a decommissioned diesel boat. It was a prideful day aboard the Key West when they made their first dive signified by the AH-OO-GA! Sailors who left the Key West and went to other boats longed for their days spent with the klaxon, when their new command had the digital squelch diving alarm.

Hearing the rumble of the low pressure blow system, Quinn steadied himself by putting his hand on the bulkhead as the boat made a short bob to the surface. Once his legs acclimated to the rocking on the surface, he continued aft. He found the forward control room door shut, which was somewhat odd, but as he tried to open it, the door hit the messenger of the watch who was stooped down getting equipment ready to man the bridge.

While Quinn waited patiently for the young sailor to finish his duties, he heard the clanking of Lt. Turno's harness as he ascended the stairs from middle level to the command passageway. As Lt. Turno waited in line with Quinn for the door to be cleared, they heard the same clinking of a harness coming up from middle level. The XO emerged from the steps wearing the same orange harness. Quinn watched as the awkward moment turned to disappointment on the face of Lt. Turno. The XO said nothing to Turno; he just stared at him. Turno knew that to protest would be useless; the XO had a propensity for bumping the oncoming OOD (Officer of the Deck) when it came time to man the Bridge. After a few days of being submerged, some sailors would be clawing at the bulkheads; the XO was the unofficial leader of the Claustrophobia Club. He was not a greedy man, until it came to the opportunity to breathe air that had the glorious absence of machine, chemical, and foot odor. Sweat accumulated on his brow as his eyes pled with Lt. Turno not to object.

Quinn couldn't help but think the XO looked like a shaved squirrel. The man had a small frame, which, in many cases, was beneficial to a submariner. Yet, in the XO's circumstance, the small build combined with uncanny bushy eyebrows and features that seemed to be pulled into the center of his face undermined any authority he aspired to have. It was the XO's brilliance as an engineer that carried him to his current position, unfortunately for him that was as far as he could ride it. Any hopes that the Navy had for him were dashed when he was unable to glean any leadership qualities from Captain Maddox. For now, he was just biding his time until an instructor's position opened at Annapolis.

Lt. Turno said nothing, although he made no attempt to disguise the disappointment on his face. He simply reversed his direction, called out, "Down ladder," then grumbled as he descended the steps back to middle level.

Quinn could understand Lt. Turno's disappointment. Even the least claustrophobic sailor, such as himself, relished the thought of standing atop the submarine as it sliced its way through the ocean's surface, breathing non-synthetic air. In fact, as Quinn stood waiting for the door to open, he couldn't remember what excuse he had formed to bring himself to the control room. It was kind of an unconscious habit of his to come up to Control when he knew the boat was surfacing, with semi-hopes of having to make the ascent to the bridge for some trivial task which may give him a glimpse of the million star sky that only the black canvas night of the desolate ocean can give.

When the door to the control room was finally cleared, the XO, lacking the usual cordialness that accompanied his demeanor when in port, hurried his way past Quinn, and announced to Captain Maddox that he was ready to man the Bridge. Captain Maddox coolly tried to settle the XO's nerves. "Hunker down shipmate," he said, "we need to get your lookout up here too."

At that moment, Petty Officer Pope came lumbering through the aft door of the control room. His bright orange harness tightly fit over his submarine coveralls. "I'm ready to man the bridge, Chief of the Watch," he said in his

Gomer Pile-ish manner. Before Chief Meyers could acknowledge him, the Nav piped up, "Excuse me, Chief of the Watch, I need Petty Officer Pope to get some TPS reports ready for the next transmit." The Nav's nervous glance was met by Captain Maddox's steady gaze.

Chief Meyers, obviously annoyed with the Nav's last minute request, replied with a bit of a sneer, "Can't we just have him man the bridge with the XO, then I'll have him replaced in fifteen or twenty minutes?" "I have to have the reports ready for the transmittal at 2330," the Nav retorted.

Chief Meyer's annoyance was starting to border on insubordination, "Pope isn't the only radioman on board this boat."

The Nav quickly went for checkmate, "No, he's not, but Petty Officer Walker is working on a Crypto problem at the moment."

Chief Meyers' face reddened as his blood pressure rose. There was no argument that could be made to this, since Crypto was so top secret, nobody in the crew, with the exception of those directly involved with radio operations, knew what Crypto actually was. Chief Meyers did not have the need to know, so he wasn't sure if this meant a hardware problem, a software problem, or a problem with a game of solitaire. Simply put, it was the ultimate trump card and could not be argued against.

Covering his anger with the thinnest of veils, Chief Meyers huffed, "XO, you're going have to wait a minute while I have my messenger go scrounge up a replacement lookout." The XO rolled his eyes dramatically, as if he were a thirteen year old girl.

If Quinn had been thinking clearly, he would have jumped at the opportunity to man the bridge. However, while Chief Meyers and the Nav had been trading barbs, he noticed Ms. Collins slip in through the aft door and he had migrated towards her.

While Quinn was busy flirting, Scarpa came in through the forward control room door clad in the orange harness required to go up top. Chief Meyers was giving his messenger the order to go find a qualified lookout, when Captain Maddox interrupted him. "Chief of the watch," Captain Maddox said as he was doing a visual sweep on the periscope, "Petty Officer Scarpa is just going up to check the scope's faring. That'll only take thirty seconds or so." The XO shifted his weight to move slightly away from Scarpa.

"Petty Officer Scarpa," Captain Maddox said sternly, "are you on watch now?"

"I'm the oncoming Aux of the Watch, sir," Scarpa said, not revealing any emotions for or against becoming the lookout.

"Chief of the Watch," the Captain continued, "tell the off going Auxiliary Man of the Watch he will be relieved a half hour late. I'm sending Petty Officer Scarpa to the bridge as lookout. The cooks can save a plate for him." Captain

Maddox looked up from the scope to see the pathetic desperation on the XO's face. He quickly went back to the scope. "Man the bridge," he snapped.

As the XO and Scarpa started up the ladder to the bridge hatch, Chief Meyers sent the Captain's orders tumbling down the chain of command. Seeing his opportunity missed, Quinn turned his attention back to Ms. Collins. "How 'bout we go down and I see if I can score us some early midrats," Quinn said, forgetting he was talking to someone who didn't understand statements so heavily laden with submarine lingo. "If we're lucky it'll be pillows of death."

Perplexed, Ms. Collins tried to decipher Quinn's riddle. "I'm not sure what you said, but I think you were trying to seduce me."

With a shy laugh Quinn clarified himself, "What I said was, 'Maybe we can go get some midnight rations.'" Still seeing a look of confusion on her face, he went into deeper clarification, "That's the midnight snack the galley serves. If we're lucky it will be pillows of death...that's ravioli."

"Why would we be lucky if its ravioli?" she asked earnestly.

Noticing the way the submarine coveralls could not hide her meticulously maintained figure, Quinn realized nothing which had come out of a Chef Boyardee can had probably ever touched her lips. Still he tried to make her realize it could be worse, "Once you have the rice pilaf you'll start looking forward to the ravioli."

Le Poignard

"Sir, we've located the Key West," the sonar man called out. "It sounds as if they just commenced a low pressure blow. They're surfacing."

Reno smiled at his executive officer, "Prepare the drone."

"Sir, we are supposed to be on a break," De Panafiue reminded him.

Reno pursed his lips and shook his head as if he were about to correct a naive child. "My dear friend, we've played by the Americans rules far too long already, our mission is to use our weapon to its fullest potential without letting the Americans know what we can do."

De Panafiue matched his Captain's excitement, "Prepare the drone!"

Looking like a massive sea turtle breaching the surface, the rounded sail of the Poignard quietly emerged from the depths. Once the apex of the sail was approximately a meter above the surface, two panels at the centerline sunk downwards breaking the continuity of the nearly seamless surface of the shell. After lowering ten centimeters, each panel slid to the side, one to port and one to starboard. Once the panels were clear, a pedestal type mast raised from the opening. At the top of the mast was what would have been the ultimate Christmas toy for any tech-savvy boy; France's latest version of an unmanned drone. The top of the drone was the size and shape of a truck tire. Its flat black color and quiet rotor system had inspired its creators to call it the "Whisper

Wheel". Though, to their disappointment, none of the military men picked up their nickname, they simply called it what the Americans had been calling theirs, a drone. The outer ring was stationary while the center "rim" began to spin. As the drone lifted off the pedestal, a pair of bars which the clamps on the pedestal had been secured to retracted.

"We have lift-off of the drone sir."

Captain Reno looked over at the drone technician's monitor. The video feed from the drone dimly showed the shell-shaped sail of the Poignard as the panels returned to their seamless position. "Can you brighten that up?"

"Yes, sir." The tech turned a virtual dial on his screen and the image seemed to go from black night to near daylight.

"Very good." Captain Reno looked back to his periscope monitors. The drone hung in the air a few meters above the water. "Let's try the cloaking, shall we?" Reno said, almost giddy.

"Initiating the Lumicloak System."

The outer surface of the drone let off a momentary glow then seemed to almost disappear. A star which had been blocked from view on the periscope monitors by the position of the drone was now visible on the screen. "That is amazing," Reno whispered. "Swing it around in front of the moon!"

The technician swung the drone around, located the moon in his monitor, and then positioned the drone between the moon and the periscope. Captain Reno, as well as the other crew members, watched as the drone slipped in front of the moon. It looked as though someone had slid a sheet of glass in front of the celestial body. The cloaking technology was rather rudimentary, but it seemed to work. The shell of the outer wheel was essentially a high definition monitor which projected the image from the opposite side of the wheel. This cloaking image was pulled off by sixteen cameras around the circumference of the wheel creating a seamless image, giving the faux appearance of looking right through the machine.

"Let's go find that American sub, shall we?"

USS Key West

Scarpa stood straddling the lower bridge hatch as the XO struggled to undog the upper hatch. The XO's breathing was becoming heavy and labored. There was no way to be sure if it was from the physical exertion, or if it was panic setting in.

"Would you like me to open the hatch, sir?" Scarpa asked without betraying the disdain he surely must have felt toward such a feeble man having a position of authority over him.

"No!" the XO snapped as he grunted. He strained for another ten seconds before letting his muscles go limp. His shoulders dropped in exhaustion, and then, as if by his own cognizance, he ordered Scarpa to climb up and open the hatch. As he descended into the bridge trunk, he was griping about the A-Gangers not keeping up with their maintenance on the hatches. Scarpa did not give the XO the satisfaction of acknowledging the verbal jab.

Scarpa was the boat's most knowledgeable Auxiliary Man, or A-Ganger as the division was less formally called. He may not have taken much pride in the Navy or even in being a submariner, which was commonly known to be a much tighter knit community within the general culture of the Navy, but he did take pride in his work. The fact that he superbly maintained the systems that everyone aboard depended on, yet took for granted, was his only glory.

As he climbed the ladder, he made no attempt to recover a wrench which slipped out of his pocket. The wrench was securely fastened by a four foot lanyard to his belt so it would not fall overboard if it slipped out of his hands while working. The tool bounced wildly when it had reached the end of the rope. The XO displeasingly guarded his face from being hit with the initial wild bounce of the wrench, but he did not say anything to Scarpa, fearing it might slow his progress on the hatch.

Upon reaching the hatch, Scarpa firmly grasped the wheel and with a quick jerk, he broke the seal. "I can take it from here, Petty Officer Scarpa," the XO persisted, but Scarpa simply ignored him. He knew he would have to open the clam shells as well. The clam shells were the two steel doors which made up the last obstacle before they would be free of the submarine. The clam shells covered a free flood area in the sail, which meant their handles were exposed to all the elements of the open sea and would require the use of the wrench Scarpa carried as well as all the strength he could muster to open them.

After exerting a considerable amount of effort, he was able to loosen the handles and emerge into the glorious air. Even for someone as unsentimental as Scarpa, being the sole life breathing the virgin air of the black night seemed to have the same mystical effect as it did on all other sailors. He stood in the bridge with his head and chest rising from the submarine like one of its periscopes. He scanned all 360 degrees of the horizon. It was as if he was standing atop a world where he was alone.

The moment was gone when he could no longer ignore the whining of the XO trying to claw his way out of the boat like a cat trying to escape a tub of water. Scarpa hopped onto the top of the sail and let the XO up to the world. The XO hung his head over the side, taking deep breaths in his nose and exhaling out his mouth as if he had just completed a marathon. He did this for the next five minutes without saying a word while Scarpa set to work hooking up the bridge communication box. When he finally lifted his head, Scarpa immediately recognized that the XO no longer suffered from claustrophobia, but now his ailments were that of seasickness.

Once the XO had composed himself, he began communicating with the control room. As the XO was busy giving permissions to do such housekeeping tasks as pumping sanitaries and ventilating the boat, Scarpa attached his harness' lanyard to one of the safety hooks in the sail and crawled back to the periscope to perform a cursory inspection of its faring. The XO had just given an order to bring the ship to course one-six-five when Scarpa called out to him.

"XO!"

The XO turned around and cupped his ear so that he could hear Scarpa over the boat's churning of the water at an all ahead full bell.

"Sir," Scarpa shouted, "could you ask control to have the Captain check the periscope now?"

"Was there a problem?" the XO interrogated.

Scarpa held up a piece of rubber. "There was a gasket pinched in the faring," he explained. The XO nodded then spoke into his comm. mic. Scarpa couldn't hear the exchange the XO was having, but he noticed the scope panning around, so he made his way back to the bridge platform. As he reached the platform, the XO told him Captain Maddox was on the scope and said that everything was fine.

"So, that's it," the XO said, settling back, obviously feeling better, "we just made our last turn of the watch." Scarpa listened as he rummaged in his jacket's breast pocket. "So now we just sit here and enjoy the night until we get relieved," the XO said with a freshness in his voice which had been absent since the boat left the pier.

Scarpa's hand emerged from his pocket holding a cigarette, "Request permission to burn a smoke, sir."

The XO turned to see Scarpa ready to light up his cigarette. Stress returned to the XO's face, "Absolutely not, Petty Officer Scarpa!" Scarpa did not look surprised. Some of the boat's junior officers would let the lookouts catch a smoke while they stood watch in the bridge together. It was a technique the young officers would use to try to gain an equitable reputation among the enlisted ranks, which was a task Annapolis had no course to prepare them for. Unfortunately for the officers that let this little infraction slide, they did not realize that if an enlisted man did not respect their leadership before being allowed to break the rules, it only weakened the officer's authority in his eyes. However, on the flip side, if an officer had already gained the blue shirt's respect, and let the protocols relax a bit, then the reverence toward the officer would deepen. It was a catch twenty two for those officers who just could not manage to leap the hurdle of respect which was so important to leadership.

The XO turned back to scanning the hidden horizon which lay off the bow, satisfied that his authority had prevailed. Scarpa promptly lit his cigarette. Since he was standing atop the sail and behind the XO, the XO did not notice. Scarpa had taken a few drags off his cigarette when the acrid odor finally settled upon the XO's senses. As soon as the XO was able to discern the smell of the burning tobacco as it mingled with the smell of the chemical air coming up from the bridge hatch, he whipped back around to face Scarpa.

Scarpa did not look at him; he had observed the XO peripherally but did not acknowledge the squirrelly man's rage. The XO looked up at Scarpa in obvious disbelief. Under normal circumstances, the XO avoided confrontation at all costs, but this type of flagrant insubordination infuriated him. His fists clenched with rage. He had complained to Captain Maddox about being bullied by some of the blue shirts. Captain Maddox, rather than going on the witch hunt the XO wanted, convinced him he could tolerate little snipes a bit longer until he was teaching officers in training. Captain Maddox soothed his anger with fantasies of only dealing with young men who came from decent backgrounds; men who were taught how to respect authority. No more games of walking a tight rope with the enlisted, where if you try and be too authoritarian you fall, or if you try and be too appeasing you fall off the other way.

The XO seemingly let himself falsely believe there was a great fissure that divided nineteen year olds who were in college from those who were enlisted. Captain Maddox knew, even as he tried to convince the XO otherwise, it did not make a difference, whether a dog is a mutt or pure bred, if they smell fear they go right for the jugular. At the moment, the XO looked as though he was done waiting for that far day to come. It was as if he decided that by taking a stand against Scarpa now and making him pay for his insolence, he would somehow gain respect from the crew. His head seemed to be swimming with possibilities as he yelled almost incoherently with rage at Scarpa.

"This is the last straw, Petty Officer Scarpa!" he sputtered as he turned from Scarpa and reached, with trembling hands, for the communications box. "I'm getting you re-" Before he could finish, Scarpa raised his twelve inch crescent wrench over his head and brought it crashing down with such tremendous force upon the XO's skull, it split his head open from the top of his crown to the corner of his eye.

The XO crumpled onto the deck grate. The grate was the only thing that kept him from falling to the control room. Immediately, he began to convulse with seizures. Scarpa jumped into the small space where the XO's foot was making a racquet as it involuntarily kicked the hitch pin which held the deck grate in place. As Scarpa lifted the XO's body, he hadn't anticipated how many thousands of capillaries would be opened up from such a blow. Blood drained from his head like a faucet. Scarpa struggled to remove his jacket. Frantically, he pulled his harness straps off of his shoulders, removed his jacket and wrapped it around the XO's hemorrhaging head. He could see sailors passing twenty feet below the bridge hatch. Knowing it was almost habit for them to look up to the bridge when the boat was on the surface, Scarpa worked quickly to hoist the

XO to the top of the sail. It would be hard for anyone who peered up as they passed underneath to see anything distinguishable. They would only be able to make out faint shadows silhouetted against the night sky; however, suspicion would be drawn immediately if some unlucky sailor looked up only to get a face full of blood spilling down from the hatch.

Once he had the XO on top of the sail, he climbed up himself. The XO's initial violent convulsions had settled into subtle tremors. Scarpa could hear muffled groans coming from the olive green jacket wrapped tightly around the XO's head. In the crisp glow of the crescent moon, Scarpa caught his breath as he watched the hull number, stenciled on the back of his jacket, heave up and down with gasps from the XO. With an uncanny rhythm, Scarpa's rate of breathing matched that of the XO's. His slowed after being spiked by the moment of exertion. The XO's breathing slowed with the onset of shock.

After a minute or two, the groaning turned into mumbling, so Scarpa calmly slid the XO over to the starboard side then, with a shove of his foot, pushed the XO overboard. The XO did not simply slide into the ocean, his harness was still attached to the boat, and he had to contend with the fairwater plane on the way down. Newer classes of submarines, even some of the later Los Angeles class subs, were outfitted with bow planes below the waterline. The Key West happened to be one of the last submarines built with fairwater planes for stability control. The massive wing-like structures jutted out of the port and starboard sides of the sail and had never been much of any consequence to the XO, but on this night, as his ankle bones shattered against the starboard plane, its relevance was unmerciful. When his feet crashed against the fairwater plane, he let out a yelp like a wounded dog. The combination of his angle of impact as well as his complete lack of reflexes sent his body tumbling headlong toward the deck below. His fall came to a sudden halt, just shy of the topside deck, as the harness's lanyard went taught. He was lurching back and forth, as he hung limp like a boxer's heavy bag, his feet just six inches above the deck.

Scarpa unhooked his own harness, and then hopped onto the fairwater plane. The six foot drop, which had been devastating for the XO just moments before, was no big deal for a sailor with their wits about them. Scarpa made his way carefully to the back edge of the fairwater plane. The sea spray made the surface slick, and the twelve foot drop to the rounded deck below could spell disaster for him. He swung himself onto the lanyard which dangled the XO like a piñata and shimmied down to the deck. He even used the XO for hand and foot holds as he neared the bottom. He was equally as careful getting his footing topside when he reached it. Standing on the side of the sail was precarious when the boat is simply pulling in or out from the pier, but standing on the side of the sail while the boat is running at an all ahead full bell was bordering on suicide. As submarines cut through the water at high speeds, the ocean completely covers the bow. When the water crashes against the sail, which protrudes upward from the deck, it is like splitting Niagara Falls with a giant wedge. Standing on the starboard side of the sail, Scarpa was able to keep his footing only because the towed array faring ran the length of the boat. With its hump-like shell, the faring gave an extra foot to the precarious walkway.

Wasting no time, Scarpa set to work loosening the straps of the XO's harness. After freeing the XO, he began to make his way aft carrying the semiconscious man like a roll of wet carpet. When he reached the back of the sail he was out of the greatest danger. He had a somewhat wider span of deck to maneuver on, although the span was only about four foot wide down the centerline. When stationary, the topside deck only gave about ten feet of safe working area before the curved hull would become a slide into the drink, but at the current speed even the sliver of deck down the centerline would have surf wash over it from time to time.

Scarpa positioned the XO into a fireman's carry and made his way toward the stern. As he neared the aft-most portion of the deck he could see the outline of the boat's thirty foot rudder protruding a few feet out of the wake. Behind it, the water churned wildly with each revolution of the boat's heavily torqued screw. Every few seconds, as the valley between wave crests would dip the surface to within a few inches of exposing the enormous blades of the screw, the sea would be thrown into the air with a dull glow as its reflective properties caught the light cast upon it by the stern lamp fixed to the top of the rudder. Scarpa dumped the XO onto the deck.

Le Poignard

"Sir, the drone is within one kilometer of the American Sub."

"Very well, what is your altitude?"

"One hundred and seventy five meters, sir."

Captain Reno stepped over to the technician's station and studied the image of the Key West growing larger on the screen as the drone made its approach. Even with the enhanced optics, the submarine looked like nothing more than a sliver of black ice in the water.

"That's what I love most about submarines," Reno remarked just over the technician's shoulder.

"What's that, sir?"

"Even a sub twice the size of ours is barely visible on the surface, the ultimate weapon of the sea," Reno let the sentiment linger before he gave his next order. "Bring the drone down to," Captain Reno searched his technician's face for any doubt of the drone's abilities, "two meters above the surface."

The XO wasn't as ambitious about risking the new drone. "Captain, isn't that cutting it a little too close?" he asked respectfully.

"The Key West was in dry dock last spring," Captain Reno explained without taking his eyes off the monitor. "We don't know what type of upgrades they may have gotten, and while the cloaking seems to work as its designed, it will be a lot easier to hide it in the noise of the waves than in the clear sky."

"Besides," the technician offered up, obviously as excited about the test as his Captain, "we have a few options for auto hovering." The technician brought up the options on his screen. "It's equipped with a TFR, a Terrain Following Radar, which provides precise altimeter readings so you can set it to stay at a specified distance above the water, so it automatically adjusts its hovering system to ascend or descend with the sea." He set the drone to follow the protocol. "But you may find the resulting video leaves you with a queasy stomach." Captain Reno and De Panafiue nodded their head in agreement of the theory, but the young technician began to turn green. He quickly changed the auto hover settings to one more suitable for his weak stomach. "The one I prefer keeps it at a steady altitude, hovering at an average of two meters above the swells."

"Zoom in on that periscope," Captain Reno said as the first signs of concern began to peek through his cool demeanor, "let's make sure the optics aren't staring dead at us." The tech made the adjustment.

"It appears whoever is on the scope is not scanning this way, or at least not toward the drone."

"It looks as if the scope is fixed in one position," De Panafiue assessed.

"Zoom out," Captain Reno instructed. "See if we can ascertain what he is looking at."

The tech zoomed out and instantly saw what the scope operator was watching. "There's someone working on the deck."

USS Key West

As Scarpa unwrapped his jacket from the XO's head, the XO began to mutter the word, "why" over and over. Scarpa said nothing. He simply began to shove the XO into the sea with his boot. As the cold sea washed over his legs, panic arose within the XO. He clumsily fished into his breast pocket, pulling out a picture.

He held the picture in front of his left eye, his right pupil having been blown by swelling on the optic nerve, and studied the faces of the three ugly little girls. He knew they were ugly, but he had loved every detail about them since before they were born. He loved how their eyes would study his mouth as he read them bedtime stories. It was as if they watched brightly colored words float out of his mouth to paint pictures in their imaginations. He loved the way they had inherited a complete lack of artistic ability from him. His stateroom, when not borrowed by a T.V. newswoman, would be adorned with the most hideous drawings and he would have absolutely no idea what the images were supposed to represent. But they could do math; boy, could they do math. He especially loved that there were three of them, a prime number, indivisible. He stared at the picture trying to draw strength from his little angels.

A wave washed over the stern and did the rest of Scarpa's work for him. The XO made a feeble attempt at swimming. Unfortunately for his family of five, his effort was no more than a few thrashes of the water by his limp arms. Scarpa watched as the XO made a last ditch effort to survive. Mustering all the strength he had left, the XO managed to cling to the rudder for a second or two before being swept under. As the XO felt the suction of the screw pulling him toward his death, the math wiz must have been mortified at the thought that by losing him; his family would be down to four. Composite numbers had always made him uncomfortable.

Scarpa studied the wake just behind the screw, unsure of what he might expect to see from the surface. He had, on two occasions, deployed as a support element during covert SEAL operations. On those missions, he and Quinn merely went along to make sure the SEAL team's equipment rigs were deployed safely and that no damage came to the submarine while the SEALs and their inflatable ribs made their ascent to the surface.

During those missions, Scarpa had witnessed the intimidating screw making turns to keep the boat moving forward at a mere two knots. Even at that slow speed, the massive blades had been a haunting image, as they glowed eerily in the dark sea exciting the bioluminescence with each slash through the water. He and Quinn talked afterwards, wondering if they would have been able survive if one of their safety lines had snapped and they had been pulled into the screw. There could be no doubt the XO would be killed, but he just waited, as if he expected to see a massive pool of blood turning the wake red like it was a shark attack. As the seconds passed, he seemed to resign himself to the fact that if there were any visible signs on the surface of the horror which had just taken place beneath, the boat was moving much too quickly for any of the evidence to reach the surface before it had moved passed the area of the wake made visible by the moon and the stern light.

Le Poignard

"We're witnessing a murder!" As if the operation of the new drone hadn't had the entire control room distracted enough from their duties, De Panafiue's outburst caused the helmsman to turn almost completely around in his seat. As the helmsman strained his neck to try and get a glimpse of the drone's monitor screen, he put a full turn on the rudder. The excessive rudder caused the sub to bank as it turned to starboard. Feeling the change in his balance, Captain Reno looked up at the periscope screens and noticed the video feed submerging.

"Mind your helm!"

The helmsman, realizing his blunder, turned back and worked to bring the boat back to the surface. "Get us up, Helm! We don't want to lose our control signal!" When Captain Reno saw the periscopes break the surface, he turned his attention back to the drone monitor.

"Captain! We've got to stop him," De Panafiue pleaded.

"What are we supposed to do?" Reno asked, obviously displeased with the moral dilemma he had been thrust into. "This is happening eighty five kilometers away."

"We could radio them and let them know what is happening on their deck!"

"Somebody is watching them through the periscope," Reno talked it through as much for his benefit as for his crew's. "Most likely it is a high ranking officer, they should have security coming topside any moment." The men watched the screen. The seconds seemed like an eternity.

"Unless whoever is watching is part of it," De Panafiue said softly.

"That is what I'm afraid of," Captain Reno conceded. "If that is the case, I would hate to reveal our country's most secret technology because of some American love tryst gone awry."

"It would be rather hard to explain how we knew what was happening on the deck of a submarine so far away," De Panafiue added.

USS Key West

Satisfied the XO was dead, or if he miraculously survived the ordeal, he would be dead before there was a chance anyone would locate him, Scarpa turned to make the dangerous trek back to the sail.

When he reached the aft escape trunk, he noticed the lens of periscope number one was facing him. He paused, outstretched his hand and held up his thumb.

Things were quiet in the control room, where it was rigged for night. Since there were no lights on, the only illumination came from the soft red glow of the control panel's gauges. As the control room party went quietly about their business, Captain Maddox faced aft looking into the periscope. As he peered at Scarpa standing gravely on the deck giving him the thumbs up sign, he swallowed hard. He had been witness to Scarpa's cruelty at the stern and gave no outward sign of the horror which had taken place topside. Watching through the periscope gave him a sense of separation, as if he were watching two actors portray a heinous act on screen for entertainment. He had worked so hard at compartmentalizing his emotions for the last few months, years even, that it did not affect him as it should have. It was as if he were a completely different person than that of the supportive superior officer who had but a few months earlier dined with the now murdered XO, his wife and three daughters. He watched Scarpa as he made his way forward until he was close enough to the sail that he slipped into the blind spot directly beneath the scopes.

Captain Maddox took a deep breath, steeled himself, then popped the scope handles into their upright stowage position and turned the hydraulic wheel overhead to send the scope downward. As the main body of the periscope began its descent followed by the thinner smooth steel shaft which penetrated the hull, the Captain announced in a clear and determined voice, "Down periscope." He did not let on to the inhumanity he had just witnessed. "Chief of the Watch, the scope seems to be working fine," he said as his eyes met the Nav's. "Scarpa has taken care of everything."

Le Poignard

"Close in behind her," Captain Reno instructed the drone technician, "see if that poor soul pops up in the wake."

"Aye, sir," the tech acknowledged as he maneuvered the joystick to swing the drone behind the Key West.

"Ease it up to fifty meters so we get a better field of view," De Panafiue added.

"Up to fifty, aye," the tech repeated. Then taking his own initiative he said, "Switching to forward looking infrared."

"Good call," Reno said, bolstering the technician's confidence. They all scanned the screen in silence.

"It's been two minutes, Captain," De Panafiue said, checking his watch.

"There!" the tech shouted as he pointed to a bright white dot which had just popped up in the blackness which filled the screen.

"Zoom in!" Captain Reno ordered. The tech zipped the drone down to just a few meters above the lifeless body.

"He's face down, sir." the tech observed. Captain Reno nodded his head slightly as he weighed his options.

"There's nothing we can do for him now," Reno finally said. "Catch back up with the Key West. Let's see what that sailor is up to."

"Yes, sir," the tech said. Then he added, "But we'll need to get the drone headed back soon; its power supply isn't limitless."

"Very well. See if you can get close enough to attach a sonar amplifier to the rudder."

"Sonar amplifier?" De Panafiue asked, not having been completely briefed on the drone's capabilities.

"The drone is equipped with an amplifier, which can be affixed to the surface of any ship you wish to track," Reno began, but his enthusiastic technician couldn't hold back from expanding the explanation.

"Once it is attached to the boat it amplifies any sound resonating from the target. You see, it's not as detectable as a tracking device which emits a rhythmic pulse. Their sonar technicians are aware their ship is putting out minor transient noises into the water; they just don't realize they've been amplified to carry farther."

USS Key West

Scarpa climbed back up to the top of the sail using the XO's useless lanyard. As he reached the bridge he noticed all the blood. He knew the XO had been bleeding profusely, but he had been so busy dealing with it that he did not take the time to process how messy it had actually been. "Looks like a damned murder scene," he said softly, apparently not putting any emotional equity into the logic that that was precisely what he was looking at.

He began to try and clean the mess with the XO's jacket, but there was just too much blood. The more he tried to sop it up, the more it seemed to smear, making it appear worse than it had been. He stopped his attempts to clean it. A cursory inspection would reveal the attempts to hide the blood, so he decided to camouflage the situation. He pulled out his pocket knife and reopened the centimeter long cut on the ridge of his hairline in the center of his forehead. Immediately, blood began to ooze from the wound. He noted the time on the glowing hands of his dive watch. "Crap, too soon."

CHAPTER 10

The Nav nervously adjusted the band of his watch as he compared it with the clock on the wall in the tiny radio room. Petty Officer Walker sat tinkering with a potentiometer dial on a piece of radio gear. The Nav stood over Petty Officer Pope as he filtered through the latest batch of radio messages. The man practically hit the overhead when the door buzzer went off. Pope looked at the Nav with innocent suspicion as he reached over and turned the knob to the radio room door.

As the Weps entered, his shoulders seemed to take up half the room. Being on the upper level and close to the outboard, the overhead in Radio sloped downward quickly, giving the Weps little head room. "I need Petty Officer Walker," the Weps announced. The Nav and Walker exchanged panicked looks.

"What for?" the words fumbled out of the Nav's mouth.

"I need him to put together this BRC report for me so we can get it transmitted before we dive again."

"Pope can do that for you," the Nav said in a tone more pleading than pacifying.

Irritated, the Weps raised his thunderous voice, "I have the morning watch, and I'd like to get some rack time before hand, not teach some newbie how to format a BRC report!" The Nav knew this was the case, and since he could not counter with any excuse the Weps would not easily dismantle, he relented.

"Go with the Weps," the Nav said to Walker. Walker looked at his watch.

The hair stood on the back of the Weps' neck. "What, do you have a date?" he raged. Walker stood and dejectedly walked out the door. "I think you computer geeks have fried your motherboards," the annoyed Weps said. Usually, he was respectful of everybody, but what should have been a simple task seemed as if he were asking them to carry a child for him.

As the door shut behind the Weps, the Nav stood with his mouth agape. He, once again, checked his watch and then looked disparagingly at Pope.

Scarpa pinched the mostly burned cigarette between two blood-stained fingertips. Before lifting the cigarette to his lips, he spit the blood out which had trickled down into his mouth as a tobacco chewer spits the leaf particles out after a chew. His face was a bloody mess at this point; twenty five minutes had passed since he had disposed of the XO. He took one last drag, and then flicked the still burning butt into the ocean. He hopped down onto the deck grate, grabbed the microphone from the comm. box, keyed it and screamed, "Man Overboard, starboard side!" Before he could reach the alarm on the box, Chief Meyers had already jumped up from the ships control panel and had the general alarm blasting away below decks.

Scarpa then balled up the XO's Jacket and heaved it as far as he could away from the boat. He could hear commotion erupting below as he hit the jacket with the spot light. A look of desperation crept across his face as he saw the jacket get sucked into the screw. The absence of a floating target to draw everybody's attention would leave only the messy bridge and his bloody face for others to dwell upon.

In Radio, Pope was having the beginnings of a panic attack as well. He couldn't decide whether he was going to stand up or sit down. "I'll send out a Mayday!" he exclaimed. The Nav had not planned on this situation; he had been counting on Walker. He and Walker had worked together for the last two years, and at one point he had gained the junior Petty Officer's undying loyalty by covering a mistake which could have threatened to strip Walker of his security clearance and would have resulted in a dishonorable discharge at the least, ten years in the brig at the most. It was a risk the Nav would not have taken had his career followed an ideal path.

One evening two months back, Captain Maddox opened up to the Nav in a very dark conversation where the two men finally aired their grievances about the Navy. Captain Maddox seemed to turn from a path filled with endless complaints to a path which led to unpatriotic actions; actions the Nav didn't seem particularly opposed too, especially when the opportunity came with a chance to become extremely wealthy. In their initial conversation, Captain Maddox instructed him to make at least one concrete ally among the crew. He already had that in Walker, so he took his chance, banking on the presumption Walker was as disenfranchised with the service as he was.

Now, all of his previous courting of Walker was useless. As Pope's finger was seconds away from hitting the transmit button, the Nav did what he had to do to keep the situation from spinning further out of his control. He swung the component Walker had been working on over his head.

Pope was about to send the Mayday, when he noticed the Nav's reflection in the computer monitor. The reflection startled him. The Nav's face was contorted as if he were a starving man about to take a bite of a dead rat. Pope turned quickly in a fright, but before he could find out what caused the Nav's face to be so wretched, everything went black.

Scarpa was desperately searching the black waves for the XO's jacket when he heard the clanking of one or two people fast-climbing the ladder to the bridge. If he could at least spot the jacket it would create a diversion for the time being and stay off any questions which, if brought too quickly, might easily shoot holes in his story.

From below, he heard Quinn's voice yelling to him, "Up Ladder!" No sooner had Scarpa hopped off of the deck grate, Quinn blasted it open with the palm of his hand and with almost unnatural speed was on top of the sail scanning the waves beside Scarpa. Lt. Turno had followed Quinn up the ladder. Though his ascent was not accomplished with the same gusto as Quinn's, he never-the-less was quick about taking control of the boat.

"This is Lt. Turno, I have the deck and the con!" he informed control over the communications system. "Helm all stop! Right full rudder!" The helm had already responded with an all stop bell when the initial man overboard announcement went out, but still procedure required the order be given. The screw stopped churning the water as the boat made a wide arc turning to starboard. When Quinn momentarily took his eyes off the sea and glanced at Scarpa, he saw for the first time the bloody mess that was his shipmate's face.

"What the hell happened up here?" Quinn said, grabbing a handful of Scarpa's coveralls, pulling him closer to inspect his bloody face.

Quinn detected a hint of panic in Scarpa. According to the Captain's plan, the inquiries were not supposed to start this early. He and Captain Maddox had discussed the best method of rendering the XO incapacitated. Captain Maddox had urged him to strangle the XO, but Scarpa pressed that if his body were discovered, it would be apparent it had been a murder. Blunt force, on the other hand, would more likely mimic an injury caused by a fall, or being minced up by a nuclear powered blender. Captain Maddox had reluctantly agreed to Scarpa's plan, the argument having been laid out thoughtfully and point by point;

however, it still was unsettling to him that the underlying factor to Scarpa's case was that it seemed to fit his personality better.

Scarpa, as good a case as he had made, had not anticipated the buckets of blood the injury would produce. Now, his impromptu act of using his blood in an attempt to cover up the XO's, a detail which seemed relatively minor at the moment since no one had yet noticed, threatened to cast immediate and justifiable doubt upon his story. The panic, which seemed as though it was about to engulf him, quickly evaporated, as he spotted the jacket out of the corner of his eye.

"There!" he shouted.

Quinn saw it too. He relinquished his grip on Scarpa and jumped down onto the starboard fairwater plane. As he landed, he went down to a knee to cushion the impact. There on the fairwater plane, sticking to the thin layer of moisture, he saw a thousand tiny white specs. It was the remnants of cigarette ash. At the moment it did not raise any red flags. He knew lookouts who smoked would sometimes talk the officers into letting them have a cigarette while on watch. Quinn never could understand the desire sailors had to fill their lungs with chemicals the moment they left an environment where their lungs were filled with chemicals. Nevertheless, it was a litmus test sailors would perform on the officers.

With the detail of the ashes safely locked away in his subconscious, Quinn took the few running steps he could manage then made a diving leap into the ocean. Had adrenaline not been making the decisions for him, he would have jumped in feet first. However, in an attempt to maximize his trajectory, he instinctively dove in, head first. Unfortunately, the ocean did not assist him in his effort. What should have been a fifteen foot drop to the water, turned out to be almost twice the distance since the boat, having come about nearly one hundred and eighty degrees, caught up with the swells from its own wake.

The ocean seemed to run away from Quinn as he fell. The unexpected valley between the swells caused him to over rotate and land flat on his back. As he hit the concrete-like surface of the water, he felt all the air, which he had filled his lungs with anticipating a long-fast swim underwater, reflexively leave his body. Because of the irregular landing, he only penetrated the water a few feet. After a few ugly kicks, his face broke the surface and he tried to replace the fleeting air, but his body seemed only to be able to produce dry heaves which sapped him of every last cubic inch of air in his lungs. *Dear God*, he thought, *All those months of dive school and I'm going to drown because I couldn't jump feet first like they teach everyone with a pulse the third day of boot camp.*

As a Navy Diver, the training regiment he and all Divers went through ensured they were in top physical condition. The reason Divers went to such great lengths in their training was to make certain they could handle any situation which may come up underwater. It also meant they had very little body fat. In other words, their bodies were absent any natural buoyancy, so they sank like rocks.

Quinn felt himself beginning to sink. He flailed his arms, but lacking the oxygen his muscles needed for energy, he felt as though he had cinder blocks attached to them. A concussion in the water registered on his ears. He felt Scarpa grasp the inner pit of his elbow. This time, when his head broke the surface he was able to gasp in a few breaths. He looked up and saw Lt. Turno hitting the water with the spot light about forty yards from their position. Scarpa said nothing, he just began to swim. After a few good breaths, Quinn felt his strength returning and began to follow.

Captain Maddox had one foot on the bridge ladder when the Nav screamed "FLASH TRAFFIC" over the comm. system. The news of a highly important message halted the Captain's upward progress. Dealing with a flash message trumped any assistance he could give in the bridge. "Bring it to me, Nav!" he said as he stepped off the ladder.

"Captain!" the Weps objected to the change in his direction. The Weps' noticeable irritation with Captain Maddox for not continuing to the bridge showed his loyalty to his troops. While the Weps' gut instinct went against mission protocols, Captain Maddox knew he was right to question him. Showing the crew they mattered above anything else would ensure their loyalty and bring about a better chance at mission success than simply following protocols.

"There's nothing I could do up there to improve the situation, Weps," the Captain retorted.

The tension broke when Lt. Turno called down from the bridge, "Control-Bridge, it looks like Scarpa and Quinn have him!"

"Chief of the Watch," Captain Maddox snapped, "Have the COB and a recovery team get topside ASAP!"

Chief Meyers gave an abbreviated repeat back, "COB-team-topside-ASAP-aye."

Captain Maddox and the Weps locked eyes. The Weps quickly busied himself, flushed with shame that he had questioned Captain Maddox in a crisis moment, a moment when it really counted. In all the exercises of the past, he had trusted in Captain Maddox implicitly, and now when the Captain would need more support than ever, he folded. Captain Maddox knew the Weps was following the right instincts, but he would beat himself up for questioning him in front of the crew.

In the midst of all the commotion in the control room, Ms. Collins walked in facing her cameraman and began to give a narrative of the unfolding situation. As sailors bumped into the intrusive pair, they remained the consummate professionals, reporting as if they were in the middle of a hurricane. As Dave panned his camera across the control room, Captain Maddox turned just in time to be blinded by the unit's 1500 watt light.

"What the hell!" he exclaimed as he brought his hand up to shield his eyes. "Chief of the Watch, have Ms. Collins and her assistant removed from the control room." As Chief Meyers gave his dutiful repeat back, Ms. Collins let her arrogance get the best of her.

"You can't," was all she managed to get out when Captain Maddox erupted in a torrent of anger.

"I can't? I can't?" he spat as the veins in his forehead and neck began to bulge. "I assure you I can, sister! This is my submarine! Chief of the Watch, have these two escorted to their stateroom and post a guard outside her door. She is not to leave her stateroom until further notice!" As Captain Maddox turned his attention back to more pressing matters, Ms. Collins turned and headed toward her stateroom.

Normally, in this type of situation, she would have tried to stand her ground. She was known in the business to be tough as nails. She had had the most heated exchanges on camera with Prime Ministers and Presidents. She always pushed back hard, drawing strength from her opposition. Dave seemed astonished she had backed down so easily. He lagged behind a moment, almost as if he were expecting her to come back in a firestorm of her own. When he saw her continue to march down the command passageway, he quickly followed.

She entered what had been the XO's stateroom prior to her coming aboard and slumped down in front of the door. Tears began to roll down her face. There came a soft knock at the door. She scooted her body away from the entry and the door opened slowly. She peaked up, having buried her head between her folded arms and bent knees as if she were an ostrich and her limbs were sand. She saw Dave come through the door, while a rather burly sailor stayed behind in the passageway.

"Is that our prison guard?" she asked in a nasally voice as she wiped tears from her reddened cheeks.

"I guess so," Dave said as he averted his eyes, studying the overhead, obviously uncomfortable with the sight of the hard driving Stephanie Collins in such a vulnerable state.

"I'm sorry," she apologized. Dave shrugged it off, as if there were no need to. "I don't understand this," she continued.

"It's this place," he justified for her, "It's all these guys right on top of us, all the time. There's nowhere to go, there's no peace. Going to sleep isn't even an escape because I feel like I'm sleeping in a coffin."

She laughed, sniffing up the remaining tears, "Did you see that tall kid? How do you think he feels?"

"Or the Weapons Officer; that guy's a giant, how can he even cope?"

"Still," she returned to her apology, "I don't know what came over me, I mean I've been insulted by world leaders. I've had producers tell me my butt is too big and my chest is too small. I'm too pretty to be taken seriously. I'm too ugly to put on camera, and never one tear, but this guy says boo and I cave."

"I'm telling you, it's this place," Dave insisted. He had been in situations with her where he was scared but she stood her ground and never once had he ever seen her waver in her resolve.

"It's not this place, it's him."

"Who?"

"Captain Maddox," she said with reverence. "Did you see the way the men look at him? They would do anything he asked. I've sat across the table from countless world leaders and I've never seen such loyalty."

The Nav came tripping into the control room. He passed off the clipboard containing the flash message to Captain Maddox as if it were a hot potato. The Captain's eyes raced back and forth across the message as if he were reading it for the first time. He tried to pace out in his mind how long it would take to read and comprehend a message of such apparent importance. The fact was, every word of the message was familiar to him because he was its author.

When he thought the delay was sufficient, he began barking orders to the crew with no explanation. "Chief of the Watch, get those guys back on board as soon as possible. Weps, when their feet hit topside, dive the ship." Everyone in the control room looked as if they were sitting on pins and needles.

"Dive the ship, aye," the Weps said, trying to recover himself in the Skipper's eyes.

As a mysterious elation soared in the hearts of every sailor in the control room, the future took another turn for the unknown.

"They don't have him!" Lt. Turno's voice cracked over the comm. system. The informal announcement took everyone off guard. Nobody was sure of what they had just heard. Not a muscle moved in the control room as they waited for more information. After an eternal two seconds, Chief Meyers keyed the mic to ask the bridge to clarify, but just before he did Lt. Turno's voice came over comm. box again. Chief Meyers' reflexes were not quick enough. The momentary break in communication while he keyed and released the mic was enough of an interruption to block out Lt. Turno's entire message.

"Damn it, Chief!" Captain Maddox sputtered.

Chief Meyers, realizing his mistake, did not let the Captain's outburst rattle him. He did not wait politely to see if there was a follow up message. Immediately, he was on the horn asking the bridge to "Say again".

Everyone's heart sank as they heard Lt. Turno return with, "They don't have him! It's just his jacket! Just his jacket!"

"Abort the dive!" the Weps immediately ordered.

"Continue with the dive!" the Captain snapped. The Weps looked at him in horror.

"Captain, there is no way I am letting you dive this boat while the Executive Officer is still out there." The Weps took a stand, "We're are not abandoning him!"

Captain Maddox crossed the control room and slammed the clip board into the Weps' chest. "Why don't you get off your high horse and read this." The Weps flipped up the boards security cover and skimmed the page-long report. His eyes darted from key word to key word. He did not read it verbatim, but he managed to glean the key phrases 'highest national security', 'chemical weapons', 'possible hundreds of thousands dead', and 'intercept'. His testosterone levels jumped immensely, but as the Nav filled him in on what should have been obvious, he looked less like the confident Weps and more like a junior officer.

Captain Maddox watched the Nav in action. The Nav was explaining the situation to the Weps openly and quite boisterously so the entire control room party would hear. The Nav explained that Pope had put in the distress call with the exact coordinates at the time the XO went overboard. He told him that SARs (search and rescue) would be on the scene within three minutes, and that they were better equipped and had a greater ability to find the XO. The Weps seemed to shrink as the Nav pointed out that if the XO were rescued and had any sort of significant injuries, a surface ship would be better equipped to treat him, since they were equipped with trauma centers and all the Key West had was a table on the crew's mess and Doc Comstock.

HMCS Comstock was the boat's only fully trained medical person. As a Hospital Corpsman qualified for independent duty, he had been a battle field medic with the Marines. He had the training and the knowledge to perform emergency surgeries, but the crew was not confident he would really care one way or the other if it ever came down to saving one of their lives. In most cases, if someone in the crew came to him complaining of an ache or a pain, he'd accuse them of being a sissy, hand them a dozen or so Motrin and say, "get outta my face."

As a Marine, he had seen what he referred to as "real injuries", so he didn't have much tolerance for submariners and their "whining", as he put it.

He was also a bit of a drunk, so usually he suffered from DT's the first week or so underway. The image of Doc Comstock with anyone's life in his hands wasn't too comforting, even though most of the crew still remembered him pulling a bullet out of a SEAL they extracted from Syria while on deployment the previous year. He patched the kid up so well that when they pulled in to port, he walked across the brow and off the boat with the rest of his team.

Captain Maddox watched as the Nav chiseled away at the Weps' self-assuredness. He didn't think the Nav would be able to follow through with the plan without him having to do ten tons of damage control to stop the leaks the Nav would inevitable leave in their story. Not only did the Nav effectively sideline the Weps, but he did such a thorough job of rationalizing why they would leave a fellow officer in the open ocean to fend for himself, he could almost see the smoke rising from the brakes on the blue shirt rumor train.

The blue shirts, rarely being privy to what was really going on, would often start a locomotion of rumors to fill in their informational gaps. Sometimes the rumors would be so outrageous by the time they finally filtered back to Captain Maddox's ears that he would worry about the mental faculties of his crew. After all these years, it still blew his mind to what ends boredom could drive seemingly practical minds.

When the Nav was finished, Captain Maddox piled on, "The worse thing in the world for the XO would be to have us blindly chopping through the water back and forth looking for him." He could see that the Weps already fully understood, but he was trying to quell any opposition he might receive from him in the near future. "If he's not dead already, we'd surely kill him." He turned to Chief Meyers, "Chief, I want this boat running fast and deep yesterday!"

As he turned back to the Weps, he could see mist forming in the big man's eyes. He had an intimate knowledge of the same constrained flood of tears he worked so hard to hold back the moment he was told he would have to sit out the first Gulf War. As he felt empathy beginning to spring up for the Weps, he tried to quash it by looking away. He did not expect the Weps to challenge him so quickly. It was a testament to the character of the man that in the moment he noticeably strayed off course by stepping down from the ladder in the midst of the XO's peril, the Weps was there trying to correct him. His judgment was impeccable, which was the reason Captain Maddox felt the need to destroy him. The Weps was the best officer who had ever served under him.

"Weps, have all the off-watch Weapons Division personnel in the wardroom in five minutes," Captain Maddox commanded. Without waiting for a response, he walked out of the control room, and took momentary refuge in his stateroom.

Quinn and Scarpa were treading water about ten yards off the boat's starboard when the forward escape trunk hatch popped open. The COB climbed onto the deck followed by Carter and Grant. The two cooks slung a cargo net over the starboard side of the hull. Quinn held up the XO's jacket and yelled to the COB, "It's just his jacket, COB! We've got to keep searching!"

The COB strained to get down on one knee. He stretched out his hand and motioned for them to come closer, "I know, but you guys had better get back on board, we're about to dive." Logic did not allow Quinn's mind to comprehend the words the COB had just spoken. Scarpa, whose conscience gave no such impediment, immediately started swimming toward the boat. Quinn's lack of action prodded the COB to repeat himself.

"You've got to come on board. We're going to dive soon." As the COB restated, one of the sailors who had joined Lt. Turno in the bridge stopped sweeping his spotlight across the endless black waves in search of the XO, and focused his beam upon Quinn who was still treading water. The intense glare pounding down upon Quinn not only made it nearly impossible to see the COB, it also added to frustration of the moment. The COB could see Quinn was still in disbelief.

"We just received some sort of Spec Op. Come on son."

The idea was ludicrous to Quinn. "But the XO is out here, we have to find him!" His voice strained with defeat as he tried to implore that the search continue.

"The choppers will be here any second," the COB said, pleading with his eyes, "They're better equipped to find him, come on." He beckoned with his hand as if he was trying to get a reluctant puppy back in its collar.

Scarpa had already climbed back on board, when Quinn slowly began making his way toward the hull. The short swim felt as if it were the longest distance he had ever swum. His strokes felt heavy and slow, yet his mind raced with questions. *Why wouldn't they continue with the search, even if SARS would be there any second? What was so important they would leave one of their own?* Nothing was making sense to him. As Quinn neared the cargo net, the COB returned to his usual stern tone, "National Security waits for no man." Then, as if Quinn needed some real motivation, the forward ballast tanks started to vent. The dive had been initiated before the hatch was even shut. As the filling of the ballast tanks shot a geyser of air and water nearly forty feet above the bow, Quinn's pace quickened.

The light, which had been such a nuisance, no longer illuminated his face and Quinn saw that everyone had disappeared from the bridge. He knew he'd better get back on board PDQ or he'd be left there treading water, alone. Of course, he might come across the XO, but with each passing moment that thought held less and less comfort. *For all I know the XO might be an all-you-can-eat buffet for the sharks by now,* Quinn thought. He had climbed about half way up the makeshift ladder when he felt Carter and Grant grab his arms and lift him the rest of the way as if he had been a piece of drift wood they had come across floating in the water. Their adrenaline had obviously been heightened as well by the sight of the bow dipping below the surface.

As the small party made their way to the topside hatch of the forward escape trunk, they noticed it was slowly coming shut. Scarpa had already made his way down the ladder to middle level and was pumping the manual hydraulic lever to shut the hatch. Of the four men remaining topside, Carter went first. No discussion on the matter was needed. It went without saying, a few more pumps and he wouldn't be able to fit through the opening. Grant followed, and then before the COB could object, Quinn gently nudged the old man into the hatch. As Quinn was sliding through the last sliver of an opening, the first waves began to crash over him.

Lying on the deck directly below the hatch, Scarpa spit out seawater as it rained down upon him while he pumped the lever. Quinn hung from the upper hatch's locking wheel, attempting to use his body weight to assist the hydraulic pressure in shutting the hatch. "You'd better not slip!" Scarpa yelled as he looked at Quinn dangling fifteen feet directly above him. With just four inches left before Quinn could turn the wheel to dog the hatch, the forward escape trunk became submerged. Water blasted in from the entire circumference of the hatch. At once the spray seemed to form a thick column of water that converged on Quinn's head and shoulders. It may as well have been concrete pouring in on him. The weight of the water was more than Quinn's vice-like grip could bear. His fingers were easily stripped off the wheel, and he reached out grasping at anything that would save him from the eminent fall. Luckily, his reflexes were quick enough to snatch the third rung down on the ladder. He pulled his body tight against the ladder and out of the main shaft of water. Scarpa, however, received the column of water as if he was a tiny insect and the giant finger of Poseidon was smiting him into the deck. Fortunately for the two divers, and for the fate of the entire crew for that matter, the pressure of being submerged worked to their advantage. With the presence of two atmospheres of sea pressure pushing against the hatch, the remaining four inch gap closed itself.

Quinn, recovering from yet another beatdown from the sea, managed to climb back to the upper hatch. While it was completely shut and the column of water had dissipated as quickly as it had formed, it still was not sealed. Had they not experienced the torrent of a few seconds prior, the spray, which was still sneaking through, would have seemed like more of an emergency to them. Quinn leisurely reached through the shower, spun the wheel to dog the hatch, and what had seemed like an underwater apocalyptic event moments earlier was no longer evident, not even by a single drop seeping in. Quinn let his feet find their way down the ladder, but when they touched the deck his legs failed him. He collapsed in a heap of exhaustion. Sucking wind on the deck next to him was Scarpa, equally depleted.

After a moment, Quinn found the strength to resume the interrogation he had begun on top of the sail. While still lying on his back, he reached over and grabbed the collar of Scarpa's coveralls. As he pulled Scarpa close to him, he used the leverage to raise his head and shoulders a few inches off the deck, "What the hell happened up there?!"

Before Quinn could get any answers, his interrogation was cut short yet again. The COB, who had stepped off the ladder just before all hell broke loose, lifted Quinn to his feet, "Stop pussyfootin' around." Quinn didn't have the strength to hold on to Scarpa as he was lifted. "The Captain wants the Weapons Division posted in the wardroom five minutes ago," he said as he pushed Quinn through the galley.

CHAPTER 11

Moments later, Quinn found himself wet, shivering, and standing at attention with the rest of his division when Captain Maddox entered the wardroom. Judging by the subtle reactions of his companions, Quinn felt as if the shock of the Captain's appearance was a shared sentiment. The Captain seemed as though he had aged ten years in the short but eventful hour since Quinn had last laid eyes upon the man. He realized whatever personal torment he felt about leaving the XO, it must have paled in comparison to the crippling anguish the Captain was surely contending with.

Searching internally, Quinn began to understand his view of the situation was more about regret of a task left incomplete rather than genuine concern for the XO. Of course, when he was in the water, he would have given his life to ensure all possibilities were exhausted to save the man. But in retrospect, those feelings were diminished. He even began to feel a tinge of guilt beginning to build. It was brought on by the onset of relief that it was not he who was left behind. However, the ignoble thoughts of, *I'm glad it's him out there and not me*, were relegated to a deeper, more selfish part of his subconscious which would not be touched in a relatively light moment of inward reflection. For the most part he was focused on trying to empathize with Captain Maddox's frame of mind.

Besides, it wasn't as if he had any angst towards the XO, it was just the opposite. On most occasions when he had been around the XO he had been filled with sympathy for the man. The XO always had an air of being the consummate fish out of water, or more accurately, a lost puppy. Now, Quinn's feelings had not been changed towards him, just amplified. However, as he studied Captain Maddox, who had fallen heavy into his chair at the head of the wardroom table, he found it painful to imagine the inner struggle he was going through. As he watched Captain Maddox's eyes dart back and forth across the charts the Weps was laying out, Quinn could tell his vision was not affixed on the tangibles before him. He tried to imagine what thoughts were flashing in his Captain's mind. He envisioned a day in the future, as the Captain tried to offer trivial condolences to the widowed mother of three.

Quinn's upbringing had created in him a powerful imagination. At one time it had been a tool used by him so he could escape to far off places, if only in his mind. Coincidentally enough, places much like his current station. But as he grew older, he developed his knack for high fantasy into an unrestricted means of empathy. On long deployments, he would quietly study his fellow sailors, and with exacting details, he would live life in his mind through their eyes. In fact, if any of his companions ever attained the skill to be able to see into his mind, it would have shaken them to the core. If they could see the incredibly precise recreations of their lives Quinn had pieced together, he would have been labeled a prophet, or a witch, depending on if the accusing sailor was more familiar with the writings of the Apostle Paul or J.K. Rowling. This ability, to mentally walk a mile in another man's shoes, lay at the very core of Quinn's leadership skills and was the main reason his shipmates naturally migrated to him although Quinn had no clue his thought processes were different than anyone else's.

At the moment, dissecting the way he internalized emotional events was the furthest thing from Quinn's mind, for he was fully engulfed in one of his out of body scenarios. In his mind, he was Captain Maddox standing in the foyer of the XO's colonial era home just off the Chesapeake Bay in Newport News, Virginia. Not even the lace of a black veil could filter out the redness in the exhausted eyes of the widow who stood before him. She was a homely woman, no doubt married for the intellectual stimulation she could provide rather than the status she would attain as a trophy wife. On this day however, she held herself with a grace and a poise which had been long forgotten by the royal courts of the world. What beauty she held had always been in her posture, albeit a bit bony. The fantasy was so complete; Quinn could even smell the lilacs as their scent wafted through the house. As the Captain, he offered his most heartfelt condolences to the aggrieved widow. She, knowing the high regard her husband carried for the man, instantly wrapped her arms around his neck and sobbed into his chest, repeating the words "thank you" over and over.

Then, without thinking, he let the lie slip out. "We did everything we could." As soon as the words slipped past his lips, he felt as if a dozen small fish hooks sank themselves into his heart. The woman, not for a second doubting his sincerity, switched her words of thanks to words of reassurance as she repeated "I know you did" over and over. Each time the phrase was uttered, it felt as if the barbs which pierced his heart were all tugged in opposite directions. The tugs gained in veracity as his mind suppressed the screams of, *We didn't! We didn't do everything possible! We left him! We abandoned him! We left him alone, in the middle of the black ocean, in the middle of the black night! We left him in a world so black; he wouldn't even be able to catch a glint of light off his wedding ring to give him hope! We left him to die!*

As the heart-wrenching scene played out in Quinn's mind, he suddenly felt the full weight of the crushing responsibility which came with being a Commanding Officer. In what was a rare thaw for Quinn, he let his emotions slip out. A tear rolled down his shivering cheek.

The tear went unnoticed by almost everyone. Captain Maddox had been lost in his own thoughts; however, they were not as singularly tortured as Quinn had guessed. While he was beginning to second guess the method used to sideline the XO, the reality of it had not quite begun to consume him. His main focus was on the obstacles which lay ahead in the operation Scarpa had initiated. The first phase was complete and so far as he could tell, things had gone according to plan.

The tear that slid down Quinn's cheek caught Captain Maddox's eye. He had spent so much time preparing for this night and he had managed to become so emotionally detached that it didn't process in his mind that the crew would be affected on any great terms. That is why he saw the tear, but thought it was only seawater from Quinn's still soaked hair dripping down his face. Seeing Quinn trying to hold still at attention, while obviously uncomfortable, seemed to bring Captain Maddox back to the present. The men jumped as he screamed, "Grant!"

Petty Officer Grant popped his head into the wardroom through the wardroom pantry door, "Yes, Captain."

In a much cooler tone Captain Maddox made a request of him, "Petty Officer Grant, get a towel for Petty Officer Quinn."

"Get a towel for Petty Officer Quinn, aye, Cap'n," Grant dutifully replied then slipped out the door as quickly as he had emerged.

Quinn, relieved at the thought of warming up, thanked Captain Maddox.

"At ease, gentlemen," the Captain ordered. The men shifted from attention to parade rest. With their hands neatly clasped behind their backs and their feet uniformly shoulder width apart, it was hardly a casual stance as the directive implied, but their necks were free to turn so they could give the eye contact needed for the briefing.

Captain Maddox got down to business. "I know it has rattled more than a few of you to leave the XO out there, but two points. First, the XO is safer now that there is not a big submarine chopping through the water. If we had visual contact on him it would have been a different matter. Searching blindly with a submarine is like searching for ants on a sunny day with a magnifying glass." He could see some looks of understanding, but still frustration was a common thread among the sailors.

"Second," he began, "we have received a time-sensitive special operation." He could see the flicker of hope returning in his sailors. Nothing made the adrenaline flow like the sound of a special operation. "Now, I'm afraid I can't go into the details with you, but the first phase is preparedness. Your torpedo room is still three quarters of the way full of exercise torpedoes; I need it empty in the next forty eight hours." In most cases, an announcement which contained news implying a day or two of work without sleep would have been met with the loudest groans of displeasure the sailors thought they could get away with in front of their Captain; however, as Captain Maddox had predicted, the excitement was barely contained. "We'll be running fast and deep the entire time," Captain Maddox continued, "just let the Officer of the Deck know when you're ready to launch and he'll slow." The sailors, forgetting where they were, began to chatter with anticipation. Captain Maddox raised his voice to settle them as he finished, "We're not going to risk any damage to our tubes by doing high speed launches."

The Weps spoke up with what seemed like renewed enthusiasm, yet he still did not speak with his usual bravado of authority. "What of the War Shots, Captain?" Among the exercise shots were four fully capable Mark 48 ADCAP torpedoes.

"After you've shot off all of the exercise torpedoes, load the four remaining War Shots into the tubes."

Quinn waited for what seemed to be an uncomfortably long time, then posed the question which should have been the next words out of the Weps' mouth, "What status should they be at, sir?" Captain Maddox shot his eyes up at the Weps. It pleased him that the Weps had not thought to ask. It showed him that he had already tipped him off balance.

"Make them ready, set tube three for snapshot," Captain Maddox ordered.

A shudder of excitement soared through the whole division. The men of the Torpedo Division had the torturous job of maintaining some of the world's biggest fireworks, but rarely, if ever, had the chance to shoot them off. The simple task of loading them into a tube and making them ready to launch, however remote the possibility, was enough to make them giddy. They had no particular malice against anyone or any nation per se, but being boys, the thought of blowing something, anything up, was cool.

Captain Maddox saw the glimmer in their eyes. It amazed him how easy it was to excite bored sailors. Just then, the buzz in the room ceased and everyone perked up like prairie dogs as they heard the keying of the 4MC, the boat's emergency communications system. The half a second of open air was followed by the Nav's steady voice, "Emergency Medical Technician to the radio room."

Everyone jumped as Captain Maddox's open hand slammed down on the table. "What now!" he exclaimed. The 4MC's announcement was followed by the Chief of the Watch's reiteration of the request to the whole crew over the 1MC. Then the growler phone, located under the wardroom table at the Captain's chair, gave off a throaty ring. Captain Maddox answered with no protocol whatsoever, "What happened?" A silence hung in the air as he listened to the explanation. "Is he alright?" he asked, with all traces of his growing panic absent from his voice. "Have Doc take a look at him and keep me informed."

Captain Maddox looked up at the men staring expectantly at him. He knew curiosity was gnawing at their information-starved souls, but he didn't satisfy their craving just yet. He switched the dial on the phone under the table from memory and gave a sharp turn of the growler handle, then he said, "Chief of the Watch, make a general announcement reminding the crew that we are on a submarine and they need to stow their compartments for sea so nobody else gets a bump on the head."

Before he could hang up his phone, Chief Meyers was making the announcement to the entire crew. Captain Maddox looked up at the expectant Weapons Division. "Petty Officer Pope had a piece of equipment fall on his head," Captain Maddox said as he scanned their faces, searching for suspicion. The Nav's voice, which had been calm as it came over the 4MC, was frantic on the phone with Captain Maddox. He explained how the Weps had come for Walker, and he was forced to take action before Pope spoiled the plan. As Captain Maddox had listened to him, he portrayed a look of someone having a grocery list read to them. Now, as he explained to the Weapons Division a fabrication of what had happened, he wondered if the Nav's voice had been too loud; if everyone had heard the words bleeding out of the earpiece. So much had transpired in such a short time, he wondered if it was too much for the crew to try and process, or if their sensory preceptors were in overdrive with suspicion. If there was any suspicion among the sailors which stood before him, he could not read it.

He continued with his briefing, "Once the torpedo room is emptied, we need to prepare the weapons shipping harness." This order, he could see, sincerely piqued their interest. He would have left this detail out longer if he could have, but constructing the elevator system, which was used to load torpedoes, was a complicated enough process to handle when the boat was moored to the pier. He knew it could not be sprung upon them to try and do at the last possible second while at sea. Before any questions could be posed to him, he dismissed the meeting.

The sailors left the wardroom buzzing with speculation as they filtered down the middle-level passage way. Quinn, however, turned and zipped aft to the wardroom pantry where he found Grant listening with a cupped ear on the door which led to the wardroom.

Quinn grabbed Grant by the shoulder. Grant jumped. He quickly slapped his hand over Grant's mouth to keep him from making any more noise than he already had. When Grant had seen who it was, and his breathing had calmed down, Quinn removed his hand.

"You're a sneaky cat," Grant said in what he thought was a whisper; "You'll have to teach me your noise discipline techniques."

"My what?" Quinn asked.

"Noise discipline," Grant explained, "That's SEAL speak for stealthiness."

"Why didn't you just say stealthiness?"

Grant put his hand on Quinn's shoulder and looked up as if speaking to the heavens, "Forgive him, Captain Marcinko." Captain Marcinko, of the famed SEAL team six, was Grant and Carter's hero. They had even erected a makeshift shrine to the original Rogue Warrior in the galley.

Quinn knocked Grant's hand off his shoulder. "You're creeping me out, Grant," Quinn said with a laugh. He always enjoyed Grant's uncanny ability to get off subject. "Stay on target, Red Leader," Quinn reeled him back in as he reached for the dry towel Grant was supposed to bring to him.

"Well," Grant started, as he looked around to make sure no one else was in the two foot by four foot room, "Carter thinks we're goin' after a Taliban submarine." Quinn waited for Grant to crack a smile. He felt a little deflated when he realized his greatest intelligence source was serious.

"You tell Carter he'll be serving up mouse eggs for breakfast before we destroy a Taliban submarine," Quinn said as he shook his head to the side to remove the water from his ears.

"Is that some sort of Talibani delicacy?" Grant asked earnestly.

Realizing his statement of impossibility had not been able to make the connection, Quinn resisted the urge to go in to details on the differences in reproduction between mammals and reptiles. He thanked Grant for the dry towel and added, "You and Carter keep up the intelligence gathering, just tell Carter to leave his imagination out of it."

CHAPTER 12

It had been a long two days for the Torpedo Division. No one had had a chance to take much more than a twenty minute nap or two. They had been loading and shooting the exercise torpedoes for the last two days. It wasn't just the Torpedo Division who had lost sleep, much of the crew found it hard to get any solid rest with the concussions of torpedo tubes launching their contents every two hours or so.

The torpedo room, which had been full, now only had the four war shots left on the trays. The weapons handling team just finished loading the last exercise shot into torpedo tube one. "Torpedo tube one breech door shut."

"Breech door shut, aye," Quinn responded from the Weapons Control Panel. "Locking breech door," he called out as he pressed the button to seal the door. The heavy brass ring, which encompassed the breech door, rotated, creating a hydraulic seal which could withstand the pressures of the deep sea. "Flooding tube one," Quinn said as he went down the check list almost robotically as he had done so many times in the last forty eight hours. After the rumble of the tube filling with water, Quinn went on to the next step. "Equalizing tube one." He pressed the button, but the sound of the tube equalizing with the outside sea pressure was absent.

Quinn looked down and found the tube equalization button on the control panel flashing. "Oh come on--not now!" Quinn said aloud as he hit the button over and over. Exhausted, he regretfully called to the control room over the comm. box. "Control-Torpedo Room," Quinn sighed and waited for a response.

"Control, aye," the Officer of the Deck responded, awaiting his report. "Control-Torpedo Room, we're having a problem with the equalization valve on tube one. We're going to have to unload tube one and reload the shot into tube three."

"Very well, get it done and report."

Quinn was about to begin the long process of transferring the exercise torpedo to the lower tube when Captain Maddox's voice came over the comm. box. "Petty Officer Quinn, we don't have time for that," the Captain said harshly. "You can't tell me you don't know a way to override it."

"No sir, I can't tell you I don't know a way to override it."

"That's what I thought; I want that torpedo jettisoned in seconds, not minutes."

"Aye, sir." Quinn hung the mic back up and looked over at his team. "Well, you heard the man," Quinn said with a smile. "Seconds, not minutes." Quinn loved that about Captain Maddox. Common sense could at times trump protocol.

"Override the equalization valve manually," Quinn directed as he set to work opening the control panel. Hearing the muffled rush of seawater into the torpedo tube, he set the control panel to bypass the sensor on the automated equalization valve. "That's it," he said, having tricked the computer into automatically thinking the tube equalization valve cycled. "Let's shoot this dud and load the real ones."

Le Poignard

"Captain, they're opening their muzzle door again," the sonar technician noted.

"Very well," Captain Reno stated routinely. It was a starkly subdued scene compared to that of the one which unfolded nearly forty eight hours earlier in the control room of the Poignard. As they were finally closing the distance in their chase of the Key West as it raced down a southerly course, sonar picked up the firing of a torpedo. In those first frantic moments there was no way to tell that the Key West had fired an exercise torpedo. All they knew was that they were the only other contact in the vicinity and a torpedo had just been fired. After it was established the shot had not been fired at them, the crew let out a communal sigh of relief, but it wasn't until about the third shot that the feeling of routine began to set in.

Each time the Key West slowed to shoot off one of its exercise torpedoes, it gave the Poignard a chance to shrink the distance which the Key West had opened due to its head start on the mysterious run south.

USS Key West

Captain Maddox sat working at his stateroom desk when Quinn knocked on his open door. "Enter," he said. Quinn took a step forward and said nothing as he waited for Captain Maddox to finish reading the report he was scanning. Captain Maddox looked up to see Quinn holding out a pistol belt with the pistol in the holster.

"The Weps told me to bring you a weapon, sir," Quinn said.

"I think we need to start calling him Lieutenant Commander Rambo," Captain Maddox said as he stood. Quinn pulled a Colt .45 pistol from its holster and drew the chamber back so he and Captain Maddox could see that the pistol was not loaded, as was the official procedure for the transferring of small arms.

"One Colt forty-five, number Zero-One-Seven. The chamber is free and clear," Quinn said, handing the pistol to Captain Maddox.

"The chamber is free and clear," Captain Maddox repeated after a quick inspection. He tried to release the chamber, but he wasn't quite as proficient at it as Quinn.

"Here, sir," Quinn said, as he released the slide lock.

"Thank you," Captain Maddox said, a little embarrassed.

"Three clips, nine rounds each," Quinn said, as he pulled two of the clips out to show Captain Maddox and then slipped them back in their pouch on the gun belt. The third clip he handed to the Captain. Captain Maddox turned the Colt over and clumsily inserted the clip into its slot. Quinn gave him a nod as if he were a father watching his son load a BB gun for the first time on Christmas morning. Captain Maddox, knowing the young men in his crew usually look like a bunch of Jack Bauer wannabes when they hand off weapons to each other, rolled his eyes as if to let Quinn know he realized how stiff he looked.

"I want you and three of the boat's best shooters topside to cover me," Captain Maddox ordered as he slipped the pistol into the holster and strapped it around his waist.

"Sir, I'm still in the dark," Quinn reminded him. "What *is* the situation we will be in?" Captain Maddox was taken aback by this. He had been so focused on keeping the operation a secret from the crew, he neglected to brief the men on the basic information they might need to save his life.

As he ran through the operation in his head, trying to think of any other holes he may have left unplugged, he tried to suppress his fear. He sat back down, looked again to the papers on his desk. "We're going to be surfacing and coming alongside a merchant ship," Captain Maddox explained. Quinn wasn't expecting a personal briefing but he wasn't about to object. "We're taking on some cargo through the weapons shipping hatch."

Quinn interrupted, "Sir, if we're using the weapons shipping harness I will be tied up with that. I'm the team leader."

The Captain spoke in a blunt manner, "I'm sure there is another Torpedo Man who can replace you. I want you heading up the security detail."

"Yes, sir," Quinn acknowledged flatly, trying to hide his excitement. Being a security team leader during a special operation sounded much cooler than operating a hydraulic elevator.

Captain Maddox continued, "They will be sending down a brow for me. I will be going up to the merchant ship to inspect the packages before they are sent down."

"Will we be going with you?" Quinn asked.

"No, it will just be me," Captain Maddox said.

Quinn shook his head in disapproval. "A security detail won't do you much good staying down on the deck."

Captain Maddox was happy to see Quinn easily transform into the security team leader. He began to doubt his reluctance to bring Quinn into the fold of his plans. Quinn was certainly ambitious enough, and he definitely could handle fluid situations with ease. Yet, he had a bright career ahead of him, and there was no malice in his character. It's not to say he believed Quinn was without flaws; he just didn't have any which Captain Maddox could exploit as he had done with the others going along with his scheme.

"If things go badly up there, not only will my hands be tied, but we will be sitting ducks in an exposed lower position," Quinn said, trying to convince the Captain to bring him along. In Quinn's mind he tried to convince himself he was looking out for his primary asset, but truth be told, his lust for action was what drove him to try to form a boarding party.

"No, Quinn," Captain Maddox said, "if things go bad they go bad, duty above all else." Captain Maddox's words were inspiring. If Quinn were to one day have a command of his own, he hoped he would lead as courageously as the man before him did.

"We'll at least try and look really tough, sir," Quinn said. Captain Maddox did not have to look at Quinn to see the broad smile which adorned the young sailor's face, he knew it was there and just knowing it made him smile. Quinn was hoping to get more information but they were interrupted by the Nav. "Sonar has picked up the contact, sir," the Nav said from the doorway of the stateroom. Captain Maddox rushed to the control room.

Le Poignard

Captain Reno entered the control room in response to the beckoning of his Executive Officer. "Have we got a clue why he is running south like a mad man?"

"It appears as though he may be coming to a rendezvous point with this surface contact, sir," De Panafiue said as he brought up a simulated graphic on the plot display.

"Do we have a satellite overhead?"

"Not this far south, Captain," the technician answered. "We didn't know to request one down here."

"Are there any American satellites we can pull images off of," Captain Reno asked as he pulled up distances between his boat and the one he pursued.

"I'm trying, sir," the tech answered as he dashed away at his keyboard as if he were performing a piano concerto. "I was booted out of CENTCOM's system again, and I haven't been able to find an open path back in."

"Are we close enough to use the drone?" De Panafiue asked.

"We're on the outer rim of its range," Captain Reno explained. "We'd have to bring it back as soon as it reached them."

"Not necessarily, Captain," the technician broke in with a glimmer of hope. "If we don't use the Lumicloak system, coupled with the fact we are heading toward the target at top speed, we could squeeze in five to ten minutes of surveillance." Being in new territory with the fresh technology, Captain Reno did not see the harm in trying.

"What's the worst that could happen?" Captain Reno asked. "We find that we don't have enough juice to make the trip and we bring it back with no more or no less information than we have now."

De Panafiue was not so optimistic about his Captain's non-consequential depiction of his worst case scenario. "Or the American's could find out we're hacking into their DOD systems and spying on their apparently secret operations and they decide to treat us as a threat to their PATRIOT Act."

"Point taken, Mr. De Panafiue," Reno said with no hint of taking the Executive Officer's concerns into consideration.

"You know what they say, Captain," De Panafiue added, "what happens underwater..." He added nothing to the comment to try and drive home the point that submariners always run the risk of never being heard from again each time they dive.

USS Key West

As Captain Maddox entered the control room the Nav followed, briefing him all the way. "It seems he has just come upon his waypoint now sir," the Nav said.

Captain Maddox called out, "Sonar, what's the range to the contact?"

Over the speaker the sonar shack replied, "Twelve thousand yards, sir."

"Twelve thousand yards!" Captain Maddox exclaimed. He opened the door to the sonar shack and spoke directly to them. "Why are we just now picking him up?" The sonar men looked to Petty Officer Bowden, who was the sonar supervisor on watch. The skinny man's Adam's apple plunged downward then rose sharply as he swallowed.

"He's not hardly moving, sir," Bowden explained. "We're the one's makin' all the noise."

"Officer of the Deck, all ahead two thirds," Captain Maddox ordered as he turned back to control. His order to slow was the only thing Bowden could take as a response. Captain Maddox's eyes darted around the control room, "Where the hell is the Weps?" he screamed.

"I'm here, sir," the Weps said as he carefully entered the control room carrying a ceramic mug filled with coffee.

Captain Maddox's eyes blazed when he saw the Weps coming in. "I'm sorry, Mr. President, we lost your billion dollar submarine because the Weapons Officer couldn't use the Messenger of the Watch to go get himself a frickin' cup of coffee. Get me a damn firing solution on that contact," Captain Maddox huffed like a Tasmanian devil.

The Weps didn't dare bring up the fact that he wasn't actually on watch, and that the Fire Control Technician already had a firing solution brought up on screen. He simply stopped what he was doing just as everyone in the control room had. Captain Maddox looked around at everyone staring at him. Outwardly this enraged him. Inwardly, however, he was quite pleased with his performance. The more off-balance he kept them the less time they would think about what they were actually doing. He knew they would all carry out their duties in the safest, most professional manner, that is how he had trained them, but if they spent the majority of their time preoccupied with their Captain's behavior they would miss the obvious foul smell this operation had to it.

"Man Battle Stations!" Captain Maddox ordered. Immediately everyone was back to doing their jobs as the rest of the boat's crew was roused from their normal duties by the Chief of the Watch's announcement to "Man Battle Stations."

Santa de Juarez

Luis Cortez scanned the black horizon with his deep brown eyes as he stood on the deck of the Santa de Juarez. His companion stood next to him drawing broad sweeps with his binoculars on the same blackness. Cortez noticed a stirring in the water. Like a great whale coming to the surface for air, the USS Key West seemed to slide upward, silently, just twenty meters off the starboard, matching the slow speed of his own ship. The Key West's course, at first glance, seemed to be parallel; yet, after a moment, Cortez could see they were closing slightly.

The surfacing maneuver had been pulled off with such precision, Cortez's companion had not even noticed and was still scanning the horizon. "I don't think they're going to show," the lookout said.

Cortez did not rebuke the man; he simply reached up and gently pushed the binoculars down from the man's face and said, "They are here." The surprised fright on the man's face was echoed in the expressions of the rest of the crewmen who were nearby.

A wickedly handsome smile flashed across Cortez's face. He was on the verge of using one of the United States' most sophisticated weapons of war for his own profit. The operation would certainly make his mark in the world of crime, terror and politics. The profits and prestige this one coup d'état would bring would make him the King of South American drug cartels. His profits would be off the charts since he managed to get a partner to pay for the entire operation, not wanting any payment in return, and the cherry on top was that the United States Government was providing the transport vessel.

CHAPTER 13

Quinn stood at the top of the ladder in the forward escape trunk. Just behind him were Petty Officers Scarpa, Thomas, and Jackson. The four ship's divers were dressed in black-lycra skin suits and had M-16s slung over their shoulders. Behind them was the COB leading a troop of sailors who would set up the weapons shipping harness.

Captain Maddox made his way through the crowd below. When he came shoulder-to-shoulder with the COB, he yelled up to Quinn, "We're on the surface now." The men on the ladder steadied themselves, already aware of their position because of the rocking motion. "Let's pop the hatch and get into position!" he ordered.

Quinn pressed his back against the hatch that he had already undogged. His legs were on the highest rung of the ladder he could manage. Grunting like a dead lifter, Quinn pushed up as hard as he could, straightening his legs and thrusting the hatch upwards. He gathered his wits about him as he looked to the port side to see the massive wall which made up the starboard side of the merchant ship. After letting his brain settle for half a second, he scrambled onto the deck, swung his M-16 around to the ready position and scanned upward for possible targets on the ship that towered over him.

As the rest of Quinn's security team came to the deck swinging their guns around as if they were extras in a made-for-TV action movie, Quinn knew they were coming to the same conclusion he had just moments before. The problem facing them as a security team was they were overwhelmingly outgunned. At least two dozen men stood in various positions across the deck and upper levels of the merchant ship, each with one type of assault rifle or another.

None of the guards had their guns drawn or ready. Most had their weapons slung over their backs; some leaned casually with their arms resting on their weapons for support. They all stared at the small security contingent as if they had been rudely interrupted. "Tell me I didn't just hear a record scratch," Quinn said as he scanned the barrel of his M-16 across the deck.

"Is it secure?" Captain Maddox's voice echoed up from the escape trunk.

"Cha," Scarpa grunted as he straightened out of defensive posture. The men above started to point and laugh. "They don't have a thing to worry about, Captain," he said as he let the shoulder strap take the weight of his gun.

Captain Maddox came out of the hatch. "I see," he said. "Stand strong boys, they may put up a good front, but in the back of their minds they know we could sink their ship and leave them for the sharks." He looked up and saw Cortez smiling down on him.

As the Captain neared the top of the steep brow which had been lowered for him, he looked over his shoulder at the Key West. His submarine looked like a shard of black ice in black water. The movement of his crew under the work lights, which had been masked in red to minimize the distance the light would travel, took on a nightmarish vision for him. As the men finished the preparations of the weapons shipping harness, the red glow they were bathed in seemed to trigger vertigo in Captain Maddox.

Suddenly the vision of Scarpa tossing the bloodied XO into the ocean came back to him. His head spun and he reached to steady himself on the brow's handrail but his hand misjudged the distance and his wrist glanced off the rail causing his chest to come crashing down onto it. As his head hung over the edge, he experienced the nausea the sea uses to poison new sailors.

Quinn jumped onto the foot of the brow ready to make the fifty foot ascent to assist his captain. However, Captain Maddox, being just a foot from the top, found it was Cortez who grabbed his arm to steady him. "I get a little seasick myself," Cortez said. "Of course, I am not used to the sea."

Captain Maddox took a firm grip of his arm. "It's not the sea, I think it's the heights," he lied. He did not want to betray the fact that his head was swimming with angst.

"Ha," Cortez bellowed, "I guess that's why you are not on aircraft carriers."

Quinn watched as Captain Maddox and Cortez disappeared off of the brow and onto the deck of the merchant ship. Quinn's head flashed around and his eyes locked on the Weps'. "Weps, ask Control if they have a visual on the Captain." The Weps looked up to the merchant ship and saw that he too could no longer see the Captain. He tilted his head to his shoulder and spoke into his radio. Quinn heard the response come across the airwaves.

"Topside-Control, we have a visual on the Captain through the periscope." Knowing the control room had a visual on Captain Maddox did not ease Quinn's misgivings. The thought of being able to see the Captain get shot was no comfort to him.

The Weps' radio crackled once more, this time it was Captain Maddox's voice that came across. "I'm fine. I'm just inspecting the cargo," he said. Hearing the usual coolness in Captain Maddox's voice seemed to send a wave of reassurance to all those within earshot. "Weps, have the men stand by to receive, they are sending down the first container." The roar of a diesel engine seemed to swallow up the sound of the waves lashing against the sides of the two vessels. The men below could see the exhaust from the crane puff out and immediately get blown out of the small area illuminated by the lights. The crane hoisted what seemed to be a familiar canister to the men aboard the submarine.

As the first stainless steel cylinder was lowered from the deck of the merchant ship to the readied crew aboard the Key West, it seemed to them to resemble the canisters that contained the submarine's UGM 109 Tomahawk missiles. While roughly the same dimensions, the cylinder was absent any of the usual markings found on ordinance. It was simply a nondescript metal cylinder, twenty feet in length by approximately twenty one inches in diameter. Its sleek body was only disrupted by what appeared to be bolts holding the cap on.

A hatch opened onto the helipad of the Santa de Juarez. Sanchez stepped through the opening dressed in his cook's uniform. He paused as soon as he was clear of the hatch, pulled out a cigarette and lit it. The red glow of another cigarette increased as a man standing in the shadows took a drag from his own. "Buenas noches," Sanchez said. His conversations with others outside of the galley were filled with the usual pleasantries, but beyond that they lacked any substance. He had worked on many other merchant vessels but the crew of this one seemed to be extremely guarded.

"Are we stopped?" he asked, noticing the lack of the wake's usual glow from the bioluminescence.

"Yes," the other man curtly replied.

He waited a half a second for the man to offer more of an explanation. When he could see the man would volunteer no more, he asked, "Why?"

The other man frowned and said, "We're off-loading some cargo." Then the man took two quick drags off his cigarette, flicked it over the side and disappeared through the hatch.

Sanchez waited for the door to latch, then made his way over to the edge of the helipad. He peered forward and could see the crane swinging one of the cylinders over the side. He strained to see over the side but the ship's life boat obstructed his view so he could not make out what type of ship was receiving the cargo. He tossed his cigarette as he hurriedly made his way down the stairs to the aft deck. He tried to peer over the side again but the curve of the fantail still made it impossible to see what vessel was taking on the mysterious cargo.

He shot back through a hatch which held a stairwell and quickly skipped down two levels. He opened a hatch door leading to the starboard side of the ship so carelessly, it surprised the two guards who were leaning against the railing watching all the action. They turned with a start and raised their weapons, pointing them right at the Sanchez's head. His forward progress came to an immediate halt.

"What are you doing?" said one of the guards. "You have no business up here."

"I was going to be sick," he bluffed. He slapped his hand over his mouth, puffed out his cheeks and lunged for the railing. He expected the guards to be more concerned with keeping their shoes clean rather than the diligence of their duties. To his surprise, they closed the space between them and gave him a shove which toppled him over onto his backside.

"Go use the head!"

"If you don't want to be sick you should learn to cook better!"

The guards laughed as they shut the door they had just sent him sailing backwards through. Redirecting his efforts, Sanchez rapidly made his way down through the bowels of the ship. He stopped in front of a door labeled "Utilities", put his hand on the door knob, checked over his shoulder, and then he slipped inside.

USS Key West

Ms. Collins sat on the floor of the XO's stateroom listening to the banging going on in the passageway. After rolling her eyes for the hundredth time at her camera man, she finally screamed, "What the hell are they doing out there?"

"I don't know," Dave said with disinterest as he played HALO on his laptop. "You're the reporter, why don't you ask them?" She shrugged off the suggestion with the sarcasm it was meant to have, but after a moment the idea must have taken root.

She stood up and started beating the door with her fist and screaming, "Hey! Hey! You out there!"

After a minute of her incessant banging, Dave was tired of it. "Would you give it a rest already, they're not going to open it." As soon as the words left his lips, the door knob began to turn.

Ms. Collins looked at her partner and gave him an "I told you so" look which could have only been matched by a kindergartner. The door opened and a young Petty Officer with broad shoulders stood so obtrusively in the opening, it was as if the door had not even been opened. Ms. Collins began to speak before he could say anything, "I just wanted to-"

The young man talked right over her, "Ms. Collins, we are performing very dangerous operations, and safety is paramount."

"Well that sounded completely scripted," Ms. Collins said as she slid her hand holding her cell phone around the waist of the Petty Officer. As he reached down to remove her hands from his waist she snapped a picture of the passageway.

"Ms. Collins, you need to stay in your stateroom and be quiet or I will be forced to take further measures of restraint upon you." He gently but firmly pushed her back into the stateroom and closed the door.

"That did a lot of good," Dave said as he restarted another game.

"More good than you know," she said with excitement. "Let's just see what was making all that noise out there." She plugged a USB cable into her phone and popped the image up on Dave's laptop.

"Where is that?" Dave asked, not being able to recognize the area in the picture.

"I think it's the torpedo room."

"When did you take that?

"Just now, when I reached my hand into the passageway."

"But where's the floor?"

The Nav stood at the front of the control room watching the gleaming container being lowered from the weapons shipping hatch. The container was being lowered on a hydraulic elevator that was erected where deck plates had been removed from the middle level and the command passageways. He could see into the torpedo room three decks below, where sailors were strapping down and stowing the containers as fast as they were coming off the crane.

Captain Maddox's voice came over the handheld radio, "Weps, number fourteen is coming your way. Four left after that."

"Aye, sir," came the brief response from the Weps.

The air of routine which had seemed to settle in was suddenly broken by a near hysteric call from the radio room. Walker's voice, usually flat and emotionless, cried out shrilly, "Nav, get in here!"

To Walker, it must have seemed as if he had just lifted his finger to un-key the mic, when the Nav flew through the door. "What is it?" His voice matched the tone of Walker's call.

"There's a rat aboard that ship; listen," Walker said, as he pulled up a transmission he had just intercepted. "It took me a few seconds to realize its proximity." The Nav listened to the message. It was in typical military code, but it didn't take a brain surgeon to figure out the gist of it.

"That sounded like coordinates." As soon as the words had passed the Nav's lips, an alarm started flashing on a computer screen just behind Walker. He swung around on his bench seat and started researching the cause of the alarm.

He looked with horror at the Nav, "Whoever sent that message had enough clout to get a DOD satellite to change to an intercept course."

"Get me an ETA on that bird, and block that transmission!" the Nav yelled over his shoulder as he flew out the door.

Quinn was not feeling any less anxious, but he was getting the sense that relief would be upon him soon, as he heard the call that only four more containers were left. However, all feelings of forthcoming relief were lost when he saw the look in the Nav's eyes as the Nav sprang out of the escape trunk and hurriedly make his way toward the brow. To Quinn, it looked as if the Nav was trying not to heighten any suspicions as he strode up the brow towards the deck of the merchant ship, but as he reached half-way he quickened his pace to a run and began shouting to Captain Maddox.

His shouts were masked by the rumble of the crane's engine, so his cries remained unnoticed by Captain Maddox. When the crane's engine went idle so the men on the deck of the Key West could remove the cables from the container, the shouts suddenly aroused everyone's attention. Now, all eyes were on the Nav as he made it to the top of the brow. A few of Cortez's men brought their weapons to the ready position and fixed their sights upon the Nav. Cortez motioned for his men to back down with a subtle hand gesture as he and Captain Maddox met the Nav at the top of the brow.

Quinn made his way forward to see if he could glean any information from reports over the Weps' radio. Quinn heard Captain Maddox order the Weps to have his men "double time it."

The Weps looked up at Quinn. "Petty Officer Quinn, you and the rest of the security detail get over here and help us get these down!"

Quinn didn't protest. He gave a sharp "Aye, sir!" then turned his head just in time to see the Nav, Captain Maddox, Cortez and a few of the other men disappear from sight.

Santa de Juarez

Sanchez crouched in the broom closet he had turned into a makeshift communications center. He was switching through channels on his radio, repeating the same desperate call in a hushed tone, "Dragon, this is Salamander. Did you copy my last? Over." Again and again he would punch in a channel he had locked in his memory and repeat the same.

He suddenly froze as the handle on the locked door of the closet was tested. Slowly he placed his communicator back into a box of latex gloves. The handle shook violently. He stretched out his right hand reaching for a suppressed Jericho 941 pistol he had fastened to the underside of a shelf holding cleaning products. Before his fingers could loosen the duct tape which held the pistol, the door was kicked open. He had but a moment to look up and see the shoulder stock of a rifle, then blackness.

Sanchez grimaced in pain as he opened his eyes slightly. Two pairs of hands grasped him under his arms. He was being dragged across the body of a man who had been shot in the head. His fingers made a grasping motion as if he thought he had actually been able to reach his gun.

Cortez came rushing down the corridor followed by Captain Maddox and the Nav. The trio saw two of Cortez's goons dragging a man, in a cook's uniform, away from a closet which had a body protruding from its doorway. When the men saw Cortez, one of them spoke up, "We found the spy!"

The other man added, "He killed Diego!" Captain Maddox and the Nav halted, but Cortez slowly walked past the men holding Sanchez's limp body.

He walked to the closet and studied the lifeless corpse. Diego had a small hole in his cheek under his left eye, but a great deal of his brain matter was on the overhead of the passageway. Cortez cocked his head to the side studying the barrel of Diego's rifle still in his right hand. Cortez let out a singular laugh which came deep from within his belly. "That spy did not kill Diego," he said as he walked back towards Captain Maddox. "It was his own stupidity," he declared. Then paying no mind to the men holding the spy, he explained to Captain Maddox and the Nav, as if he were a criminal defense lawyer, just how Diego had erased himself from the earth. "The ignorant fool did not have his safety on. When he hit that man with the butt of his rifle, he also shot himself."

Cortez waited, as if the two US Naval Officers would applaud his conclusion. The Nav looked at his watch impatiently. Captain Maddox just stared at the body of poor Diego. He had never seen a dead body before.

The sheer horror of the scene struck him dumb. He was not listening to Cortez's presentation. He looked at the massive pool of blood which continued, even then, to grow. Cortez had gingerly tip-toed through it as if it had been a spilled bottle of merlot. Captain Maddox's thoughts were now of his son and the horrors he must have witnessed in Afghanistan.

His son wouldn't talk about it much, but when he did it was as if he were describing a movie. He could hear pain in his son's voice during their conversations, but could tell BJ was working hard to mask it so he did not push him to reveal his emotions. He knew now, even though his son's life had been cut abruptly short, he held a grisly knowledge that aged him well beyond his twenty-four years. What pained him most about seeing the bloody scene which lay before him was the thought that the horrors his son had endeared on numerous deployments must have been a hundred times more brutal than this.

The pain he was feeling could be likened to the pain of a father finding out his daughter had lost her virginity at much too tender an age.

"Kill him."

The blunt words, which were spoken with no emotion, snapped Captain Maddox back to the present. Cortez repeated himself as he stared coldly into Captain Maddox's eyes. "Kill him." Captain Maddox struggled to comprehend the order.

"Kill him now and spare him the cruelty that will come upon him from Diego's amigos if he is left on this ship alive." Cortez did not seem to care one way or the other how his spy would die; he seemed as if he were more interested in gaining power over Captain Maddox.

"Kill him now!"

Sanchez, seeming to drift in and out of consciousness, struggled to lift his eyes. Captain Maddox was shaking his head unable to speak any words in protest against what was being asked of him. The Nav was growing more and more impatient. "We're running out of time," he said, as if he were so singularly focused on his watch he had no comprehension of any of the events which were going on around him. Captain Maddox was not pleased with the Nav and looked at him scornfully as if he were suddenly a pawn of Cortez. Though he did not realize it, the Nav's words had brought him back to an operational mindset.

He knew that if they did not resolve the current dilemma quickly, the satellite, which was changing its orbital path, would soon beam images of his boat back to the Pentagon and all would be lost. He began to justify in his mind reasons for doing, what a few moments earlier, had been implausible. He thought of tortures which might be performed on this poor soul who had the unfortunate position of being caught between a rock and a hard place. He thought of his son and how he wished he could have spared him from the last cruel days of his life. Reaching down he pulled his pistol from its holster.

He took a few steps forward and closed the distance between himself and the men holding the Sanchez. A thought flickered in his mind, he might shoot the two goons along with Cortez, then he and the Nav would carry the spy back to the submarine. That thought was fleeting however; he knew they would be cut down before they made it topside. Now his justification turned to the Nav. He knew it was he who convinced the Nav that their careers were over and he needed to come along with him in this scheme to line their pockets with riches a Navy pension couldn't hold a candle to.

As if his thoughts had somehow betrayed him, Captain Maddox saw a gun seemly appear out of thin air in Cortez's hand and the barrel land against the Nav's temple. The Nav, as if in a haze of disbelief, continued to check his watch, not even acknowledging the peril of his situation.

"Do it now or he dies," Cortez hissed.

"We're running out of time," the Nav implored, still not seeming to grasp the threat against his life, even with the cold steel of the barrel pressed firmly against his temple.

Sanchez lifted his head. He saw the familiar insignia of an American Naval uniform and it brought a smile to his face.

"Captain," he muttered with delight, as though he had not realized the voices he heard talking of his death in his dreamlike state included the American Naval Officers.

Captain Maddox stepped toward Sanchez who still hung heavily by his arms in the grip of the goons. He put his pistol to the side of the man's head, closed his eyes and squeezed the trigger. Nothing happened. Sanchez grimaced as he realized the Captain had meant to execute him. Captain Maddox opened his eyes wondering if there had been some sort of divine intervention.

Cortez pulled away the pistol he had been holding to the Nav's head and drew closer to Captain Maddox. He seemed to be the only one able to move in real time. He grabbed Captain Maddox's wrist, pulled it upward and outward so that he might see the inside of the Captain's pistol.

"Looks like Diego could have used a few gun safety lessons from you," Cortez said as he reached over with his hand still garnishing his own pistol and chambered the first round into Captain Maddox's pistol.

"Now Captain, you may continue," Cortez said as he let the Captain regain control of his own hand.

Sanchez looked up and implored softly to the Captain, "I'm an American."

Understanding these words could have a tide-changing effect on Captain Maddox, Cortez pressed him once again. "Do it now or you do not leave this ship alive!" He now pointed the barrel of his weapon at Captain Maddox.

Sanchez, regaining a bit more of his wits, started to struggle in the clutches of his captors. He raised his voice, "I'm an American!" Both Cortez and Sanchez could see the struggle in the eyes of Captain Maddox.

Cortez now pulled no punches, "You might be able to take a bullet, but will your submarine be able to take a shoulder fired rocket directly down one of its open hatches!"

The decision had been made. Captain Maddox's eyes welled up; he closed them tightly, turned his head, gnashed his teeth and let the muzzle end of his pistol press Sanchez's thick black hair against his scalp. Sanchez began a fierce struggle but the goons held him even tighter. The man on the right even pressed his knee into the nape of Sanchez's neck putting pressure against his head to steady him.

"Do it!" Cortez screamed.

Sanchez let out one more horrid cry, "I'm an American!" As soon as Sanchez's tongue hit the roof of his mouth to make the 'n' sound, the shot rang out.

It seemed to Captain Maddox to be the most horrible clap of thunder he had ever heard in his life. He had never fired a weapon, except for on the naval base gun range, and then he had been wearing hearing protection. Here, in the tight corridors of the merchant vessel, the shot seemed to go on ringing for minutes, but what shattered his heart was that the words "I'm an American." seemed to reverberate throughout the corridor without end.

He barely noticed the screams of the goon who lay on the floor clutching the bloody mess which moments before had been his knee holding Sanchez's head steady. The bullet not only traveled through the skull of Sanchez, but it also tore through the knee the goon was pressing against the American Operative. Cortez laughed it off.

"It seems I need to review gun safety with my entire crew," he said as he slowly guided Captain Maddox's hand down to holster his pistol.

USS Key West

"There it was again," Rubber exclaimed.

Petty Officer Bowden looked annoyed as he peered over his training manual at Rubber, "Are you still hearing things?"

Rubber's mouth dropped as if he could not believe the words coming from his supervisor. "Yeah, I am, it's my job. I'm a Sonar Man. That might be a question on your test."

Bowden rolled his eyes as he pushed his glasses up his nose. "What was it, another gunshot?"

"Yes, it was," Rubber said. He unplugged his head phones. "Here, listen."

He replayed the noise for Bowden. Bowden now listened with a look of sincerity on his face. Rubber played what sounded like a sharp metallic pop amidst the crackling of the sea state. The sincerity which had been on Bowden's face was now washed away by cynicism. "That could be anything," he said. He listed off the possibilities as he settled back into his chair. "It could be a door slamming, or somebody hitting something with a hammer."

Rubber did not stop protesting. "*Or* it could be a gunshot!"

Bowden seemed to be losing his patience. "It's a merchant ship, not a submarine. They ain't trying to be quiet!" Rubber turned and pulled the book out of Bowden's hands before he could reopen it.

"The Nav ran up there because he found something out from radio, then he and the Captain disappear from view. A few minutes later, I hear a gunshot. Then, a few moments after that I hear another and still no Captain and no Navigator. For all we know they are laying inside that ship dead."

The argument seemed to show some validity to Bowden. After all, he was not stupid, just preoccupied. The heavy curtain that separated the Sonar Shack from the control room was pulled briskly to the side. Lt. Turno stood in the doorway with a look of displeasure on his face.

"What's all the noise in here?" he snapped. Rubber said nothing; he just pushed Bowden with a look. Bowden swallowed hard.

"Petty Officer Rubber thinks the Captain and the Nav might be in trouble," he confessed. At that moment the three heard someone call out from the control room, "We have a visual on the Captain and the Nav."

Lt. Turno shot Petty Officer Bowden a cold look. "Next time the Sonar Shack decides to use ESP rather than the sonar consoles you're paid to use, keep it to yourselves." With that, he left in a huff.

Bowden turned his anger towards Rubber. "Well, that's great, Rubber!"

"Bowden, I'm telling you, something-"

Bowden cut him off, "I don't even want to hear it. How am I supposed to go to him for a letter of recommendation now?"

Rubber tried unsuccessfully to answer his question, "He's not going to…"

Again, Bowden cut him off, "Not another word, Rubber."

Rubber sat there as though he were debating another try. This time Bowden preemptively cut him off.

"I don't want to hear another word out of you for the rest of this deployment. Even if the entire Russian and Chinese submarine fleets are tailing us."

"Noted," Rubber said softly under his breath.

"Not another word!" Bowden retorted.

Captain Maddox, the Nav and Cortez emerged onto the deck of the merchant ship as the last of the containers was being lifted. Captain Maddox walked as if in a haze, while the Nav seemed as though he could not make it to the brow fast enough.

"We need to dive as soon as possible," the Nav implored.

"We don't have time to load the last container," Captain Maddox said to Cortez.

"Are you going back on our deal Captain?" asked Cortez. Captain Maddox picked up his pace as he headed to the brow.

"It was you who allowed a spy on board!" he forcefully reminded Cortez.

The Captain noticed four armed men waiting at the top of the brow. They had a more militaristic look about them than the other men aboard the ship. At their feet were two hard shelled shipping cases, about four feet in length each. When they noticed Cortez coming they squatted down, each grabbing a handle on the end of the cases and lifted them.

"These men will escort the cargo," Cortez explained. Captain Maddox whirled on his heel to face Cortez.

"They will do no such thing!" he protested. "That wasn't the plan!"

"You have no choice," Cortez said. "My activities are no secret to your government; they *know* I'm a criminal."

At that moment, a young man came running up to Cortez and handed him a sheet of paper. As Cortez looked at it, a smile crossed his face. "Of course your actions could be devastating to anyone you care about." Cortez turned the paper to reveal a picture of Captain Maddox, taken with a surveillance camera, executing Sanchez. He felt his stomach tie into knots.

The Nav pulled at his arm. "We've got to go, sir!" Captain Maddox offered no further argument. He turned and followed the Nav down the brow. Cortez gave the armed guards a nod. They turned sharply and filed in behind Captain Maddox.

Quinn looked up and saw the Nav running down the brow, followed by Captain Maddox, who looked as if his mind were a thousand miles away. Behind him were four armed men. Quinn tried to assess whether the men were hostile or friendly. He took no chances. "Eyes on Charlie Oscar!" he yelled to his security detail. The men all brought their weapons up and took aim at the newcomers carrying the cases down the brow. The Weps heard the yell and took his attention away from the last container that was sliding down the hatch. The Nav was yelling, "We need to dive! We need to dive!"

Captain Maddox seemed to return to the current situation. His pace quickened. "Weps!" he yelled.

"Aye, Captain," the Weps called as he made his way aft of the sail.

"We need to dive ASAP" he informed him. The Weps took notice of the armed entourage coming down with Captain Maddox.

"Who are these men?" the Weps questioned. Captain Maddox's frustration came to a hilt.

"How many times do I need to give an order? Dive this boat!"

The Weps was taken aback. "But Captain, it will take some time to disassemble the shipping harness." Captain Maddox looked at the massive steel structure that was constructed on the bow of the submarine.

"Jettison it," he ordered.

"Captain, we can't-" the Weps began to reason.

"Unbolt the damn thing and push it overboard," Captain Maddox pressed. "I assure you, it can be done!"

"Who are these men?" the Weps demanded as his concerns trumped his obedience.

Captain Maddox reached the foot of the brow. Tired of the Weps ignoring the order to dive, he pulled his pistol from his holster and fired two shots into the air. He now had everyone's attention on the deck.

"Listen up!" he yelled. "This boat will be underwater in one minute. Those still topside can swim home." As he stepped onto the deck and made his way to the hatch, it took the men a moment to process his order. Once they had, there was a flurry of activity topside.

The rest of the security team went forward to work on the shipping harness, but Quinn watched every step the armed men took as they made their way behind Captain Maddox. As he disappeared down the hatch, the four men stood around it exchanging glances. Quinn was not sure what kind of detail it was but he could tell they had never been on a submarine before. That ruled out SEALs, but they had be some sort of American Special Operations unit; *maybe CIA*, he thought.

The men looked to one another. After exchanging glances, their eyes seemed to rest on the youngest of them. Quinn made a mental note of their gazes; *so he's their leader.* The man they all looked to seemed to be the least likely candidate to be the head of the group. He was a soft looking man in contrast with his gruff companions. *He must be an officer*, thought Quinn. As soon as the thought flashed across his mind, it was immediately contradicted by the thought that he would soon join the commissioned ranks. He let the ongoing debate within his own mind distract him from making any more useful observations of the men as they fumbled their way down the ladder with their cargo.

"Quinn, get up here," Scarpa shouted as he and the other men topside were fighting with the weapons shipping harness. Quinn slung his M-16 around to his back and dashed forward. They were unbolting the last piece of the harness that impeded the hatch, when Quinn made it to the bow. He could see a pair of hands reaching out of the open hatch ready to assist in shutting it. He looked down to see Sparks straddling what normally was the deck of the command passageway. Sparks was performing a delicate balancing act, trying to keep his size fourteens holding onto the one inch strip of steel which protruded from both port and starboard bulkheads. Under normal circumstances, the thin strips of steel which ran the length of the passageway would have deck plates bolted to them, but since they still had not reconfigured the interior of the sub, if one of Sparks' big feet slipped he would have a fifteen foot drop down to a torpedo shipping tray made from the hardest Pennsylvania steel tax dollars could buy.

"Hold on Sparks, I'll get this pushed down to you," Quinn said as he grabbed the top of the weapons shipping hatch. Below him, and just aft of Sparks, he could see Captain Maddox leaning out from the control room as far as the safety chain which roped off the passageway would allow.

"We're venting the ballast tanks in thirty seconds!" he screamed as the hatch came shut. "You heard the Skipper, thirty seconds," Quinn reiterated as he jumped onto the hatch pushing it down the last half inch so that Sparks could dog it.

He joined the men trying to push the weapons shipping tray overboard. Even with half a dozen sailors pushing, the tray seemed immovable. It was designed with an extraordinarily heavy base so when missiles and torpedoes were tilted to a near vertical position to begin the descent down to the torpedo room, the tray would not waver.

"It's no use, Weps," Stoney declared. "We'd need half the crew up here to move this." To Quinn, this seemed a bit of an exaggeration, but it was clear the men they had weren't going to push it overboard without some help.

The COB, who had been straining right alongside them, said, "Let's just leave it here and let the ocean take it off."

"We can't take the chance that it'll hit the sail or the screw," the Weps grunted as he pressed his back against the tray and tried to use his massive legs to push it over.

"I guess it must be made of Kryptonite," Stoney said making jest at the Weps' uncanny resemblance to Superman. The remark momentarily lightened the mood, but the bit of laughter somehow zapped their strength, and the tray now felt even heavier. Their efforts had only given them about three inches of movement on the forward end of the tray. They were all taking a moment to regain their breath and strength when the ballast tank vents opened. As the geysers blew into the air, the men redoubled their efforts.

Le Poignard

"Captain," the drone technician called out, "the drone is approaching the merchant vessel."

"Very well," Captain Reno responded. "Transfer the video feed to periscope screens."

"Aye, sir." The tech reconfigured the video feed so the drone's bird's eye view showed on the main screens in control. De Panafiue studied the image alongside his Captain.

"It looks as if the Key West is moored next to it sir."

"It does," Captain Reno agreed. "There seems to be a cluster of activity on her deck."

"Is that its weapons loading system?" De Panafiue asked as the images grew clearer due to the drone closing the distance.

"Bring up Jane's profile for the L.A. Class subs." As if anticipating Captain Reno's request, the technician was clicking through the profiles of American subs as listed in Jane's Almanac of Fighting Ships. Once he had found the L.A. Class profile he sent it to the screen adjacent to the drone feed.

"Here it is, Captain."

"Does it have an image of its weapons loading system?"

As the tech flipped through the various images of the subs, De Panafiue cried out, "They're venting their ballast tanks!"

USS Key West

Desperately, Quinn looked around the deck to see if there were any items which could be of use. Among the miscellaneous tools strewn about, he noticed a length of rope and the top piece of the shipping harness. He jumped over to the rope and tied it around himself. Stoney, who noticed what Quinn was doing, seemed to be in awe of the speed with which he tied a bowline knot around his waist. He probably didn't realize it was a skill that was hammered into divers at dive school. "What the hell are you doing?" he yelled to Quinn, trying to compete with the noise of the air and water rushing out of the ballast tank vents.

"Anchor me!" Quinn shouted as he struggled to lift the top piece of the harness. The top piece was nearly fourteen feet in length itself and was arched upward along the centerline so it would hug the torpedo when it was latched on. Stoney grabbed the free end of the rope.

"Give me a hand," Quinn shouted. He was immediately helped by some of the sailors clearly relieved to see any semblance of a plan which didn't involve them getting a hernia.

The sailors helped Quinn maneuver the long shank of steel. At his direction, they placed one end under the base of the tray in the middle where it wasn't completely flush with the deck. The other end of the top piece protruded perpendicularly sticking out to the port side of the boat. The curve of the submarine's hull made a natural fulcrum for Quinn's lever. With Stoney as his anchor, Quinn nearly sprinted out to the end of the steel lever with the agility of a Cirque Du Soleil performer. Once at the end, he spread his legs into a stance as if he were riding a horse.

"Ready," he called out to the men who were stupefied as if they were watching a Harold Lloyd film. Quinn clapped his hands twice as if to wake them from a trance, "Let's go!" They all turned and pushed again against the tray. The bow was beginning to dip noticeably lower in the water. Like a schoolyard daredevil riding the teeter-totter standing up, Quinn rocked his weight downward. "One, two," he counted as he bore down on the lever. "Three!" He squatted all his weight onto the end of the beam. The tray rose upward. Scarpa saw it was working, but must have realized Quinn wouldn't be enough of a counter weight by himself to finish the job. So with a great leap he plunged himself out to the end of the lever to double up the force on it.

His chest caught the lever right at Quinn's feet. The sudden lurch downward caused Quinn to lose his footing. He felt his weight taking him backwards, so he heaved forward and came crashing down on top of Scarpa. The force which was created was enough to lift the base of the harness. It went slowly at first, but with the men still pushing, once the harness passed its counterbalance point, the men had to jump back from it to get clear. Its roll off the sub was so violent, had it not been for the clang of the lever as it shot back against the merchant ship, the men never would have turned to see Quinn and

Scarpa being carried away by the current between the two vessels. Stoney ran aft attempting to make it to the starboard side of the sail before the slack in the line went taught and pulled him overboard as well. As it was, Stoney was able to make it a few paces back from the forward edge of the sail and use the protruding mass itself as a giant cleat in an effort to save himself and his shipmates.

As the current pulled Quinn and Scarpa, Stoney's shoes began to lose their grip on the non-skid surface of the sub. He had managed to stave off disaster long enough for three others to come relieve him from his burden of trying to hold them alone. Meanwhile, the rest of the party went along the narrow port side of the sail to try and pull the castaways up. Every step they took was guarded, as to not multiply the dilemma. As they made their way aft of the sail, they were able to begin pulling the men upward. They did not have to pull them up very far since the boat was sitting so precariously low in the water, but Quinn's heart raced as he strained to hold onto Scarpa who did not have the luxury of a safety line attached to his body. His eyes darted back and forth from the safety of the deck to the massive hull of the merchant ship which threatened to slide right over the top of the Key West as it submerged.

The men were able to get ahold of Scarpa and haul him up. Then Quinn's outstretched hand was grasped and he found his feet on the deck again. Once more the hatch was being pumped shut as he was the last to slide through it. Unfortunately, this time around, Scarpa had not been below decks giving them a head start shutting the hatch and the steady flow of the ocean came down upon him as he cleared the upper hatch ring. Seeing the ocean pour into middle level where a team of men were still trying to pump the hatch shut, Quinn reacted. In a moment of haste, before descending the ladder any further, Quinn kicked the latch holding the escape trunk's lower hatch open. The heavy weight of the hatch, as well as the force of the ocean pouring down upon it, brought it slamming shut with a deafening crash. Clearly miscalculating how long he would have before the escape trunk completely filled with water, it seemed to be less than half a second before he found the small space to be completely void of any air or light.

Le Poignard

"There it is, Captain," the tech said as he popped an image on the screen of a Los Angeles Class submarine with its weapons shipping harness assembled on its bow.

"They just pushed it overboard!" De Panafiue exclaimed. Captain Reno looked back to the live scene. Sure enough, the metal monstrosity which had adorned the deck like a tacky hood ornament moments before was now gone.

"Run me a play back on screen three!"

An alarm started to flash on the technician's counsel. "Are we out of time on the drone?" Captain Reno asked, hoping he was wrong.

"No sir, we've got about three minutes and forty five seconds," the tech informed him, adding, "if you want to play it safe. The alarm is letting me know an American DOD satellite I had been tracking changed its orbit."

Captain Reno came over to inspect his screen closer, "Do we have images off of it?"

"No sir, I wasn't able to get back in, but it's definitely switched to an intercept course."

"Captain," De Panafiue asked, "why do you suppose the Americans would be diving so quickly when one of their own satellites is on its way to do a flyover?"

"My guess is whatever they loaded with that shipping harness wasn't in the scope of their intended mission."

"The Key West has submerged and is changing its course," Sonar informed the control room.

"Did they get all their sailors below?" Captain Reno asked as he turned back to the screen showing the drone feed. The technician switched to thermal imaging.

"There doesn't appear to be anyone treading water," De Panafiue said as they studied the lone merchant vessel sitting on the surface.

"Get that drone back here and then let's get out of the Key West's way," Captain Reno said as he puffed out his cheeks in disbelief of the Key West's actions.

USS Key West

Events had happened so quickly, Quinn only had a chance to take a shallow breath. The sudden combination of weightlessness and pitch dark made him lose his bearings immediately. He tried to calm his nerves as he reached for his dive watch. The bright LED light on the watch gave off enough luminescence for him to find the battle lantern which hung in the escape trunk. The light gave him some comfort, but his oxygen levels were running low. He could see the upper hatch was flush with the locking ring, but he had other concerns before he set to sealing it. He knew no one was going to be able to open the lower hatch with five hundred gallons of seawater sitting on top of it, so using the light from the battle lantern, he began to study the escape trunks emergency air valves. It was hard enough to decipher which valve was which with the sting of the saltwater against his eyes, but it had been years since he had been through the training at submarine school on how to actually operate the escape trunk's emergency air system.

Stoney, Scarpa, and the other sailors lying on the deck were surprised when the ocean suddenly stopped intruding in great droves into the boat.

"What happened?" Stoney asked.

"The lower hatch came shut," answered one of the sailors looking up at the hatch which was shut but not sealed.

"That was lucky," Scarpa said, spitting salt water onto the deck. Stoney peered up at the hatch. A bit of spray was still coming in but he knew it would stop as soon as it was sealed. He looked around for his friend who he had been tied to topside. The rope was still around his waist but the other end had an empty loop where it had been attached to Quinn.

"It wasn't luck," he cried out as he jumped to the ladder, "it was Quinn!" His ascension of the ladder was Olympian, but his push against the hatch was to no avail.

"Come on! Give me a hand," Stoney said as he strained with all his might. Another sailor bounded up the ladder to assist him, but was no help in budging the hatch.

"There's no way you're gonna lift it," Scarpa said, as he offered no assistance. The Weps popped back in from the crew's mess where he had retreated to, to make room for those coming down behind him.

"Let's get that hatch sealed," he ordered.

"Weps, Quinn is still up there!" The Weps didn't hesitate to jump onto the ladder and try to push with his massive arms.

"Let's get this open," he grunted. Stoney looked down at Scarpa who was simply being a spectator.

"Scarpa, he saved your life up there, do something!"

"He was just returning the favor," Scarpa said coldly. "We're even." Stoney looked at Scarpa, as if he couldn't believe he would just stand there. All he could do was scream Scarpa's name as he pushed.

"Scarpa!" his voice cracked with desperation.

"Don't give yourself a hernia, *Stoner*," Scarpa said. "Quinn's fine." He pointed to a gauge at the foot of the ladder. "Look at the emergency air gauge." Stoney looked at the gauge, exhaling in relief. Just then a metallic tapping came from the hatch to the tune of "A Shave and a Haircut". Stoney pulled out his Leatherman and tapped back a reply, "Two Pence"

CHAPTER 14

Quinn had changed into a pair of dry coveralls then set about to collect the firearms he had issued to a select few in the crew. Though he and Scarpa had both lost their M-16's during the struggle to remove the weapons shipping harness, he felt sure no reprimand would come of it. He was not, however, looking forward to the mountains of paperwork he would have to go through to justify the loss to the Naval Investigators.

After collecting the weapons from the members of the security detail who did not lose their rifles, Quinn made his way to the control room. There, he found tensions high as Captain Maddox and the Weps were having a heated debate over whether the newcomers should be allowed to carry weapons aboard the submarine.

"We should have our own armed security team then," the Weps implored as his voice hinged on screaming.

"I'm not going to turn this place into the O.K. Corral," Captain Maddox said, absent any of the usual diplomacy in his voice. Quinn loitered back by the navigation plots. He had had no time to reflect on any of the events which had taken place over the last few hours, but his uneasiness was building.

"These men *are* the security detail!" Captain Maddox yelled. Quinn noticed the leader of the group, who had come aboard with the mysterious cargo, bristle with importance as he stood flanking the two officers.

Quinn sensed the stranger sizing up the crew. His eyes darted back and forth registering reactions from the men at Captain Maddox's words. Knowing his reactions would be cataloged in the memory banks of this intruder, much the same way he was compiling his own assessment of the man, Quinn consciously masked his own tells as best he could. He hunched his shoulders forward, and walked slothfully toward Captain Maddox and the Weps. He buried his eyes into the clipboard he carried. Absent was the sense of purpose his strides usually exclaimed.

The sound of Quinn's feet scuffing the deck like a lazy teenager alerted Captain Maddox to his approach. The Captain looked at Quinn puzzled. Quinn began to worry he was trying too hard to be inconspicuous; the last thing he wanted to do was to paint a target on his forehead. Any look of suspicion Captain Maddox did betray was gone in a flash. It was apparent to Quinn the Captain had more pressing issues on his mind than trying to figure out why a second class petty officer would be moping.

Captain Maddox returned his attention to the Weps. "Petty Officer Quinn is here for our weapons," he said as he unbuckled the belt that supported the holstered pistol. "He will put them in the gun locker and that is where they are to remain locked up." He handed his belt to Quinn. This time they did not go through the usual procedure of making sure the chamber was free and clear and the number of rounds were declared as they exchanged possession of the weapon.

The Weps let Captain Maddox's words and actions hang in the air for a moment, as if the Captain would realize his error and rescind his order. No such reversal was spoken. With a grunt, the Weps unfastened his gun belt and with the same lack of procedure, he slung it into Quinn's hands. Quinn latched the belts together and hung them casually over his shoulder as if they were the straps of a back pack. He noticed the eyes of the unnamed outsider searing Quinn's embroidered name tag into memory. A chill swept over Quinn. He was not exactly comfortable with this man knowing he controlled the keys to the gun locker.

"COB," Captain Maddox called out.

"Aye, sir," the COB replied as he broke off a conversation in the Sonar Shack and turned his attention toward the control room.

"Take Mr.-" Captain Maddox paused. He saw the collective look of doubt shoot across the faces of the crew as they realized their Captain didn't even know the man's name. Nowhere did the look solidify quite as apparent as on the stone-set face of the Weps.

"Ramirez," the man offered up in English with a thick Spanish accent.

"Take Mr. Ramirez," Captain Maddox continued, "and his companions to the torpedo room." Quinn's eyes jumped, betraying him, and he saw that Mr. Ramirez had noticed the uncontrolled flinch.

"He and his men will bunk in there, since that is where their duties lie." Captain Maddox directed.

"Aye, sir," replied the COB. "You and your men can follow me." Mr. Ramirez gave a nod to the members of his team and they followed the COB forward through the command passageway, which had just been restored to its normal condition.

Captain Maddox headed out of the control room just behind the COB and the other men. He went immediately into his stateroom. Once inside his stateroom, his physical appearance drastically changed. In the absence of watchful eyes, his knees finally completely buckled. His hand shot out to his desk to keep from falling over. The jolt to the desk sent the picture of him and his son tumbling to the floor. As he looked down at the picture, his back was hunched, his eyes burned with what felt like acidic tears. In a matter of seconds, he turned into a tired, beleaguered old man.

Ms. Collins perked up as she heard the door lock to the head that was shared between the XO's and CO's staterooms. Captain Maddox had left the door from the XO's stateroom to the head unlocked so she and Dave could use it at their leisure, but he kept the door which led to his stateroom locked at all times. He had never used the lock before, but now that he was using the XO's stateroom as a brig, it came in handy.

Ms. Collins did not pay much attention to the comings and goings of Captain Maddox. She had stopped trying to plead with him after about the fifth time he used the head and paid no attention to her harassment. She sat on the deck reviewing video footage on her laptop which they had already shot, when some muffled sounds could be heard coming from the head. She paused the video on the screen and listened intently. It sounded as if Captain Maddox were throwing up. The fact that it was difficult to hear the sounds emanating from the other side of the door seemed odd to her. Privacy, or the lack of it, had been the hardest aspect of the submarine life for her to get used to. The bulkheads being so thin, as well as having louvered vents in the door, made every sound which came from the head seem as though it couldn't be any clearer even if the door was wide open. This made bunking with Dave, who's stomach didn't agree with submarine food, unbearable.

When the muffled heaves ceased, they were replaced by the clear sounds of Captain Maddox breathing heavily, as if he had just finished his annual physical training test. She was about to cusp her ear against the vents when she noticed the door bow out slightly as the Captain sat with his back against it. She waited a moment as he regained control of his breathing. Once it sounded as if he had composed himself, she said softly, "Is everything okay, Captain?"

Dave, lying in the top rack, had been thumbing through a less than academic magazine he had borrowed from a member of the crew, when he took notice of the emerging interview. As he started to shift his weight in the rack, Ms. Collins halted him by putting a finger up to her pursed lips. He took extra care not to make a sound as he reached down to grab the camera off the desk.

Inside the head, Captain Maddox rolled his eyes to the heavens as if to say, *Can't I get a moments peace?* He sighed heavily and responded to her question with a question of his own, "Why are you here, Ms. Collins?"

"So you can tell the American people and the world your story," she snapped off as if she were giving a perfectly prepared answer in a job interview. She expected a response, but none came.

As Dave lifted the camera to his position, the USB wire that still attached the camera to the laptop, pulled taught, then popped out and slapped the deck as it fell. Ms. Collins eyes twitched with a flash of anger. Dave cringed and mouthed the word "sorry". As he started recording Ms. Collins' interview with the door, she fired off more reasoning. "I'm here to tell your son's story."

"I never asked you to come tell my story," he said, naively thinking she might back off.

"But the American people did," she said with a softness which was legendary for opening up the toughest emotional shells.

After another long beat of silence, she heard the Captain relent, "What do you want to know?" She probably didn't plan on getting the interview through a door like a Catholic Confessional, but at this point she seemed to be happy to get anything.

"Why don't you start by telling me what kind of boy your son was?" As she asked the question delicately, her face showed nothing but jubilance. She scribbled editing notes on a legal pad. She didn't seem concerned with the camera catching the mismatch between her exuberant expressions and her somber voice. Once the excitement wore off, she would put on a face more fitting the subject matter. Those were the shots that would make it into the interview. For the opening of the interview she would use the voice track as she flipped through a slide show of Captain Maddox's family pictures; like the one he kept on his desk of him and his son.

At some point in the interview, she would probably show the now infamous video of BJ Maddox, or portions of it, or maybe just stills from it. It didn't really matter; America's love for Sergeant B.J. Maddox was endless. There were T-shirts and coffee mugs with the young sergeant's image on them with the word "perseverance" inscribed across it. Ms. Collins didn't need to be told this interview would be the highest rated special of her career.

"My son," Captain Maddox began, "was the greatest *man* I ever knew." He said this with special emphasis on the word man. As the interview progressed, she continued scrawling notes as fast as her hand could fly. She was writing down questions she did not want to forget to ask, as well as ideas for her narrative.

When it seemed she had enough background, and that Captain Maddox might be ready to delve into the meat of the interview, she asked him the question every reporter in America had been waiting to ask him.

"How did you find out about your son's death?"

Captain Maddox had managed not to relive that fateful day over and over in his mind as so many of the parents of fallen soldiers did.

"Did the Army send representatives to your home?" She must have realized she was getting ahead of herself so she added, "Were you even home?"

Captain Maddox took a shallow breath. It seemed to be cut short by a massive twitch in his diaphragm. After a few short breaths his breathing became deeper as tears began to roll down his face. As difficult as it must have been for her to imagine the bear of a man crying, it seemed she was tuned in enough to notice the subtle signs. She waited, giving him as much time as he needed. After what seemed like two full minutes, he began to speak in a very weak voice.

"I was visiting my wife in Washington," he began. He cleared his throat and continued in a stronger, yet fragile tone. "It was about quarter after six; we had just sat down to breakfast when Nancy's cell phone rang. She jokingly said 'They usually wait 'til six twenty to start hounding me.' She looked a little dismayed when she read the caller ID. It was Nora White, the President's personal secretary. She asked Nancy if I was with her and said the President would like to meet with us as soon as possible. When she told us there was a car waiting for us out front, neither my wife nor I could imagine what would be so urgent."

"Did the two of you ever meet with the President before?" Ms. Collins asked, seeming afraid to interrupt him now that he was on a roll, but intuitively the reporter in her must have known that's what her viewers would be wondering.

"That's just it, I had only met him at two different Senatorial social functions, and it was for the briefest of moments, just a hand shake really. Nancy had obviously met him in the course of her duties as a Senator, but she had never had a private meeting with him."

"What did you talk about on the ride to the White House?"

"Nothing. She figured she would take advantage of the chauffeured ride and busied herself responding to emails. I took the opportunity to research an assignment I was working on."

"What type of assignment?" Ms. Collins asked, letting the investigative reporter get the better of her.

"I was asked to come up with a report on imaginative ways the submarine force could be better utilized in the war on terror." Realizing he had somehow fallen under the spell she was famous for and had become a little too comfortable answering her questions, he quickly added, "But that's classified. So if you report that, I'll have to kill you." His attempt to lighten the moment with a classic military line pierced his heart as he suddenly remembered it had been less than an hour since he had killed someone.

Ms. Collins laughed off the line, thinking that is what he wanted, but she heard nothing in reply. Finding the silence too nerve racking to linger in, she pressed on, "What happened when you arrived at the White House?"

Switching from one horrible event in his mind to another, Captain Maddox continued, "We were escorted to the Oval Office. Inside we were greeted by General Mason, Speaker Daniels and the President. The President asked us to have a seat then he leaned against his desk and assured us he was doing the single hardest thing he had to do since taking office. Then he told us that B.J. had been killed in action." The words hung in the air, just as they had that day in the Oval Office.

After the longest pause since beginning the interview, Ms. Collins asked, "Do you need some time, Captain Maddox?"

She heard him blow his nose then utter faintly, "No."

He hadn't talked to a soul about his son's death in the three months since, and as much as he did not want to admit it, there was something therapeutic about it.

"No," he repeated after blowing his nose once more. "You won't get another chance for an interview so we'd better get this over with now." She clearly hadn't anticipated he would be so difficult to get to talk. Usually the military types were so full of themselves, they would trip over each other trying to get interviewed hoping it would lead to an analyst position for a news organization in their retirement.

Not waiting for him to tell her again to continue, she pounced, "What happened next?" Captain Maddox, getting lost in his own thoughts, did not hear her.

"I'm sorry," he beckoned her to repeat.

She repeated her question with more clarity, "How did you feel having the President tell you of your son's death?"

Annoyed at her emphasis on the fact that it was the President who informed him his son was gone, he became abrasive.

"It didn't matter that it was the President! It could have been a damned junior ROTC cadet coming to my door telling me!" He began to regret being so forthcoming with the details. He could sense that she thought the President calling him into the Oval Office to tell him was icing on the cake.

Realizing her mistake, she tried to railroad past her gaff, "How did it feel, hearing that your son had died?"

He wished now he had just told her, "a guy came to the door, told me and left." He refused to answer what he considered the dumbest question in the history of journalism, and simply said, "I'll leave the knowledge of those horrible feelings to those parents who carry the same burden as me, and pray for the ones who don't share our grief; may they never know it."

Ms. Collins decided to stay away from the questions dealing with internal issues for the time being and tried to bring it back to the sequence of events. "What happened after you were told?"

Captain Maddox replayed it in his mind. He remembered the President saying those awful words 'killed in action'. When they were told, Speaker Daniels arm shot around Nancy first, thus, it was his shoulder she cried into. The President and General Mason averted their eyes. It wasn't that they hadn't been in the presence of grieving parents; in fact over the past few years it was a position they had found themselves in all too often. Their discomfort was due to the fact that Daniels was blatantly letting his affection for Mrs. Maddox show, at a time when he should have known to take a step back.

To Captain Maddox, even though their marriage had been more of a long distance friendship over the last decade, Daniels deserved a punch in the face. However, he wasn't about to create havoc in the Oval Office. The worst part of it was that Nancy was so shattered by the news she had no idea whose shoulder she was sobbing into.

Captain Maddox kept the details of who comforted his wife to himself. He was not willing to turn his son's death into fodder for the tabloids.

"Did you wonder why the President was telling you in person?"

"Not at first. I just stood there listening to Nancy's sobs, replaying BJ's whole life in my mind. After a few minutes it dawned on me, so I asked the President about it. He told us that BJ was a true American hero. At first I thought he was just feeding us the same tired line he told every parent, or spouse, or child of a fallen soldier, and I must have given him an unenthusiastic thanks or something. He grabbed me by my arm, looked me in the eye and told me, 'Your son's selfless actions have saved millions of lives!' I couldn't for the life of me grasp what he was getting at. The only thing that flashed through my head was Pat Tillman's poor family testifying before congress about being lied to by the military about their son's death."

"Did you say anything to the President?" Ms. Collins asked, seeming to pay true attention to Captain Maddox's words and forgetting she was actually interviewing him.

"I pushed him away and told him he better not try to pull any of that Pat Tillman BS. That was one of the greatest kids of his generation who had it all and gave it all for his country and they put his family through the ringer just to try and get some good P.R. I told him, 'Just because my son's mother is a Senator, we're not going to use that as ammunition against the people who say politician's families don't make the same sacrifices that most average Americans do.'"

"So is it true," she asked, "everything they've told us about your son?"

"Everything they have come out with is true," he replied. She pondered his words, and then asked, "What haven't they come out with?"

"I haven't paid much attention to the media lately," Captain Maddox said apologetically. "What's the latest that has come out?"

"Well," Ms. Collins said, running through the chronology of the events of the past few months in her mind, "last week I interviewed your son's C.O. He said their ranger unit had been actively tracking weapons shipments through Afghanistan. Your son was part of a small contingent of the unit that stumbled upon a massive transport caravan. The four men, including your son, did not retreat. They held their ground, even though they were outgunned."

"Outgunned!" Captain Maddox snorted indignantly. "It was a hundred and fifty against four!"

"I know," she said, seeming to be caught up in the fantastic story the country seemed to have an endless appetite for, "NBC released the drone video of it last week." Then, losing herself in her own fascination with the story, she said with tempered excitement, "People are comparing your son's last stand with that of King Leonidis and his Spartan warriors."

"If only they had gotten air support," Captain Maddox said under his breath. The words must not have been as soft as he intended, for Ms. Collins heard them, and not realizing they were simply the woeful longings of a father, she took them as permission to take the interview down another avenue she wished to get on record.

"Pakistan denies giving support to the group," she said antagonistically, trying to provoke a reaction she had not been able to drag out of any of her interviewees in Washington.

"You can't block U.S. Military transmissions with signal scramblers purchased in an Afghani market," scoffed Captain Maddox. She started to say something in obvious hopes of inciting an even more damning statement against Pakistan, when he interrupted, "Don't bark up that tree." Unwittingly, he used the same verbal road block the President had used on him.

Tired of having the Pakistan door shut in her face, she went back to the topic she was having success with. "The video shows your son's daring dash at the transport vehicles, Hollywood couldn't have produced anything that looked more dangerous or heroic." She paused but he said nothing.

His silence must have made her think back to his earlier statement about the truthfulness of the government. "Hollywood didn't produce it, did they?" she asked in the tone of a child on the verge of putting the Santa Clause mystery together.

"No," he said with a slight laugh at her conspiratorial connotations, "there's no soundstage where they fake lunar landings and military actions."

He let his mind slip into the images of the video. As it replayed in head, his mind took a more omniscient view. The scenes played out in his imagination, not as if he were watching the black and white thermal images from a bird's eye view perspective of the drone, but as if he were there, next to his son.

"So your son planted his personnel location transmitter on the truck, sacrificing himself."

"Regrettably."

"Regrettably?" Ms. Collin questioned as if there were some threshold which could be passed, where pride could trump grief. "Sir, that truck contained fifty nuclear warheads. It was stopped because your son made the ultimate sacrifice; he put the lives of countless millions ahead of his own."

As she lectured Captain Maddox, he began to fill with rage. She took his smoldering silence as permission to continue with her lecture. "It would be an understatement to say your son is anything less than the greatest hero the world has ever known."

He could not contain himself. Even though he had been personally briefed by the President, and reminded repeatedly by the Secretary of Defense of the extreme classification of the information he had been privy to, he couldn't hold back any longer.

"It doesn't matter!" he screamed. "There were two trucks! We only took out half the shipment!"

"What are you saying?" Ms. Collins said in disbelief.

"That's what they're not telling the American people. My son's sacrifice doesn't make a damn bit of difference. You'll wake up one morning and millions of people will have died anyway."

A wave of shock swept over Ms. Collins as she looked up to be met by the ghostly pale gaze of Dave. At that point she must have sensed she was about to lose the interview, and even though the shock of the news she had just heard was still fresh, her journalistic instincts kicked in.

"Do you think that would have made a difference to your son?" The Captain did not reply. "Wouldn't you have done the same thing?"

"I never got the chance!" Captain Maddox screamed back. It was a statement which surprised even himself. He had been so reluctant to accept his son's place in history, telling himself his grief was too great to share his son's memory with the world. He never, for a moment, entertained the thought that his own lack of martial glory would be the reason his son's death was so hard to accept.

She must have sensed her unbridled time with Captain Maddox was slipping away, so she pounced on the question America would be waiting on the edge of their seats for her to ask. "Did you see the video?" she asked as sympathetically as she could.

The pause which came next was so long, it seemed the interview had just ended. She was about to give Dave the sign to kill the camera when she heard

Captain Maddox clear his throat of a soft sob. He began to speak as if he were in great pain.

"The day it hit the airwaves, I didn't feel like talking to anyone. I didn't go back to work after lunch. I drove out to Ft. Eustis, just to watch soldiers going about their daily business in their uniforms. The uniform I had given my son so much grief for donning. It had been two weeks since the President told me my son was dead, and I just felt closer to him by seeing the soldiers. After driving around the base for a few hours, I headed home. It must have been about eighteen thirty, when my phone started ringing off the hook. As I said, I wasn't in the mood to talk to anyone so I turned it off. It didn't dawn on me that my friends were trying to warn me."

His breathing became more rapid as his near gasps chopped off every word.

"I came home, poured a drink, stood in front of the TV," his voice cracked as it raised an octave.

Hearing the pain in his voice, tears began to run down Ms. Collins' cheeks. The day which he was speaking of, she had been flying around the news room after a contact in Pakistan had delivered the video to her. While Captain Maddox had been spending the afternoon grieving the loss of his only son, she had been in meetings, fighting with the network heads about the viewable content on the tape.

"When I turned it on the screen was black, but I could hear chanting and I heard," he began choking on sobs, "I heard my son screaming. The screen was black but I knew it was him, I knew it was his scream. I knew every sound my son made. I knew the sound of his sneezes, I knew the sound of his coughs, I knew the sound of him breathing in his sleep, and I knew it was my son screaming in horrible pain. I would have turned the TV off but I couldn't. I was frozen. I heard men chanting in a language I didn't understand, but my son did. I heard him defiantly screaming back at them in their own language. I heard the sounds of violence. I heard two men scream in pain."

He paused as he tried to get his breathing under control. Ms. Collins wiped her tears away as if they burned. She was forced to live the moment, not as a reporter removed emotionally from the story, but as a parent having their heart afflicted with the most painful moment of their life. She looked as though, for the first time in her career, she felt regret after asking a question.

"I heard *my son* scream the word 'perseverance,' then I heard gurgling! Gurgling! The last sound I ever heard my son make!"

The words, *my son*, seemed to pierce her heart. She had seen the video in its entirety, with the exception of the end; she had covered her eyes when the young American soldier was decapitated. Now, hearing the complete heartbreak in his father's voice, she choked on her apparent self-loathing. She had fought so hard to put the tape on the air. After a few moments of silence, the Captain broke it. Venomous anger filled his voice as he spat.

"Then *you* came on the screen and told *me*, I had just listened to the last moments of *my* son's life."

Then, in an uncharacteristic break from submarine discipline, Captain Maddox slammed his elbow against the door, jostling Ms. Collins' head back. She felt the blow through the door, having had her sobbing face pressed against it. Through tears and snot she whispered, "I'm sorry, I'm sorry." Returning to submarine protocols, Captain Maddox quietly slipped back to his stateroom, leaving her to grovel to the head door.

Hearing Dave's tearful gasps, she noticed him still pointing the camera at her. Burying her head between her knees, she slapped the air with her trembling hand signaling him to shut it off.

CHAPTER 15

Quinn was squatted in the ward room passageway performing an inventory of the weapons as he checked them back into the gun locker. "One clip-nine rounds," he said repeatedly as he checked the clips and put them back in their place. Scarpa came around the corner as Quinn was counting the rounds in the magazines which had been issued.

"Seven, thirteen, six," Scarpa interjected, trying to throw off Quinn's inventory count.

"Thirteen?" Quinn questioned with exaggerated surprise, "I didn't know A-gangers could count up to thirteen." Scarpa shot out what was a little more than a playful kick at Quinn's ribs. Quinn quickly pulled in his elbow to cover his ribs and take the blow.

"Sure we can count past thirteen," Scarpa said with a rare smile. "It usually goes like this; I banged your sister twelve times, I banged your sister thirteen times, I banged your-" Quinn, in the rare instance of not having a wittier comeback, rapped Scarpa in the shin with a pistol.

"Ow! Bastard!" Scarpa blurted out as he jumped backwards.

"Oh, that didn't hurt, you baby." Quinn laughed.

Scarpa stooped and rubbed his shin, "At least I wasn't counting the number of guys who banged her." Quinn tried to ignore him and returned to his counting. "I don't think there's a nuke on board who could count that high," Scarpa continued to run with the joke.

"Isn't there a head that needs to be unclogged or something?" Quinn said with a hint of venom in his remark. He was now starting to get a little impatient with Scarpa.

"Actually, the wardroom head needs a new valve handle on the faucet," Scarpa said as he pointed down the short passageway to the Officers' head at the end of it, "so I need to get by you."

"Don't let me keep you from your duties," Quinn said as he slid himself and the pile of guns he had in his lap closer to the gun locker. He held the heavy door of the gun locker with one hand so if the boat pitched suddenly, the door would not swing into Scarpa's leg as he stepped over the top of him.

"Hey, Scarpa," Quinn said in a hushed voice, "do things seem kind of off around here?" Scarpa looked at him as if nothing could be more ridiculous.

"Like what?"

"I don't know," Quinn shot back sarcastically, obviously insulted by Scarpa's haughtiness, "maybe the fact there's a bunch of guys we know nothing about running around here with automatic weapons."

"So what?" Scarpa said, blowing off any idea of impropriety with the situation.

"Well, what about having to jettison the weapons shipping harness?" Quinn continued his hushed assault on Scarpa's perceptiveness.

"I don't know," Scarpa said as he pulled a can of Skoal from his pocket, "maybe the clock was about to strike midnight and the sub was going to turn into a pumpkin." Quinn was starting to get aggravated with Scarpa's laissez-faire attitude. As he was about to pile on more strange happenings, Scarpa cut him off. "Dude, it's a Spec Op. Nothing is ever normal about a Spec Op."

Scarpa shook his canister of chewing tobacco with three rapid snaps as if he were playing an intense game of rock, paper, scissors. Then, he pulled a neatly packed wad of tobacco out and shoved it deep in his mouth between his gum and cheek. As Quinn watched the mechanic feed his nicotine habit, he remembered the white specs of cigarette ash on the fairwater plane. He knew of all the officers, the XO would have been the least likely to let Scarpa smoke up on the bridge. Remembering that Scarpa lay at the center of one of the most disturbing factors in his uneasiness, the loss of the XO, he decided not to press the issue any further.

"You're right," he said as he consciously tried to change his demeanor. "I guess if you don't have the need to know things always seem mysterious."

"Pretty much," Scarpa said taking Quinn's last statement as a capitulation. He started to turn into the head, then he paused and said, "Do you want to play chess after watch?"

As alarm bells went off inside of Quinn's head, he managed to squeak out, "I'll be there."

In all the time Quinn and Scarpa had been on board together, Scarpa had never asked Quinn to play chess or vice versa. Three years earlier, while on a very uneventful deployment, Quinn had challenged and beaten just about everyone on board. One evening, in the mess decks, Quinn had just won a quick match when Scarpa, who was sitting at the next table over, made an especially rude comment about Quinn's style of play. Quinn scooped up his board, set it up in front of Scarpa, and made the first move.

After three hours, Quinn found himself defeated for the first time since he had been on the sub. The match had been extremely close, and from that day on Quinn never squared off against anyone but Scarpa. Neither kept track of the number of wins or losses, or at least neither admitted they did, but since the very first impromptu match there had never been an invitation to play by either party. It was simply understood that when one was sitting in the mess deck the other would arrive and the match would start. It was never planned.

Scarpa nodded at Quinn then went inside the head and shut the door behind him. Quinn felt like his head was going to explode. There was so much going on which did not make any sense. The only conclusion he could come to was that he needed to be on his toes.

As he removed the last gun from its holster, he started to go through the mundane routine of counting the rounds in the clip. His mind was so preoccupied; he almost failed to realize he counted nine rounds in the clip, when in actuality there were only five. After realizing his mistake, he picked up the pistol he had taken the clip out of and cycled the chamber. One round popped out. He emptied the rounds out of the magazine just to be sure. Only six rounds including the one which was in the chamber. He checked the inventory number on the pistol against his issue list. It was the pistol he had issued Captain Maddox.

His mind was now in overdrive. He felt as if he had three pieces to a thousand piece puzzle. At once, it came back to him that Captain Maddox had fired off a couple of shots topside. His mind began to ease its pace. *That's right, the Captain fired three rounds into the air*, he thought, *no, it was two*. He replayed the scene in his mind. He had been looking right at Captain Maddox when he pulled his pistol out. He was sure. He distinctly remembered Captain Maddox squeezing off two rounds. *But I didn't chamber a round for him*, Quinn thought.

Quinn had issued Captain Maddox a .45 caliber Colt M1911. If he had issued him one of the boat's Beretta M9 nine millimeter pistols, a round would not have needed to be chambered. Having a double-action trigger, simply squeezing the trigger on the Beretta would have automatically chambered, and then fired the first round. However, with the Colt, the trigger mechanism was single-action, meaning the chamber would need to be manually cycled to load a round. Even if stress had altered his memory, and Captain Maddox had actually fired three rounds, Quinn knew he would not forget the Captain cycling the chamber first. It would have stuck out in his mind as seeming a little too Hollywood for Captain Maddox. So the question lingered, *when did the Captain chamber and fire the first round?*

Exhausted from thinking about all that had transpired in the past 48 hours, Quinn placed the items and the inventory list back into the gun locker and started to shut the door. He hesitated. Then, unzipping his coveralls half way, he reached into the locker, pulled out one of the Berettas, slapped in a clip and then shoved the weapon into his coveralls.

As Quinn secured the locker, he did not notice Scarpa spying on him through the slightly ajar head door.

Later that night, just before the watch sections were going to change, the Nav made a rare trip down to the lower level. As he reached the foot of the ladder he could see Scarpa taking logs in the auxiliary machinery room. Scarpa looked up and noticed the Nav coming towards him. "Petty Officer Scarpa," the Nav called out in a voice that was trying to be hushed, yet loud enough to be heard over the whir of the machinery. Scarpa turned his back and walked further into the depths of the machinery room. The Nav followed Scarpa to where he had stopped to take a reading off the CO_2 scrubbers.

"Scarpa, I'm talking to you," the Nav said impatiently as he grabbed Scarpa by the arm to get his attention.

Scarpa slapped his hand away. "I know, but I don't think you want to stand right in the doorway so any limp dick strolling by can eavesdrop."

The Nav, feeling inept in his covertness, relented, "You're right, good point."

Not waiting on the Nav, Scarpa continued to fill out the readings on his machinery logs. The Nav jumped back into his mode of urgency, "We've got a problem."

Scarpa, now taking interest, stopped to listen. "What is it?"

"It's Petty Officer Pope," the Nav continued, "I didn't have any choice but to knock him in the head. He was about to put the entire mission in jeopardy!"

"So what's the problem?" asked Scarpa not seeming to match the Nav's sense of urgency.

"I don't know if he saw me," the Nav said, bordering on panic. "He was turning around as I hit him."

"You hit him pretty good though," Scarpa said, almost hinting at admiration. "He's pretty much in a coma. If he hasn't come out of it by now, I think you're safe."

"But Doc says his condition is showing signs of improvement. If he comes to, he might remember what I did."

Scarpa looked as if he were deeply considering a remedy to the situation, but then he coldly stated, *"You've* got a problem." He started to return to his duties, when the Nav grabbed him by both arms and started to shake him as if he were a disobedient child.

"We're in this together," the Nav said almost completely uncontained. "I need you to take him out!"

Scarpa flung his left arm up and outward in a circular motion, clamping down an over hook on the Nav's right arm. At the same moment, he shot his right hand up, easily stripping the Nav's weak grip, and caught the Nav by the throat. His powerful fingers squeezed the Nav's neck, pinching off the man's airway. As he squeezed, he pushed his weight down on the Nav, bending him backwards over the auxiliary hydraulic pumps.

Scarpa eased his grip slightly to allow the Nav to take a few gasps of air. He put his mouth right up to the Nav's ear. "We are not in this together," Scarpa hissed. "I am in this with the Captain, and in case you are as blind as you are ignorant, there is a much bigger problem than Pope." The Nav winced in pain as the metal pump dug into his lower back. In this new world of deceit he had entered, rank carried no protection. Before that moment, he had never been physically attacked by a subordinate.

As Scarpa chose to let oxygen make its way back to the Nav's bloodstream, he continued his tirade in the Nav's ear. "Why are you worrying about a guy lying unconscious in his rack, when you have a whole crew asking questions about what the hell is going on aboard this submarine?" He shoved the Nav away and disappeared around the corner. The Nav stood up trying to compose himself.

A few minutes later the Nav made his way through the mess deck. Normally, the crew's mess would be filled with off-watch sailors carrying on as they played video games or watched movies, but as the Nav walked through, the silence was deafening. There were a number of off-watch sailors but they seemed to be huddled into small groups, talking in hushed whispers. The few sailors who did look up and take notice of him seemed to pierce him with accusatory eyes. He quickened his pace, and sprang up the ladder to the navigation equipment space.

When the Nav entered Captain Maddox's stateroom, he was shocked to find Captain Maddox in such an abysmal state. The man he looked to for reassurance had all but disappeared. In front of him sat Captain Maddox, elbows resting on his knees so his hands, clutching two fistfuls of hair on the side of his head, kept him from falling headlong to the deck.

"Captain," the Nav said softly, "sir?" Captain Maddox did not acknowledge his presence in any way. "Sir, may I have a word?" the Nav

145

implored. The Captain slowly raised his head. Not waiting for a reply to his rhetorical question, the Nav addressed him. "Sir, if I may, I don't think the crew is following the plan as blindly as we had hoped they would." Captain Maddox looked as if he struggled to comprehend what the Nav had said. "Captain, the men are very uneasy."

Captain Maddox pulled himself to his feet, walked over to his sink and splashed some water on his face. The Nav waited to say anything more. Once the Captain had toweled off his face, he asked the Nav, in a thin voice, what he meant. Out of the necessity, and unconscious mimicry, the Nav replied in the same nearly inaudible voice. "The crew, Captain, I think a lot of them are freaked out right now."

"Freaked out," Captain Maddox repeated, "they're freaked out, eh?" He began to raise his voice. The Nav motioned with his hand to keep his volume from creeping any higher. In a raspy forceful whisper, he got in the Nav's face, "What about you Nav! Are you freaked out too?"

The Nav tried to calm him by speaking in an even tone, "I'm fine Captain." The technique had not worked, Captain Maddox spoke with even more force to his voice, but he managed to keep his volume low enough to not be heard outside of the room.

"You're fine? You're fine?" he railed. "It didn't bother you at all to see your Captain blow that kids brains out?"

"Actually," the Nav said still attempting his calming tactic, "I haven't had a chance to give it much thought." It seemed he was not lying. Until Captain Maddox brought it up, it appeared as though he hadn't given it a fleeting thought.

"Well I'm glad that one of us won't be losing any sleep over it," Captain Maddox said, seething with disdain.

The Nav seemed to realize Captain Maddox wasn't upset with anything he had done, but was upset with the way events had transpired. "We made our bed; we have to sleep in it." The Nav's unintentional play on words came across a little condescending, but after months of the Captain Maddox's relentless diatribes against the Navy and how it had callously tossed them aside, he seemed to be losing his patience with his Captain's lack of fortitude.

Captain Maddox was a bit stung by the Nav's remark. It wasn't the Nav's lack of candor that bit at him; it was the fact that he had foreseen having to prod the Nav at every turn. Now, it was the Nav who verbally knocked some sense into him. He collected himself as he returned to his bunk. He sat down, clinched up the sheets as he balled his hands into fists, drew a deep breath, and then released the tension. As he looked up at the Nav, his resolve was renewed for the moment. In a voice that more resembled the calming tones of the Nav's, he asked, "What exactly do you mean the crew is *freaking out*?"

Appearing to be relieved that Captain Maddox had not abandoned ship mentally, the Nav explained what Scarpa had said to him. However, he did leave out the reason why he had been conversing with Scarpa in the first place. He, as well as Captain Maddox, knew after being involved in a special operation there usually was an intoxication that affected the boat. Even the nukes, who came off watch from the engine room, not having any idea of what had transpired, would be caught up in the buzz which would erupt into a party on the crew's mess. Captain Maddox stood up and began to pace the small room.

"That does worry me, Nav," he said.

The Nav scooped up the picture of Captain Maddox and his son off the deck. Captain Maddox turned to see the Nav hanging the picture back in its spot on the bulkhead. "Thank you," he said under his breath. Before the Nav could acknowledge him, he started thinking out loud. "We've got a day and a half of running fast and deep," he said. "That is a lot of down time with nothing to distract them."

"We could run through some drills," the Nav blindly threw out the suggestion.

"No, that is the quickest way to fan the flames of mutiny."

"We could fabricate another flash message." The Nav couldn't even finish the thought before Captain Maddox vetoed the idea.

"That would just create even greater suspicion," Captain Maddox said, adding, "It might *freak 'em* out even more."

The verbal jab noticeably irritated the Nav. Captain Maddox seemed to be making fun of his use of slang, obviously forgetting that moments earlier the Nav was on the verge of slapping him to keep him from going into hysterics like a high school drama queen.

"That's it," exclaimed the Nav. Then, lowering his voice he explained himself. "We need something that is not only going to distract them, but will lift their spirits."

"What would that be?"

"Well, we came within a hundred miles of the equator." As the Nav said this, Captain Maddox immediately saw what he was getting at.

"Shellback!" the Captain exclaimed.

As part of Naval tradition, when a ship crosses the equator the crew holds a Shellback ceremony. The Shellback ceremony was an initiation. Sailors, who had previously crossed the equator, and had been initiated, were known as Shellbacks. Sailors, who had not yet reached this nautical milestone in their journeys at sea, were known as Pollywogs.

There were no formal guidelines to the ceremony, but it usually consisted of some mostly harmless hazing, such as a prequalifying medical exam performed with tongue depressors that had been soaked in jalapeno juice. Usually an ominous riddle was read aloud over the 1MC to make the Pollywogs think they had to show up to the initiation with a shaved leg. The catch was they were not sure if it was supposed to be the right or left. The whole thing had been so tamed down over the last few decades for fear of reprisals against Commanding Officers who presided over the Shellback ceremony that many boats did away with them and just handed out certificates.

"Talk to the COB, have him inform the crew," said Captain Maddox.

"Yes, sir. Also, I'll talk to Petty Officer Ruddick and remind him that as the Quartermaster of the Watch during a Spec Op, he cannot discuss the coordinates of the ship with anyone." With that, the Nav left the Captain's stateroom.

Later that night, as the crew buzzed with excitement about the impending Shellback ceremony and tried to figure out who among them were the Shellbacks and who were the Pollywogs, Captain Maddox lay in his rack tossing and turning. In his dreams, he found himself standing in the passageway of Cortez's ship. Just as it had been in reality, two guards held a captured spy. He was again holding his gun to the spy's head. Cortez, like before, was shouting *kill him*. Only, this time he was not pointing a gun at the Nav's head, he was pouring gasoline onto a duffle bag which was filled with neat stacks of one hundred dollar bills. Captain Maddox shouted, "No!" but Cortez pulled out a Zippo lighter, and held it over the bag. Captain Maddox turned to the spy and pulled the trigger. Before the man's lifeless body had crumpled to the deck he turned to see Cortez dropping the lighter. Instantly, the bag was engulfed in flames. He ran to the bag, dropped to his knees and started beating the flames with his bare hands.

As he made an impossible attempt to put out the flames with his hands, his skin began to blister and blacken. Even with the excruciating pain, he was undeterred. He was starting to make some progress in dampening the flames when the blood, which had been pooling from the dead spy, started to seep into the duffle bag. He scooped the bag up and held it over his head. As he did this, he looked at the spy's lifeless body on the deck and realized it was his son.

"BJ!" he exclaimed, and began to run towards his son's corpse. His remorse was overwhelming. He wanted to get to his son and hold him, but as he ran towards him the corridor seemed to stretch longer and his son's body began to get further and further away. The faster he ran, the more the distance grew. His feet sloshed in the blood which was now ankle deep as he ran, still holding the flaming duffle bag over his head.

Realizing he would never reach his son, his legs gave out. He fell face down into the endless pool of blood. The duffle bag tumbled over and the flames were extinguished by the blood.

Captain Maddox sat straight up in his bunk as the general alarm was going off.

CHAPTER 16

Captain Maddox came stumbling into the control room just as the COB was following up the general alarm with an announcement of reveille and a call for the crew to post up for the Shellback ceremony, which would commence as soon as the galley crew had secured from breakfast. The COB's words trailed off when he looked up and beheld Captain Maddox.

When the Nav talked to the COB about having the Shellback ceremony, he had mentioned that Captain Maddox was looking a little rough. After a night of anything but peaceful sleep, Captain Maddox, standing before the men in nothing but his stretched out whitey tighties, looked like a schizophrenic hobo.

"Skipper," the COB said in a voice thick with concern, surprise, and horror, "you look like dog squeeze."

Everyone in the control room party was clearly happy to have the COB there, he was the only who dared tell Captain Maddox the truth, and he had a way with verbiage which was, if not poetic, definitely colorful. Hearing the tone of the COB, Captain Maddox became aware of the way his crew was gawking at him. He began to realize he was wearing his toils on the outside. He nervously rubbed the two day beard growth adorning his chin. In a flash, the tirade he was about to beset on the COB was gone. He simply said in a low voice, "COB, let that be the last time you use the general alarm for anything but an emergency." Without waiting for a response, he turned and walked back to his stateroom.

The COB, who, under normal circumstances, would put on a show about how "he was the old man of the boat" as if it were some sort of justification to do things he would jump down other people's throats for, stood speechless. As Captain Maddox disappeared out of the control room, the COB offered up a quiet apology.

"It will be the last time, sir."

Everyone sat as if frozen. Then, the COB slapped his hands together in a thunderous clap which seemed to shatter the ice encasing the sailors. His voice boomed, "Let's fry us up some Pollywogs!" The sailors' moods in the control room began to liven up again, although a dark cloud seemed to be ominously hovering over their excitement.

Later that morning, when the Shellback ceremony was in full swing, Captain Maddox managed to put on a better face. He presided over the ceremony playing the part of King Triton, passing judgment on the Pollywogs and determining if they would be bestowed with the honor of becoming a Shellback.

The deck of the crew's mess was covered with a mixture of rice, beans, ketchup, mustard and any other food supplies the cooks felt they had an abundance of. After going through a rigorous exam in the lower level, they would be brought before King Triton. Coming before the King of the Deep meant a Pollywog had first crawled with his face down and his hands behind his back through the cooks' concoction on the deck to grovel at the feet of the King.

At this point, the Pollywogs thought they were done. They had already endured the medical exam, which left their eyes watering and their mouths burning. Then they were sanitized in an ice cold shower, and finally, after failing the riddle (no matter if they shaved just their right leg, just their left leg, or both) they had to drink bilge water, which was a combination of apple juice, brown food coloring and cottage cheese. They were then sent up to middle level to go before the court.

When they reached middle level they were blindfolded, made to believe they were having half of their head shaved and then forced to crawl to the King for judgment.

The King did not show any mercy. He would sentence them to retrieve a ruby from the Sea Witch. The Sea Witch was played by Senior Chief Brady, a Nuke Machinist Mate who had one of the biggest bellies on board. His head was adorned with a makeshift turban and he sat shirtless on top of one of the tables. His large belly was smeared with peanut butter, and a cherry was pushed into the cavern which he called a belly button. Being Pollywogs, they technically had not formed arms yet so they would have to retrieve the ruby (cherry) without the use of their hands. After they deposited the ruby at the foot of King Triton's throne, he would declare the honor of Shellback upon them.

Captain Maddox was pressing on in good form. He had cleaned himself up and merely looked like any of the sailors who had not had much sleep in the last few days. The ceremony was progressing quickly due to the fact the boat had crossed the equator on a deployment a year earlier. This meant there were less than two dozen Pollywogs to be initiated. This pleased Captain Maddox. The pomp and circumstance would have its diversionary effect without subjecting him to an entire day of torturous acting.

Quinn, having been through the Shellback ceremony on two previous occasions, didn't feel the urge to take part this time around. His mind was mostly preoccupied with piecing together the informational gaps in the events of the past few days. He walked across the backs of the Pollywogs who were crawling on the deck. He wasn't necessarily doing it to be mean, he just didn't want to get his shoes dirty on his way to the galley. Besides, the Pollywogs were blind folded and wouldn't be able to tell who it was. As he came to the galley door, he found Carter and Grant watching the ceremony. They caught him as he sprang through the door.

"Hey, Quinn," Grant greeted him, "I figured you'd be down in lower level torturing these guys." Quinn went to the back of the galley looking for anything good to eat that the guys might have hidden.

"I'm not into it this time around," Quinn said as he checked out the strawberry chiffon pies in the pie rack. "May I?" he asked, pointing to the pies.

"Sure," Carter said with sarcasm, "we made 'em just for you." Quinn paid him no attention, mostly because he knew they would have made themselves at least one extra pie.

"What's buggin' ya, Quinn?" Grant asked as he pulled out a pie and sliced him off a piece.

"Thanks," Quinn said, as he took the desert. "I just feel like this isn't our same boat." He hesitated, waiting for the same condescending reaction he received from Scarpa. Grant pounced as if he was waiting for someone to broach the subject.

"Dude, I was just tellin' Carter that things are rotten in Denver."

"Denmark," Quinn politely corrected.

"Yeah, there too," Grant agreed.

"Talk to me, Goose," Carter said, coming to life. He seemed not to accept Grant's suspicions, but was more than willing to jump on Quinn's band wagon, "what do ya got?"

"Goose?" Quinn questioned. "Don't you think I would be Maverick and you would be Goose?" He was happy whenever he could relate in loose conversation.

Making word plays on literary references came naturally to him, but when it came to movies, he was usually at a loss. His movie watching experience was limited mostly to what he had seen on the boat, and the guys tended to watch a few select movies over and over. He had seen Top Gun, however, so as the occasion presented itself he didn't breeze over the opportunity to connect as if he had had a normal upbringing.

Before Carter could explain why he was more suited to be cast in the role of Maverick, a case he was eager to make despite outweighing the character by a hundred and eighty pounds, Grant interjected, somewhat offended.

"I thought I was Goose," he said, as if he was a spurned sibling playing a game of dress-up.

"Didn't Goose die?" Quinn asked, laughing. "Why would you want to be the guy that died?" Grant was about to explain, when Quinn decided to bring the conversation back to topic. He found with Grant and Carter it was quite easy to get lost on a tangent.

"Anyway," Quinn started to explain, "I've been going over everything in my head and things aren't adding up."

"Yeah, like why are we having a Shellback ceremony when we didn't cross the equator?" Grant asked, as if the question could no longer be held back.

"What do you mean?" Quinn asked. He didn't have the slightest clue what Grant was talking about.

"Shut up, you idiot!" Carter said, throwing his towel at Grant. "Ichabod here thinks we didn't cross the equator," Carter added, acting as if Quinn would find it as inconceivable as he did. Ignoring all Carter had to say except the Sleepy Hollow reference, Quinn repeated his question.

"I ask again, Mr. Crane, what do you mean?" Grant seemed none too pleased with the insinuation that he looked like Ichabod Crane, or with how fast Quinn had picked up on it. Ever since his fifth grade teacher showed the class Disney's take on the Washington Irving classic, he had been plagued by his obvious resemblance to the unfortunate character.

"What I mean is exactly what I said," Grant grunted as he threw the towel back at Carter. "We never crossed the equator."

"How do you know that?" pressed Quinn.

"He doesn't," said Carter, with the exhaustion of someone who had been arguing the same point all day long.

"Yes, I do," said Grant as he sprung into action, "check this out." He reached his hand down into the sink where he had some pans soaking. He pulled the rubber plug and the standing water began to swirl down the drain. "You see, the water always drains counter-clockwise," Grant explained. "If we had gone below the equator, it would have switched directions and drained clockwise." Quinn found himself starting to side with Carter.

"Is that real?" he asked.

"Sure it is. I saw it on Mr. Wizard when I was a kid." Grant rebutted.

"So you pay attention to the way the water drains every time you do dishes?" Quinn asked earnestly.

"I do," Grant said.

"Well, it just switched directions," Quinn said, noticing the draining vortex of water had switched to a clockwise rotation. Grant stared at the water in disbelief.

"I think your theory is all wet," Quinn said as Carter added a rim shot sound effect.

"Okay, so maybe there's nothing to that," Grant said without giving up, "but the kicker is when I asked Ruddick, who was the Quartermaster on watch at the time we would have crossed, he told me he couldn't talk about it."

Quinn, not yet hopping on board with the theory, said, "It's classified, he can't talk about it."

"I know that, but it's Ruddick we're talking about here," Grant continued to defend his point emphatically. "Even if we hadn't crossed the equator, he would have tried to convince me we were sittin' off the coast of North Korea." Quinn knew, as well as anybody, Ruddick was an embellisher. He knew Ruddick would try and convince anyone he was eight feet tall if he thought there was a chance they'd believe him.

"He just said 'it's classified' and that's it?" Quinn asked.

"That was it, end of story, he just turned and walked away," said Grant.

"Walked away?" Quinn said as if he needed anymore clarification.

"Yep," said Grant proudly, seeing that not only was Quinn coming around, Carter had stopped trying to pretend he wasn't interested, "just walked away."

"That is weird," Quinn agreed.

"You didn't tell me that," Carter said in a hushed voice as if their little group had just taken on the tone of a cabal.

"I didn't think I had to," said Grant scornfully.

"Whoa, you two aren't lovers are you?" Quinn joked at their almost spousal-like quarrel.

If Carter and Grant sometimes seemed like a married couple, it was completely understandable. Their time in the Navy had been spent almost completely together. They entered boot camp on the same day, and while they were not in the same company, their barracks shared a courtyard at Great Lakes Naval Training Center. When they arrived at the Mess Cook School, they recognized each other from brief encounters at boot camp and quickly became friends. After Mess Cook School they went on to Submarine School together. Thinking their time together had ended, but not their friendship, they were sent off to their new commands upon graduation from sub school.

Grant went to the Key West and Carter went to the Chicago. When Carter arrived on board the Chicago, it was the day before they went into an extensive dry dock refurbishment and that meant there would not be a galley for him to work in for two months. The day Grant arrived aboard the Key West, he was greeted by a slob of a sailor named Seaman Bill Pudnam who said he would take Grant under his wing. After showing Grant everything he needed to clean, Pudnam, being extremely hung over, stole away to the fan room to take a nap.

While taking a nap, he inadvertently pulled the rip cord on the life raft he was using as a pillow and found himself imprisoned in the small room by a wall of inflated rubber. Being only one of two life rafts on board the submarine, the Captain was not happy when it had to be destroyed to free Pudnam. Reducing the boats life raft inventory to one, the Key West was no longer certified, under naval regulations, to be deployed until the life raft was replaced.

When the Supply Officer informed the Captain there was none to be found in the base warehouses, the Captain turned to his fellow C.O.s to see if any boats were willing to part with theirs. Finding all the boats on the pier unwilling to give up their seagoing status to wait upon the navy supply system, a call was made to the Chicago, who would not need theirs for the next few months. When a pudgy cook named Carter came strolling down the pier carrying the raft which was to be handed over, the Captain procured him as well, since Pudnam had been dismissed from the Key West a half hour before Carter's fateful arrival.

So when Grant and Carter sometimes took on the role of a bickering couple, it was because they had spent nearly every waking hour together for the last three years. Some couples could be married for twenty years and not spend as many hours with each other as a submarine could force upon its crew.

"Ya know, I was talking with Rubber last night and he told me he thought he heard two gunshots over sonar yesterday," Carter said almost in a whisper. Quinn went white as a ghost.

"When did he hear them?" Noticing the paleness which had come upon Quinn, Carter's tone became even more serious.

"Yesterday," Carter said stammering, "while we were loading those things on board."

"Why," asked Grant, "what's that mean?"

Quinn's mind shifted to all ahead flank. He was trying to put everything he had already had questions about together with the information he had just received. "I'm not sure what it means, but-" Quinn was starting to form a thought when the door to the galley burst open.

Schmidt started to come in. "Where can I get a towel?" His blindfold was pushed up revealing only one eye with the rest of his face covered in food stuffs.

154

"Don't drip that crap in here," Carter shouted as his towel went flying at Schmidt's face. "Go rinse off in the bilge!" Carter rolled his eyes. "He's your nub," he said to Quinn. Quinn, blowing off the jibe, returned to his thought.

"Okay, we have to have a meeting, but we can't have it in here. There's too many people in and out of here," said Quinn.

"What about VLS?" Carter offered up.

"It's too close to the torpedo room," Quinn said. "I don't know if all those goons can understand English, but it's too risky."

"How about the aux tank in lower level birthing," Grant suggested.

"That would be perfect," agreed Quinn.

"I don't know," said Carter reluctantly, "there's gotta be somewhere better. What about back in the engine room?"

"Nothing will look more suspicious than a bunch of coners taking a little stroll in the engine room," Quinn said. "The aux tank it is."

"Who all is going to come?" Carter asked. The three exchanged glances, a question none had thought about until that moment.

"What about Ruddick?" Grant asked.

"Ruddick?" Carter questioned. "Are you an idiot, or did you forget he's wrapped up in this Rubik's cube of deceit." Grant shrank from his suggestion.

"Rubik's cube of deceit?" Quinn questioned Carter's corniness.

"Yeah, ya like that?" Carter said, puffing out his chest.

"Yeah," Quinn said with a smile. "You just come up with that or have you been working that out in your head for a while?"

"Came up with it just now," Carter beamed.

"Just like that," Quinn said with a snap of his fingers.

"Just like that," Carter said, imitating the snap, adding, "Ya know he said Ruddick, I thought Rubik's, hence the-"

Grant interrupted. "Guys, can we get back to our trivial pursuit?"

Carter and Quinn looked at Grant as though he ruined their day.

"His was clever," Quinn said to Grant. "Yours, not so much."

Carter brought the conversation back to reality. "We've got to have Rubber there."

"Definitely," Quinn agreed, "and I would add Sparks, but that's it for now."

"Why Sparks?" Grant asked, "Does he know something too?"

"I'm not sure if he knows anything," said Quinn, "but even if he doesn't, he's very resourceful and I think I speak for us all when I say we can trust him." Carter and Grant both nodded in agreement.

"Then it's settled, we'll meet in the Aux tank in fifteen minutes." Quinn was assuming his natural role as the group's leader. "Carter, you round up Rubber, I'll get Sparks." Quinn looked at his watch, "Show up first at sixteen twenty two, the rest of us at two minute intervals, Rubber will be second, Grant you're third, Sparks will be fourth and I'll be last." Quinn held out his watch, "Gentlemen, synchronize your watches!" Carter held out his cell phone and Grant held out his iPod, these being the items they kept track of the time on. "When I pictured that in my head, I didn't realize it was only going to point out how technologically deficient I am," Quinn said in mock sadness.

"Whatever you guys do, don't let Scarpa see you," Quinn warned.

"Why?" asked Grant. "Is he mixed up in this too?"

"We don't even know what *this* is yet," said Quinn, "but if *this* turns out to be truly a *this*, then I'd lay money down that Scarpa is up to his ears in it." Quinn started out the door when Carter quietly gave him a motherly warning.

"Be careful."

Quinn turned, smiled and shot back, "Veni, vidi, vici." The two looked at him blankly. Turning back, he treaded carefully through the chaos which was still taking place on the mess deck. *I am a Caesar with no Empire yet*, he thought to himself, *or maybe I'm Brutus.*

When the agreed upon time came, Quinn slipped quietly out of aft crew's berthing and slid down the ladder to the lower-level berthing compartment. When he entered the darkened space, he noticed Carter, slightly illuminated by the dim deck lights, kneeling next to the Aux tank hatch. Carter lifted the hatch door in the deck plates and without saying a word motioned for Quinn to head through the small opening. Quinn wasted no time making the descent into the absolute bottom of the boat.

The auxiliary tank was a small space that the cooks used to store dried goods. Unlike most compartments on the sub, it was pretty well sealed, making it an ideal place to have conversations which could not be easily overheard. As Quinn came down the short ladder, Grant turned on his flashlight. The red filter he had over the lens basked the compartment in an eerie glow. Quinn could see Rubber and Sparks had made it. They were seated on cartons of flour that were stacked up in between the frames of the inner hull. Sparks' knees were crammed up in his face. He spoke up before anyone else had a chance.

"Okay, Quinn's here, now would somebody tell me why I am?"

"I'll get to it," Quinn said in a tone which let him know it wasn't going to be a waste of time. "Isn't Carter coming down?" Quinn asked Grant.

"He said he'd stand guard," Grant replied. Quinn looked at Grant as if waiting for a further explanation. "Alright man," he admitted reluctantly, "he can't fit down the hatch anymore."

Looking at Sparks and Rubber, Quinn said, "Thanks for coming, guys."

Almost in unison, they replied, "No problem."

"Now, I don't know how much Carter and Grant told you," Quinn began.

"Nobody told me a thing except that I had to come down into this crummy little tank," Sparks complained.

"Yeah, Quinn, I'm out of the loop," seconded Rubber.

"Sorry about all the secrecy, there wasn't really any time to explain," Quinn said. Sensing a relax in their posture, Quinn took it as a sign of forgiveness. "I'm not sure if the two of you have noticed anything weird going on the past few days, but I don't even feel as if I am on the same boat we left port in," Quinn said. The others related the fact that they were feeling the same way, and began to spontaneously list all the strange happenings aboard the Key West.

"The Eng jumped down my throat this morning about something stupid," Sparks began "The only thing that saved me was that the evaporator was on the fritz again and he had to go deal with that mess."

"Don't be too hard on the Eng, I don't think he's gotten any sleep since we left port," Grant defended.

"Rubber, is it true that you heard two gunshots yesterday?" asked Quinn.

"Well, there is no way to tell if they were gunshots," Rubber tried to back off his earlier statement to Carter. "I don't really have anything to compare it too."

"What I have to tell you guys does not leave your lips," Quinn warned. They all shook their heads in compliance. "No, I'm serious, do not tell this to anyone. I have a feeling our lives might be at stake at this point," Quinn emphasized his warning. They all agreed verbally to keep their mouths shut. "Yesterday, I issued weapons to the officers and to the security detail. When I inventoried the weapons and ammunition upon return, there were three rounds missing from the Captain's pistol." They all were speechless. "So you can see why I became very interested when Carter told me you thought you heard two gunshots yesterday," said Quinn.

"So you think the gunshots I heard came from the Captain's gun?" asked Rubber.

"I saw him fire two rounds topside," Quinn stated, "so I'm thinking one of the shots you heard came from the Captain's gun."

"So what does all this mean?" Sparks asked.

"I don't know," Quinn admitted, "but what I do know is that I am not sure who is in control of the submarine anymore."

"Do you think the Captain is taking orders from those guys who came down with the cargo?" Grant asked.

"These are all questions we need answers to," Quinn said.

"The way I see it," Sparks offered up, "the first question is to find out what's inside those containers. If we know what we're dealing with we'll have some place to start."

"How are we going to do that?" asked Rubber, "Aren't those guys supposed to shoot anyone who comes close to them?"

"We need a diversionary tactic," said Quinn. Sparks snapped his fingers.

"That's it!" he exclaimed, "Grant, what was it you caught on fire in the oven that created all that black smoke?"

"Which time?" Rubber kidded.

"It was only once," Grant punched Rubber in the arm, "and it was pineapple upside down cake."

"That's right, it spilled in the oven when we took an unexpected angle," Quinn remembered.

"I've got an idea that just might work," Sparks declared.

"You see, Grant," said Quinn, "I told you he was resourceful."

CHAPTER 17

"Sparks, what's your status?" Quinn asked over the phone.

"I'm in position," Sparks said as he hunched in front of the ventilation control panel in the fan room.

"Grant, status?"

"We'll be ready to go in about fifteen seconds," Grant said as he held a flexible ventilation duct hose to the galley's ventilation port on the overhead.

"Okay, let me know when you're set," Quinn said as he and Rubber removed their EAB masks from the storage bags. "We're standing by."

Grant was using EB Green duct tape, an essential tool on any submarine, to attach the duct hose to the overhead port. Carter stood in front of the open stove. In one hand, he held a pan full of melted butter and in the other he held the open end of the duct hose. As Grant made an airtight seal on his end of the hose, air started to blow out Carter's end.

"I hope this works," Carter said reluctantly.

"The galley is ready to commence Operation Info-Gather," Grant declared over the phone.

"I thought we were going to call it Operation Sneek-a-Peek," Sparks protested from his end.

"I was more partial to calling it Operation Blue Lightning, but, hey, to each his own." said Quinn.

Grant, getting impatient, blurted out, "Who cares, just get it going!"

"If you insist," Quinn said, "Stand by...in three...two...one...go!"

Sparks, who was standing by at the ship's fan controls, reversed the galley's fan, turning the galley's ventilation port into an induction port. Then, he aligned the ventilation system to redirect the air it took in from the galley and exhaust it into the torpedo room.

At once, Carter noticed the air cease to blow from the hose. The duct hose he held had been transformed into a giant vacuum. He tossed his melted butter into the open oven. Immediately, black smoke poured out of the oven, only to be sucked into the ventilation duct he held.

In the torpedo room, two of the foreign guards kept watch over their cargo. Thick-black smoke began to bellow out of the overhead and quickly filled the room.

Abandoning all sense of decorum, the two goons bolted from the room out the aft door. As the aft torpedo room door came flying open, it blocked any view the guards would have had of Quinn and Rubber, who had stationed themselves in the Battery Well access port. As soon as the two guards had stumbled their way up the ladder to middle level, Quinn and Rubber slipped unnoticed into the torpedo room.

They quickly made their way to the forward end and plugged their EAB masks into the air manifold. They began a cursory inspection of the containers, looking for any sort of access panel in the smooth steel cylinders.

"Do you see anything?" shouted Quinn. Rubber slid his fingertips over the cold surface; feeling for a crease, or a bolt, anything which might indicate a way in.

"I can't feel anything," Rubber said, as he depended more on touch and less on sight as visibility shrank to almost nil.

Having no luck on the body of the container, Quinn moved his search to the forward end. "There's a cap here," he said as he pulled out a small screw driver.

Coming down the ladder from the upper level command passageway, Ramirez saw his two inept associates come stumbling up from lower level. In Spanish, he yelled at them, "Return to your posts!"

"But there's a fire down there," one of them replied. The acrid odor of smoke was just starting to creep up to middle level.

"All the men aboard this ship are trained to handle fires; you need to secure the cargo!" Ramirez shouted unsympathetically as he pushed the two down to lower level.

As the smoke was starting to diminish from the oven, Carter threw in a second round of melted butter. Once again the black smoke instantaneously poured out.

"That's probably enough," Grant said to Carter. Carter gave him a quick nod of agreement.

"Initiate diversionary tactic number two," Grant shouted into the phone as he ripped the ventilation duct from the overhead and stuffed it in the cabinet under the sink.

Sparks again repositioned the fans, this time setting the galley ventilation to its normal setting.

The return of normal ventilation was enough to start pushing the black smoke from the galley into the mess decks. Carter snatched up the 4MC emergency phone and alerted the control room of the fire in the galley as Grant slipped his EAB mask on and handed him one.

Within seconds, the announcement, "FIRE IN THE GALLEY!" came over the 1MC followed by the general alarm alerting the entire crew.

Quinn and Rubber had just loosened a third screw on the cap when the alarm went off. "That should buy us another minute or two," Quinn said as he was able to see some movement in the cylinders cap.

"I'm not sure if it's going to be enough time," Rubber said, as he noticed the black smoke already begin to thin out as it made its natural progression to the upper levels. Just then, a white powdery substance began to flow out of the cylinders head where Quinn had made a gap.

"Oh crap!" Quinn exclaimed as he saw the substance. He looked around for something to catch it in.

"There!" Rubber yelled, pointing at a cup behind Quinn. Quinn grabbed the cup and dumped the coffee in it onto the deck. He put the cup under the makeshift spout as Rubber began to tighten the screws back down on the cap.

Ramirez and the other two came down the ladder to lower level when the announcement came over the 1MC regarding the fire in the galley.

"You see, the fire is in the kitchen," he said, as he pulled three EAB's out of an emergency gear locker and handed them off to his two companions.

Ramirez pushed the two through the door. The first man through the door took the starboard side, the second man, followed by Ramirez, went to the port side.

As Rubber was tightening up the last screw on the cap, Quinn noticed a figure come around the corner. Though the smoke was still thick in the compartment, it had dissipated enough so the goon who had taken to the port side could see the two shadowy figures in the forward part of the torpedo room.

Quinn scooped up the mug containing the contraband, grabbed Rubber by the collar, and shouted, "Let's go!"

Noticing the two figures after he had plugged into the overhead manifold, the man bolted forward after Quinn and Rubber. Forgetting the hose from his mask only gave him about six foot of slack. The man felt as if someone had reached down through the overhead and tried to snap his neck. As he reached the end of his hose, his head was jerked backwards as his feet continued his body's forward momentum. This brought the man crashing to the deck flat on his back.

As Quinn and Rubber slipped past the weapons control panel in the forward section of the room, Ramirez was slowed by having to crawl over his companion. Hearing the commotion on the port side, the other goon left his search of the starboard side and came aft to offer any assistance he could. Ramirez, finally making his way to the forward end of the torpedo room, intended to give chase by the same route in front of the weapons control panel. However, his pursuit was cut short when he was brought to the deck having slipped in a puddle of coffee.

With the starboard side unguarded, Quinn and Rubber were able to make a hasty retreat up the forward torpedo room ladder to middle level and then slip unnoticed into the forward crew's berthing compartment.

When Ramirez managed to make his way up the forward ladder, all he could see was a mass of sailors flaking out fire hoses and charging down the passageway with fire extinguishers. He dropped back down the ladder and, with the air starting to clear up, ripped his EAB mask off in disgust.

As the boat made its way up to periscope depth to ventilate, Carter and Grant bravely put out the "fire" with the galley's fire extinguishers. The COB made his way through the crowd of sailors trying to get in on the fire fighting action.

"What in San Antonio is going on in here?" the COB barked.

"Sorry COB," Grant explained through his EAB mask, "we were trying to make a pineapple upside down cake in honor of the newest Shellbacks."

Pulling the remains of what was once a desert out of the oven, Carter explained, "I think we might have used too much butter."

"You think?" the COB said, bristling with too much anger to be mistaken for sarcasm. "The two of you would burn water trying to boil it," he continued to rail.

Quinn and Rubber had made their way to the towed array space. The towed array space was one of the smallest compartments on the submarine. Under normal conditions, only one or two Sonar Technicians would occupy the space as they worked the controls to let out or reel in the sonar array.

Quinn pulled off his EAB mask to make a closer inspection of the contents in the coffee mug. "What are you doing?" Rubber grabbed his arm in alarm. "What if that's anthrax?"

"Then I'm dead already," Quinn said carelessly. "Anthrax kills through contact." Rubber looked at his hands, which were covered with the white powder.

Just then, a knock at the door not only made Rubber jump, but also Quinn, who had been trying to play it cool. The door cracked open and Sparks poked his head in.

"Did you guys find anything out?" he said, as he maneuvered his large frame into the already cramped space. Regaining his composure, Quinn held out the coffee mug.

"This was inside the cylinder." Sparks looked in the mug. Upon seeing the white powder, he pressed his back against the door to get as far away as possible.

"Is that anthrax?" he asked, as he pulled his t-shirt over his nose and mouth.

Quinn was starting to feel the weight of how irresponsible his actions were. He now faced the reality that he might be responsible for not only the death of himself, but quite possibly the deaths of the entire crew.

"I sure hope it's not," Quinn said gravely, forgetting all the suspicions which drove him to his actions.

Taking the mug as if he had already accepted his death, Rubber asked, "You don't think it could be cocaine, do you?"

Suddenly, the pile of life jackets tucked away in the corner erupted. Stoney emerged from underneath the pile.

"Cocaine?" he asked, bright eyed. "Who's got cocaine?" Quinn and Rubber had practically jumped into Sparks' arms when Stoney popped up. As his heart came out of his throat, Quinn picked up a life jacket and started beating Stoney with it.

"What the hell are you doing?" he asked, straining his voice so it did not turn into a shout.

With his arms raised in front of his face to shield it from the life jacket beating, Stoney explained, "I didn't want to take part in that dumb drill so I came up here to nap."

"You idiot," Sparks chimed up, "that was a real fire."

"It was?" Stoney shrugged.

"Yeah, you're lucky we started it, otherwise you'd be dead," Rubber said, seeming to fish for Stoney to ask why they had started a fire.

"Whatever," Stoney said, blowing him off. "Somebody said something about cocaine."

"Here," Quinn said offering up the mug to him, "what do you think?" Stoney looked at the contents of the mug.

"What if it's anthrax?" he asked.

Before Quinn could answer, Sparks and Rubber blurted out simultaneously, "Then we're already dead." Quinn shot them a bitter look.

"You said it first," Rubber reminded him.

Stoney continued to inspect the mug, "Where did you get this?" Rubber started to open his mouth, but Quinn piped up before Rubber could say any more.

"It doesn't matter," said Quinn.

"I don't usually partake in the cola," Stoney assured them. "I usually prefer to dance with a little girl named Mary Jane." It was a statement which brought little surprise to the faces of the trio. "But I have been acquainted with this little flirt," Stoney confessed. He licked his pinky finger, dipped it into the powder and dabbed a sample on the tip of his tongue. Suddenly, as Quinn and the others watched in horror, Stoney's whole head turned purple. Drool started to come out of the corner of his mouth, his eyes rolled back in his head and he collapsed backwards. The three stood panic stricken; none of them could move a muscle.

After a few silent moments, Stoney's corpse, as it was now assumed to be, started to chuckle. As he sat back up, the others started to breathe again.

"Yeah, it's cocaine," he said, completely absent of any gloating at the prank he had just pulled off.

"Great," Quinn blurted out, "the Captain makes this huge bust and what do I do; I set the boat on fire just because I wasn't in the know."

"Hey now, Captain Pity Party," Rubber cut in, "remember why we decided to do this."

"Yeah," said Sparks, backing him up, "you were the one who laid out the evidence of mysterious things going on here."

Rubber added, "Like the goon squad, and the missing bullets."

"Not to mention the missing XO," Sparks reminded him.

Pulling himself up to his feet, Quinn slowly got back into the conspiratorial mode. "You're right," he relented, "things still don't add up if it was a simple confiscation."

"Yeah," Sparks continued, "do you think we would have tossed the weapons shipping harness over the side if we were just filling in for the Coast Guard?"

"Wait a minute," Stoney interjected, "what are you guys getting at?"

"That's just it," Rubber answered. "We don't know."

"Ah, there's the rub," Quinn said thoughtfully. Stoney looked at him with his head cocked to the side as if he were a perplexed dog, "The what?"

"It's the conundrum," Sparks tried to clarify. Still looking confused, Stoney asked, "Again, the what?"

"The puzzle, the obstacle, the impediment," Rubber snapped impatiently. "I'm going buy you a Thesaurus when we pull in."

"A whatasaurus?" Stoney asked again. Losing his patience, Rubber began hitting him with a life jacket.

"Jeez, I'm kidding, I'm kidding," Stoney said laughing. Rubber ceased his attack.

"This is serious, Stoney," Rubber lectured him.

"I know, but he's over here," Stoney said pointing to Quinn, "talking like he's in a play or something."

"Okay guys," Quinn said, getting them under control, "It's clear we don't have enough intelligence."

"I'll say," added Sparks.

Quinn shot him a look as if to say, *don't get it started*. Sparks pointed to Rubber and Stoney as if to plead a nonverbal case. "We need to find out what is being said behind closed doors," Quinn said.

"Is there anyone in the wardroom we can approach?" asked Rubber.

"Normally, I would say the Weps," Quinn answered, "but there's something funny going on between him and the Captain right now."

"Funny ha ha or funny strange?" Sparks asked, as he tried to sit down and stretch his legs across the entire space.

"They've been on edge," Quinn said, "kind of at each other's throats."

"I noticed the same thing," added Rubber.

"Man, we just need to bug the place," Stoney piped up.

"If only it were that easy," Quinn said.

"I can do it," said Sparks.

"Well, fill us in, Mr. Second Class Interior Communications Specialist," Quinn said, referring to Sparks' rank and rate.

"I can set up the phones to act as an open mic; leave the line open to a phone of our choice," Sparks explained.

"Brilliant, my man," Quinn said cheerfully. "Let's do it."

"Where?" Sparks asked, getting back up to his feet.

"The Captain's stateroom," Quinn said confidently.

"The Skipper ain't just gonna let you waltz into his stateroom and start messin' around with his phones," Rubber said, "especially if he's involved."

"Good point," Quinn sighed, as if his big plan had just been deflated.

"It can be done without going into his stateroom," Sparks assured him.

"It can?" questioned Quinn.

"Sure," Sparks said confidently, "someone can do it from the outboard."

"Great," Quinn said, "get to it."

"I can't do it," objected Sparks.

"Why not?" asked Quinn, well aware of Sparks' reasoning.

"Dude," Sparks exclaimed, "look at me." He stretched himself out to remind Quinn of his full height. As he straightened out his spine, he did it with a little too much gusto and cracked his skull on the overhead. "Ow," he exclaimed, shrinking back to his normally hunched stance and rubbing the top of his head.

"You see," he said as he winced in pain, "I'm too big to be crawling around in the outboard."

The outboard was the area of the submarine which lay between the frames of the hull and the bulkheads which had been constructed in the living quarters to make the submarine feel fit to live in. In the small space hidden behind the false wood paneling, there was a jungle of communication wires, hydraulic lines, power lines and anything else the engineers could cram in the space. All of it ran in and out of the frames for the entire length of the submarine. Quinn knew it was a tight fit, even for the most spry of sailors. It would be nothing shy of a miracle to get all six foot six of Petty Officer Sparks to make the precocious trek; however, there was no other option.

"You've got to do it, my friend," Quinn persisted. Sparks couldn't even believe Quinn was actually trying to talk him into it.

"Listen to you, my friend, my buddy, my pal," Sparks said mockingly. "No. No way."

Quinn continued to try and sweet talk him, "Come on, man."

"Oh, come on, man, nothing. I'm not doing it!" Sparks said emphatically. Quinn tried to appeal to his sensible side.

"If not you, than who else?" Quinn asked. "I certainly don't know the communications systems well enough to do what you proposed. Do any of you?" He gestured to Rubber and Stoney.

"What about Popper?" Sparks suggested. "He's an I.C. man too and he's a foot shorter than me and the only thing smaller than his waist is his shoulders." It was true; physically there was no better candidate than Seaman Samuel Popanov whom everyone referred to as "Popper".

"Yeah, but," Quinn argued, "that kid can't keep his mouth shut. He's like his own personal brand of Mountain Dew coffee. He'd get us caught in a second."

"Say no more," Sparks cut him off in a tone of defeat. "You're right. I'll do it." Sparks' words trailed off at the end so his surrender was barely audible.

Quinn knew he had him when he put forth Popper as the only other candidate. There was no amount of exaggeration which could be heaped on Popper's chattiness. On one deployment, Captain Maddox had "unofficially" ordered him to stop talking for three days.

"When should we do it?" Sparks asked.

"I figure now is as good a time as any," Quinn said, "with everyone still running around securing from the fire."

"Alright," Sparks said, "let's go get my gear." The pair turned and headed out of the towed array space. As if he could see the smile come across Stoney's face with eyes in the back of his head, Quinn turned around and confiscated the coffee mug from Stoney's hands.

"First, let's dump this in the head," Quinn said.

Sparks kept talking in a morbid tone, as if he hadn't heard any more Quinn had said. "I'll probably get stuck back there and you'll leave me to die."

CHAPTER 18

Quinn prepared an access point in the Combat Systems Electronic Space (C.S.E.S.) for Sparks to be able to crawl into the port side outboard. C.S.E.S. was the forward-most compartment on the upper level of the submarine. The plan was for Sparks to climb into the outboard from there and shimmy his way aft, past the XO's stateroom, until he was adjacent with the exterior bulkhead of the Captain's stateroom. From there, Sparks would be able to tap into Captain Maddox's phone without the risk of being discovered.

Quinn worked fast as he unbolted a locker that held firefighting equipment. He pulled the locker off its base and removed the last few items from the corner, to reveal a small opening outlined by high pressure air pipes. Sparks looked at the opening and protested once more.

"There's no way I'm fitting back there."

Quinn stepped behind him and pushed him towards the small hole, "Come on, quit being a baby, you'll fit." With a groan, Sparks put his small tool bag in his mouth and squeezed his shoulders into the opening. He wriggled and writhed and got all but his feet into the outboard. When his large boots got to the opening, they became caught up in some of the power cables.

"You're not going to be able to maneuver out there with these boats on," Quinn said as he slipped off Sparks' boots.

"Come on man, leave my boots on," Sparks beckoned.

"Forget it," Quinn said. "You'll have more toe dexterity to push yourself through."

"Toe dexterity," Sparks muttered. "I'll show you my toe dexterity, right up your ass."

Quinn pretended not to hear Sparks' last remark. "You're doing great man, all you have to do is squirm your way aft another twelve feet and you should be there." There was no reply from Sparks this time so Quinn went to work putting the D.C. gear locker back in place. As Quinn covered the hole, Sparks noticed the light diminish significantly. He hollered back to Quinn in the loudest tone he could manage without alerting anyone to his presence in the outboard.

"Quinn!" he called, "Quinn, what are you doing?"

"I have to put this back," Quinn explained, "otherwise it might raise suspicion." Quinn did a cursory tightening of the bolts then tried to reassure Sparks, "I'll come back for you, don't worry." With that, he was out the door and left Sparks to his task.

After leaving Sparks, Quinn headed down the ladder to middle level. As he stepped into the passageway, he saw the COB marching toward him. The COB looked especially exhausted. The shear pace of events over the last two days, combined with organizing an impromptu Shellback ceremony and then having to fight a fire had left the man drained. His eyes followed the deck plates as he walked. The flash hood from his EAB mask was still hanging around his neck. Quinn could see that his hair was drenched from sweat.

"Everything under control, COB?" Quinn asked in a voice which matched the exhaustiveness of the COB's look.

"It's fine," the COB said, absent any emotion. Seeing the toll the excursion of the fire emergency had taken on the COB, Quinn's itching sense of guilt returned. Whether it was out of guilt, or an overbearing sense that he was in over his head, Quinn made a snap judgment. Deviating from his own plan, Quinn asked the COB if he could have a word with him in the Chief's Quarters. With a sigh, the COB seemed to reluctantly agree.

"Sure," the COB said, "what's one more thing to deal with today?" Quinn didn't say anything else, he just followed the COB into the Chiefs' Quarters.

As he entered the Chiefs' small stateroom, Quinn's eyes scanned the head and the sleeping quarters to make sure the conversation would stay private.

"Have a seat," the COB motioned him to sit at the small table. "What's on your mind Quinn?" the COB said, feigning real interest.

"Well COB," Quinn began as the COB poured himself a cup of coffee, "there are some events which have occurred that have been bothering me." The COB rolled his eyes in his usual "could care less" way.

"Well, let me just bring the entire hamburger flippin' fleet to a screeching halt so that we might set your mind at ease," the COB snapped. Quinn shifted uncomfortably in his seat. The COB tugged on the pin on his coveralls, "Does this say Chief of the Boat or Oprah 'I give a crap' Winfrey?"

"Come on, COB," Quinn said trying to appeal to any soft spot which might be buried underneath the COB's crusty exterior, "I'm serious. I think there are less than honorable intentions driving this boat right now." The COB scoffed at Quinn.

"Listen to you," the COB shot out with a laugh. "Less than honorable intentions," he said mockingly. "You don't need to go to Officer Candidate School. After a statement like that I think we could have the Skipper award you a commission right now."

Even though Quinn was growing annoyed with the COB, he was also growing more confident he could bring the COB into the fold.

"COB!" Quinn yelled slamming his hand on the table and finally getting the COB's real attention. Returning to a hushed voice, Quinn said, "We are transporting the mother lode of cocaine in the torpedo room." The COB's face grew very grave. Suddenly, Quinn felt a wave of anxiety wash over him thinking he may not have given Sparks' mission a chance to find out more, yet he also felt relieved that he would not be responsible for all the decisions from here on out.

"How do you know this?" the COB asked. "I don't even have the clearance to know what we are transporting."

"I peeked." confessed Quinn.

"You what?" said the COB, raising his voice.

"There were just too many things unaccounted for," Quinn tried to explain.

"Things don't add up for you so you just decide to shrug your shoulders at national security," the COB lectured.

"It wasn't like that, COB," Quinn said with the timidity of a mouse.

"It doesn't matter what it was like," the COB said as his anger peaked.

Quinn didn't say any more. He ran through all the events in his mind which had led up to this point. Inwardly, he became critical of every decision he had made; every decision, except the one to come confess to the COB. He pondered if it had been fate which brought him and the COB together in the middle level passageway. If gone unchecked, he wasn't sure to what ends he would have brought himself and his shipmates.

Just as he was about to apologize to the COB for his actions, the COB's mood changed. Sitting down at the small table across from Quinn, the COB made a confession of his own.

"I *would* take you directly to the Skipper," the COB said, "if I wasn't just as bothered by the way things have gone in this operation." Suddenly all of

Quinn's self doubt vanished. This was the exact reaction he was hoping for in that split second decision to pull the COB aside.

"We just have to figure out where to go from here," the COB said. Quinn straightened up in his chair ready to have a strategy session. But before Quinn could lay out how he planned to continue with what he had already done, the COB started probing Quinn to find out what he already knew.

"Do you have the evidence anywhere?" the COB asked.

"No, I flushed it," Quinn said, feeling a little silly now, since he hadn't had the forethought to plan on trying to convince anyone else.

"That's not a big deal," the COB said. "I'm sure there is plenty down there."

Their conversation came to a halt when there was a soft knock at the door.

"Excuse me," the COB said as he slid out of his chair. The COB went over to the door and cracked it open a few inches. From his vantage point, Quinn could not see who was at the door. There was an over head locker in the entry way which hung down just enough to obscure his view of the face of whoever it was.

Quinn noticed the COB making a gesture with his hand to keep it down. He wasn't sure if the COB was motioning to him or the person at the door. A general alarm started to go off inside Quinn's head.

"Who else have you told about this, Quinn?" the COB asked.

"You're the first, COB," Quinn lied.

The COB stepped back into the compartment followed by Ramirez. Instantly realizing the double cross, Quinn was determined not to say anything else. Resisting the urge to even try and lecture the COB, Quinn held his tongue as the two impatiently interrogated him. Quinn studied Ramirez's movements as he grew more and more agitated. He came to realize he was wrong in his first assessment of Ramirez; the man moved with the physical grace of a fighter and never took his finger off the trigger of his weapon. He seemed as though he was playing a part when he first came aboard. Yet, now it was apparent that Ramirez was trained in the art of killing and was ready to display his talents at the drop of a hat.

While Quinn was well versed in fighting, he lacked the combat training in killing techniques. His fighting experience had been tempered by the presence of a referee whose main job was to ensure the emerging sport of Mixed Martial Arts did not lose its licensing by any state commissions. His only choice was to try and endure whatever they had in store for him. Unless he felt the situation had grown completely desperate, he would not act.

The time of desperation seemed to be approaching faster than he anticipated. In his frustration, Ramirez pounced on Quinn. He pinned Quinn's thigh to the chair with one knee while pushing upwards with the barrel of his MP-5 under Quinn's jaw. Quinn's heart raced. He was contemplating trying to knock the barrel of the gun away but he was almost certain Ramirez would be able to squeeze off a round before any of his efforts would be effectual.

Fortunately for Quinn, it seemed neither the COB nor Ramirez yet possessed the authority to start taking the lives of any sailors, no matter how belligerent the sailor had become.

"Get off him, Ramirez," the COB said, jerking the arm of the foreigner. Quinn thought for sure that would have been the motion which brought his end. Apparently, Ramirez's control was every bit as good as Quinn had given him credit for.

"We have to find out what the Skipper wants us to do with him," the COB said. Upon hearing Captain Maddox was still at the head of the operation, Quinn's heart sank. He still wasn't sure what was going on, but his feelings on the situation were much bleaker than they had been fifteen minutes prior.

"Take him down to the VLS compartment just forward of the torpedo room and have one of your men stand guard," the COB directed.

"Let's go," Ramirez said as he lifted Quinn by his arm. As Quinn stood, he felt the barrel of Ramirez's weapon press into his spine.

"When you lock him in there, be sure to cut the phone line," the COB reminded Ramirez.

The COB led the two out of the chief's quarters. He rounded the corner of the middle level passageway, made sure the coast was clear, then motioned for Ramirez to bring Quinn. Quinn glanced over his shoulder at Ramirez. He pressed his finger to his lips, and then he gave a jab with his gun to get Quinn moving.

They only had to go about three feet aft to get to the ladder which descended to the forward torpedo room. With the COB's large frame blocking the passageway there was little chance anyone who rounded the corner heading forward would be able to tell there was any suspicious activity going on. Nevertheless, they were discovered by Schmidt when he came out of the forward crew's berthing door which was directly opposite the ladder leading to lower level.

Schmidt's eyes flashed from the gun at Quinn's back, to Quinn, to the COB, to Ramirez then back to the gun. The COB didn't waste any time trying to explain the situation to Schmidt. He grabbed Schmidt by the back of the neck, shoved him into the ladder well.

"Lock him up too."

Quinn caught Schmidt and prevented him from falling. "Don't say anything, just go," he whispered to Schmidt.

The two descended the ladder, followed by Ramirez. The COB watched them make their way forward, and then headed up to the command passageway.

Ramirez gave Quinn a hard shove as he went through the VLS door. Schmidt tried to catch Quinn, but his momentum carried them both to the deck. Then pulling out a knife, Ramirez cut the phone line and took the handset with him. Finding no way to lock the door from the outside, he took off his belt, removed his pistol from its holster and shoved it into the waistline of his pants. He then looped the belt through the door's handle and around a pipe. Cinching the strap down, he was able to make it tight enough to act as a sufficient lock. He motioned to one of his team members in the torpedo room to come to him. When the man approached, Ramirez said, "Make sure nobody goes in or out of here until I get back." The man nodded his head in agreement, and then Ramirez ascended the ladder.

"What's going on, Quinn?" Schmidt asked impatiently, as Quinn began to empty out every locker in the compartment.

"To tell you the truth, I have no clue," Quinn confessed. "All I know is that we are transporting a butt load of cocaine in those containers and I'm not sure that it's on the up and up."

"Why did the COB have us locked up?" Schmidt pressed.

"I have no idea," Quinn snapped. "Apparently the COB, the Captain and possibly more, are trying to pull a fast one." Quinn paused as his thoughts spilled out, "I'll bet the XO was the first to get in their way."

"Wait, what are you getting at?" Schmidt began.

"The XO was murdered," Quinn finished the thought. "If that's the case then we're probably next." Schmidt went white as a ghost. Quinn continued to pull the contents out of the lockers with even more veracity.

"There's something else that doesn't seem quite right," Schmidt said.

"What's that?" Quinn asked, as he surveyed the items he had pulled out of the locker.

"Ramirez's accent," Schmidt began. "It doesn't fit, it's not Spanish."

"What do you mean?" Quinn questioned. "I'm not bilingual or anything but I could tell they were speaking Spanish."

"They were speaking Spanish, but Ramirez's accent wasn't Spanish."

Quinn studied his Nub thinking, *there just might be more to you than we think Seaman Schmidt.*

"So you're a linguist these days," Quinn said, masking his internal thoughts.

"Not exactly. Before my Dad died he used to hire migrant workers on the farm. Every season we'd get a few families, sometimes they'd be from Peru, sometimes from Mexico. I not only learned Spanish but I can usually tell you which country they're from."

"Why didn't you tell me this earlier?" Quinn lectured. "We could have had you spying on these guys and telling us what they're saying."

"They don't exactly say that much," Schmidt said, "but what I can tell you is that Spanish is not Ramirez's first language."

"So, can you tell what his first language is?" Quinn asked hopefully.

"No," Schmidt said, unwilling to surmise, "but I can tell you, he learned Spanish in Europe, most likely in Spain. There's a pretty big difference in the Spanish of South and Central Americans."

"Schmidt," Quinn said, happy to know at least a little bit more information which may come in handy, "you just might earn your Dolphins yet."

The two stood and surveyed the items Quinn had pulled from the locker. A few cans of Pepsi, a small tool bag, and some training manuals were all they could scrounge up.

"We need to figure out how to communicate with somebody without getting shot," Quinn said gravely.

Le Poignard

"We've caught up to them, sir," De Panafiue Reported as Captain Reno entered the control room.

"They're making an awful lot of noise," the sonar technician announced.

"What do you suppose they are doing?" Captain Reno asked.

"It sounds as if they are at periscope depth, ventilating, sir."

"Bring us up to periscope depth" Captain Reno ordered.

As they came near the surface, Captain Reno raised the scope. The periscope on the Poignard was about a third the thickness of the scope on the Key West, so when it breached the surface it was even harder to see than that of its predecessors. The men looked at the screens. Once they shifted to thermal imaging, they could see clouds of smoke bubbling up out of the water just aft of the Key West's snorkel mast. The Key West had had to slow and come to periscope depth so they could replenish the air within the sub. They did this by raising their snorkel mast to take in fresh air, while the smoke filled air was pushed out through exhaust vents on the aft portion of the sail just below the waterline.

"Lucky break for us," De Panafiue stated. "They must have had a fire." At that moment everyone in the control room jumped as a high pressure air reducer popped a relief valve in the lower level, causing high pressure air to blow into the pressure hull. Forgetting the Key West momentarily, it took the crew a few seconds to realize what had happened. The sound of high pressure air being released into the boat was very similar to the sound of sea water rushing in. It did not take but thirty seconds for one of the crew members to get the reducer secured, but by then the damage had been done to the submarines stealth.

The sonar technician looked at his screen, "Sir, that was pretty loud, they'd have to be deaf not to hear it."

CHAPTER 19

Rubber walked into the sonar shack and found it to be in a flurry of activity. "What's going on?" he asked. No one paid him any attention. They just kept the conversation amongst themselves going.

"That's got to be it," Petty Officer Bowden said to the tech on watch.

"Got to be what?" Rubber asked, again trying to figure out what all the commotion was about.

"Hold tight," Bowden said to Rubber as he grabbed the mic and gave a slight smile.

"Control-Sonar, we've picked up a transient from a possible submerged contact bearing two-one-six." Rubber looked at the screen. His face flushed with anger. On screen was a transient from a faint contact he had picked up two days ago when Bowden blew him off. He was about to argue the point until he saw the fire in Captain Maddox's eyes when he ripped open the curtain from the control room

"You've got a what?" Captain Maddox screamed. Suddenly all of Bowden's confidence melted away. He began to stammer as he tried to explain.

"Uh, we've picked up a possible submerged contact, sir," he said feebly.

"Where did it come from?" Captain Maddox demanded. Mustering up some courage, Bowden attempted to hypothesize on the situation.

"It's awfully quiet sir, it's possible that it's the French boat."

"What?" Captain Maddox said as he began to flip through the various sonar screens with the deftness of a skilled technician.

"It's possible he followed us out of the operations box when the exercise closed last week," Bowden said, further digging his grave.

"What would make you think that?" Captain Maddox asked in a very deliberate tone.

"We had picked up some signs that maybe-" Bowden started to say when Captain Maddox spun around, grabbed him by his lapels and forced him to his knees as he berated him.

"You had signs, you had signs!" he screamed.

Everyone in the control room became silent as Captain Maddox flew into a rage, the likes of which had never been witnessed by a sailor attached to one of his commands. "We are on the most sensitive mission of my career and you failed to inform me you had anything other than saltwater in our wake!"

Captain Maddox threw Bowden to the deck then stormed back out into control, continuing his rage.

"Lower that scope! Get me a firing solution on that bastard! Dive, make your depth five hundred feet; Helm, all ahead full." His orders were swiftly repeated and initiated.

The fire control technician on watch piped up, "Sir, I have a preliminary firing solution."

Le Poignard

Aboard the French submarine, Captain Reno watched the periscope's display screens, hoping nothing would come of the transient which had just emanated from his boat. Seeing the periscope of the Key West submerge, his fears were confirmed.

"They've increased their speed," the sonar man reported. "They're diving!"

"Dive!" Reno called out. "Dive!"

USS Key West

As the angle of the Key West steepened, Sparks fought to maintain his position stretched out among the pipes in the outboard. He was working frantically, with his fingers mingled among the wires of the phone circuitry for the Captain's stateroom, when the boat pitched hard to port. He grimaced as he contracted every muscle in his body to hold his position like a snake scaling a wall. Try as he might, the angle became too much for him to bear, he let go of the cables and pliers he was holding and tried to brace himself. It was too late. His body slipped falling only about a foot, but it was enough to wedge his large rib cage between a hydraulic pipe and the exterior bulkhead of the Captain's stateroom.

He groaned in pain as he heard his tools sliding down the outer hull destined to end up in the bilge.

"Do you have a firing solution?" Captain Maddox demanded.

Working frantically at the fire control station the tech called out, "the firing solution is locked into the computer, sir!"

Captain Maddox, coming over to the fire control station, called out, "Snapshot tube three!" When the illuminators indicated the tube was ready, he swung the firing lever over to the firing position. The control room shook as the torpedo was fired.

Le Poignard

In the control room of the Poignard, the sonar man on watch suddenly jumped to his feet and screamed.

"They've fired a torpedo at us! It sounds like the real thing!"

De Panafiue repeated this information as if Captain Reno himself did not hear the shriek.

"The Americans are shooting at us!" he said, in a near panic.

Captain Reno started barking off orders in hopes of saving his boat.

"Full dive! All stop! Take on as much water as possible! Stand by to deploy countermeasures!"

The men in his control room started to perform the tasks he was piling on without hesitation. "Make ready the sanitary tanks for discharge!" he ordered.

"The sanitary tanks?" De Panafiue questioned.

"Yes, the sanitary tanks," Captain Reno snapped. "I want a five second burst from the sanitary tanks the moment we deploy the countermeasures, then shut everything down!"

USS Key West

Schmidt was watching Quinn fiddle with the phone box when the torpedo was fired. The deafening crash of the torpedo tube took them both off guard. "What was that?" Quinn exclaimed. Schmidt looked at him stupefied, as if Quinn really expected him to have an answer. "We just fired off a war shot," Quinn answered himself. "Who the hell are we shooting at?" Again, Schmidt looked at him blankly. Quinn stood up, taking his attention away from the empty phone box. "Things just escalated to a whole new level."

"What does that mean for us?" Schmidt asked.

As Quinn's eyes darted around the room with an abundance of nervous energy, he replied, "That means if we are shooting at somebody, then somebody might shoot back at us!" Quinn's eyes fixated on a fire extinguisher. "And if somebody's going to be shooting at us the last place I want to be is locked up down here." He darted across the small compartment to the fire extinguisher.

"Give me a hand!" he directed Schmidt, as he pulled it out of its storage bracket. "We're getting out of here."

Le Poignard

"Countermeasures deployed," De Panafiue screamed. As Captain Reno acknowledged him, another sailor turned and reported.

"Five second burst of the sanitaries complete."

"Very well," Captain Reno acknowledged as he made his way to hover over the sonar man's shoulder, "shut everything down."

The monotonous humming of equipment which normally filled the background noise of the submarine went completely silent. The buzzing from sonar's hydrophones was the only sound which could be heard. The crew listened nervously as the ominous whir of the incoming torpedo intensified. They all stood as if frozen in time, some held their hands over their hearts as if they were beating too loudly and needed to be muffled.

USS Key West

In the Key West's sonar shack, Captain Maddox stood over the technicians as the sound of the torpedo churning through the water grew weaker and weaker as it headed for its intended target. "It should be closing one thousand yards now sir," Bowden said in a whisper. After a few more seconds of the same enraptured silence which was gripping the French boat, there was a loud explosion, heard first through Sonar's speaker system, then it reverberated right through the hull.

There were no cheers throughout the control room as had been the case during the firing of the exercise torpedoes during the war game scenarios. There was a moment when no member of the crew, not even Captain Maddox, knew what to expect. Only a handful of the crew had even been aboard a submarine which had fired a live torpedo, and the few that had, had only shot at barges intended to be sunk. None in the crew had ever fired a torpedo at another submarine. Finally, Captain Maddox broke the silence.

"Did we get them?" The sonar technicians scrolled through their screens, none brave enough to answer their captain. "Well?" he said, demanding a reply. Bowden, having taken enough abuse, held his tongue.

"There is the large explosion here," Rubber said, stepping forward and making a circular motion over a large mass of static on his screen with his finger. "I don't see any secondary explosions, but the contact is not being picked up by sonar anymore." Captain Maddox studied the screen with as much knowledge as any of the technicians.

"What about those readings there, to the southwest?" he asked, pointing out a small area of disturbance on the screen.

"That appears to be just some biologics, sir," Rubber deduced. "Here, I can bring it up for you." He isolated the hydrophones that were picking up the disturbance, then handed Captain Maddox a pair of headphones. The Captain listened with one ear. After a moment of listening to the cracklings and poppings of what was obviously sea life, he handed the headphones back to Rubber.

"Keep your ears peeled," he said to the entire sonar crew. "If you pick up even a blip of anything out of the ordinary-" He paused a moment, then continued, "or hell, anything just plain ordinary, inform me immediately."

Le Poignard

Inside the sonar shack of the French sub, the sonar man reported in a whisper. "Captain, the ADCAP went for the countermeasures and," he stuttered in amazement, "the fish, it's like they are masking us." A smile started to creep across the face of Captain Reno. "Here, listen," the technician insisted as he flipped a switch turning on a speaker. The same sounds of sea life heard by the Key West were amplified as they came out of the speaker. "The fish, they are all around us!" the technician said, overcome with joy.

"The sanitaries," De Panafiue said.

"That's right, my friend," Captain Reno said, "We threw out a dinner cloud of human waste."

"The fish-" De Panafiue started.

"They cannot resist," his captain finished his thought.

USS Key West

As Captain Maddox stepped back into the control room from Sonar, the COB came through the forward control room door followed by Ramirez at the same time the Weps came through the aft door, each demanding to speak to the Captain.

"What the hell was that?" demanded the Weps.

"Captain, I need to see you in your stateroom," the COB insisted. The Weps shot a venomous glance at the COB, then at Captain Maddox.

"Do you mind explaining to me why we just fired off a live torpedo?" the Weps seethed.

"Captain, we have a problem that urgently needs your attention," the COB pressed.

Losing his patience, Captain Maddox yelled, "COB, I'll be with you in a moment." This had the momentary effect of shutting the COB up. Then he turned to the Weps, "Mr. Copaletti, have you forgotten I am the Commander of this submarine!"

The Weps, not backing down, snapped, "And as the Commander of this submarine, you cannot just go around, like a cowboy, shooting torpedoes at who knows what!"

"It was an enemy submarine!"

"A what?" the Weps gasped. "I wasn't aware the rules of engagement specified any active enemies with submarines."

"The R.O.Es state that anyone trying to interfere with this mission is an enemy and can be engaged as such. Yourself not withstanding!"

"What *is* this mission?" the Weps dared to ask.

"You would know if your judgment was worth a dime!" Captain Maddox shot back.

The sailors in the control room were dumbstruck. They had never known an incident of such outright insubordination by a senior officer. The Weps couldn't mask his wounded pride, having Captain Maddox question his judgment in front of the entire control room party. Up until a few days ago, the Weps had looked at Captain Maddox as the greatest mentor he had ever known. But now it was clear, Captain Maddox carried no positive regard for him as an officer, and even though the Captain's career had plateaued, his opinion was still considered to be golden in the Navy.

"You will back down, Mr. Copaletti, or I will have you relieved of your position," Captain Maddox seemed to bite off every word as he continued to harangue him. The Weps must have realized he would be of no use to the crew if he were relieved of his position, so he did as he was ordered and backed off. With a conciliatory apology, the Weps stepped back into the fire control center.

Turning to the COB, Captain Maddox laid into him with the same harsh tone. "What is it, COB?" he snapped.

"We've got a problem that I need to speak to you in private about, sir."

Captain Maddox stared at the COB for a few moments, getting his breathing under control. He looked around the control room at all the sailors. None would make eye contact with him. Noticing Ramirez standing behind the COB, he knew he'd better retire to his stateroom.

"Let's go," he said as he walked out, followed by both the COB and Ramirez.

Inside the radio room, Walker busied himself preparing radio reports to transmit the next time the boat came up to periscope depth. The Nav rushed into Radio seeking refuge from the fireworks in the control room. Seeing the Nav, Walker said, "Sounded like world war three in there."

"The sooner we reach the drop point the better," the Nav sighed.

"How close are we?"

"We're approaching the coast of Florida now, but the sun will be up soon, so we'll hug the coast most the day as we make our way north."

"The sooner the better," Walker said.

"If we can just keep things under control for a few more days, we'll be golden," the Nav said as he collapsed into his seat and began flipping through the pages of the most recent download. "Is this all we got?"

"That's all I had time to get before we dove," Walker informed him.

"Let's get the floating wire strung out," the Nav said. "I'd like to be able to give the Captain a more comprehensive report of what is happening with the battle group before we join back up with them."

"Aye, sir," Walker replied as he made preparations to send out the ship's floating antenna.

Sparks was struggling to free himself when he heard Captain Maddox enter his stateroom. The Captain slumped down on his rack, sitting with his back pressed against the outer bulkhead. When he did, the bulkhead bowed outward into Sparks' already compressed rib cage. He resisted a groan as the added weight upon his chest cavity made breathing even more painful.

"What is so urgent you needed to pull me out of the control room when we've got an enemy sub out there?" Sparks heard Captain Maddox ask. Though his voice was slightly muffled coming through the bulkhead, he could still make out his words quite clearly since only a thin sheet of wood paneling separated them.

The COB stood flanked by Ramirez in front of the Captain. Captain Maddox looked drained. The emotional toll the operation would take on everyone involved had been grossly underestimated.

"We've got a problem with the crew, Skipper." Captain Maddox clasped his hand over his forehead and leaned forward, taking some of the pressure off Sparks.

"What now, COB?"

"It's Quinn, sir," the COB said flatly.

"What is it about Quinn?" Captain Maddox asked in a regretful tone.

"He's a hemorrhoid, sir."

Captain Maddox held up his hand to stop the COB. "Spare me the personal commentary COB."

"He went snooping around the cargo, sir." The COB paused.

"And," the Captain said, insisting the COB continue.

"Well, he found out what was in the containers and he is questioning the motives behind this operation." Seeing the look of despair which came over Captains Maddox's face, Ramirez jumped in.

"You said your crew would be easily distracted."

"And the majority of them have been," Captain Maddox tried to defend his earlier assurances.

"Well, apparently you have under estimated your crew," Ramirez snapped.

"Just a few," Captain Maddox returned in a tone meant to remind Ramirez he was still on his submarine.

As desperate as the situation was for Sparks, he couldn't help but let a smile slip across his face hearing the news that a select few sailors, himself included, were not letting whatever seemingly devious plot these men were trying to unfold go unchecked. Yet at the same time, the news of Quinn being found out cast a shadow of bleakness on his situation.

"Where is Quinn now?" Captain Maddox asked.

"He and Seaman Schmidt are locked in the VLS compartment," the COB said.

As Captain Maddox drew a deep breath considering his options, Ramirez was starting to show signs of impatience.

"Well, we've got him neutralized for now," Captain Maddox said, trying to forestall any more events which would cause him to suffer further mental fatigue.

"There aren't enough rooms in this place to lock up all of your sailors," Ramirez snapped.

"This is Quinn we're talking about, sir," the COB reminded Captain Maddox. "You know he's not just going to sit there and give up." At that moment there was a knock at the stateroom door.

The COB opened the door and Scarpa slipped in. Captain Maddox looked up, seeing Scarpa standing before him, he said, "Your timing is impeccable, Scarpa." Scarpa glanced around to the other men in the room.

"The COB said you wanted to see me, sir."

"He did, did he?" Captain Maddox said, flashing a scowl at the COB.

"I took the liberty, Skipper."

"So you did."

At that moment, Captain Maddox was brought to his feet as an announcement came through his comm. box, "Conn-Sonar we've regained submerged contact designated sierra eight."

As Captain Maddox started to bolt out of his stateroom the COB blocked his exit.

"We need to know what to do about Quinn," the COB pressed. It was obvious he held no soft spot in his heart for Quinn, or any other sailor for that matter, so he seemed to be looking for a quick resolution.

"The sooner we get rid of any potential problems, the more chances this operation has of success."

Sparks listened, shaking his head no, as if trying to will Captain Maddox into making the right decision. A look of horror flashed across his face as he heard Captain Maddox bend to the wishes of the COB and Ramirez.

"Take care of him," Captain Maddox said rashly as he pushed his way past the men.

The COB grabbed ahold of Scarpa and said, "Do it quickly and quietly." Then, he and Ramirez followed Captain Maddox out of his stateroom and into the control room.

CHAPTER 20

Schmidt stood by as Quinn removed the last screw from the small porthole window in the VLS compartment door. Carefully, he handed the screw to Schmidt as he made sure the Plexiglas window did not drop to the floor bringing unwanted attention before he was ready. Then, as he removed the window piece, he whispered, "Alright Schmidt, post yourself at the electrical panel." Schmidt went over to the port side of the compartment, and opened the cover of a small circuit breaker box. The panel only held four circuit breakers so Schmidt was able to situate his fingers to throw them all at once.

"Remember," Quinn gave some last minute instructions, "as soon as he goes down, throw all the breakers." Schmidt acknowledged him with a nod. Quinn's shoulders dropped from the ready position in frustration.

"Seaman Schmidt, even though what we are about to do is probably criminal, and we're most likely going to be court martialed for it, if we want any chance at success, we still need to maintain military integrity."

Schmidt smiled at Quinn's continued efforts to turn him into a competent sailor. "When he goes down, throw all the breakers, aye," Schmidt said the repeat back with hushed zeal.

"Ready?" Quinn said as a smile flashed across his face. The forthcoming action suited Quinn better than the inaction of being held prisoner, waiting for someone else to decide his fate.

"Ready," Schmidt affirmed.

Quinn pulled out his pocket knife, squeezed his arm through the small port and blindly slashed at the web band which held the door shut. He felt his knife miss a few times, but eventually he made two solid swipes at the strap. Then, he heard the guard, who had been posted to watch them, rattle off something in Spanish. Quinn imagined it was equivalent to the English word "hey". He pulled his arm in, tossed his blade to the side, and then he picked up the fire extinguisher and loaded a can of Pepsi in its cone as if it were a mortar.

The guard came to the door and predictably looked through the port hole. The only thing he would have seen was a silver circular object in a dark shaft. At that moment, Quinn squeezed the handle of the fire extinguisher and shot the guard at point blank range with the twelve ounce bullet. The man immediately fell backwards, screaming pain, as the can had enough velocity to fracture the bones around the man's left eye socket.

As he fell backward, Schmidt threw the circuit breakers and the torpedo room went dark. Quinn pulled on the door with all his might and was able to break the last few threads of the strap which had remained intact. Lifting the fire extinguisher over his head, he brought it down upon the guard with as much force as he would use to split a piece of firewood with an ax. Intending to deliver a blow that would merely incapacitate the man, Quinn felt a pit instantaneously grow in his stomach as the man's skull crumpled under the force with which he had brought the metal cylinder down. A warm liquid splashed across Quinn's face and he was happy the lights were off to conceal the scene from his eyes, although he was sure the scene couldn't look any worse than he imagined. As he stepped over the man, he heard him choking as his brain functions were ceasing to operate.

Growing up, Quinn had murdered his uncle a thousand times over in his mind. The night their confrontation in the yard came to a head, Quinn stopped before he had killed the old man. After that night, seeing his uncle limp around the farm brought no feelings of satisfaction. As the man who had tormented his childhood grew weaker, Quinn took no triumph in his victory. When he came to realize the injury he had given his uncle was the most significant contributing factor to the man's death in the pig sty, it became a weight Quinn had carried ever since. The weeks he had been locked in with the giant hog were the worst weeks of his life. To this day, he woke up to nightmares where he was in his uncle's place, paralyzed as the giant hog began to devour him. The guilt of what he had done to his uncle would hit him in moments when it seemed to be the furthest thing from his mind. It didn't matter if he was alone, or if he was out with the guys, it would randomly hit his conscience like a truck; pulling him away, putting an unusual distance between him and the rest of the world.

Now, as he cautiously stepped down the darkened passage and loaded another can of Pepsi into his improvised mortar, he pushed any thoughts of the man, whose life he had just ended, into a compartment of his mind to be unpacked later. For the moment, he couldn't afford to predict whether he would be haunted by this man's face, as he was haunted by his uncle's. Later he would analyze if it was his hatred for his childhood tormentor which kept his uncle a fresh corpse in his mind. He could only hope, since he had no particular malice toward the unfortunate man, it would be but a surface memory, easily justified by necessity and washed away with time, rather than compounding his guilt.

"Where is he, Sonar?" Captain Maddox shouted as he entered the control room. Inside the sonar shack, Bowden was working frantically to isolate the signal.

"We'll have it narrowed down in about five seconds," Bowden cried out. At that moment, the phone in the sonar shack right next to Rubber growled.

Rubber answered in a hushed voice as not to disturb Bowden who had taken over his console in order to help get a firing solution for Captain Maddox.

"Sonar," he answered, covering his mouth with his right hand.

"Rubber?" he heard the voice on the other end ask in a grim tone.

"Yeah, Sparks, is that you?" he said as he stepped back from the men fixated at the sonar consoles.

"Yes," Sparks said in an extremely strained tone.

"What's wrong, you sound hurt," Rubber asked cautiously. His eyes darted over his shoulder to make sure nobody was listening to his conversation. The other men in the space took no notice of him.

Without explanation of his own dire circumstances, Sparks said, "You've got to save Quinn. The Captain and COB are traitors; they sent Scarpa to kill Quinn and Schmidt." Rubber stepped back, twisting away so his back was to the other men in sonar.

"Say again."

"The COB and the Captain just sent Scarpa to kill Quinn and Schmidt. They're holding them in VLS," Sparks said as he labored a breath in between each word.

Sparks tried to reposition himself to make it easier to talk. Using his forearm, he pushed his body upward in an attempt to relieve the pressure on his ribs. Just when he felt as though he could expand his chest to take a full breath, his arm slipped off the pipe sending his body crashing further into the wedge it had been in. It was only a fall of four inches, but the jolt was enough to send the phone slipping out of his hand. Not being able to move the mass of his body, he tried to recover the phone using just the fingers of his left hand.

He managed to snag the cord of the dangling phone with two fingers. As he used his fingers to cinch the cord towards him little by little, he could see the rough patch job he had done on the line starting to unravel. Lacking any tools or tape, and the freedom to use both hands at the same time, he had bitten through the existing phone line, stripped the wires with his teeth and twisted them together, patching his phone into the Captain's line.

Now, as he tried to recover the phone, he wished he hadn't been so hasty with his work. The phone's handset hung several feet below him and he was trying desperately to recover it. As the handset was pulled upward, it became ensnared in some electrical wiring. As he tugged, the phone's spiral cord started to stretch out. With about six inches before he could get his hand on the line's patch job, it broke. The phone hung three feet below him, but there was no way he could snake his long arms down to reach it.

Rubber heard the line cut out. "Sparks, Sparks are you there?" he called. He waited for a moment but then felt as if he had better not waste any time.

"I got it!" Bowden shouted as Rubber hung up the phone.

Captain Maddox did not congratulate him; he simply walked out into the control room and called out, "Man Battle Stations!"

Quinn could hear the other guard calling out in the dark to his friend.

"Felipe," the man called out in a horse whisper. As Quinn's eyes adjusted to the dark, he could start to make out the silhouette of the man about ten feet in front of him. Suddenly the announcement came over the 1MC. "Man Battle Stations!" Then, following standard procedure, the announcement was immediately followed by the illumination of the boat's emergency lighting.

Quinn stood completely exposed in the passage way in front of the guard. The guard hesitated a moment before he comprehended what was going on. The hesitation was long enough for Quinn to squeeze off a shot from his makeshift cannon. This time the shot was not at point blank range, so the guard had time enough to react. He lifted his arm, taking the blow on his wrist. As the man stepped back into the narrow passageway between the midships and the starboard torpedo stowage trays shaking his hand in pain, Quinn dropped the fire extinguisher and charged.

He was able to reach the guard before the man had time to raise his weapon. Quinn caught the guard with a left hook. It did not knock the man out though. The left hook was never Quinn's strongest punch, but he feared if he threw a punch with his right hand the force would turn the man into him and he would find the barrel of the man's gun pointing right at his chest. The left hook did as Quinn had intended. It caused the man's head to twist to the left. His shoulders followed this motion and Quinn found, not only the gun turning away from him, but the man's back became exposed. Quinn side-stepped to the left, and was able to get behind the man.

From behind, Quinn threw his left arm over the man's left shoulder grabbing onto the barrel of his weapon. With his right arm he was able to reach around and slide his thumb onto on the gun's safety lever, locking the trigger. Then, he pulled the gun into the man's throat to use it as a choking instrument. At the same time he lifted his right foot and dug his heel into the back of the man's knee putting extreme pressure on the goon's anterior cruciate ligament.

Unfortunately, as adeptly as Quinn had adjusted his fighting style to neutralize an opponent with a weapon, his left side was vulnerable. The man threw back his elbow as hard as he could, landing the point of the blow in Quinn's ribs. The pain was so sharp that Quinn instantly gave up his heel attack to the man's knee. He did, however, manage to bear enough of the pain and maintain his grip on the weapon. The guard, getting both his stout legs solidly underneath him, bent over at the waist, twisted, and then shot backwards smashing Quinn's lower back against the solid steel of the torpedo storage tray.

Pain shot through Quinn's spine as the guard propped a powerful leg up on the adjacent torpedo tray and crushed his weight back into Quinn. As excruciating as the pain was, Quinn did not relinquish his grip on the man's gun. Quinn glanced forward to see where Schmidt was and why he hadn't joined in the fight. He saw Schmidt timidly trying to pluck the gun away from the guard who lay dying just outside VLS.

"Hurry up, Schmidt!" Quinn grunted. Schmidt, seeing the perilous situation Quinn was in, let his adrenaline become unhindered. Grabbing the man by the hair on the side of his head which wasn't caved in, Schmidt pulled him up to a sitting position so he could pull the gun strap off the dead man's shoulder.

Finally, prying the weapon away from the lifeless man, Schmidt turned, facing the embattled Quinn, brandishing the gun. Quinn's eyes widened and he forgot about the pain in his back as he saw Schmidt raise the weapon. He could see the panic and the intent to shoot in Schmidt's eyes as he prepared to fire.

"No!" Quinn screamed. The guard he was wrestling with took notice of Schmidt.

Instinctively, both men shifted their weight together and threw themselves to the ground as Schmidt squeezed off a five round burst.

As Bowden busied himself trying to lock in an exact position for the elusive French submarine, Rubber slid out the forward sonar shack door into the starboard side of the CSES compartment. Opening a drawer on the small workbench just outside the sonar shack, he pulled out a socket wrench and quickly ratcheted off a bolt on an access panel to the sonar system's mainframe computer. He was in a race against time and from what Sparks had told him, the situation for Quinn was dire, but before he went anywhere, duty demanded he put forth his best effort to stop the madness Captain Maddox was trying to unleash.

In the control room, Captain Maddox was finalizing the firing solution for the French sub. The Weps, with renewed vigor, protested his current course of action.

"You cannot fire upon an allied submarine!" the Weps protested vehemently. Captain Maddox ignored him as he grabbed the mic.

"Torpedo Room-Control, make ready torpedo tube number one!" The Weps picked up his mic at the fire control station.

"Belay that order Torpedo Room!" Captain Maddox looked at the Weps with scorn.

"Mr. Copaletti, you are relieved from your post!" he screamed. He reiterated his last order to the torpedo room. "Torpedo Room-flood tube one!" The Weps continued to try and argue with him but Captain Maddox merely blocked him out. He was focused on the tube indication lights from the torpedo room, which at this point had not changed.

Suddenly, the Nav could be heard yelling for Captain Maddox as he rushed out of the radio room. Running in through the aft control room door, the Nav said in a panicked voice, "Captain, Walker just pulled this off the floating wire." He handed Captain Maddox a reel of paper which had not been organized on to a clipboard in the usual manner for the Captain.

Working quickly in CSES, Rubber removed the access panel off of the AN/BQS-5, the sonar system's mainframe computer. He carefully reached in, and with a sharp tug disconnected a circuit card from the motherboard.

Bowden sat next to the other sonar technicians working at what would be considered light speed for Bowden, trying to track the intermittent signal from the French boat. To his obvious horror, the screens went momentarily blank then came back on filled with what seemed to be a random pattern of ones and zeros.

"No!" Bowden said in shock. "No, no, no, no, no!" he said, speeding up his verbal reaction with each utterance of the word "no." He began to hit the sonar console, gently at first, but gaining quickly in intensity.

As the Weps continued to berate Captain Maddox, the Captain's eyes flashed across the paper the Nav had handed him. He didn't read every detail, but the important ones stuck out rather quickly.

The details Captain Maddox was able to pull off at a glance were: "To: Roosevelt Battle Group From: Group Commander Adm. Perry. French submarine reports being fired upon by rogue U.S. submarine...detailed evidence...periscope video of officer killed topside...unauthorized rendezvous with merchant ship tied to Maltanado drug Cartel...unauthorized receipt of unknown cargo...known weapons on board three Mark 48 ADCAP torpedoes...possible unknown weapons..."

Then the message was closed with a personal note: "Mike, if you are in control down there, I know things have been tough, and did not work out as you had planned. Just surface your boat and we can talk about it. If someone else has gained control of the Key West you will be sent to Hell shortly. Vic."

Captain Maddox had not expected this. In all his contingency plans, being spied on by a French submarine was never in the realm of remote possibilities. He felt the barbs of panic set in upon his heart. He handed the report to Ramirez who had been standing just behind him as if he was second in command.

As Captain Maddox's mind raced with possibilities, most of which did not turn out favorable to his objective, Petty Officer Bowden broke his train of thought.

"We lost sonar, sir," Bowden said in a panicked voice as he stood in the sonar shack's doorway.

Bowden stood there timidly, seemingly worried about another tongue lashing from Captain Maddox which might affect his reviews for his Chief's promotion board. Neither he, nor anyone else in the control room, could have expected what came next.

Captain Maddox assessed his life in a split second. His failed career, his failed marriage, the loss of his son, and now the mission which was supposed to set him up for a wealthy retirement, and be carried out so that no sailor who served under him would be the wiser, was failing too. The action which he was so reluctant to do on board the merchant ship came as if it were second nature now. As Ramirez read through the report, Captain Maddox snatched the pistol from Ramirez's waist and fired off a round at Petty Officer Bowden.

The shot rang out in the control room just as a short burst of automatic weapons fire echoed up from the torpedo room.

The bullet ripped through Bowden's abdomen, just under his lower left rib and sent him hurtling backwards into the sonar shack. The Weps moved toward Captain Maddox, but Ramirez, dropping the report, snatched up his MP5 that hung loosely over his shoulder and popped off two rounds. One round missed, lodging itself into one of the fire control computers, the other pierced the Weps' thigh, dropping the big man instantly.

The rest of the crew in the control room found themselves in shock. The young sailor sitting at the helm, without realizing it, had put a fifteen degree right rudder on as he turned to watch the action. Cuffing the young sailor on the ear as if he had suddenly been transported back to the Navy of two decades ago, the COB snipped, "Mind your helm."

Grant, hearing the gun shots, poked his head out of the ward room pantry just in time to see Scarpa and one of the foreign guards heading down the ladder to lower level.

Schmidt, after firing off the five rounds which penetrated the container in a neat row starting in the exact spot Quinn's head had been moments before, found his gun locked up.

"It's jammed," Schmidt called out.

Quinn, who had the wind knock out of him from the force of hitting the deck flat on his back with not only his own weight, but that of the guard coming down upon him, managed to grunt out the word "Good" in response. As Quinn struggled with the man on the ground, he managed to gain control of the man by wrapping his legs around the guard's legs. This, along with the fact he had not released his grip on the man's weapon, kept the man from getting the upper hand.

"Hit him!" Quinn cried out as he struggled to maintain control. Schmidt stepped forward and prepared to swing the gun like a baseball bat. Having one close call with friendly fire already, Quinn did not want to push his luck. "Not with the gun!" Quinn said in a fearful tone. "Find something else."

Schmidt tossed the gun to the side and started to glance around the room for anything which might be used as a weapon. The guard, realizing how desperate his situation was becoming, started to thrash his head around trying to catch Quinn's face with a blow from the back of his head. Quinn tried to avert this desperate assault, but he could not put up much of a defense. The guard caught Quinn square on the bridge of his nose. Pain rocketed through Quinn's sinuses; however, he managed to bear it and keep his grip until the man caught him with a second blow.

Trying his hardest not to, Quinn released his grip and his hands shot up reflexively to defend his face. The guard felt the grip slacken and immediately sat up to attack with his weapon. At that moment, Schmidt brought the torpedo room's stainless steel trash can down upon the man's head. The man slumped back, unconscious. His heavy head came crashing back down on Quinn's face for one last devastating blow.

CHAPTER 21

As Quinn pushed the limp man off of him, another call came over the 27MC to flood torpedo tube one. Out of the corner of his eye, Quinn noticed Schmidt disappear around the corner, but didn't give it much thought. Quinn stood and tried to stretch out his throbbing back. He was about to take the gun from the injured guard when he was startled by the sound of rushing water filling a torpedo tube. Letting go of the gun, he rushed to the weapons control panel.

"Schmidt! What the hell are you doing?" Quinn yelled, finding Schmidt standing at the controls for torpedo tube one. Schmidt pulled his hand away from the console as if he had been caught with his hand in the cookie jar.

"They said to flood the tube."

"Yeah and *they*," Quinn shouted above the noise of the flooding tube, "are the son of a bitches who are trying to have these bastards kill us!"

"Don't touch anything else," Quinn warned as he turned his attention back to retrieving the gun.

Expecting the man to be in the same heap on the deck where he had left him, Quinn was startled to find the man getting to his feet with the barrel of his gun trained on Quinn's chest. "You die now," the man said in broken English as he rubbed his head.

Before Quinn could even think of diving for cover, a wrench came swinging, seemingly out of the overhead, and caught the man in the back of his skull. This time Quinn saw the man's eyes roll into the back of his head as he went down for the count. Frozen in his tracks, Quinn saw Stoney struggling to crawl out over the top of the steel cylinder on the upper torpedo stowage tray.

"Stoney!" Quinn said in disbelief, "what are you doing up there?" Stoney, squeezing his head and chest through the few inches of clearance between the cylinder and the overhead, explained.

"I was just making a closer inspection of this cargo."

"I don't care what you were doing back there," Quinn said as he reached up to give him a hand. "Your timing couldn't have been better." Just as Quinn started to pull him out, another guard rounded the corner at the aft end of the torpedo room. The guard saw his companion lying on the deck and the two likely culprits over him. Quinn, seeing the man, yelled.

"Take cover!"

As the man raised his weapon, Quinn dove back in front of the weapons control panel. Stoney was able to slip back into the hole he had been climbing out of like a cockroach sliding through a paper-thin crack.

The guard sprayed off nearly twenty rounds into the already perforated cylinder. Three of the four thin metal straps which held the cylinder in place were severed by the volley of lead. The only strap which remained intact was the aft-most one.

Just outside the aft torpedo room door, Grant and Carter heard the shots as they prepared to enter. Grant, with a large meat cleaver in hand, made silent gestures to Carter. In ultimate stealth mode, Grant signaled that he would take the starboard side upon entering and Carter was to take the port side. Carter nodded in the affirmative. Grant spun the meat cleaver in his hand and made sure he had a tight grip. He looked down at Carter's hands and saw that he was holding a plastic spatula. Grant's eyes widened as a silent scream seemed to be frozen on his face. In a whisper, Carter explained.

"I was cooking eggs when you told me to follow you. You could have told me to grab a weapon!"

Grant rolled his eyes, nodded three slow and distinct nods, and then burst through the door. Immediately, he went starboard and Carter followed, turning to the port.

Grant came around the corner of the torpedo stowage tray and found the guard squatting trying to see if he had a shot underneath the cylinder at Stoney. Grant leaped in the air, let out the SEAL team battle cry, "HOOYAH!" and planted a kick square in the lower back of the guard. The kick sent the guard sprawling out onto the deck.

As Grant landed gracefully with his feet under him, Stoney called out from behind the cylinder, "Grant, the strap!" Not missing a beat, Grant spun around as if throwing a killer back fist punch and split the thin-metal strap with his cleaver. Stoney saw the strap, which had been under pressure, snap back like a broken rubber band.

"Dude!" Stoney cried out in amazement, not being able to see the meat cleaver in Grant's hand, "did you just karate chop that?" Grant had jumped backwards, expecting the cylinder to simply roll off the tray and come crashing down on top of the guard. Unfortunately, the chocks, which held it, provided enough of a lip to hold the canister in place even with all the straps off.

"You're a bad ass, Grant," Stoney continued. "I'm never messing with you again."

"Shut up and push," Grant said, as he saw the guard starting to recover. He began to pull on the container, trying to get it to roll.

Hearing Grant's voice, Quinn peeked around the corner. He saw the goon grimacing in pain as he tried to stand. Cocaine showered down upon the man out of the holes he had shot into the cylinder.

"Don't worry, Grant," Quinn said as he jumped up to give a hand in trying to roll the cylinder from his forward position, "I forgot to grab his gun, too." Grunting, Quinn called out to Schmidt who was still standing in front of the weapons control panel, "Schmidt! Give me a hand." No response came from Schmidt.

"Now, Schmidt!" Quinn ordered. He glanced over his shoulder at Schmidt when he still did not get any response. He could see Schmidt staring doe eyed at him. *Oh man*, Quinn thought, *I was wondering how much of this the kid would be able take before he snapped.*

"Schmidt," Quinn yelled as he started to feel movement of the cylinder, "snap out of it!" Schmidt continued just to look at him.

Quinn focused back on the cylinder and saw that it was starting to rock up on its chocks. Grant had grabbed a fire-fighting ax and was using it as a lever. Looking back at Schmidt, Quinn noticed tears starting to well up in the young sailor's eyes. Quinn's efforts slackened when blood started to come out of Schmidt's mouth.

"Schmidt!" Quinn screamed with concern as he let go of the cylinder.

Fortunately, as the container rocked up, Stoney was able to get a little more of his body behind it. With Stoney's greater leverage, and the lightened load as the container's powdery contents continued to spill out through bullet holes, the loss of Quinn's effort didn't matter. The cylinder came crashing down upon the last lucid guard as he began to stand. The force, with which the container came crashing down, surely crushed the life out of the two guards as well as blasted the cap off the cylinder, spilling more of its contents in the forward end of the torpedo room.

Quinn barely noticed the cylinder's crash, which echoed throughout the forward compartment, as he slowly approached Schmidt in disbelief. Schmidt reached his hand backward. Feeling his back, then bringing his hand forward to inspect it, he and Quinn were both startled by amount of blood which covered it. Schmidt stumbled forward. Quinn caught him and lowered him to the deck gently.

Movement in Quinn's peripheral vision caused him to whip his head around. Scarpa was coming at him slashing down with an already bloodied knife. Quinn was trapped. He tried to react but Scarpa had caught him with no defense. He knew he would not be able to stop the knife from piercing his flesh, he just hoped he would be able to twist enough as to not let it be a debilitating wound.

"HOOYAH!"

The SEAL battle cry, obviously working as intended, gave pause to Scarpa's attack. Carter, moving with surprising speed for a man of his size, sprang from behind Scarpa and wrapped the assassin in a massive bear hug. However, before Quinn was able to leap over to disarm him, Scarpa shot his arms upward as he dropped his hips to the deck. In a split second, he had slipped Carter's bear hug, turned and made two slashes with his knife. The first slash opened up a twelve inch laceration across Carter's large gut. The second came lower, catching Carter's inner thigh. The cut went deep and was more devastating than the superficial laceration on his midsection. The cut in the thigh dissected Carter's femoral artery. Stumbling backwards, Carter collapsed on the deck.

"Grant!" Carter cried out with mortal panic in his voice.

Quinn had brought Schmidt down onto his lap so his reaction wasn't fast enough to save Carter. By the time Quinn was able to hop to his feet the damage had been done.

Once again, the call came down to make tube one ready. Scarpa swung around and leaped toward the weapons control panel. Quinn managed to get between Scarpa and the controls. All his attention was focused on controlling and neutralizing Scarpa's knife hand. Quinn managed to grab Scarpa's right forearm as he slashed towards him. Using Scarpa's momentum, Quinn stepped to the inside and brought Scarpa crashing into his raised right elbow. The point of Quinn's elbow caught Scarpa on the left cheek bone, forcing his head to snap to the right. Thinking he had hurt Scarpa worse than he really had, he concentrated his efforts on twisting Scarpa's wrist, trying to force him to drop his knife.

Scarpa must have realized Quinn's focus on his knife hand and he simply let his arm go limp, dropping his knife. Quinn, surprised by the ease with which he was able to disarm Scarpa, hesitated momentarily. Scarpa didn't let the opportunity pass. He jerked his limp arm away, spun quickly and brought it swinging back around violently.

The wild punch caught Quinn in the temple. His hesitation, which allowed Scarpa to slip his arm away, didn't last but half a second and just before the punch landed, he was able to anticipate what was coming and rocked his head to the right so the blow wouldn't land with full force. Although the punch hadn't rocked Quinn as hard as it was intended, the bench seat in front of the weapons control panel tripped him.

As he hit the deck Scarpa did not take the opportunity to attack him, he turned his attention to the weapons controls. As he went to push the "Open Muzzle Door" button, Quinn yelled to him.

"Scarpa, no! Tube one isn't equalized!" Scarpa looked at the indicator on the weapons control panel. It was illuminated green, only because Quinn had never reversed the work-around he had set up when they were shooting off the exercise torpedoes.

"It's too bad we never played poker," Scarpa said as he pushed the button to open the muzzle door, "you're terrible at bluffing."

As the muzzle door came open there was a loud bang which resonated within the tube. The tube, not being equalized, was subjected to a surge of sea pressure that jammed the torpedo up against the locking bolt.

Quinn kicked out at Scarpa, catching him in the knee. Scarpa stumbled back, giving Quinn time to get to his feet. He was just about to press the button to shut the muzzle door when the torpedo fired.

The torpedo tube cycled but the torpedo did not leave. The torpedo's motor kicked to life. Its hum became louder and louder as it reached maximum RPMs without ever leaving the tube.

Startled by the firing of the torpedo, Quinn was nearly caught off guard when the attack from Scarpa came again. Rather than risk being tripped again by trying to duck backward to avoid the punch, Quinn stepped into Scarpa. While stepping in, he brought his left shoulder up to his ear; this allowed his shoulder to let Scarpa's blow glance off of it while he wrapped his hands around the back of Scarpa's neck in a Muy Thai clinch. That is, he was able to reach his hands back behind Scarpa's neck and interlace his fingers into a locked grip.

Scarpa, being a street brawler, wasn't trained to deal with such a technical fighter. To an untrained fighter, the position Quinn had gone for would seem to be a disadvantage. Scarpa confidently threw a few punches thinking Quinn's hands would be too tied up to stop them, but Quinn quickly neutralized Scarpa's blows by shifting either elbow without releasing his grip and it rendered the punches harmless. The same was true for any inside punches. Scarpa tried to sneak an uppercut in on Quinn, but again Quinn, having control of his head, could sense any subtle changes in his body weight and simply squeezed his elbows together before Scarpa could slide the punch through.

Losing any control of the situation, Scarpa tried escaping the clutch Quinn had him in. He tried to straighten his body from the hunched position Quinn was keeping him in. He had a couple of inches on Quinn and must have thought if he could straighten his back he might be able to break Quinn's grip.

Breaking Quinn's grip would not be so easy however; years of bailing hay had given Quinn forearms and a grip that Popeye would have been jealous of. As Scarpa drove his hips forward and his head back, trying to straighten up, Quinn used Scarpa's momentum to lift himself off the ground, driving a knee into Scarpa's ribs. Doubling over in pain, Scarpa found himself back in the same hopeless position.

Scarpa then tried instantly to retreat by ducking out of the clinch. Again, Quinn brought his knee up, this time landing it on Scarpa's nose. The power with which Quinn threw the knee was so great; it not only broke Scarpa's nose, it also broke the grip he had. Scarpa staggered backward with the hazy look of a fighter seeing a thousand flashes of light popping in his eyes. He grabbed hold of the torpedo storage tray to keep from falling.

Quinn's adrenaline kept him from mentally acknowledging how bad the kick had hurt his knee. He stepped forward into the aisle to continue the attack against Scarpa. As he did so, he could see Grant dragging Carter towards the back of the torpedo room. The sheer amount of blood on the deck and Carter's ashen color seemed to evaporate any adrenaline which was coursing through Quinn's veins. Suddenly, the pain in his back, knee, and face seemed to materialize for the first time.

Stoney, hearing the commotion in the forward part of the torpedo room, slid off the tray and ran; hunched over, on top of the cylinder he had just sent crashing down on the two guards. As he came to the front of the cylinder, he could see the cap had been knocked off by the impact and its powdery contents spilled about the deck. He took a running step off the cylinder and turned his foot, preparing to plant it on the deck and bound off, changing his momentum from a forward direction to a leap towards the port side in hopes of coming to Quinn's aid. What his foot planted on, however, was not a powder covered deck. His foot landed on something metal and round. This caused his ankle to roll and his body to continue forward as he crashed to the deck.

"What the hell!" Stoney exclaimed as he nursed his ankle. He looked back at the cylinder and noticed something cone-shaped jutting out from the powder. He crawled over to the object and pulled it out of the cylinder. It was about three feet long and ten inches wide at its base which tapered up to a rounded point.

"Quinn!" Stoney yelled. "I think we got a nuke warhead over here!"

Quinn, with pain shooting through his knee, answered without taking his eyes off of Scarpa. "What are you talking about?"

197

Stoney used his hand to brush the white dust off what appeared to him to be a warhead.

"I think there are nukes packed in with the coke!"

"Are you sure?" Quinn yelled.

"No, not really," Stoney answered, "I've only ever seen one in a James Cameron movie."

At that moment, Quinn realized they were shouting over the noise emanating from the torpedo tube. He looked at the breech door. The shiny brass of the door seemed to have a red tinge to it.

"Hot run!" Quinn shouted.

"No, I think it was *The Abyss*," Stoney shouted back.

"HOT RUN TUBE ONE!" Quinn screamed above the noise.

Stoney looked up and could see the tube starting to glow red from the heat. As he jumped to his feet, a sharp pain shot through his ankle, but it didn't stop him from flying to the 4MC.

"HOT RUN TORPEDO TUBE ONE!" Stoney screamed into the emergency phone.

Quinn, taking his attention off Scarpa, began trying to manually shut down the torpedo. He attempted to manually cut the control wire to the Torpedo by pulling the cutter handle on the breech door, but it was too hot to the touch. He turned to look for something he could insulate his hand with, but found Scarpa bringing a knife down upon him. In desperation, he threw up his arms and dropped to the deck instinctively attempting to keep his vital organs from being stabbed. The knife came down on his forearm. A quick twist of his wrist protected his ligaments from being slashed, but the tip of the blade jabbed into the radius bone of his lower arm.

Landing on the deck in front of tube three, water started to rain down on Quinn from the breech door of tube one, which was stacked just above tube three. The hot drizzle quickly became a spray as the door began to lose its watertight integrity. As he lay on his back, he could see Scarpa coming down in another relentless knife attack. Scarpa looked as though he was hoping to strike a more devastating target, when Quinn shot his foot upward. Quinn's heel caught Scarpa at the base of his sternum, knocking him back against the torpedo tray gasping for air.

At that moment, Quinn flinched as he heard what sounded like an explosion. The torpedo tube's breech door had weakened to the point where the sea pressure easily overcame it and it blew off the tube as if it were nothing more than a mere spitball. The two inch thick brass door rocketed aft, not slowing a bit as it ripped Scarpa's head and shoulders from his body.

Seeing the column of sea water blasting into the boat like the spray from a giant fire hose, Stoney tried to call out flooding into the 4mc, but the words failed him.

What was left of Scarpa's body crumpled down on top of Quinn. Letting out a stream of profanities, he struggled to kick the half corpse off of him. As he scurried across the port aisle, he noticed Grant and Carter were gone from the aft of the room. Once clear of the sea water column, Quinn jumped to his feet and hit the Flooding alarm which was inches from the spot where Stoney stood frozen with fear.

Immediately, the boat shifted to a steep up-angle. The roar of the flooding made it so Quinn could not hear the usual sound of rushing air which unmistakably indicated an emergency blow, but the speed with which the boat had taken the up-angle let him know that someone had thrown the "chicken" switches. He figured they must have been thrown before he had even hit the flooding alarm for events to happen so quickly. The angle the boat took forced Stoney to readjust his balance. The action seemed to bring him back to reality.

"We've got to get Schmidt out of here," Quinn yelled. The two scooped up Schmidt and headed toward the ladder at the front of the torpedo room. As Quinn walked backwards holding Schmidt's upper body, Stoney, who had Schmidt by the legs, motioned with his eyes for Quinn to look toward the deck.

Quinn looked down and saw it lying on the deck. In the middle of a pool of white powder was the ominous cone shape. He had never seen a nuclear warhead either, but to him it didn't seem like there was any other explanation.

"How many?" Stoney yelled.

"Say again!" Quinn shouted back as they continued to move.

"HOW MANY?" Stoney yelled trying to super annunciate with his lips.

Quinn understood. Judging by the size of the warhead, and then mentally comparing it with the size and number of cylinders, he came up with a rough calculation as they rounded the corner to the ladder. "AT LEAST FIFTY," he shouted.

"Let me give you guys a hand," a voice shouted down at Quinn and Stoney. They looked up and saw Rubber reaching down from middle level.

"Take him," Quinn directed, lifting Schmidt up so that Rubber could take hold of his shoulders. As Rubber lifted, Quinn and Stoney pushed from underneath.

Rubber pulled Schmidt back on top of himself in order to get Schmidt through the hatch. Quinn followed right behind. As Rubber rolled Schmidt off of him, he was startled by the glazed-over expression on Schmidt's face. He checked his pulse, but felt nothing. As Quinn hoisted himself through the hatch, Rubber said, "He's gone, Quinn."

Quinn knew as much from carrying him, he had just not let the fact sink in. He looked into Schmidt's eyes and saw no signs of life. Wiping tears from his own, he took the silver dolphin pin from his coveralls and pinned it to Schmidt's.

Looking down the ladder, Quinn saw Stoney disappearing into the torpedo room. "Stoney!" he yelled. Stoney sloshed back through the water, which was now ankle deep in the lower level and rising quickly. "What are you doing?"

"I'm just going to grab the KPOC's for us from down here. Go ahead, I'll catch up." Not waiting for any further protest from Quinn, Stoney was gone again.

"We need to get up to control, the Captain's gone off the deep end," Rubber told Quinn. Figuring Stoney would just be a few seconds behind, Quinn let his mind shift gears.

"How so?" Quinn asked.

"He's shooting people," Rubber said emphatically.

"Who?"

"He shot Bowden and that Ramirez guy shot the Weps."

"Hold on," Quinn said, as he disappeared through the forward crew's berthing door. By the time Rubber had pulled himself up to his feet, Quinn reemerged from the berthing compartment brandishing the Beretta pistol he had swiped from the gun locker.

"I stashed this in my rack," Quinn explained. "I wish I would have kept it on me; Schmidt might still be alive."

Quinn bounded up the ladder to the command passage way followed by Rubber. As they came to the top of the ladder, they could hear Ms. Collins banging on the stateroom door. The sailor, who had been posted as a sentry, apparently abandoned his post at the sounding of the flooding alarm.

"Ms. Collins is in there, get her out," Quinn ordered Rubber as he headed toward the control room. Quinn entered the control room and quickly trained his pistol on Ramirez.

"Drop your weapon, Quinn," Captain Maddox yelled. Quinn glanced over at him, but then immediately focused his attention back toward Ramirez. He wasn't surprised Captain Maddox was pointing a gun at him, Rubber had prepared him for the Captain's frame of mind, but he knew Ramirez, given the chance, would not hesitate to pull the trigger. As it was, Quinn had caught Ramirez by surprise and the pretend Spaniard did not have a chance to raise his weapon.

"Captain," Quinn tried to reason, "I don't think you have the full picture of what's going on here."

Annoyed, yet hesitant to fire off a round into Quinn as quickly as he had Bowden, Captain Maddox said, "I think I know more than you."

Losing his temper at his captain's arrogance, Quinn snapped back, "Did you know the boat is sinking?"

"We're on the surface now," Captain Maddox stated, "I'm sure the damage control team will have things under control in a matter of minutes."

Ms. Collins came bolting up the command passage way to control followed by her cameraman and Rubber.

"WE LOST A TUBE DOOR! THE BOAT IS FILLING WITH WATER!" Quinn screamed. The news blasted through the control room like a shockwave.

"Captain, we've got to abandon ship," Chief Meyers pleaded. "That's beyond the capacity of the boats pumps!"

Quinn could sense the way the news deflated Captain Maddox. "Do you know what's in those containers down there?" Quinn asked in a sympathetic voice. His softer tone withdrew a confession from Captain Maddox.

"Narcotics," the Captain said as he lowered his gun and his gaze toward the deck.

"Ha!" Quinn blurted out, bringing Captain Maddox's fallen gaze back up to attention. "The coke is just the packing material for the nuke warheads." Captain Maddox looked at him in disbelief. "There's got to be at least fifty warheads down there!" Quinn screamed. Ms. Collins turned to make sure Dave was rolling. Apparently knowing exactly why she was turning to him, he held up his thumb as if to reassure her that things were as juicy as they could get.

Captain Maddox suddenly focused on Ramirez

"I think the double-crosser has been double-crossed," Quinn said to Captain Maddox, his voice now lacking any sympathetic tones.

Chief Meyers, not waiting any longer for an official order, picked up the 1MC and called away, "ABANDON SHIP!" The sailors in the control room were too transfixed, too scared to move.

"GO! ALL OF YOU, TO THE FORWARD ESCAPE TRUNK!" Captain Maddox ordered. Most of the sailors in the control room headed for the aft door. Two sailors helped carry Bowden from the sonar shack. As they passed Captain Maddox, his eyes reddened as he restrained his tears.

Another sailor offered to help the Weps, who had managed to pull himself up onto his uninjured leg. The Weps pushed him away, telling him to go.

Unable to hold her tongue any longer, Ms. Collins piped up, "Those war heads are probably the rest of the ones your son died keeping out of Al Qaeda's hands!"

Everyone's attention was on Captain Maddox. The voyeuristic human impulse had intrigued everybody's curiosity and they waited to see the news hit him like a city bus. Dave, who had been doing his job long enough to realize this was the money shot, tightened his focus in on Captain Maddox. Quinn, however, did not take his eyes off Ramirez. He felt as if he were experiencing the emotions as his captain was, so he did not feel the need to see what sort of facial contortions the news of the warheads would illicit. The air in Captain Maddox's lungs left him in a great rush as if he had just been punched in the gut. And so it was, the skeleton crew left in the control room stood staring, as they watched the soul ripped out of a man. That is why no one saw the Nav coming.

Picking up the only weapon he could find in a split-second reaction, the Nav tackled Captain Maddox and began jabbing at his jugular with the pointed end of a quartermaster's compass. As he stabbed like a madman, he shouted incoherently about "giving everything up for him".

Chief Meyers was the first to react, trying to stop the Nav, but he had been behind Captain Maddox so it was difficult for him to fight off the Nav with the weight of the Captain pressing back against him. He called out for Quinn's help.

Quinn took three steps backward, reaching behind with his left hand in a blind attempt at grabbing the Nav without taking his eyes off Ramirez. He thought his eyes only dropped for a split second to get his bearings, but Ramirez who had been intently transfixed on the only person who posed a threat to him, dodged the moment Quinn's gaze failed.

When Quinn returned his attention to his target, Ramirez was gone. In the small control room, it didn't take long for Quinn to reacquire his target; but with insane speed, Ramirez had leapt behind Ms. Collins, snatched a fistful of hair at the base of her skull, and tightly pressed the stout muzzle of his MP-5 into her lower jaw.

"Drop your weapon!" Ramirez shouted as he crouched behind Ms. Collins, trying to make the most of his petite shield.

"Give it up, Ramirez!" Quinn coaxed as he stepped to the starboard side of the room, trying to get any sort of line of sight on his target, "there's nowhere to go."

Ramirez pulled Ms. Collins around and stepped back into the command passageway so no clear shot was available. He began to shuffle backwards down the slope of the passageway.

"Ramirez, you won't be able to open the weapons shipping hatch," Quinn tried to bargain. "Even though we're on the surface, at this angle the bow is still under."

"Shut up, you fool!" Ramirez snapped, showing frayed nerves for the first time. "This operation is not over!"

While Quinn was locking horns with Ramirez, the struggle still continued in the control room. Rubber was about to hit the Nav with a sound powered phone, when the bulk of the adrenaline-jacked Weps knocked him to the deck as he sailed past. Coming from behind, the Weps nearly crushed the Nav's larynx as he wrapped one of his massive hands around the smaller officer's skinny neck. Grabbing the Nav's belt with his other hand, he lifted the Nav into the air as if he were made of paper. He then slammed the Nav down, wedging him between number one periscope's shaft and its guide rod. As the Weps held the Nav down, Rubber leapt over and twisted the periscope's hydraulic activator wheel.

The Nav's screams became progressively louder and more panicked as the smooth shaft of the periscope slid upwards, rubbing against his side. As the body of the periscope ascended from the deck it lifted the Nav towards the overhead. The Weps let go of the Nav as he flailed, trying to free himself.

The hydraulic pressure worked too quickly and too powerfully for the Nav to save himself. The periscope pinned the Nav to the overhead, and slowed as it compressed his body. However, it did not stop until the unrelenting pressure crushed his bones as if they were made of toothpicks.

Dave nearly herniated a disc in his back twisting the camera back and forth trying to capture all of the events as they unfolded. The viewfinder seemed to give him a separation of reality in which he did not react as though he was in any danger.

Hearing the events escalate in the control room, Walker began to destroy any evidence which could be incriminating toward him. When the call came in to abandon ship, he pulled out a flash drive and uploaded a data eating virus into the systems hard drives. After the process was confirmed, he left his destructive activities and frantically headed out the door. As he ran from the radio room into the navigation equipment space, he could see the Weps hoisting the Nav into the air in the control room. He felt no draw of loyalty toward the Nav, and he quickly looked for his closest escape route before the Nav could try again to recruit him to help in his dire circumstances.

As the boat's down angle became more drastic, he could see sailors struggling past the foot of the ladder in middle level as they headed aft to escape the rising water. Horror seemed to grip Walker when he saw lower level had completely flooded and now middle level was beginning to fill. He grabbed the safety chain which acted as a parapet for the open ladder well and swung his feet down.

"Down ladder aye!" Grant snapped bitterly as Walker's feet almost caught him in the head.

As Quinn and Scarpa fought, Grant had dragged Carter out of the torpedo room's aft door. He had been treating Carter's wounds with the submarine sailors' bandage of convenience rather than choice, EB Green tape, when he heard the explosion of torpedo tube number one's breech door blasting off. As he finished up the makeshift tourniquet on Carter's thigh, water began to fill the lower compartment. Grant's skinny arms struggled to haul the stumbling girth of Carter up the ladder to middle level. He shouted for help to the sailors who ran past the ladder well headed for the escape trunk. Whether they did not hear him over the commotion, or they had all apparently adopted an "every man for himself" attitude, Grant pressed on, alone in his attempt to save his brother in arms.

Walker's sleeve got caught up on the safety chain and by the time he managed to free himself, Carter and Grant had already trudged through the water filling the crew's mess and were at the escape trunk ladder. Walker dropped into the water, which was now nearly waist deep, and climbed aft through the crew's mess.

As he was approaching the escape trunk, what sounded like a half a dozen voices could be heard inside the small trunk yelling down to Carter and Grant.

"There's no more room!"

"But, he's hurt," Grant implored as he stood behind Carter pushing him up the ladder. Carter was lucid enough to hold on to the ladder and had made it up to the fourth rung.

Not willing to wait for Carter and Grant to ascend into the trunk ahead of him, Walker lowered his shoulder and checked Grant as if he were at home playing hockey on the frozen lakes of Wisconsin. Grant hit the wet deck and skidded into the cold stores refrigerator. Next, Walker jumped up, grabbed Carter by the back of his collar, and yanked him off of the ladder sending him crashing to the deck. Just as Grant had scampered to his feet, a surge of water came up through the auxiliary machinery room access hatch at the foot of the escape trunk ladder.

"C'mon, Carter," Grant said, helping Carter to his feet, "we'd better make for the escape trunk in the engine room."

Walker tried to weasel his way up the ladder into the already overcrowded escape trunk. The sailors in the trunk, who had witnessed his assault on Grant and Carter, seemed to feel no sympathy for him as they kicked at his hands and head. One of the sailors unlatched the escape trunk's heavy lower hatch and screamed, "Stand clear! Stand clear!" As the heavy hatch came crashing down, it struck Walker in the head knocking him off the ladder. He reached out, grasping at anything to break his fall. Unfortunately for Walker, the first thing he managed to grab hold of was the hatch ring which formed the base of the seal for the two hundred pound hatch. The hatch, under normal circumstances, would have been slowed by its heavy spring, but due to the overcrowding in the escape trunk, a sailor had been standing on top of it when it was unlatched. This caused it to slam down, severing three of Walker's finger tips on his right hand. His screams echoed up into the escape trunk as he hit the deck.

After assisting Carter through the engine room's watertight door, Grant was about to continue aft when the Eng came flying around the corner at the far end of the passageway.

"Dog that hatch or we'll all die!"

"Sir, Carter's hurt, he needs a hand," Grant said, but the Eng apparently had not heard or taken notice of the plight of the two cooks.

"It wasn't my fault!" the Eng exclaimed as he disappeared around the corner.

Water began to spill over the lip of the watertight door as Grant set to work shutting it. The watertight door to the engine room was unlike any other internal hatch on the boat. It literally separated the boat into two compartments. The design was intended to save a reasonable portion of the crew if there was a catastrophe on either the end of the boat. The hatch was constructed so that it would be able to be closed against great pressure. The mechanics for this consisted of a large hand wheel which turned a small screw shaft that would pull the hatch shut. The effect was a reduction gear that allowed an 18 to 1 ratio; that is, one man would have the strength of eighteen.

Grant turned the wheel as fast as he could. "Come on! Come on!" he beckoned it to close even faster. When there was approximately four inches before the hatch was sealed, he heard someone yell on the other side and then a foot came jutting through the opening at the bottom of the hatch. Grant was about to reverse direction which he had been turning the wheel, when he noticed Walker's face peer through the small, yet thick, porthole in the hatch.

"Open the hatch, you prick!" Walker scowled. Grant most likely would have instantly opened the hatch for any of his other shipmates, but the cruelty Walker had employed on Carter and him moments earlier had sealed his fate.

Rather than reversing course, Grant doubled his efforts. Walker screamed as the thick steel hatch compressed tightly on his leg. It had closed so quickly that he was not able to pull his leg free. Grant continued to shut the hatch, which began to break the skin on Walker's leg. Walker writhed in pain and beat at the door with his undamaged left hand.

Grant continued spinning the wheel as the water began coming through with greater force. Even if he had reversed direction at this point, the incoming rush of water most likely would have carried him away before he would have been able to let Walker through, and then reclose the door. Walker's leg showed no sign of impeding the door's progress toward sealing the compartment. However, two muffled pops, the breaking of Walker's tibia and fibula, shot what was left of Grant's nerves. He could no longer muster the mental or physical strength to continue turning the wheel, which would have had no trouble severing Walker's lower leg.

Being completely spent, Grant dropped backwards onto the deck next to Carter and tried to catch his breath. Walker's eyes peered desperately through the porthole. Instantly, his blue eyes had transformed into psychotic bloodshot orbs as he used every last drop of oxygen in his murderous screams. The water, which had been spraying through the hatch at the bottom, seemed to march evenly up both sides of the oval hatch.

Walker's screams were abruptly cut off as the water overcame him. A frightening amount of water blasted through the hatch with only an inch or so left unsealed around the circumference. As Grant backed away from the hatch, the last he saw of Walker was his bloody fingertips scratching at the porthole glass.

Grant tried to get Carter to his feet, but his friend had slipped into unconsciousness.

CHAPTER 22

Ramirez continued to backslide down the command passageway, followed by a resolute Quinn. "There's nowhere to go, Ramirez," Quinn continued in a stern voice. "Just put the gun down and you might survive this thing."

Ms. Collin's pleaded with her eyes, unable to speak with the barrel of Ramirez's weapon thrust so firmly against her throat. Ramirez, reaching the forward end of the command passageway, stepped down onto the ladder which led to middle level. When his foot hit the second step, it landed in water.

"The two levels below us have already filled with water," Quinn shouted. "You can't go that way!"

Tears broke and ran down Ms. Collin's cheek as she heard Ramirez begin to hyperventilate. Quinn heard him taking the deep heavy breaths as well. "Ramirez, stop!"

Ramirez cried out, "Allahu Akbar!" Then, he shoved Ms. Collins forward, let off a stream of bullets, and disappeared into the water below. Quinn did not flinch as the bullets sprayed past him. He kept his aim, and after Ms. Collins had fallen to the deck, he returned fire. He walked swiftly past her and continued to fire into the watery void until his clip was emptied. As the last casing was ejected from the chamber, he stood above the stairwell searching for any sign of Ramirez. Ramirez was gone.

His gaze was broken when he heard the grunt of pain from Ms. Collins. He spun around to see her trying to crawl toward the control room with a limp right arm. The dark blue of her coveralls was becoming increasingly darker as oxygen-rich blood seeped into the fabric.

"Stephanie!" he cried as he leapt to her side. He turned her over and could see that one of the bullets had pierced her shoulder just above her clavicle. "Stephanie, hold on! Rubber! Give me a hand!"

Without hesitation, Rubber slid down to them and helped Quinn carry her into the control room. They put her on the deck just in front of the conning station and began to address her wound.

"Camera guy," Quinn snapped, "put that thing down and give us a hand." Dave, for the first time, pulled his eye off the viewfinder and looked to Ms. Collins for orders.

"Keep rolling!" Ms. Collins forced out through gritted teeth. Dave, quite happily put the camera back to his face.

"What, are you trying to win an Edward R. Murrow award?" Quinn asked.

"A second one," she answered, just before she let out a painful cry.

"Chief Meyers!"

"Yes Quinn," Chief Meyers responded.

"Check to see if we can get to the aft escape trunk."

"Check to see if we can get to the aft escape trunk, aye," chief Meyers repeated the order as if it had come from the Officer of the Deck, not someone two pay grades his junior. He gingerly let Captain Maddox, who he had been attending to, sit back against the ships control panel and then headed aft to check the escape route.

"I'm going to put some heavy pressure on your wound to try and stop the bleeding," Quinn said, trying to prepare Ms. Collins for the forthcoming pain. "This is going to hurt."

"Okay," she said softly, all brashness gone from her voice. Quinn applied the pressure needed on her wound. She grimaced, but no scream came.

"Chief Meyers, what are we looking at? We've got to get her off of here!"

Chief Meyers came hustling back from the navigation equipment space. "Water level's just about up to the deck plates," he reported regretfully.

"We're not getting out that way," Rubber stated.

"The bridge hatch, drain it!" Quinn snapped. Rubber jumped up and turned the valve to drain the bridge hatch.

"It might be under water," Chief Meyers spoke aloud everyone's fear.

"We'll have to take the chance," Quinn replied. "Rubber, we can't wait all day! Get that hatch open!" Rubber climbed the ladder leading to the hatch and undogged it. As he did, a small amount of water came down, but quickly dissipated.

"Well that's one hatch, let's hope we get lucky with the next one," Rubber said as he pushed the hatch open and latched it in the upright position. He climbed to the next one and tried to turn the wheel but was not successful. He yelled down, "If the Weps can handle it, I'm going to need him on this one."

Quinn looked to the Weps, who was finishing up applying a makeshift pressure bandage on his own wound. "Do you think you can make it up there, Weps?"

"It's either that or die, isn't it?"

"That's the way I see it."

"Well, I plan on seeing my wife and kids by the time this day is over," the Weps said optimistically as he hoisted himself up. Rubber jumped down the ladder and moved to the side to make room for the Weps.

"She's all yours, big guy."

The Weps stopped his hobbled ascent and stared at Rubber. "I'm still the Weapons Officer to you, Petty Officer Prophylactic."

Rubber cringed as the Weps headed toward the upper hatch. "Camera guy, you're next," Quinn said. Dave did not react; he just continued to shoot the video. "Dave, up the hatch now!" Quinn shouted in such a manner, it broke the media trance Dave had been caught up in. Immediately, he moved to the ladder.

"Here, I'll hand it up to you," Rubber said, holding out his hands to take the camera from Dave.

"Great," Dave said as he trustingly handed over his Panasonic HPX 2000 camera, "hand it up to me when I get in the middle so I can shoot Stephanie's escape."

"You bet," Rubber replied with a grin. As Dave hoisted himself up the ladder, Rubber looked to Quinn. Quinn gave him nod. A smashing sound alarmed Dave as he climbed past the lower bridge hatch. When he looked down, his face instantly reddened with anger as he saw Rubber smashing his camera against the ladder.

"What the hell are you doing?" Dave screamed, coming back down a few rungs.

"The world doesn't need to see that," Quinn said as Rubber tossed the mangled camera down the passageway.

"You're going to protect him?" Dave questioned indignantly.

"We're not protecting him," Quinn explained coldly, "we're protecting the memory of his son."

Suddenly a rush of air burst past them all and the water began to rise visibly faster. "The upper hatch is open," the Weps called down.

"We've got to move quick. Chief Meyers, get the Captain," Quinn ordered.

Chief Meyers took hold of Captain Maddox, preparing to lift him to his feet.

"No," Captain Maddox said weakly, "leave me."

"Captain, just stand up with me," Chief Meyers pleaded.

"Leave him," Quinn said.

"We can't-"

Before Chief Meyers could state a case for not leaving Captain Maddox, Quinn cut him off.

"It's his choice," Quinn snapped, "besides it's a tradition that's been around longer than any of us." Quinn locked eyes with Captain Maddox. "Personally, I think he's taking the easy way out." Captain Maddox's gaze fell to the deck. "Now help me with Ms. Collins!" Chief Meyers reluctantly let go of Captain Maddox and moved to assist Quinn.

"Dave, get your ass up that ladder and help us with her," Quinn barked. Dave had been stuck watching the saga of Captain Maddox's decision to stay unfold as if he were still filming it. He nodded his head as though he were a witless moron without his camera and scrambled up the ladder. As Quinn and Chief Meyers carried the limp-bodied Ms. Collins to the ladder, Rubber stepped back, knocking open the door to the Captain's stateroom. A banging, which had not been noticeable above the commotion in the control room, was now audible. Curious, Rubber turned and looked to the source of the banging, the outer wall of the Captain's stateroom.

"Sparks!" he remembered out loud. "Quinn, Sparks is still in the outboard!"

Quinn felt his skin grow instantly cold as thousands of his capillaries constricted with the shock of realizing he had forgotten Sparks. "Dave, grab her," he said, handing Ms. Collins up to her colleague. He ran over to the bulkhead and started banging back on it. "Sparks!" he yelled through the bulkhead, "I'm going get you out of there!" Quinn looked quickly around the room. Seeing nothing which might help, he bolted out the door to go find something he could use.

In the outboard, Sparks' legs were now immersed in water as it was rapidly rising. "I knew you wouldn't forget," Sparks called back thankfully. "You've got to get me out of here fast!" Sparks waited for a response, but heard none. "Quinn," he called out. Still, he received no response. "Quinn!" he screamed. He waited another moment. When he still hadn't heard back from Quinn, he started to panic. He began to bang his head against the bulkhead again. His head was the only appendage he had enough freedom of movement with to pound out a distress call.

His restricted flailing ceased immediately when an ax blade came crashing through the bulkhead about four inches from his face. The blade stuck there momentarily, wiggled a bit, and then was pulled free.

"HIGHER AND AFT! HIGHER AND AFT!" Sparks screamed. The next swing came crashing through about two inches higher than the first. "NOT HIGHER ENOUGH!" Sparks directed.

After a few good blows, Quinn was able to stick his fingers through the wood paneling and get a grip. With the help of adrenaline, he was able to pull nearly half of the bulkhead off. The opening was big enough for Sparks, and about 200 gallons of water, to come spilling out onto the deck.

Quinn helped Sparks to his feet. Sparks tried to take a deep breath, but as his lungs filled with air, a sharp pain shot through his midsection. "Aww!" he exclaimed, "I think I broke some ribs because of you."

"But you're a hero, man." Just as Quinn made his remark, Sparks caught him with an unexpected punch to his ribs. Quinn doubled over in pain. "Ow! You bastard!" he exclaimed. "You don't know what I've been through."

"Quinn," Rubber interrupted their not so happy reunion, "Weps just hollered down from topside. He said we don't have long 'til the water spills over the top of the sail."

"Let's go," Quinn prodded Sparks from behind. His lumbering friend winced his way up the ladder, climbing with one hand and guarding his ribs with the other. Just as Quinn and Rubber were about to make their egress, they noticed an eruption of bubbles at the forward end of the command passageway where the water was now creeping up the deck. A figure emerged from the water wearing an EAB mask. Quinn drew the Beretta, which he had tucked in his belt, but his heart sank when he remembered he had emptied his clip. He aimed anyway.

"Don't shoot," Stoney yelled, showing his hands. Quinn lowered his empty pistol, while Stoney ripped the EAB from his head. "I can't believe that actually worked," Stoney said, looking at the EAB mask in amazement.

"Are you crazy?" Quinn blurted out. "We have to get off this boat! What were you doing fartin' around down there?"

"I was just getting some extra KPOCs," Stoney claimed as he pulled a bundle of KPOC life vests up from a tether he had attached to the life vest he was wearing.

"Just hurry up," Rubber insisted, growing increasingly impatient.

"Okay but-"

"But nothin', let's go," Rubber grabbed him by the arm and led him to the ladder like a bouncer escorting an obnoxious patron out the door.

"But, that bad guy was headed down to the torpedo room."

Quinn grabbed Stoney by the arm and spun him around. "Ramirez?"

"Was that his name?" Stoney asked.

"Yes," Quinn answered. "Was he wearing an EAB?"

"Yeah," Stoney recalled, with little concern.

"Come on," Quinn began to move the two sailors toward the ladder, "you guys head up, before it's too late."

"What are you going to do?" Rubber asked, noticing Quinn hadn't included himself.

"I've got to stop him."

"What's the point?" Rubber tried to convince him it wasn't necessary. "The boat's going sink in a few minutes."

"If he sets one of those nukes to detonate, it won't matter if we get off the boat; it will vaporize the water and everything in it for a half a mile."

"I'm coming with you then," Rubber bravely offered.

"No," Quinn refused, "it will be hard enough swimming around trying to find an EAB connection alone; if there were two of us we'd just get our lines tangled." Rubber seemed relieved Quinn had given him an out. It was no secret he never felt that comfortable in an EAB during fire drills; it would take no stretch of the imagination to understand the panic he would feel being submersed in one. "Stoney, hand me your EAB."

"Sure," Stoney said handing him the mask.

"This thing worked underwater for you?" Quinn questioned him.

"It was getting a little dicey down on lower level where the water pressure was higher, but it did the trick."

"Here, let me see it," Rubber said grabbing the EAB and pulling out his Leatherman. He adjusted the screw on the top plate of the regulator manifold as tight as it would go. "That'll raise the rate of air delivery to the max, should give you an extra fifteen feet or so."

"Thanks," Quinn said as he took back the mask.

"The air is going to come at you quick, so you'll just have to relax. Don't breathe it as fast as it wants to come; you'll hyperventilate," Rubber warned.

"Alright, you guys get out of here."

"Good luck, Quinn." Stoney shook his hand then headed up the ladder with the gaggle of KPOCs swinging like a pendulum at the end of the lanyard. It was then that Rubber and Quinn noticed EB green tape on all the seams of the life vests, as well as a white residue leaking out one of the frayed edges.

"Really, Stoney," Quinn yelled up after him, "the boat is sinking and that is what you were risking your life for?"

"I don't know what you're talking about, man," Stoney hollered back innocently.

Rubber turned and faced Quinn. He put his hand on Quinn's shoulder, "Good luck."

"Thanks," Quinn said genuinely, "I'll need it, now go."

Rubber gave him a nod and began his climb to the surface. Quinn began to don the EAB when Captain Maddox called out to him. Quinn ducked back into the control room and found that Captain Maddox had pulled himself up into the Chief of the Watch's chair. Quinn answered him softly as if he were about to take an order from him.

"Yes, Captain?"

Captain Maddox studied him for a moment, then turned and gazed at the ships control panel. "I remember the first time I sat at the ship's control panel, not this one of course, but I was a wet behind the ears Lieutenant JG, fresh from the academy and scared to death."

"That's nice, Captain, but I have to go stop a guy trying to blow up the boat," Quinn interrupted impatiently. "There's no code that says *I* have to go down with the ship."

As if he didn't hear him, Captain Maddox continued, "Seems like it was yesterday."

"Good bye, Captain," Quinn said as he turned to leave.

"He's not going to blow up the boat, Quinn," Captain Maddox suddenly blurted out.

"Say again, sir."

"He's not going to blow up the boat. He's got an inflatable Zodiac boat down there."

"What are you talking about, sir?" Quinn asked, suddenly feeling like he could take a little time to pump the Captain for some intel.

"The plan was to ferry these guys up to Saint Catherine's Sound in Georgia, and under the cover of night, they would off-load their cargo and take it upriver with their inflatable boats to a waiting truck."

"And what were you supposed to get out of the deal?"

"I was going to have a seventy-five million dollar retirement fund to disappear with."

"And the nukes?"

"I had no idea about the warheads. I convinced myself I was just going to bring that garbage in, people could shovel it up their noses and I wouldn't give a damn." His resolve melted and he began to weep. "I've gone against everything my son died for. I've betrayed my son."

"Even if he manages to get the boat launched, he won't get far," Quinn began to rationalize. "I mean, we're still out in the middle of the Atlantic, the battle group will take him out by daybreak."

"We're within twenty five miles of the coast."

"What!" Quinn exclaimed as he darted over to the Quartermaster's plot.

"We were avoiding the Battle Group by hugging the coast."

"Captain," Quinn looked at the chart in horror, "we're only thirty miles from Miami! There could be a million people dead in an hour!"

Quinn noticed the tube indicator light for torpedo tube number three at the fire control station light up, indicating the muzzle door had been opened.

"He's trying to go out the tube!"

Quinn wasted no more time talking with ghosts. As Captain Maddox's apology echoed after him, he slid down the command passageway, putting on his EAB as he went and dove down the stairwell to middle level.

As Rubber climbed toward the top of the bridge, he noticed Quinn fly by underneath the hatch. Then, water which had been spilling over the top of the sail rapidly became a steady stream. He was a mere four feet from the surface when, assisted by the ever increasing down angle of the boat, the force of the water became too great for him to climb against. He clung to the ladder with all his strength. He looked down to see the water rising in the compartment below and found he could not lift his head against the pressure of the water spilling over him. He tried to breathe, but the spray was so great it was like being waterboarded. When his grip finally failed, he fell off the ladder only to be met by a press of water shooting up the hatch. In a matter of seconds, he found himself free of the submarine and kicking towards the surface.

CHAPTER 23

Quinn entered the water and let his eyes adjust to the lower visibility before he began his search for an EAB manifold. He didn't need to search long. He knew where every EAB manifold was on the boat, but he did have to orientate himself to swimming in the middle level passageway. He found the manifold just above the ladder which led to lower level. As soon as he inserted the fitting on the end of the air hose into the manifold's receptacle, a blast of salt water shot into his face. The sting to his eyes was unexpected, but it was followed by breathable air which set Quinn's mind at ease.

The air did come faster than Quinn was used too, causing him to concentrate on taking shorter breaths than normal; the danger being hyper-inflated lungs. Once he got used to the rhythm with which he would have to breathe, he descended to lower level. He would have liked to have had a weight belt on to help keep him grounded sufficiently. Also, it would have made him more stable if it came to weightless hand-to-hand combat. However, he knew he couldn't afford the time to make a pit stop at his dive locker. As it was, he had very little body fat, so being overly buoyant was not a significant problem.

As he swam into the torpedo room, he noticed the warhead he and Stoney had seen spilled onto the deck was missing. Cautiously, he peered around the weapons control panel and saw Ramirez loading some equipment into torpedo tube number three, the lower tube on the port side. Quinn saw him climb half way into the tube as he pushed a bundled self-inflating zodiac boat down the shaft. Seeing his opportunity, Quinn unhooked his EAB. He quickly covered the end of the fitting with his thumb in an attempt to reduce the amount of salt water which would dowse him the next time he plugged in. Using the small metal handles on the individual components within the weapons control panel like little ladder rungs, he pulled himself around the corner and towards the port side. Piecing a plan together as he moved, he spotted the manifold he would plug into when he reached the port side. What little of the impending attack he had begun to visualize quickly diminished when he noticed Ramirez shimmying his way back out of the tube. Quinn began to backpedal as if he were an inept diver in a Jaws movie.

At first, Ramirez did not notice Quinn. His mask was halfway filled with water and he was preoccupied with trying to clear it out. Quinn made a mental note to thank Rubber for his last second adjustment to his mask's regulator; that is, if he ever saw him again. He tried to move slowly, not making any sudden movements that would catch Ramirez's eye. He was contemplating making a rush at Ramirez while his vision was impaired, but in the moment of hesitation, Ramirez finally blew the water out of his mask. The shocked look on Ramirez's face told Quinn he had been stunned to see him. The stun effect only lasted a half a second though, and Ramirez raised his weapon.

Quinn didn't know if the MP-5 could fire under water, but the ratcheting pops he heard as he retreated answered his question. Although it sounded like it fired, as Quinn ducked back behind the starboard side of the weapons control panel, he did not notice any bullets cavitating past him, nor did he feel any strike his body. As he plugged back into the manifold, he realized the shot of adrenaline had used up his brains oxygen supply faster than he expected. He worked at calming his mind like he had been forced to do during Pool Week in dive school, a week where the instructors went MMA on the students underwater to teach them not to panic.

Once Quinn had replenished his oxygen and his nerves sufficiently, he dared to take another look. He made a quick glance, but hadn't noticed any movement, so he chanced a longer gaze. When he studied the area a bit longer, he saw no sign of Ramirez. Hesitantly, he kicked his feet and floated out from his hiding place. He knew if the weapon had fired under water it was ineffective at a short distance, but coming up against it at point blank range would leave him as food for the sharks. He cautiously made his way to the port side of the room, watching for any sign of Ramirez preparing to pounce on him. As he neared the end of the weapons control panel he knew he would be coming to the most likely spot to be waylaid. His heart began to pound like a child playing hide and go seek. He felt as if he were about to get ambushed and he did not even have a weapon. A trip to the dive locker began to seem like it would have been the smarter choice, now that he was feeling vulnerable. He would have felt much more secure with the heavy steel of his eight inch dive knife in his hand.

Unfortunately for Quinn, the particular spot he decided to search for a weapon happened to be the area of the torpedo room where all the training manuals were stowed. A manual on hand-loading a torpedo wasn't going to do him much good at this point, but then a glint on the deck caught his eye. After a closer inspection, he found Scarpa's buck knife resting at the foot of the bench seat. He scooped up the knife and shoved off into the aisle between the tube bank and the weapons control panel. No Ramirez.

He peered down tube three, but saw only blackness. He pulled one of battle lanterns, an emergency 12 volt boxed flashlight, out of its holder at the edge of the tube bank and aimed its shaft of light down the tube. Near the end of the long tube, he could see Ramirez kicking frantically to push the equipment into the open ocean. He knew with the restricted movement inside the torpedo tube, he would not be able to swim it's length fast enough to catch Ramirez and if Ramirez got out with a boat there would be no stopping him without having one himself.

He turned to inspect the hard shelled cases stored on the lower torpedo stowage tray. Both cases were opened. In the foremost case, he saw what looked like a rubber area rug rolled up. This was no doubt the second Zodiac boat. In the aft case, he found an electric motor, which appeared to be in working order. Ramirez had obviously not anticipated anyone following him, so he apparently saw no need in wasting time sabotaging the second boat.

Quinn gathered the items and stationed them in front of the torpedo tube to prepare for his escape. Peering down the tube once more, he saw that Ramirez had been able to kick his way out of the tube. When Quinn turned back to gather the equipment, the motor was missing. He scanned left and right with no sign of the motor. His heart seemed as though it was in his throat. There was a flash of light above him which made him jump. His heart rate slowed a bit when he realized it was just the dim glow of the emergency lights refracting off of the motors propeller. The electric motor surprised Quinn with its buoyancy. He had to pull it down so it would not float away. It seemed to be oversized for an electric motor, so Quinn assumed it was intentionally designed with foam-filled buoyancy chambers to prevent the loss of a motor in a critical situation.

However, at the moment it created a snag in the plan for Quinn. Without swim fins, he didn't think he would be able to create enough thrust to push it down the torpedo tube to make his escape. Swimming the twenty one foot length of the torpedo tube in one breath would be difficult enough without extra baggage. With the torpedo tube being only twenty one inches in diameter, arm strokes would be impossible. Quinn would also have to contend with the fact that the submarines current down angle meant the swim was not only going to be twenty one feet in length, he would also be swimming down about eight feet, all while trying to push a floating object.

Ramirez was able to do it, Quinn thought with near fatal pride, *surely I should be able to.* However, just before he was about to make a go of it, he remembered Ramirez also had the dense weight of the warhead which surely must have helped to pull him down the tube. Quinn's eyes flashed around the compartment for an object which he could use to pull him and his equipment down the tube like a free diver's weighted sled. *The tool bags,* he remembered. Like an astronaut, he leaped effortlessly across to the bench seats in front of the weapons control panel. He pulled out the tool bags filled with the TDU weights they had used in place of bar bells. The dense weight of the bags made Quinn struggle to bring them in front of the tubes. He unlashed the webbing strap which secured the garbage can and used it to tie the two weight bags together. Then, wrapping the free end of the strap twice around his hand, making it tight enough that it wouldn't slip, but not so tight he wouldn't be able to easily cast it off once he cleared the torpedo tube, he took five deep breaths to store up the largest amount of oxygen he could.

Having his brain sufficiently oxygenated to last him at least two minutes, Quinn unplugged the EAB mask, tossed the weight bags into the torpedo tube, followed by the electric motor, and then the inflatable boat which he hugged with his left hand knowing that would be the one thing he would need to be holding once free. The weight bags worked exactly as intended. Quinn didn't even need to kick his legs; he just held on for the ride. It only took a few seconds before Quinn heard the zipping sound of the canvas weight bags sliding down the steel of the torpedo tube go silent. He knew this meant they had cleared the tube. He loosened his grip on the strap, preparing to jettison the bags so they could continue their descent into the abyss, when he came to a complete and sudden painful stop.

As the electric motor cleared the tube it quickly shot upwards. Although it was clear of the tube, the motor's powerhead became wedged in the void just above, where the outer hull hung over the tube so that when the muzzle doors were shut there would be a smooth, non-cavitating surface. With the motor's powerhead wedged, its midsection and lower unit blocked anything else from exiting the tube. Quinn had no idea what had happened. The dim light from the torpedo room did not filter all the way down to the end of the torpedo tube. He began to shimmy his way past the rolled up boat. As he climbed over the rolled rubber, which took a little over half the diameter of the tube, he was forced to blow out what little air he had in his lungs. The struggle getting past the boat had his muscles metabolizing the oxygen content in his blood stream much faster than he had anticipated. He knew he could hold his breath for about three minutes while holding still, but only about a minute and ten seconds if he was exerting himself.

The thought of going back to the torpedo room and plugging his mask back in to breathe while he contemplated alternative options seemed like the best idea, but it was not really even a viable option. Quinn would have to try and swim backwards to get there since turning around in such a tight space was impossible. He had no choice but to press on. Finally, he was able to squeeze past the boat, but the midsection arm of the motor hung in front of the mouth of the tube like a stalactite preventing a desperate spelunker from entering an enormous cavern.

He grabbed the arm with both hands and tried to shake it violently from side to side with only a hint of movement. Then he arched his back up, pressing it against the curve of the upper portion of the tube and pushed the arm downward. It worked. Quinn was able to pull the motor down from the void then push it out so it began its ascent to the surface. However, the exertion had left Quinn's lungs trying to gasp for air. He concentrated on closing off his throat while his diaphragm instinctively contracted trying to draw in air. The battle between the muscles of his upper throat, consciously being tightened, and the lungs trying to replenish themselves with air which was not available caused a croaking noise which seemed to be amplified by the water surrounding his body.

Quinn reached back and pulled the rubber boat free. Once in the open blackness, he felt along the edges of the rubber boat for the air release pin. Still fighting his own body's attempted gasps for air; he found the pin and yanked it. The rushing sound of air being released into the boat mimicked the sound of the water rushing into the submarine. He tightened his grip as he felt the relief of a quick ascent. The little air which had been left in his lungs began to expand as the sea pressure diminished, causing him to exhale the oxygen depleted gases.

The inflated zodiac boat acted like a booster engine, rocketing him towards the surface. As he and the boat vaulted from the water like the shuttle breaking through the atmosphere, Quinn felt as if every cell in his body gasped for air. He landed on the deck of rubber boat with his mind on nothing but the replenishment of his oxygen supply.

The thin rubber deck, combined with the swells of the ocean, made it seem as if he were on a waterbed and the events of the last few days had been long ago in a past life. Exhaustion was beginning to wear down his cognitive functions. The soft echoes of the water lapping against the rubber pontoons seemed to beckon him to sleep. He was on the verge of slipping into a deep sleep, when suddenly the whir of a motor seemed to slice its way through the ocean's lullaby, and he shot up as if an electric eel had just unleashed a charge through his system.

He searched the blackness, trying to discern the direction of propeller wash. The motor was much quieter than a standard gasoline powered outboard, which made the task of locating it extremely difficult. It wasn't until his eyes caught the glint of a faint bioluminescence trail that he was able to follow it to the direction of the sound. In the valley of a swell, he could just make out the darkened silhouette of Ramirez in his small boat. The boat was just breaking over the crest of the swell so Quinn knew he had to work quickly.

He began to scan the water once again, looking for the motor as the valley he was in seemed to begin to rise like an elevator. A panicked thought ran through his mind that the motor hadn't broken completely free and was still wedged at the muzzle end of the torpedo tube. His mind was set at ease however when he saw it bobbing about ten yards from the boat. He looked around the boat for some rope. He knew he had held onto a rope during his rocketed ascent to the surface, but after a quick inspection he realized that the rope was affixed to the boat and threaded through thick rubber eyelets on top of the inflated pontoon, specifically designed to assist swimmers in pulling themselves out of the water. Even if he had managed to detach it, it would only offer about 17 feet of line.

He dropped to his knees and began to examine the deck. He knew there had been some deviations in the flat surface, which upon reflection would have made lying on the deck quite uncomfortable. He couldn't believe that just a few seconds earlier he would have sworn it was as comfortable as a pillow top mattress in a five star resort. He tugged at an especially rigid flap toward the stern. The harsh ripping sound of Velcro tore at the silence which surrounded him. Tucked into the fold on the deck was a small tool pouch and what appeared to be a hundred feet of quarter inch nylon rope.

Le Poignard

"Sir," the drone technician called out, "It appears another inflatable has emerged." Reno stepped over to the technician's screen.

"Stay with the first one until we get some sort of idea as to what's going on."

"He's certainly not interested in going back for any of his shipmates," the technician added.

"Get in a little closer," Reno said with intense quiet interest, "let's see if we can get a read on his face."

They watched the screen as the drone dropped from its bird's eye view position to a position more level with the horizon where they could scan the features of the face.

"Got it," the technician reported. "Beginning search with US DOD personnel." The two stood by as a small window popped up on the screen and began flashing through identification photos as the computer ran its facial recognition logarithms. A smaller history window extended from the bottom portion of the inset window. The first message began to blink.

"He doesn't match up with any of the personnel assigned to the Key West," the technician redundantly informed his Captain. Reno nodded slowly in acknowledgement as he studied the face of the man in the boat. Another message popped up.

"He doesn't match with any US Navy personnel, sir," the technician said with bewilderment. "Should I see if he matches with any of the CIA personnel?"

"No, the US DOD doesn't go to great lengths to protect Naval identities, but if we go digging in CIA files, we may end up drawing a little too much attention to ourselves," Reno said cautiously. "Try searching Interpol's criminal database, but first, switch to a thermal scan on his boat."

"Switching to thermal scan," the technician dutifully reported. As soon as he switched to the thermal scan mode, the cone shaped object lying on the deck of the boat practically jumped off the screen.

"Sir!" the technician screamed.

"I see it," Reno said with the first signs of tension in his voice. "You'll have to get closer to do a biological/nuclear material scan!"

"Captain!" De Panafiue called out from the plot screen, "he's headed straight for the port of Miami!" Reno started to head to the plot where De Panafiue was standing when the technician cried out, "He's spotted us! He's shooting!"

"Get us out of there!" Reno ordered as he snapped back around, "How did he spot us!" They watched the screen with desperation scrawled across their faces. The tension came out of Reno's shoulders first. "He's not shooting at us, he's shooting behind him."

The technician had already made a quick ascent to a bird's eye view again. "The other boat," the technician pointed to the screen, "he's catching up!"

"Find out who is in that other boat!" Reno snapped.

CHAPTER 24

Quinn's Zodiac

Quinn was lying as flat as he could on the deck of the rubber boat with his feet toward the bow and his head at the stern. His face was just inches under the tiller of the motor. He had his left hand wrapped tightly around the tiller with the throttle wide open. He was swinging it wildly back and forth causing the boat to jump from port to starboard as bullets ripped past. He knew it would do no good just to stop and try to catch up later; Ramirez would just start shooting again. His only plan was to draw as much fire from Ramirez as he could in the hope that Ramirez would run out of bullets before he ran out of luck.

Quinn's luck ran out, from one perspective. Two of the rounds ripped through the powerhead of the motor, bringing his boat to a drift only powered by momentum. Once the firing had stopped, Quinn thought it safe to take a look. He popped his head up. The boat, which he had closed to within thirty yards of, was now just a black dot against the shimmering skyline of an unsuspecting Miami. He pulled out Scarpa's buck knife, which he had slipped into the pocket of his coveralls and began to pry off the bullet ridden fairing on the motor.

The inspection was difficult with little to no light, so Quinn began feeling his way around the components of the motor. He noticed one of the battery cables had been severed and it gave him hope. "Even an A ganger could fix this," he muttered to himself. He began to feel around a bit more. He jerked his hand back reflexively as hot metal seared his skin. His heart sank when he realized the smoldering edges were from a dime sized hole in the motor casing. "That can't be good," he said in disappointment. "It'd be nice if I had a light to actually see what I'm dealing with." At that moment a blue glow seemed to light up the area. Before he could process why there was a light there, he could see the motor was unfixable. Then his mind began to wonder about the mysterious light.

As he turned, the spotlight of a helicopter was the first possibility to flash in his mind, but an illuminated man standing just three feet from him on the water was never a consideration. He jumped back in startled surprise, nearly tumbling out of the boat. The man moved closer and talked to him.

"Petty Officer Quinn," the man said with a French accent. Quinn opened his mouth, but not a word came out. "Petty Officer Quinn, I am Captain Philip Reno, Commanding Officer of the Poignard."

Quinn interrupted him, "Are you dead?"

"Excuse me?"

"Are you some sort of ghost?" Quinn asked, half serious because he could not wrap his mind around how this glowing image of a French naval officer could appear in front of him.

"No, I am in the control room of my submarine, you see." Captain Reno picked up the web cam from the top of the drone technician's console and swept it around the room so that Quinn could see all the proud and amused sailors. Reno returned the camera to its original position so it focused on him, "You are seeing my image displayed on our newest UAV."

"Where's your drone at?" Quinn started looking up in the sky, "and how does it project your image down here?"

"You're looking at it," Reno said, having a little more fun than the moment should have allowed. "Turn off the cloaking," he said to the technician. The technician pushed a button and to Quinn's amazement a drone with a six foot girth seemed to materialize just off his port side. Quinn was speechless.

"This is all very top secret," Reno threw in as a disclaimer.

"Well I'll probably be dead in the next ten minutes, so I won't tell anyone."

"About that, we were not able to confirm what type of weapon he was carrying," Reno switched from show and tell to the matter at hand.

"It's a nuclear warhead," Quinn told him.

"Are you certain?" Reno asked.

"It's a long story, but that guy Ramirez is headed towards Miami to solve their condo problems."

"That *guy* you called Ramirez," the voice of the technician came from just off screen, "is Majed Abu-sief, a former resident of your Guantanamo Bay prison facility. Since his release three years ago he has climbed the ranks within multiple terrorist factions."

"No surprise there," Quinn said, and then he redirected the focus. "Can you guys take him out?"

Reno took back the conversation, "This is the first drone of its kind and wasn't equipped with any armament systems."

"You could have learned that lesson from the Americans," Quinn snipped in disappointment. "I don't suppose there's a seat on there anywhere?"

"No," Reno said, seeming to have the sudden realization that his drone was more of a toy than a piece of military hardware.

"Could you ram him?" Quinn asked trying to toss out as many options as possible.

"We could, but we have no idea what the triggering mechanism is on the warhead, so it may still detonate."

"What's the towing capacity on that thing?" Quinn asked as his farm boy twang slipped out.

"Pardon?" Reno asked not understanding the question.

"Can you tow me?" Quinn asked, holding up the rope.

"It has never been tested, but we can try," Reno offered.

"Throw off any unnecessary weight," the technician added.

Quinn unclamped the useless motor and scuttled it. He turned back to the drone. "That's it."

"I'm going to swing the drone over the top of you and bring it down slowly," the technician instructed. "There are two bars on the bottom where it gets clamped into the submarine; you should be able to tie off on one of those."

Quinn watched as the drone elevated and slid over him. As it maneuvered on top of him, it suddenly became extremely windy and noisy. Quinn could hear the technician trying to speak to him but he couldn't make it out the words over the noise.

"I can't hear you!" he yelled.

The technicians volume suddenly became louder as he gave a warning, "I said you've got a few hundred blades spinning around very fast under there, don't get your hand caught, this drone cost more than your submarine."

"I'm a little more worried about my hand than your drone!"

Reno smiled at Quinn's spirit as he watched him attempt to secure the drone. Quinn slowly reached up for one of the bars on its underbelly. When his hand was about three inches from the drone, there was a flash of light. Pain shot down Quinn's arm and he was knocked to the deck of the boat.

"Petty Officer Quinn," Reno said with genuine concern in his voice, "are you alright?"

Quinn sat dazed, as aftershocks of pain swelled through his arm. "What happened?" he asked, confused. "Did I get shot?"

"No," explained the technician, "I'm afraid there was a large build-up of static electricity, you took quite a shock."

Quinn struggled back to his feet.

"I'm sorry, I should have thought of that," the technician apologized.

"You think?" Quinn snapped. "Well, I'm not doing that again."

"You should be good now," the technician said, his words bringing no confidence to Quinn, "the charge would be mostly gone now."

"*Mostly?*"

"It should."

"It *should?* You really need to work on your sales pitch," Quinn said as he snatched up the rope once more. "Alright, here goes nothing." Quinn slapped the bottom of the drone with the rope and a small arc popped off. He repeated the motion and an even smaller arc popped. It didn't seem too bad, so he reached up and took hold of the anchor bar. He secured the rope to the drone with a double figure eight knot, attempting to maintain as much of the rope's tensile strength as possible. He then flaked out about ten feet of rope and secured the other end to the boat with the same knot.

"We're tied up," Quinn informed them. "Do you think we can overtake him?"

"We should be able to reach him just about the time he gets to the harbor," the technician predicted.

"Let's hope he doesn't get within a half a mile and say, 'hey it's a nuke, this is close enough'," Quinn mumbled.

"Hold on," the technician cautioned. Before Quinn had time to heed the technician's warning, the drone lurched forward and the tug on the boat nearly sent Quinn tumbling over the stern. Catching himself, Quinn held the safety line on the top of the pontoon. With the motor gone there was very little drag left on the small craft. The drone pulled him along at nearly double the speed the electric motor had been giving him. At times, the rubber boat would rise up off the waves and catch a bit of air, giving Quinn a few seconds of flight.

Quinn crawled to the front of the boat and tried to spread his weight out evenly across the centerline. He worried that he might catch a lopsided wave which would send him barrel-rolling. The drone had gone back into cloaking mode and Quinn was unsure if he would have been able to tell where it was had he not been able to follow the line from the boat up to it with his eyes. The only sound Quinn heard was the sound of the wind rushing past his ears. He felt as if he were a character riding a magic carpet from one of the tales in the Arabian folklore *One Thousand and One Nights.*

He watched as the predawn skyline of Miami grew on the horizon. The ride, having only taken a few minutes so far, seemed as if it dragged on and on for hours. Suddenly, Captain Reno's face appeared on one of the drone's rear facing screens. "Petty Officer Quinn, are you doing alright back there?"

"I'm getting nervous," Quinn replied honestly. "What's our ETA?"

"Abu-sief has just entered the harbor and it appears he is attempting to detonate the warhead. We've got two more minutes until you will be able to intercept him." Captain Reno paused, and then said, "We can turn around if you would like. We can get you far enough away from the blast so that you shouldn't be in immediate danger."

Quinn shook his head, "No, keep going." He did not look up at the video screen. He knew, without looking, that every sailor in the control room of the Poignard was watching him with admiration. However, he was not completely confident that he would have kept going had he not had a submarine full of witnesses watching him. If he had been alone, it would have been very easy to come to the conclusion his mission would fail and self-preservation may have been the easier route. But then the image of BJ Maddox floated through his mind. BJ did not know his hopeless plight was being filmed from high above his position. It would not have been out of the realm of possibilities for BJ to scramble up and over the top of the ridge he was on, but he pressed onward, sacrificing himself when he did not even know what type of weapons the trucks contained. Quinn knew what the weapon was and he knew what the fate of the people in Miami would be if he did not act. He was ready to see his mission through to the end.

Abu-sief's Zodiac

The man Quinn had known as Ramirez piloted his boat into the heart of Miami's waterfront. He had sped into Biscayne Bay, bypassing the outer keys, and set his boat adrift fifty yards off the mainland just south of Mercy Hospital. He had seen Quinn fall back after firing on him and although he had kept a watchful eye, he did not feel any pressing threats at this point. Although he had made a name for himself training young men to martyr themselves as suicide bombers, he had no interest in sacrificing himself to any cause. He knew his mentor, Ayman al-Zawahiri, would tell him to pray at this moment to calm himself, but he was too angry at the complete and utter failure the operation had become.

His plan had been to pull off an operation intended to completely eclipse that of 9/11. He knew, at this point, he would have to settle for destroying just one American city, not even the city of his choice. There was still a chance, however, if he did manage to set off the warhead successfully, and live, he might still be able to complete his intended coup of the Al-Qaeda network and replace Osama Bin Laden as the "Caliph" of Islamic Terror Groups.

The challenge in this plan was setting a timer to detonate the warhead. Oddly enough, through his work in Iraq, he found that men seeking martyrdom were much more reliable than electronic triggers. The U.S. military was constantly finding ways to foil IED's set to detonate remotely, but they had not found a way to stop a man, or woman in some cases, who was willing to strap a bomb to themselves and manually detonate it. He had worked for two years getting an army of martyrs in place throughout America. He had begun their training long before he had even secured the warheads. When he was able to get his hands on 100 warheads, he was elated. He hadn't even fully understood how it was he was able to get so many, but he didn't ask too many questions. After Guantanamo he was willing to take risks.

The warheads had a very intricate arming system with countermeasures to prevent tampering. They had lost five of the remaining 50 warheads during training due to effective countermeasures which had rendered the devices useless; however, they were able to harvest the warheads' nuclear material for use in dirty bombs at a later date. The system was complicated and they lacked the trained personnel to reverse-engineer the detonators. It was only through a very painful trial and error phase that they were able to design a work-around for the detonation system. However, they had decided to wait until the warheads were on American soil before they attempted to alter the triggering systems. Therefore, Abu-sief had to start from scratch, yet he wasn't wholly unprepared.

He removed the tool kit from its pouch. Holding an LED flashlight in his mouth, he began to gingerly remove the security screws from the warhead electronics access panel. Once the internal workings were exposed, he removed his watch and twisted off the face. From beneath the face he pulled out a coil of extremely thin 20 gage wire bundle which split into four distinctly colored hooks at the end. He then located the warhead's processor chip and began counting the pins which connected the chip to the circuit board. When he had counted down to the seventh pin from the top on the left side, he held his breath and slid the red colored hook around the pin. The hook had a barb on the end which fastened it securely to the pin. He exhaled and began to count the pins on the bottom of the chip.

Quinn's Zodiac

As Quinn entered Biscayne Bay, the drone changed course slightly to maneuver onto a north-westerly course to head toward Abu-sief's position near Mercy Hospital. Quinn felt the boat begin to slide across the waves in a sideways direction as it swung out from its position directly behind the drone. He remembered wakeboarding in the Chesapeake Bay with some fellow sailors and how easy it was to wipeout as the board increased speed swinging outside the wake during high speed turns. He postured up, trying to bear down his weight on the small boat's bow to gain greater stability.

Captain Reno's face appeared once more, only this time the screen seemed to be much dimmer. "Six hundred meters and closing," Reno reported to him.

Quinn strained his eyes to make out any distinctive form on the water. "I can't see a thing."

"Here, maybe this will help," he heard the drone technician say from off-screen. Suddenly, Captain Reno's face was replaced on the screen with a thermal image of a man hunched over in a small boat.

"Won't he be able to see this?" Quinn asked.

"This is only being projected on the rear of the drone, for you," the technician said as Quinn watched the number of meters to the target tick off on the screen's thermal image. "He will only be able to see what we project on the front, which is nothing but the black sky."

"Petty Officer Quinn," Captain Reno interrupted, "we haven't got much time. I would like to again stress to you the importance of keeping the technologies we have unveiled to you a secret."

"What, do you want me to pinky swear?" Quinn snapped, annoyed at the topic of conversation as he was trying to visualize different scenarios for the coming battle.

"Pinky swear?" Reno repeated, perplexed by the words.

"I won't tell anyone."

"Not even your superiors," Reno continued to pile on the stipulations.

"I won't mention any involvement by the French," Quinn reiterated, "but you'll owe me."

"Like the Godfather," Reno said trying to make an American cultural connection. Unfortunately, the reference to Don Corleone flew right over Quinn's head, having never seen the Godfather movies.

"You're going to have to back down on the speed or I'm going to shoot right past him," Quinn said, realizing he wouldn't be able to jump boats at his current speed.

"I'm backing it down to 12 knots," the technician said. Quinn felt the shape of the rubber hull returning to its normal form as the decrease in speed lessened the stretching of the rubber. "This speed should still give you a surprise approach. I also have a," the technician paused and said something in French. Quinn heard Reno clarify the translation for him then he continued, "I have a strobe light effect that we will shine at him when we get close."

The plan gave Quinn some comfort. He knew from taking a shipboard engagement tactics class at the Little Creek Amphibious Assault Base, disorientation in the first few moments of a fight can give the attacker an overwhelming advantage. Although having an automatic weapon, as Abu-sief had, trumped strobe lights. Quinn's eyes jumped continually from the screen to the black water ahead. As the boat closed within fifty meters, he thought he could see the faint light Abu-sief held in his mouth.

"Shut off the monitor," Quinn said faintly. "I've got him."

Quinn wasn't sure if his voice would have been loud enough for the drone's microphones to pick up, but the monitor went dark. As the boat closed within twenty yards, Quinn felt the speed back down just another notch. With just ten yards to go, Quinn could make out Abu-sief fairly well. Abu-sief must have sensed an object approaching him. His head jerked up sharply. As soon as it did, the drone blasted him with an array of strobe lights from the front monitors.

Quinn's zodiac bumped right up to Abu-sief's rubber boat and he launched himself at the man. Quinn rolled his shoulder forward and caught Abu-sief in the teeth as his projected momentum carried them to the bow of the little boat. Abu-sief landed on his back with Quinn at his right side. Like a surfer popping up onto his board, Quinn popped to his feet then dropped his right knee into Abu-sief's solar plexus. Abu-sief exhaled a shower of blood from his freshly cut lips. Quinn raised Scarpa's knife overhead, prepared to ram it into the throat of the man who was responsible for the deaths of a yet unknown number of Quinn's friends and shipmates, when with extreme resilience, Abu-sief posted his left leg against the rubber deck and pushed downward. The motion raised his hips off the deck and with unexpected flexibility, he swung his right leg up, cracking his lower shin against Quinn's temple.

Quinn fell forward, bouncing off the rubber pontoon. Abu-sief shifted his hips out away from Quinn and reached out with his right hand, grabbing Quinn's left forearm where the EB Green tape had been tightly wrapped to make an improvised bandage over the knife wound he had received from Scarpa. Abu-sief dug his fingernails into the wound, causing the nerves in Quinn's arm to send a muscle spasm through his shoulder and back. As Quinn writhed in pain, Abu-sief used his left hand to rain down punches on Quinn's right ear and jaw.

Using the grip to his advantage, Abu-sief got up on his knees. Having superior leverage, he brought his fist down with a vicious blow right on the hinge of Quinn's mandible. Quinn felt his jaw slide out and then quickly back into its socket. The pain was so immense, he felt as if stars were popping in his eyes. He knew this was the last thing a fighter sees before sliding into unconsciousness, however, he realized he wouldn't come to from this one staring at the lights asking his coach if he won the fight. The fact that he was able to worry about being knocked out signaled to him the punch hadn't been hard enough to finish him off, but if another one landed like that the fight would be over.

In a survival response, he jerked his left arm out of Abu-sief's grip, curled up like a turtle with his back facing his attacker and protected the back of his neck with interlocked fingers. Abu-sief hit him two more times then moved away. Quinn knew there was still an MP-5 machine gun in the boat and as soon as he felt Abu-sief move away, he turned, ready to face the next attack. However, the attack wasn't upon him. Abu-sief was at the rear of the boat beginning to lift the warhead.

"Petty Officer Quinn," Reno's voice shouted from the closely hovering drone, "if he drops that in the water, there's no way you'll find it in time to stop it from detonating!"

The voice startled Abu-sief long enough for Quinn to get to his feet. When Abu-sief saw Quinn coming he dropped the warhead and picked up his MP-5. Quinn dodged to his right as Abu-sief squeezed the trigger. He knew he wouldn't be able keep dodging bullets in a five foot wide boat, but the body doesn't stop to think about rationality when it is trying to survive. A single bullet snapped off, missing Quinn. Quinn grimaced, expecting the next round to tear though him. It never came. Quinn looked up and saw Abu-sief pulling at the trigger in vain. The one round had been the only one left in the magazine.

As Quinn got back to his feet, Abu-sief tossed the gun to the side and scooped up Scarpa's knife. Quinn looked around for anything which could be used for a weapon. The only thing lying on the deck was the EAB mask Abu-sief had worn to make his escape from the submarine. In desperation, Quinn snatched it up. Abu-sief charged at him. Quinn whipped the long air hose around. The metal fitting at the end of the hose caught Abu-sief on the cheek, opening up a superficial cut, but nothing that was severe enough to dissuade the man from attacking.

Suddenly, as if an invisible man had entered the fight, Abu-sief was knocked down hard. The cloaked drone had rammed into him with such force that he was thrown to the bow of the boat. Quinn looked at Abu-sief, wondering if it was over. He was disappointed to see the man moving. However, his movements were agonizing. He put his hand on the rubber pontoon to gain enough leverage to turn his body to face Quinn. As he did this, air began to whistle through Abu-sief's fingers.

The single bullet he had intended for Quinn had grazed the boat's thick rubber pontoon. He faced Quinn. His eyes tightened. When Quinn saw him raise his knife, he turned toward the warhead. His arm outstretched, Abu-sief plunged his blade into the rubber and rent it towards his body. As the massive fissure opened up in the pontoon, it sounded like a last agonal breath from a dying man. Quinn's next step seemed to fall away from him as the deck sank without the support of the pontoons on either side. His hopes of getting to the warhead were shattered when he saw the weight of the weapon pull the deck under as it took the boat stern first towards the sea floor.

The boat going under stern first pulled the bow toward Quinn. Quinn turned just in time to catch Abu-sief rushing at him. He was able to duck under the overhead knife swing and get behind Abu-sief as they submerged. Abu-sief struggled to face Quinn, but Quinn had wrapped his legs around Abu-sief's midsection preventing him from doing so. Quinn tried to slow his mind and his actions. He knew from his training that fighting underwater would deplete the muscles' oxygen supply rapidly.

He reached out, grasping for anything he could us as a weapon. He caught the dangling hose from the floating EAB mask. In what was more of a reaction than a thought, he wrapped the air hose around Abu-sief's neck. Immediately, Abu-sief let go of his knife and began clawing at the hose. Quinn released the grip he had with his legs, brought his feet around behind Abu-sief, and planted his knees firmly between the man's shoulder blades. He pushed against Abu-sief with his knees, and pulled back on the ends of the hose, creating an anaconda-like choke. Then, he let it loose.

Abu-sief, feeling the pressure release off his neck, instinctively inhaled. There was nothing he could do to stop it. His body reacted to the release of the choke by inhaling a lungful of seawater. The secondary reaction was to expel the seawater and try again. Quinn held onto Abu-sief as he convulsively went through half a dozen of these painful breaths. The latter attempts to breathe were very shallow, and when Quinn had made it to a fifteen count since the last twitch of his body, he exhaled and followed his bubbles to the surface.

As his face felt the air, he gasped for breath. The drone zeroed in on him and hovered just above where he was treading water. "Petty Officer Quinn," Reno called out, "what is the situation?"

Quinn tried to speak but pain shot through his jaw. He screamed in pain through gritted teeth.

"Did you get to the warhead?"

Quinn shook his head to a negative response.

"I assume Abu-sief is gone," Reno said.

Quinn shook his head in the positive.

"We need to disarm that warhead," Reno said with the coolness of someone who was not treading water with a dislocated jaw just above an armed nuclear warhead. "According to our charts, the sounding of the water you are in should be 9.2 meters deep." There was a pause. "I assume you can free dive to that depth," Reno stated. "Our records indicate you are part of your boat's dive crew."

Quinn knew he could free dive to fifty feet with swim fins on for sport, so he calculated he would be able to free dive to nearly thirty eight feet to save his and countless other lives with the absence of fins. He shook his head in the affirmative.

"Looking at the video replay," the technician's voice popped in, "it appears Abu-sief had wired what we assume to be a time delayed detonator sequence into the warhead's processor chip."

"The electronics in these warheads," Reno added, "have a thin silicone covering, making them resistant to interruption due to being submerged in water."

Quinn couldn't help but think the French gave the world's worst pep talks.

"But it is very sensitive to tampering," Reno continued. "If you can locate it, all you should need to do is remove any of the wires attached to the circuit board and the weapon's countermeasures should render the warhead harmless."

Quinn held up his thumb, and then placed the EAB mask on top of his head. He began, in his mind, to list off the parts of his body which were in pain. He had been trained to take a mental inventory of any physical irregularities he might be feeling before a dive. This was done so that a diver could establish a baseline to compare any new ailments which may crop up during a dive. In this way, divers could easily detect any early signs of diving trauma. Quinn realized there was not a single part of his body which was not in excruciating pain, so he cut the routine short for fear of losing any bit of adrenaline he had left in reserves.

He began to hyperventilate through gritted teeth, a task which was tough enough without the pain. Once he had loaded his brain up with oxygen, he pulled the mask down over his face and dove. Once under, he pushed the mask tight against his face, this burped out a small amount of air creating a vacuum seal of the mask on his face. He struggled to kick towards the bottom. He hoped he was heading straight down. The difficulty was trying to swim down thirty eight feet on the same angle. If he was off just a bit, he could wind up twenty feet away from where the warhead had come to rest, and in the dark with a limited supply of oxygen, the chances of finding the warhead would be impossible.

Quinn had been on many night dives and had above average capability when it came to body orientation under water. The challenge at this point was trying to equalize his ears to the increasing sea pressure. The EAB masks were not made for diving under water, so he had to practically crush the mask against his face in order to plug up his nose so that he could pop his ears.

He was concentrating on kicking with all his might to get to the bottom. He had his doubts he would be able to get there without swim fins. The doubt was dispelled when he crashed into the sandy bottom as if he were some sort of underwater lawn dart. He had hit the bottom just as he had scooped the water hard with both arms so his head took the brunt of the impact. When he righted himself, the compression his neck had just suffered was already being eclipsed by the burning sensation in his lungs. He knew his bottom time would only be a few seconds, so he began to search the black bottom with his hands.

Out of the corner of his eye he saw a shimmering. He turned towards it. *A light.* It was about twelve feet away. He kicked with his legs and crawled with his hands across the bottom. He got to the light. It was a small LED flashlight. He picked it up. His body screamed at him to ascend. The thought of having to swim back down was more than he could bear. He wasn't sure if he had the strength to do it twice. He picked up the light and did a few sweeps with the faint beam. Something metallic reflected the light just a few feet away. He kicked over to it. It was the warhead.

He scanned it with the light. The first eight inches of the cone were buried in the sand so that it stood on end like a premature memorial to the Armageddon it was minutes away from releasing. There was an open panel at the thicker base end of the warhead with a circuit board exposed. Quinn was out of time, he had to ascend. There was no time to study or second guess, he reached out, grabbed the circuit board and yanked.

There was a brilliant flash of light followed by a small concussion which knocked Quinn back a few feet. His legs realized he was still alive before his mind did and they pushed off the bottom with all the force they could muster. He kicked and kicked, putting one hand above his head to protect him from any collisions with unseen objects. As he rose toward the surface, the pressure eased. Breaking the surface, he ripped the mask from his head and as he had done during his panicked escape from the doomed submarine forty minutes earlier. He drank the air.

The drone spotted him and dragged his still intact zodiac boat over to his position. Quinn used the only strength he had left to pull himself into the boat and collapsed once more onto the deck. He did not open his eyes when Reno addressed him.

"Petty Officer Quinn," Reno asked with concern, sounding more like a father than a commanding officer, "is it over?"

Quinn raised one hand. He held a very weak thumb aloft. He heard the cheers erupt in the control room of the Poignard, but his heart could not join in their celebration. His mind drifted to his submarine and the state it was in when he made his escape. He thought about his friends treading water. He wondered how many had not escaped. He thought about Schmidt.

The cheering quieted down and it was the drone technician's voice which came to him this time. "Petty Officer Quinn," he said with alarm in his voice. Quinn detected the alarm. Though he thought he had used every ounce of energy his body had in reserves, adrenaline once more coursed through his veins. "I am detecting a Coast Guard patrol boat headed your way."

As fast as the adrenaline reserves had seared back through him, they receded with twice the speed. Quinn felt almost paralyzed now.

"Petty Officer Quinn," it was Reno who now spoke apologetically, "I hate to be a bother."

Quinn let out a Frankenstein-like grunt. He was expecting Reno to ask him again to keep his drone a secret.

"Before you pass out," Reno continued, "would it be too much to ask of you to untie us?"

Quinn huffed, pulled himself up with much effort, and set to work loosening the figure eight knot. The knot had become extremely tight from the strain which had been placed on it. Just as Quinn was about to give up, the knot gave. He pulled the free end of the line through the knot's coils, releasing the drone, and then he collapsed on the deck in a heap like the tangle of rope which lay beside him.

"Thank you, Petty Officer Quinn," Reno stated with the formality of a departure "It would have been quite embarrassing if the Coast Guard showed up and you were tethered to the world's most advanced UAV."

Quinn took that as another reminder to keep his promise. He grunted with contention and rolled over to sleep.

CHAPTER 25

USS Key West

Upon reaching the surface, Rubber listened for other men. Through the blackness, the Weps' voice could be heard shouting, "Get that raft over here!" Rubber swam toward the voices. One of the submarine's two life rafts had made it to the surface and by the time Rubber had reached it, Dave was hoisting Sparks aboard. Once he had him situated next to Ms. Collins, as comfortably as could be expected, he reached his hand out offering to help the Weps.

"Here you go, Mr. Copaletti."

"I don't need to take up the room," the Weps said, shrugging off the offer.

"Weps," Rubber spoke up, "we don't doubt that you can manage sir, it's just that I think we would all feel better if you got your wound out of the water."

Rubber hadn't spoken the word "shark," but the shudder that went through every sailor within earshot confirmed it was on everyone's mind. The Weps, as tough as the man was, obviously saw the wisdom in Rubber's thinking and took Dave's hand to climb into the raft.

As the sun began to brighten the glow off the eastern horizon, the sailors who had made it out of submarine had coalesced into a tight group around the one raft. The few sailors who had managed to don life vests were relegated to the outer edges of the group, while the sailors without vests took five minute shifts treading water and then taking a rest by holding onto the edges of the life raft. While the engine room's aft escape trunk had still been above the surface, sailors had been streaming out of the boat as fast as they could. However, as dawn was breaking, it had been about a half hour since that hatch had gone under. At this point, the mutterings among the group was that the entire boat would be filled with water by now.

The sub had not sunk completely; it was essentially bobbing at the surface with the stern sticking out of the water so that the rudder, stern planes and propeller screw were reflecting the red light of the morning sun. Since the coming daylight had first made the last portion of the boat left above the surface visible to the men, it had slipped down about twenty more feet, leaving only fifteen feet or so exposed, and while it's sinking seemed to pause for the time being, it was listing more and more to starboard as the minutes ticked by.

"Hey, Eng," Rubber called out to the man who seemed as if he were waking from a bad dream, "do you think if they get to us in time they'll be able to save her?"

"Right now the only thing keeping her afloat is the air in the ballast tanks, with maybe the assistance of an air bubble in the engine room. If she keeps listing like that, eventually the ballast tank grates will turn up enough and they'll lose the air they're holding."

"Help the COB get to the raft!"

Rubber looked in the direction of the distress call. He could see two sailors pulling the COB, who was in a life vest, toward the raft. As they swam closer, the COB was breathing heavily and his head seemed the deep shade of red it would turn when the man was extremely upset.

Hearing the commotion, Sparks lifted his head to see the COB's red face just inches from his own.

"Got a problem, COB?" Sparks asked in an unsympathetic tone.

The COB seemed as though he was trying to respond but only gasps for air came out.

"I think he's having a heart attack," Dave observed.

"Aw, poor COB, don't think you'll make it to your retirement," Sparks continued to egg him on. The COB shot out an arm, trying to grab at Sparks, but he missed. "What's the matter, COB, why don't you sic Scarpa on me?"

"That's enough, Petty Officer Sparks, I think he really is having a heart attack," the Weps attempted to intervene in his strained voice.

The color seemed to drain out of the COB's face, but rather than return to normal, it seemed to keep disappearing.

"His lips are turning blue," Dave said calmly, as if he were still viewing reality through a viewfinder.

"Serves you right!"

"Sparks, that's enough," the Weps cautioned.

"Weps! He deserves to die! Look around. We're lucky if we've got half the crew here!" Sparks swept his arm around gesturing at the sparse crew. Half way through his gesture, pain must have shot through his ribs and he drew his arm back sharply with a wince.

The Weps looked at the COB. The COB's expression was frozen.

"I think he just joined the rest of the crew who didn't make it."

"Did Quinn make it up yet?" Sparks asked, scanning the faces treading water once again.

"No," Rubber answered softly.

Suddenly, an eruption of bubbles began to disrupt the surface of the water. Nervous sailors began to question what was happening.

"It's the ballast tanks, the boat's list is too far," the Eng explained loudly so everyone could hear. The men watched helplessly as the stern section began to sink quickly as the ballast tanks lost buoyancy. When the tip of the screw went under, the USS Key West, a boat which had submerged thousands of times, went under for good. A soft swirl on the surface was all the evidence which marked the presence of where the submarine had been. Everyone seemed to be floating motionless, in complete silence, except for Stoney.

In the stillness of the moment, Rubber noticed Stoney, frantically kicking his arms and legs trying to stay afloat. Rubber swam over to him.

"Stoney, you having trouble?" Rubber asked him as he approached.

"No problem here, man."

"Seriously Stoney, you've got a KPOC on, and you're barely keeping your head above water." Rubber put his face underwater and could see the bundle of KPOCs hanging at the end of the taught lanyard attached to Stoney's waist.

"Stoney, you've got an anchor," Rubber said as he folded the knife out of his Leatherman multi-tool.

"Rubber," Stoney said in a panicked voice as he tried to swim backwards away from him, "I'm fine, I think those guys over there need assistance."

"Now Stoney, this won't hurt a bit."

Rubber dove down, avoiding Stoney's kicking feet. He grabbed hold of the lanyard and in a quick sawing motion with the knife, the strap snapped. He watched the bundled contraband race towards the submarine as they both headed to the bottom. Rubber was to about to kick to the surface, when something caught his eye. It looked as if the KPOCs which he had just sent hurtling towards the submarine were coming back up. The blur and sting of the sea water made it hard to tell, but as the object grew, it was obvious it was headed toward the surface.

Rubber, out of breath, kicked to the surface, inhaled quickly, then looked back at the accelerating object. It was close now and he could make out two distinct figures. Grant had one of the submarine's old Steinke hoods on, an inflatable life vest with a hood which trapped a few breaths of air, designed for escape. In one hand he had four EAB storage bags filled with air and in the other he was towing his lifeless friend, Petty Officer Carter. When he broke the surface, he took off the hood, locking eyes with Rubber.

"He's gone."

"I'm sorry, Herby," Rubber offered his condolences.

Grant's eyes scanned the grim faces of the sailors treading water.

"Quinn?"

Rubber shook his head. Their conversation ended. The quiet had settled on everyone like a fog, when a scream from the deep shot through everyone's bone. The Key West wasn't going down quietly. As the sub reached its crush depth, the metal cried out as it was tortured by the pressures of the deep. The sounds which resonated from far below were horrible. Every pop, every explosion, every screech of twisted metal battered the men. The water turned every hair on their body into a sound transducer. Each follicle on their necks acted like a needle on a record player making them not only hear the cries of their boat, but also feel them. No one said a word as the sounds haunted them. Minutes seemed like hours. After the last cry from their submarine echoed away, one sailor broke the silence as he offered up the Lord's Prayer for their friends who did not make it to the surface. When the prayer finished, the "amens" could be heard spreading out like a soft ripple across the sea.

Dark clouds began to move in and cover the morning sun as small groups of floating sailors began making their way into one huddled mass. Some sailors began demanding explanations; others began to offer up theories of what may have happened. Rubber and his group remained quiet.

After twenty minutes of treading water, the chattering among the sailors had ceased as the uncertainty of their situation had begun to sink in and most were concerned with conserving their energy. Stoney, who had been making his way closer and closer to the raft, couldn't help but try and use humor to lighten the mood. He started to hum the theme from *Jaws*. While every sailor had been thinking about sharks, none dared to utter the word aloud. No one seemed to see the humor in it the way Stoney did, and it looked as if a spontaneous water polo match had broken out with Stoney's head being substituted for the ball. Suddenly the dreaded cry rang out. The one word all of the men were afraid to hear was screamed.

"Shark!"

Sparks, who had screamed the word, screamed it in such a way, with his voice cracking on the "ar", everyone knew it was no joke. When all the attention was turned on him, his face was so contorted with pain that the sailors nearest to him began to move away, thinking he was being attacked through the bottom of the raft. It wasn't until he brought his hand back off his tender midsection and pointed that others began to see what he saw. About a hundred yards west of their position, they could see a thin line sticking about two feet above the water, cutting through the waves as if it was being driven by some primordial engine. They watched in horror as it headed straight at their group. The sailors on the fringe began to clamor over each other, looking to gain a safer interior position.

The "fin" began to climb higher out of the water as it approached. The Weps lifted his head from the edge of the raft and could see it was sticking nearly five feet out of the water.

"That's not a shark," the Weps called out, his booming voice loud enough for all to hear. Rubber could see it too.

"It's a periscope. It's a periscope!" he yelled as others began to cheer and whistle.

"We're saved," Stoney proclaimed.

"I wouldn't be so sure about that," the Weps said, sitting up. "That's the Poignard, we did shoot at them."

"Well, I'm ready to go beg for forgiveness and coffee," Rubber said as he grabbed hold of the life raft and began to pull it towards the surfacing submarine.

"And morphine," grunted Sparks.

EPILOGUE

Le Poignard

The remaining crew members of the Key West had been picked up by the Poignard. They waited topside most of the day, being fed and receiving medical treatment. Even when a light drizzle began, they were still not permitted below decks of the highly secretive French submarine. The crew of the Poignard did provide them with ponchos though. By the later afternoon, the USS Kalamazoo had pulled within a few hundred yards off the port side of the French submarine. The crew watched as four small boats were lowered into the water and headed their way to transport them over to the U.S. ship.

As Rubber was about to cross the makeshift plank to the small watercraft, everyone heard the approach of a chopper. The Coast Guard chopper circled low and one of the chopper's crew opened the side door.

"It's Quinn!" Stoney shouted.

The crew looked up and saw Quinn sitting in the cargo hold of the chopper. He was pretty banged up and had an IV threaded into one of his arms, but that didn't stop him from giving his shipmates a thumbs up and his bright smile, no matter how much pain it sent coursing through his jaw. The guys on the deck began to cheer and whistle. His smile faded when he noticed Grant holding a fist over his heart standing next to a body covered with a white sheet.

Quinn put his own fist over his heart, acknowledging the loss of Carter, a good friend.

Grant took his fist from his heart and held up a steady salute. Rubber noticed the gesture and he threw up a salute of his own. The Weps, who was waiting on a gurney next to Sparks, was talking with Captain Reno and his Executive Officer De Panafiue. When he heard the cheers, he looked up to see Quinn. Noticing the others offering Quinn a salute, he himself broke protocol and held a sharp salute to the junior petty officer. Quinn saw Reno say something to the Weps and the Weps respond without breaking his gaze. Then Reno and De Panafiue held up their own salutes. Others, who did not necessarily realize all that Quinn had done for them, gave salutes as well.

As Quinn brought his hand up to his brow to return the salute, he began to count the number of sailors on the deck. He held his hand there as a wave of shock hit him. If his estimated count was accurate, it would be lucky if there were more than fifty sailors who had made it off the boat. He dropped the salute as the chopper banked towards the Kalamazoo. He wanted to ask the pilot if there had been more crewmembers that had already been taken to the Kalamazoo, but even if his broken jaw hadn't kept him from asking, in his heart he already knew the answer.

USS Kalamazoo

Quinn waited in the Admiral's Quarters while a hospital corpsman put a sterile dressing on his forearm. Adm. Perry entered quietly.

"Are you almost finished?"

The young corpsman finished wrapping the bandage. "That'll do it," she said.

"Will he be needing anything else?"

"I'll be back in a half hour to administer more pain Meds, but that's it for now."

"We'll see you at 1930 then," Adm. Perry said, politely dismissing the corpsman.

"Yes, sir," she acknowledged, then turned to Quinn. "Next time try not to use duct tape on your wounds." Quinn shrugged and gave her a wink as she left them.

"Petty Officer Quinn, we meet again," Adm. Perry said as he pulled up a chair and set the file he was carrying on the nightstand next to the bunk Quinn was in.

Quinn tried to say, "It's a pleasure, sir," through gritted teeth, but Adm. Perry held up his hand to keep Quinn from talking. Adm. Perry had met Quinn once before at the beckoning of Captain Maddox. After interviewing Quinn, Adm. Perry had provided the letter of recommendation Quinn needed to be accepted into the Officer Program.

"You don't need to try and talk, Quinn. They told me about your jaw." Quinn was relieved once again. As bad as his jaw hurt, it made keeping the details of the French assistance from his debriefers easier. He was able to think more clearly when putting it down on paper, which kept him from slipping up. He was certain if it had been a regular interrogation he would have forgotten to use Abu-Sief's alias, which would have sent up red flags for sure.

"I read through the report," Adm. Perry paused. "Michael Maddox was one of my closest friends."

A look of panic crossed Quinn's face as the thought flashed through his mind that Adm. Perry may have been in on the plan too. His eyes began to dart around the room, searching for items which might be used as a weapon against Adm. Perry if it came down to a fight. Adm. Perry must have seen the look and recognized how his statement could be misconstrued as a threat.

"Don't worry, Quinn; I interviewed LCDR Copaletti and the rest of the crew who had been in the control room with you. Everyone's story corroborates what you have in your report."

Quinn's relief was apparent, and as Adm. Perry continued to tell him details such as the Coast Guard had recovered the warhead and Abu-Sief's body, he was only paying half-attention. Quinn was troubled however, in the split second he thought Adm. Perry may have been involved in Captain Maddox's scheme; he had identified three items in the room he could have used as weapons to kill or seriously maim Adm. Perry. Quinn valued human life. He had nearly lost his a half a dozen times in the last 24 hours trying to protect the lives of both the men in his crew, and the countless number of civilians in Miami. However, he had taken lives. The urge he had resisted the entire time growing up, under the oppression of his uncle, he was now ready to deal out in seconds. He feared, no matter what good he had accomplished, his own humanity may have been one of the casualties.

"Did you hear that, Quinn?" Adm. Perry said, startling Quinn as he slapped him on the leg. "The President!"

Quinn looked at him, confused. He had been consumed by his own thoughts.

"The President sends his thanks to you," Adm. Perry softened his tone a bit. "Of course, he can't acknowledge your acts of bravery publicly. When it came out that BJ Maddox had robbed our enemies of the chance to use nuclear weapons, it took the stock market six weeks to recover. Obviously, you could understand the panic it would create if the American public found out just how close we had come to losing an entire city population."

Quinn nodded his head in understanding. Adm. Perry pulled a sheet of paper out from his folder and set it on Quinn's lap.

"Now, this is a confidentiality agreement, classifying this mission as one of the utmost secrecy. You may at no time discuss the events of this situation, even with those involved, especially Ms. Stephanie Collins."

Quinn grabbed the manila folder which contained the agreement. He scrawled the question, "Did she sign???" across the back of the folder.

"I think she is holding out for exclusive behind closed doors access to the White House, which I'm sure she'll get."

Quinn laughed as he signed the agreement.

"But don't worry Quinn; I think you might find a quick promotion after OCS. From what I make of your little operation here, you'll make a great Commanding Officer one day."

Hey, T. Steven Sullivan here. I can't thank you enough for picking up a copy of Hot Run, it means the world to me. I hope you had as much fun reading it as I did writing it for you. I look forward to writing many more adventures for you to enjoy. As for me, I live in Florida with my wife Amy and our four children. So life is always an adventure. After being a diver on submarines in the Navy, I have gone on to become a certified Emergency Medical Technician, stuntman, actor, voice-over artist and small business owner. In my free time, I entertain and teach the kids in the children's program at my church. I also train in Brazilian Jiu Jitsu. The guys at the gym have given me a really intimidating nickname, "Cirque de Sully" I know, scary, right? Now I have a favor to ask you. Since I don't have a giant corporate PR machine behind this book, I am depending on you, the reader, to help me get the word out. Please visit my website, www.hotrunthenovel.com. This is where you can read what's going on with me and the book in my blog posts. You can also find me on Facebook at www.facebook.com/t.steven.sullivan. Thank you for your support!